S0-ARN-259

DATE DUE

THE
DEATH
OF BLUE
MOUNTAIN
CAT

Also by Michael Allen Dymmoch

The Man Who Understood Cats

THE
DEATH
OF BLUE
MOUNTAIN
CAT

Michael Allen Dymmoch

St. Martin's Press ⚓ New York

HIGHLAND PARK PUBLIC LIBRARY
494 Laurel Avenue
Highland Park, IL 60035

A Thomas Dunne Book
An Imprint of St. Martin's Press

This is a work of fiction. The characters and events depicted herein are products of the author's imagination. Any resemblance to real persons or events should be construed as coincidental.

THE DEATH OF BLUE MOUNTAIN CAT. Copyright © 1996 by Michael Allen Dymmoch. All rights reserved. Printed in the United States of America. No part of this book may be used or reproduced in any manner whatsoever without written permission except in the case of brief quotations embodied in critical articles or reviews. For information, address St. Martin's Press, 175 Fifth Avenue, New York, N.Y. 10010.

Library of Congress Cataloging-in-Publication Data

Dymmoch, Michael Allen.
    The death of Blue Mountain Cat / by Michael Allen Dymmoch.
        p.   cm.
    "A Thomas Dunne book."
    ISBN 0-312-13962-4
    I. Title
PS3554.Y6D43   1996
813'.54—dc20   95-30028
                                                               CIP

First Edition: April 1996

10   9   8   7   6   5   4   3   2   1

For
BARBARA D'AMATO,
WILLIAM F. DEECK,
and
JOAN TURCHIK

ACKNOWLEDGMENTS

The author wishes to thank the following for answers to various technical questions or for general information on topics of which the author was ignorant: Commander Hugh Holton, Detective Jack Stewart, Neighborhood Relations Officer Michael Barone, Officers Patrice Stewart, Mary Jensen and Edna White, and Tactical Officers Gerald Hamilton and David Lemieux of the Chicago Police Department; Oakton Community College instructors Associate Professor Gary Deters, M.S., Cook County Circuit Judge Bruce Lester, J.D., Mary T. Nicolau, J.D., and Dennis A. Ramsey; opera enthusiasts Yohma Gray, Miriam Schneider, Doris Blechman, and Polly Cuncannan; artist Donna Polivka; hockey fans Shelly Burger and Rich Blakley; Joe Falasco, Neil, and the gang at Falasco's Automotive; James G. Schaefer and Harold Burkhardt; the staff at *The Dellwood Pickle;* and Ron Straff, R & R Sporting Goods, Inc., Westchester, Illinois. I have taken liberties with the information given me. Any errors are my own.

Thanks also to my editor, Ruth Cavin, her assistant Elisabeth Story, publicist Karen McDermott, copy editor Nora Cavin, and cover artists Alexander Barsky and Michael Accordino of St. Martin's Press; literary agent Ray Powers; the reference librarians at the Northbrook Public Library, Northbrook, Illinois; Judy Duhl and her staff at Scotland Yard Books, Winnetka, Illinois; Janis Irvine and her staff at The Book Bin, Northbrook, Illinois; author Robert Norden; Nancy at the U.S. Post Office, Northbrook, Illinois; and Phebe Waterman and the rest of the Red Herrings. All of you helped me bring Thinnes and Caleb to life.

And thanks to Tony Hillerman for reasons obvious to anyone familiar with his work.

—mad

ONE

Caleb stood just inside the entrance to the invitation-only showing and tried to determine why the exhibition disturbed him.

The venue was wrong. The genteel Michigan Avenue museum, with its wood-paneled, marble-tiled foyer and carpeted galleries, was too conservative, too traditional for the works of "Navajo Artist, Blue Mountain Cat." They should have been displayed in the Museum of Contemporary Art.

The pieces ranged from retail-store cases of exorbitantly priced Indian "artifacts" to what the catalog described as "installation art." This seemed to refer to anything that didn't fit a familiar category, including groups of painted mannequins outrageously dressed. The collective impression was Andy Warhol meets Jonathan Swift in Indian country, and with the exception of the small oil, a desert landscape that Caleb had loaned the show, the pieces were grossly different from what he'd previously seen of the artist's work. They were out of touch with Nature and lacked the harmony and balance that was the Navajo way. Not that they were out of balance artistically. But they were slick, things an interior designer would use as props—what a skeptic would call pricey, without being lovely or loving. They were nothing like the playful, joyous things the artist had done when he was a student, works he'd signed 'David Bisti.'

All the works except the landscape were identified with a stylized cougar curled into the blue triangle of a stylized mountain. They were cynical. Shocking. Satirical. They mocked their

1

audience and their subject matter—things Western and Indian. Caleb wondered why.

Behind him, echoing his thoughts, Anita Margolis said, "Nothing short of a brain transplant could explain it."

Anita had given David his first break, his first professional showing. But measured by these pieces, that show in her Michigan Avenue gallery was a light-year distant.

She said, "What sort of monster have I created?"

Caleb turned and smiled. She was especially lovely with her dark hair swept up, pinned with diamonds, her black dress and jewelry elegant in their simplicity.

A waiter appeared with a tray of champagne in tulip glasses. Caleb accepted two and handed one to Anita.

"Honestly," she continued, "how could he?"

"Perhaps the man who's been living for his art just decided he'd like to make a living."

As the waiter moved away, a voice behind Anita said, "What do you think?"

They both turned to look at the speaker, a tall man, black eyed and dark skinned. He was dressed in a fringed, white buckskin shirt, black Levi's, and pale gray cowboy boots. His straight, black, shoulder-length hair was held in place with a headband that had Indian motifs painted on leather. The same slick style as the show. Designer Indian. In fact, the whole man seemed as carefully crafted as an ad from GQ.

"I think you'll make a lot of money, David," Anita said.

He gave her a dazzling smile and kissed her hand. Corny as it was, Caleb thought, the kiss was probably the most genuine thing about the exchange.

"A diplomat," David said. His smile faded as he realized the implication of her statement. Then he noticed Caleb and smiled again, extending his hand. "Doctor."

Caleb shook it. "David."

An unpleasant voice from behind them interrupted. "Bisti!"

David turned, and all three watched a heavy man charge up

to them. He was over six feet tall, with a flushed face and stony expression.

David's body language spoke alarm, momentarily, then caution. "I'm afraid you have the advantage."

"You ought to know a man before you libel him!"

"Ah. I take it you don't care for my art?"

"Art? Bullshit!" The man's face darkened a shade, and white blotches marked the tension locking his jaw.

Behind Caleb, Anita whispered, "Harrison Wingate."

Wingate was graying and muscular under the overweight. His silk shirt, expensive suit and shoes, and the $200 tie said money; the way he moved in them said power.

Caleb shifted so that Wingate could see Anita better, and the big man nearly choked. "Excuse me, ma'am. I beg your pardon."

There was a faint drawl to his voice that hadn't been there when he spoke to David. He ignored Caleb and glared at the artist. "You'll be hearin' from my attorney." He nodded at Anita and said, "Ma'am." He nearly knocked a waiter over as he stalked away.

Before David could explain what that was about, a woman's voice spat, "You unmitigated bastard! How can you have the nerve to call yourself a Navajo?"

Odd, Caleb thought.

The speaker was six inches shorter than David, oval faced, with the dark eyes and high cheekbones of a Native American. Her plain blouse and suit accented her jewelry—traditional squash-blossom necklace, assorted silver rings and dangly earrings. Her long, heavy hair was pulled back and pinned with a silver brooch. "You insult us with this trash!"

According to the catalog, the installation she referred to was *Native American Gothic,* a burlesque of Grant Wood's classic. In this version, a pair of dark-skinned department-store dummies—crudely whitewashed and dressed in business attire—stood in front of a cardboard-cutout hogan adorned with a gaudy, stained-glass Sacred Heart. The male figure wore a suit and, instead of a pitchfork, carried a lance strung with crude imitation eagle feathers. In his other hand, he held a skull— taboo among the Navajo—onto which rhinestone tears dropped from his cheeks. The skull was tagged: "Genuine Indian artifact, $2000.00." The female figure was painted like a cheap whore and offered the viewer a hip flask of Old Grand-Dad priced at "1/10,000 of a soul." A mirror behind the figures enabled viewers to see themselves gawking and to notice that the whitewash and the costumes of the two figures covered only their front sides.

"Wolf-man!" the silver woman spat.

David seemed more amused than offended. "It's not real, Irene." He walked over to pluck the skull from the hand of the mannequin, grasping it by the crown and upending it. "See," he said and thrust it at her. "Made in U.S.A."

Caleb edged closer. He would have sworn the skull was genuine. He held a hand out. "May I?" David shrugged and handed him the skull, the lower jaw of which was wired in place.

It was neither plaster nor plastic as far as Caleb could tell. He tapped its cranium with a knuckle and judged by the sound that it was real bone or a marvelous approximation. The words "Made in USA" *were* incised near the foramen magnum, but Caleb sensed that they were meant ironically, not literally.

It didn't seem a good time to say so. David had tensed, subtly, as if waiting for Caleb to make a liar of him. Caleb returned the skull without comment.

The artist replaced it in the installation, then lifted a champagne glass from the tray of a passing waiter and offered it to Irene. She took the glass and very deliberately dribbled its contents over the skull.

Suddenly, the museum's special-activities director slipped into the room and stopped before the Indian woman. "Miss, may I see your invitation?"

She gave him a sarcastic smile and handed him a newspaper clipping from her purse.

"This won't do, miss. I'm sorry."

"I'll bet you are."

"Come with me, please." He stepped closer to her and signaled a security guard, who moved smoothly to her other side. Neither man touched her, but she was clearly in custody.

She scowled at Bisti. "I haven't finished with you."

"Whew!" Anita said when the trio was beyond hearing.

Caleb smiled. "David, you seem to be suffering the same fate as Mr. Swift."

"The man the Irish hated because they didn't understand his *Modest Proposal*," David asked, grinning, "and the English hated because they did?"

TWO

The gallery was imperfectly reflected by the window that formed its east wall. Traffic and passersby on Michigan Avenue below showed like a double exposure through images of the moneyed set dressed to impress.

Caleb turned away from the outside view and his own distorted image. At his left, Anita leaned back against the window's guard rail and pointed to a small enclave by the elevator. "The lady with the politicians swarming around her is Lauren Bisti, David's wife."

He looked. He didn't know enough about women's fashion to recognize the work of a particular designer, but even from across the room, he knew class when he saw it. Lauren Bisti's dress was class. It wasn't trendy or titillating, but it flattered her in every way a garment could. She herself was tall and slim and naturally blond. And socially adept, he realized as he watched her handle an alderman and a senator.

They were discussing an installation titled *Red Man's Revenge,* which consisted of three white-skinned mannequins playing bingo.

Caleb studied the faces of Lauren Bisti and her entourage. Their discussion was animated by expressive body language, including wide crocodile smiles.

Anita touched his arm. "What do you suppose they're saying?"

"Probably something along the line of 'Your husband is the greatest artist alive, Mrs. Bisti.'"

"And what do you suppose they're thinking?"

They both laughed.

"Dog people," Anita said. It was shorthand for a social theory Caleb had developed—that people could be divided, roughly, into dog people, who are like canines in their need for adulation and reassurance, and cat people, self-motivated and largely impervious to social pressure. "How would you classify David?"

Before he could answer, a dark-haired woman approached them with an attractive man in tow. "Excuse me," she said. "Aren't you Anita Margolis?"

Anita turned to her and smiled.

"I'm Amanda Kent," the woman continued, pushing the man at Anita. "This is my husband, Todd."

Todd Kent held his hand toward Anita and said, *Enchanté,* Ms. Margolis."

"Anita. Please," she said.

"Todd is David's business manager," Amanda offered. She was beautiful the way fashion-magazine models are, with a face so flawless it might have been airbrushed on. But she gave the impression that her personality had only the depth of a glossy photograph.

Anita nodded, acknowledging the information, then indicated Caleb. "This is my friend, Jack Caleb. He's a patron."

"Jack," Kent repeated. "A patron." He pulled a sheet of paper, folded in three, from an inner jacket pocket and presented it to Caleb. "Then you'll definitely need one of these."

It was a price list for works in the exhibit. As he looked it over, Caleb wondered what the museum management thought of it. The glossy, official brochure didn't have prices, just artsy descriptions of the works and an insufferably flattering bio of the artist. In fact, the brochure didn't even indicate the pieces were for sale. Caleb refolded the list and put it in his pocket.

"You're not related to the Dr. James Caleb who loaned us the landscape?" Kent asked. He wasn't as beautiful up close as he'd first appeared, his features having been artfully rearranged. He had flawless teeth but thinning hair, and he wore tinted contact lenses.

"I'm he," Caleb told him. He could see Kent wonder how one got Jack from James and decide not to ask.

"Well it was very good of you. That painting tipped the balance in favor of the museum board allowing this exhibition."

I'll bet it did, Caleb thought. It may have been the only example the board had seen of David's recent work. He said, "Glad I could be of help."

Kent responded with the sort of smile that signals inattention. He was watching Lauren Bisti or the politicians. Caleb wasn't sure which.

When one of the waiters interrupted Lauren Bisti's conversation by offering the group champagne, Kent took the opportunity to excuse himself and his wife and went to join the higher-status party.

As soon as they were out of hearing range, Anita said, "Rrruff!"

THREE

Jack, darling!"

The man who slipped his arm through Caleb's irritated the doctor immensely. Ivan—pronounced *EEE*-VON—was a man for whom the clichés about catty, hostile gays had been invented. He seemed to have absorbed all the stereotypes and refined and perfected them until he presented a caricature so exaggerated that everything about him seemed to say, You can't take this seriously. Caleb suspected that he used this persona to manipulate those with whom he had business—sometimes to enrage them, occasionally to distract them from the negotiations at hand.

Ivan persisted. "What do you think of the pièce de résistance?"

"I'm not sure I've seen it," Caleb said as neutrally as possible. To show the man annoyance was to invite further provocation.

Ivan prodded Caleb's upper arm with the outstretched fingers of his free hand, ending the gesture with fingers splayed and wrist limp. "Dear, you *must!*"

Caleb firmly disengaged his arm and turned to get Anita's reaction, unequivocally calling Ivan's attention to her presence. It was a gesture. Ivan, who missed nothing, was well aware of her.

Anita took Ivan's arm and squeezed it. "Ivan, your misogyny is showing."

He gave her a beatific smile. "Nothing so sinister, my dear.

9

Just jealousy. You've managed to nab the second most beautiful man here."

"Only the second?"

"By definition, the guest of honor . . ." Ivan gave an exaggerated sigh of longing that was intended to mock as well as flatter, then flounced off.

Anita said, "What would he do if you took him up on one of his propositions?"

"That's not something I'm curious enough about to try."

The museum's architecture was peculiar. Two adjacent commercial buildings, with floors at differing heights, had been connected by a series of gently sloping ramps. The different levels divided the museum's three floors into relatively intimate galleries. And soft gray carpet underfoot furthered the feeling of coziness.

When they'd finished studying *Red Man's Revenge* and *Native American Gothic* in the gallery above the lobby, Caleb and Anita took the elevator—paneled with wood and large enough to accommodate a baby grand or a busload of art patrons—to the topmost of the two floors occupied by the Blue Mountain Cat show.

"When we've exhausted the possibilities here," Caleb told her, as they left the elevator, "we'll have gravity on our side getting to the next."

One of only two exhibits in the upper gallery, *Reverence for the Past* was an ancient-looking bone knife thrust through a bundle of currency, a bill of sale, a certificate of authenticity, and the sternum of a skeleton half buried next to a black-and-white ceramic bowl in a wooden crate of sand. There was only one other person in the room. Caleb recognized him, a professor from the University of Chicago: Matthew Dennison, PhD.

"I'd think this wasn't your métier, Dr. Dennison."

Dennison looked more like a golf pro—fit and tan—than an aging professor. He seemed startled. "Do I know you?"

10

"No reason you should. I attended one of your lectures. 'Peoples of the Southwest.'"

"Ah, yes." Dennison raised his eyebrows.

Waiting for an introduction, Caleb decided. "I'm Jack Caleb. This is Anita Margolis." When they'd completed the requisite handshakes and inanities, Caleb asked, "Are you branching out into contemporary Indian art, Doctor?"

"Hell, no—" He remembered Anita and said, "Er, excuse me."

She muttered, "People seem quite concerned, this evening, about offending my sensibilities."

"I heard a rumor," Dennison told Caleb, "that Bisti uses Anasazi artifacts to make his junk. That, for example—" He pointed to the bowl in the sand.

So much for art appreciation.

"That's illegal!" Anita said.

"Not if the piece was found on private property. Or the seller is willing to swear that it was. To read some of the affidavits, there are entire Anasazi cities buried on some private properties."

The catalog was ambiguous on the subject, saying only that the bowl was Anasazi.

"I doubt he uses genuine pieces," Anita said. "I've been offered a few from time to time. They're horribly expensive."

Genuine or ingenious? Art or artifice? Caleb was sure the ambiguity was intended.

They left Dennison studying the bowl and drifted into the next gallery, a mezzanine overlooking the floor below.

"This must be what Ivan was referring to," Anita said, pointing. *Progress.*

The installation, on the wall shared by both upper and lower galleries, looked like a ten-by-twenty foot painting springing off its canvas into three dimensions. They had to descend to the lower gallery to fully appreciate it. The part on the wall was a generic cityscape, cubist and panoramic, showing both aerial and profile views surrounded by desert. Coming out of the foreground, into the lower gallery, was the steel skeleton of a skyscraper in progress. The building's foundation, however, was a Tinkertoy construction of human bones—tiny and organized in the painted part of the picture, longer and larger and scattered like Pick-Up Sticks in the part that seemed to have broken free, so that the bones at the foremost edge of the work were life-size. They were labeled: HOMO SAPIENS NAVAJOENSIS, H. SAPIENS PUEBLOENSIS, H. SAPIENS LAKOTA, etc. A toy tractor crawling over the middle ground of the thanatocoenose had a logo that explained Harrison Wingate's wrath—a tiny, three-barred gate with a blue first-place ribbon affixed.

"Well," Caleb said, "this explains Harrison Wingate's animosity."

"Very pun-ny. Do you think David meant he's literally building on the bones of Native tribes, or digging up Indian remains?"

"We'll have to ask him." He sighed and added, "So much for my plan to save energy," as they climbed back up to the mezzanine.

Clinging to his arm to avoid falling off her three-inch heels, Anita patted his shoulder and said, "I'll overlook it if you promise we can leave soon. I'm starving."

"Our reservations aren't until nine."

"We could stop for a drink, or coffee to kill time. McDonald's would be better than this."

Caleb laughed, and they began their tour of the mezzanine gallery. Halfway through, they came upon several regular patrons of the museum in an animated discussion of David's vision of progress. They stopped to eavesdrop. All were scandalized except one elderly woman who seemed to think David was the most original artist since Picasso.

Their conversation was brought to an abrupt halt by a scream.

FOUR

Caleb wasn't given to flashbacks. The sound was real, and he reacted as he'd been conditioned to by the war, running cautiously toward it. He didn't remember setting his drink down, but he must have—he didn't hear glass breaking.

Lauren Bisti was framed in the entrance to the gallery featuring the installation with the bone knife. Her back was to Caleb. She lunged forward. He followed her through the doorway, and before her figure obscured it, he glimpsed what seemed to be David Bisti's most effective exhibit.

David himself was sprawled on the floor with the bone knife buried to its hilt in his chest. Bright blood seeped from his nose and mouth.

Simultaneously, Caleb became aware of three things.

Dismay was first, the feeling most often expressed—inadequately—by some simple utterance: Oh, God!

He noticed his own reaction next, the dismay deepening to despair. Not another artist! Not David!

Finally, there was primitive excitement—almost akin to joy—at the sight of blood. Bright, oxygenated blood. Stoplight, stop-heart red. Shocking.

He felt no guilt for this last. It was quite normal. The mind protected itself from horror with disbelief and distraction. Time enough, later, for the awful enormity to sink in. For the finality to assert itself.

Then before he could warn her not to, Lauren threw herself on the body, jerked the knife out, and flung it aside. Blood seeped from the wound and pooled on David's chest. Caleb could smell it.

Without any apparent thought for the blood, Lauren knelt beside the remains and took David's body on her lap—all in no more time than it took Caleb to register her actions. She sat on the floor, legs straight out, blood seeping onto her lap and soaking the carpet as she rocked her murdered husband, making animal sounds.

Caleb tore his eyes from the tableau and scanned the room. No bloody-handed killers skulked in any of the corners. Behind him, people piled up like cars stopped behind a wreck. A murmur of "What happened?" passed through the crowd, which surged toward the site of the tragedy until it came up against the breakwater of those first on the scene. Caleb blunted the momentum of the most aggressively curious by giving them minimal information and assignments: "There's been an accident. Please call the police and paramedics. Get a security guard. Find the director. Please stand by the front door and make a note of everyone who leaves." He kept those who questioned his authority at bay by interposing himself between them and the crime scene. With his peripheral vision, he could see Anita doing the same, standing with him to form a police line of two.

A man tried to push past, and Caleb put an arm out to stop him. He kept his voice low but put authority in his tone. "Don't come in here."

"Who appointed you God?"

Caleb kept his face neutral and raised his eyebrows.

"I'm Michael Wren," the man said. "Let me pass."

"You have a good reason to give the police for entering a crime scene?"

Wren was taken aback for a moment, then said, "Someone should help the poor bastard."

"He's beyond help."

"I suppose you're a doctor."

"I am, as a matter of fact."

That seemed to end the opposition. A man in a security guard's uniform pushed his way through; someone said, "Thank God." Wren laughed cynically.

The security guard said, "What happened?"

"There's been a violent death," Caleb told him. While the guard absorbed that, staring at the bloody spectacle, Caleb told Wren, "If you really want to help, Mr. Wren, try to get everyone to wait in one of the other rooms until the police arrive. And ask them not to discuss this until they've spoken with the detectives." Caleb watched conflicting desires—curiosity and the urge to be in control of things—contort Wren's face. The will to power won out, or perhaps—to give him benefit of the doubt—Wren's desire to be heroic won. He turned his back on Caleb and began to demand attention from the crowd.

"I've just been advised," he said, "that the best thing we can all do for now is to clear this area." He pushed his way through the crowd—parting it, to be more accurate, with the force of his personal power. Then he led everyone but Caleb, Anita, Lauren, and the guard from the room.

Caleb turned back to the guard, who looked ill but asked gamely, "What should I do?" He was young, in his early twenties.

"Keep everyone out until the police arrive," Caleb said, "even your boss."

The guard inclined his head toward Lauren Bisti. "What about her?"

"I'll see if I can't persuade her to come with us."

FIVE

Thinnes was an hour early for work. Rossi, his supervisor, had chewed him out three times in two weeks for being late, and Thinnes had had it. Rossi was never confused by the fact that Thinnes usually worked past quitting time without putting in for overtime pay.

The squad room was large and square, with standard fluorescent overhead lighting, yellow-painted concrete block walls, and a red, ceramic-tile floor. The north-south rows of tables that served as desks for the detectives were equipped with uncomfortable chairs. Each table had at least one phone. A thirty-gallon coffee urn was centrally located. The assignment officer's counter and the doorway to the stairs occupied the west wall. Other doors around the periphery led to offices and interview rooms. There were three other dicks in the room—all on the clock, all looking busy. Thinnes had taken a conspicuous seat near Rossi's office and was reading the *Sun-Times* when Rossi came in.

"Thinnes," he said without any warmup, "where's your sidekick?"

"He's not on for an hour. He'll be here."

"Yeah. Well, we got a stabbing on North Michigan. Some Indian." His tone implied that he shared Custer's attitude about Indians. He handed Thinnes a paper with the address. The number was familiar. "I don't need to remind you to be discreet."

Then why did you? flashed through Thinnes's head, followed by *Teach your grandmother to suck eggs!* But he didn't say it; he shook his head.

"Get on with it, then."

"Right."

Thinnes left the *Sun-Times* on the table. Someone might as well enjoy it; he wouldn't get back to it tonight.

When Thinnes pulled the dark blue Caprice in front of the museum, there was a single reporter canvassing the gawkers held at bay by yellow crime-scene tape. Thinnes parked in front of the line of patrol cars and the ambulance sitting at the curb with lights blazing. Out of habit, he tossed the OFFICIAL POLICE BUSINESS sign on his dash and pulled the keys from the ignition before walking back to talk to the beat cop in the second car. It was cold, but the crowd was orderly, and the copper was keeping warm while carrying out his assignment to keep an eye on things. He rolled his window down as Thinnes approached and nodded when Thinnes flashed his star. "Detective."

Thinnes pointed to the reporter. Male Cauc, early forties, five ten, 170, medium build, blue eyes, brown hair, beard streaked with silver. He was wearing wire-rimmed glasses, a black jacket, Levi's, gray athletic shoes, and a hat like John Drummond's. "Who's that?"

"He's okay," the cop said. "The crime reporter for 'News Radio.' " He laughed. "Must have a good scanner."

"Or *very* good informants," Thinnes agreed.

SIX

Anita's head appeared in the ladies' room doorway. "Jack, we need the paramedics in here!"

The two men in fire-department uniforms raced Caleb for the ladies' room. Inside, they found Lauren Bisti in a heap on the gray linoleum. Blood seemed to be everywhere.

"What happened?" Caleb asked, as the medics squeezed their equipment into the cramped space.

"I started to help her wash some of the blood off," Anita said. "When she looked in the mirror, she just fainted."

"Could you folks move out and give us room to work here?" one of the medics asked.

Without saying anything more, Anita squeezed past them and disappeared.

Caleb said, "Certainly," but he backed up against one of the toilet stalls and paused to look before he left.

In a scene familiar from the nightly news and countless TV recreations, Lauren Bisti lay on the floor between the paramedics, who were efficiently doing everything that needed to be done.

The room was surprisingly Spartan—two salmon-painted sheet-metal stalls with standard, institutional toilets; metal towel dispensers; a vanity counter with only one sink; and a mirror, centered over the sink, so small it covered only a third of the wall behind the sink. There was a single, bloody handprint on the counter. Laureen obviously had placed her hand there, perhaps leaning over to look in the mirror, perhaps to steady herself when she felt faint. The print smeared across the countertop, and where her dress brushed up against it, the front of the vanity was also smeared with blood. The floor was spotted with it.

Caleb decided he could best help by staying out of the way and was about to leave when a woman's voice demanded, "Let me through. My friend needs me."

"Damn!" one of the medics said. He looked up at Caleb. "Keep her out of here, will you?"

Caleb nodded. When he stepped to the doorway, he filled it with his bulk, blocking Amanda Kent.

She said, "Get out of my way."

Caleb kept his voice low, so she'd have to strain to hear him. "I'm sorry."

It got her attention. She said, "Lauren?"

"She's being well cared for."

"How would you know?"

"I'm a doctor. The paramedics know what they're doing."

She relaxed a little.

"The best thing you can do for her," Caleb added, "is pull yourself together and cooperate with the police investigation."

"How is she?"

"She hasn't been physically harmed but she's in shock."

She nodded dully, as if in shock herself, and turned away. Caleb stepped out of the doorway and pulled the door shut. He crossed his arms and stood guard until the medics carried Lauren Bisti out.

SEVEN

The textbooks said you were supposed to separate multiple witnesses and multiple offenders. Yeah, right. Thinnes looked around and groaned inwardly. "Give me the *good* news," he told the uniform without looking at him.

The copper pulled his notebook from his pocket before answering, and Thinnes wondered if the sudden pain in his gut was due to the .38 slug he'd stopped there some months back or to the realization that the first officer on the scene was a rookie. "Just tell me," he said wearily.

As the rookie started to answer, a second uniform hurried up. A veteran. Black, five eight, 220 pounds. Officer Reilly. "I'll take care of this, Curtis," he said. "You go see what's holding up the sergeant."

"Curtis," Thinnes said, "make a note of everyone hanging around outside and get the license number of anything parked in this block and the alleys on either side. As soon as somebody shows up with a camera, ask 'em to get pictures of the crowd." He looked back at Reilly.

"We got a call for a stabbing," Reilly told him, "and found this. Paramedics were already on the scene. Said the victim'd already been pronounced dead by a doctor."

"You got the perp?"

"Nah. Doctor who pronounced the victim seems to have taken charge—I didn't have time to get all the details but he said he couldn't finger the cutter."

"Where is he?"

Reilly laughed. "In the ladies' room. Victim's wife isn't taking it very well. They got the medics in there, too."

"Thanks, Reilly. See if you can find out who's in charge of this circus, will you? And when my partner arrives send him in—Detective Oster."

"Right."

Reilly left, and Thinnes took a deep breath. The suspect list—judging by the number of people milling around—was awesome. Where do you start with a case like this?

Get a grip on it, Thinnes! he told himself. *Start at the beginning.*

Start with the most obvious suspects—wife, business partners, lovers. Establish whereabouts. Opportunities. Motives. Figure out who stands to gain.

Fending off questions and demands from the crowd of witnesses, Thinnes found a phone near the reception desk and dialed his supervisor's number. No sense broadcasting the details to all the reporters listening on their scanners. After three rings, he heard, "Rossi."

"Lieutenant? Thinnes. I've got seventy-five of the best shod of the city's well-heeled on the scene, and they're madder than wet hornets. This Indian wasn't just some Uptown wino that wandered down here and died. You'd better send me some reinforcements."

EIGHT

The police arrived with commendable speed. Caleb glanced at his watch and calculated seven minutes elapsed between Lauren Bisti's scream and the first officer's arrival. If one allowed for the time required to decide that the police *should* be called, it had not taken them more than two or three minutes to respond.

A significant number of the guests had escaped—those who wanted to avoid the scandal, those with something to hide. The rest were trapped between the police who'd expelled them from the crime scene on the upper level and those guarding the exits. The stairs were covered with people who'd abandoned all pretense of dignity for the comfort of a seat, however unconventional. And, in spite of the injunction against discussing the case, there was a low murmur of conversation. The events taking place above, behind the barrier of uniformed officers and yellow police tape, were too intriguing to pass without comment.

Caleb and Anita staked their claim to the bottom step, with the best view of the lobby and the best chance of an early interview, but Caleb soon relinquished his seat to a pregnant woman in five-inch heels. When he got tired of standing, he sat on the floor. His suit was ruined anyway—stained with David Bisti's blood. As they watched four detectives enter and flash their badges at the cop guarding the door, Caleb told Anita, "It looks like our reservations have been canceled."

It was obviously going to be a long night.

* * *

The beat copper guarding the crime scene didn't seem bothered by the bloody death, but he was happy to see Thinnes.

Thinnes could see why. As soon as they realized Thinnes was someone with authority, the half-dozen business types swarming around the officer transferred their interest and their questions to him.

"I'm Michael Wren," one of them insisted, "a member of the museum board. I demand to know—"

"Have you given your name and statement to the officer, Mr. Wren?" He pointed to the beat cop.

"Well, no—"

"Please do so." Thinnes gave the patrolman a wink Wren couldn't see and walked away before Wren could protest.

The murder site looked like a stage set, with the body lying like an important prop under a spotlight—one of the museum's exhibit lights. The exhibit the light should have lit, a wooden crate atop a pedestal, was tipped back against the north wall of the room, tempting gravity, threatening to spill its contents onto the gray carpet.

Thinnes carefully wiped his feet on the carpet and ducked under the barricade tape for a closer look. He watched where he put his feet. The victim was a male Indian, somewhere around six feet in height, probably 175 pounds, between twenty-five and thirty-five years of age. Thinnes took latex gloves out of his pocket and put them on before putting a finger to the victim's throat, over the carotid. No pulse. He was dead all right.

There was a bloody hole in the front of his white leather shirt, and blood around his nose and mouth. None on his hands. Curious.

Thinnes looked at the rest of the room. The east wall was a huge window looking down on Michigan Avenue; the south wall had the doors and ramp down to the next gallery, as well as an ugly painting, and a fire-escape door; the elevator filled most of the west wall; the north wall was bare except for the damaged exhibit leaning against it, a sign identifying the exhibit, and architectural details of no particular interest to the police. A woman's purse lay near the body. He resisted the urge to disturb it before the mobil unit had taken photos and diagrammed its position. He didn't touch the bloody knife either.

He took the elevator back down to the lobby. Reilly had returned with a semidistracted receptionist and the information that no one had seen the man in charge—one Lewis Andrews—since he'd evicted a crasher.

Reinforcements arrived in fairly good time, in the persons of detectives Oster, Viernes, Ryan, and Swann. Oster had been Thinnes's regular partner since he'd returned from sick leave. John Viernes, Kate Ryan, and Leonard Swann were all supposed to be working days, but they happened to be in the squad room when Thinnes called Rossi. They'd been drafted because this was a heater case and Rossi was willing to pay overtime to cover his ass.

Ryan was a natural redhead, and when she didn't wear makeup—like now—her freckles stood out and her brows and lashes disappeared. She looked like she hadn't slept in days—her green eyes were red rimmed and she couldn't keep from yawning.

"Ryan, you gonna make it through this tour?" Thinnes asked.

"I just need a little coffee."

"Yeah," Thinnes said. He'd seen her mainlining it back at the Area. "They just took the victim's wife to Northwestern Memorial. Why don't you go on over there and make sure we get a statement from her before the press does? I'll give you a call before we leave here."

And if the wife was out of it for hours, no one would fault Ryan for copping a few z's while she waited. Ryan looked grateful as she nodded and left.

* * *

The doctor turned out to be someone Thinnes knew. Dr. James Caleb. The man who'd saved his life. Small world.

Neither of them bothered with pleasantries. Thinnes waited until Oster was ready with notebook and pen, then said, "Take it slowly, Doctor. Tell me exactly what you saw."

NINE

Caleb closed his eyes and conjured up the memory, describing it in detail for the detectives. Lauren Bisti's back, bared by the low-cut dress. Striking. Her elbows pressed tightly to her sides.

"Could you see her face?"

Caleb opened his eyes. "No. Only her back, only her gesture."

"So you couldn't actually see her face or expression?"

"No."

"Go on."

"I could see David on the floor, under the light that was trained on the exhibit. For a fraction of a second, I thought he was one of his installations—with the knife in his chest. Then his chest moved and I knew the blood trickling from his mouth was real."

"So?"

"It was obvious he was in shock. His face was nearly as white as his shirt and he didn't seem to be aware of us or anything."

"You were how far away?"

"About twenty-five feet."

Thinnes waited.

"Then Mrs. Bisti dropped to her knees on the floor next to him and pulled the knife out."

"You didn't try to stop her?"

"I didn't think fast enough. It wouldn't have occurred to me that anyone . . ."

He didn't need to finish. They both knew that Lauren Bisti's well-intentioned act—pulling the knife out of Bisti's chest—had probably killed him, had unplugged the hole in whatever tissue the blade had penetrated, letting the blood flow unimpeded.

"Then what?"

"She threw away the knife and lifted his upper body onto her lap."

"You still didn't try to stop her?"

"There didn't seem to be any point. All the indications were that his heart or a major artery had been hit and he'd lost a significant percentage of his blood volume into his chest cavity. If he'd been in an emergency room, with a team of prepped surgeons, he wouldn't have had much chance."

Thinnes said, "Ahuh. What did Mrs. Bisti do?"

"She just sat there, cradling his head in her arms and staring into space until Anita and I led her from the room."

"After you removed her, did the position of the body differ much from what it was when you first saw it?"

Caleb thought for a moment. "Not appreciably. There was just a good deal more blood after she— we moved him."

"How's that?"

"When the chest is compressed, whatever is in the lungs is expelled. When she lifted his upper body . . ."

Thinnes nodded.

"She didn't make any effort to avoid getting bloodied."

"She have any blood on her before she pulled out the knife?"

"Not that I noticed. Not on her back."

The interview was interesting. Interview. Not an interrogation. Caleb was fairly certain he wasn't a suspect. Thinnes's new partner, Oster, didn't seem as cynical as his previous one. Caleb had met Oster before. The detective seemed decent and intelligent. He looked like salesman Willy Loman gone to fat.

"When did you last see him alive?" Thinnes asked. He looked tired.

"The time? I'm sorry, I have no idea. Anita might know."

Thinnes asked Oster to get Anita, and Caleb was sure he'd been eliminated as a suspect.

Oster returned with her and offered her a seat. He resumed his place.

Thinnes asked her, "You were with Dr. Caleb all evening?"

"Until David was murdered. We heard a scream, and Jack ran toward the sound. I followed him, but not fast enough to keep him in sight."

She seemed very calm, and Caleb wondered if Thinnes would think that suspicious. But he must have seen every sort of response to murder in his career. He'd surely recognize the nuances of shock that were obvious to Caleb himself.

Thinnes gave no hint one way or another. He had her go over the evening for him, from their arrival at the museum to Oster's summons. Anita abbreviated. They'd checked their coats. They'd studied one or two of the pieces, observed the interchange between David and Wingate, then between David and Irene. They'd spoken with Ivan, the Kents, and several other people. They were talking to one of the museum members when they heard Mrs. Bisti scream.

"When was the last time you saw Mr. Bisti alive?"

"Just after security escorted Irene out," Anita said. "Someone came and dragged him off and we continued our tour of the show." Thinnes waited. She added, "We were looking at *Progress* when we heard Lauren Bisti scream."

"Doctor?" Thinnes said.

"That's correct."

Thinnes took them out to the lobby and pointed at the people waiting to be interviewed. "Look around," he said. Then he led them to the elevator and took them to the next floor, the one with the *American Gothic* installation. They followed him through that to the mezzanine gallery, where the rest of the witnesses were milling around. "Notice anybody missing who was here earlier?"

They looked. "Harrison Wingate," Anita said, "and the woman they threw out earlier. Irene."

"And Ivan," Caleb added.

Anita agreed.

Oster wrote in his notebook, waited, said, "Last name?"

Caleb said, "I don't know. I'm not sure he has one."

"He an artist?" Oster asked.

"A critic," Anita said. "Sort of the Truman Capote of art criticism."

"The guy who wrote *In Cold Blood?*" Thinnes asked. "I'm not sure I follow."

"Ivan's as much a celebrity as a critic," Caleb explained. "And his criticism often takes the form of sarcasm."

Thinnes nodded. "He have anything against Bisti?"

Caleb said, "Not to my knowledge. If he did, he'd attack him with words."

"Anybody else missing?"

"The museum's special-activities director."

HIGHLAND PARK PUBLIC LIBRARY

TEN

Bendix took out matches and a cigar and lit up, carefully dropping the spent match in his pocket as he created a cloud of foul-smelling smoke. He stood just outside the yellow police barrier tape that Reilly and his partner had strung across the gallery to secure the scene, and watched his men photograph and diagram the room. Bendix was the head of one of the department's top mobile units. He was out of shape and balding, cynical enough to make your average street cop seem like an altar boy and as sensitive as a steel-belted radial. He and Thinnes went way back. They got along as well as your average dog and cat. But Bendix was good.

Thinnes didn't bother to point out that the cigar was violating Illinois's Clean Air Act. He said, "How long are you going to be?"

" 'Pends on how many of 'em you want me to print." He hooked his thumb in the direction of the witnesses waiting to be interviewed.

Thinnes thought of the political ramifications of fingerprinting an alderman and a state senator. "See if you get any latents, first."

Bendix nodded. " 'Bout an hour, then."

"Let me know when you're done."

"Yeah."

Thinnes's only concession to politics was interviewing the alderman and the state senator first—after a pregnant woman and her husband. Neither the alderman nor the senator had anything useful to contribute, but both asked to be kept abreast of the investigation. Thinnes told them both the same thing: "I'll do what I can, sir." It was a useful, noncommittal answer that made him sound helpful and respectful. Never mind that what he could do was nothing at all.

"Hey, Thinnes." Detective Viernes hailed him from the doorway across the lobby and waited until Thinnes came close enough so that only he would hear. "We found Andrews." Viernes was thirty-five, five ten, and as fit and sharp as any FBI agent Thinnes ever met. He pushed the door behind him open and stepped aside to let Thinnes enter the room first.

It was an office. The desk in it probably cost more than most cars, and there were original oil paintings on the walls and an oriental rug on the floor. Andrews, the man one of the art patrons had described as hard as diamond but smooth as graphite, was stretched out on his designer couch, so shit-faced he couldn't focus when he looked up at them.

"Nothing like this has ever happened," he said, putting his words together carefully, the way people do when they don't want anyone to know how far gone they are. "Ever! I'm ruined."

He'd sober up at the station. Thinnes wished they could send him in a squad roll. He pitied the poor uniform who had to clean up the car if he puked.

Once Andrews was dispatched, Thinnes was free to use the office for his interviews. He started with the security guards and serving staff, then sent for Bisti's business manager. Later, he would interview the man in depth, probably at Area headquarters when he'd found out enough about him to judge his answers. Just now, he needed a picture—however biased—of the victim's life, an idea of what Bisti was like, a clue to what the questions ought to be.

"What do you do for a living, Mr. Kent?"

"I'm an attorney."

"Tell me about David Bisti."

"Someone will have to break the news to his mother."

"You got her address?"

Kent shook his head. "I can get it for you."

Thinnes nodded. "Tell me about Bisti."

"He was talented." As if that summed him up. There was a plaintive quality to the statement.

"He have any enemies?"

"I don't know. One, apparently."

"Arguments with anyone lately?"

"Not that I know of."

Thinnes had seen every imaginable reaction to violent death in his years as a cop, from paralyzing depression to hysterical laughter at the mention of the deceased's name. So he didn't attach much significance to Kent's apparent lack of emotion.

"How did you come to work for Bisti?"

"Lauren—his wife—introduced us. She knew I had money to invest and sold me on the idea that the work of an undiscovered genius would be a profitable way to invest it. When David got big enough to incorporate, he offered to cut me in if I'd take over the business end of things. It was a very nice arrangement."

"Hear about his run-in with Harrison Wingate?"

"No."

"Why was Wingate invited?"

"Damned if I know."

He was lying. Why? Thinnes said, "How'd Bisti get on with his wife?"

"Very well. He adored her."

"How'd she feel about him?"

"The feeling was mutual, as far as I know."

"He cheat on her?"

Kent looked startled, as if he'd never thought of it. "I don't think he'd do that."

"But you can't be sure."

"I was his partner, not his confessor."

"Are you and *Mrs.* Bisti close?"

Kent scowled. "We weren't involved, if that's what you're getting at. Lauren idolized David."

"Who would stand to benefit from his death?"

"Damned if I know!"

Thinnes waited.

Finally, Kent said, "I suppose his paintings will appreciate in value now that there won't be any more, but he wasn't Picasso." He shook his head. "It doesn't make any sense."

"How was business?"

"Very good. Until tonight. I mean . . ." For the first time he showed signs of losing control. "We had a little insurance but— Christ!—David *was* the business. You can't just go out and buy another artist."

Half an hour later, Viernes came in and held up a pile of notes. "This is all those who didn't see anything, didn't hear anything, and don't have a clue about who done it. I sent 'em home." He handed Thinnes a second, smaller pile. "This is all those who won't say a thing until they talk to their lawyers." He hooked his thumb toward the much-smaller crowd. "They're all yours." He held up one more piece of paper. "This one knows who did it but he won't talk to anyone but the chief."

Thinnes took the paper. "He'll talk to me. Send him in."

The man Viernes showed into the office was in his sixties, five ten, 190 pounds, with silver hair and faded blue eyes. He was clean shaven and well dressed. He looked carefully at Thinnes, then around the room. "You're not the chief of detectives."

"No. I'm the detective in charge of this case."

"I have to talk to the chief."

"On this investigation, I'm him, Mr. . . ." Thinnes looked at the paper Viernes had given him. "Roth." When Roth didn't respond immediately, he added, "I don't have time for games. You told the detective you know who killed Mr. Bisti. By refusing to tell us what you know, you're obstructing justice."

Roth thought about that. "If I tell you, you'll pass it on to the chief of detectives?"

Thinnes sighed inwardly but kept up a perfectly neutral front. Why did these cases always bring the nuts out of the woods? "I'll do what I can, Mr. Roth."

Roth nodded. "I read a great deal. I've read Freud in the original German. And I've read a great many true-crime stories and police procedurals. I know about these things. Mr. Bisti was stabbed, was he not?"

"I'm not at liberty to divulge that information. If you know anything, let's have it."

"Such impatience." Roth shook his head. "I know that most murders are committed by family members or acquaintances of the victim. Indoor murders, that is. Outdoor murders are, sadly, most often committed by psychopaths or drunks. Well, some indoor murders are committed by inebriated persons, but no one here fits that description. So the murderer must have been his wife."

By the time they'd interviewed everyone, Thinnes felt like lying down. His stamina seemed to have been cut out with the two and a half feet of gut they'd removed last summer repairing the gunshot wound.

The whole story was pretty routine—nobody saw anything. Nobody knew anything. No one could even imagine who would want to kill a nice man like the victim.

There were too many whose alibi was "I didn't do it" or "If I'd done it, wouldn't I be all bloody?" The relative absence of blood was no help. Bisti had bled to death into his lungs. Until his wife moved the body, there was virtually no external bleeding, and it would have been possible for *anyone* to wrap a napkin or two around the handle of the knife before wielding it. No one would've noticed. Thinnes had long since ceased to be amazed by how unobservant people are.

He'd have to talk to the alarm people and check on whoever serviced the system last—see if there was any way of circumventing the alarm on the fire door. He made a note to get the security tapes. No camera on the murder scene—no such luck—but he'd noticed the elevator and the fire exit were covered.

It was almost a classic puzzle—man killed in an otherwise empty room, no one seen leaving, no one with blood on himself. And the only ones known to have had a beef with the deceased weren't around at the time. Nearly all the suspects were people from *Who's Who,* like some bizarre American version of a classical mystery. Agatha Christie in Chicago. If it had been anybody else's case, it would have been hysterically funny.

ELEVEN

After the police released them, Caleb got the Jaguar and drove Anita home. They didn't speak in the car, but when he stopped in front of her building and started to open his door, she said, "Come up for a nightcap?"

She hadn't asked him that in years, not since he'd convinced her that he'd never be interested in a relationship. The question startled him momentarily. He could sense the need that prompted it. Tonight wasn't something you could just put out of mind. It needed explanation or at least interpretation. It needed closure. He nodded, closed the door, and pulled the Jag into the garage under the building, parking in a visitor space.

Anita didn't wait for him to get out to open her door. She stood in the drive while he set the alarm, then slipped her arm through his as they walked out. All the while, they didn't speak. Caleb waited. She would get to it, and waiting was his life's work. *Everything comes to him who waits.*

The doorman said, "Good evening, Ms. Margolis. Sir," as he waved them into the lobby.

The silence continued all the way up to Anita's condo, until she'd closed the door behind them. The door opened into a short hall. White walls. Red oriental carpet over varnished oak floor. There was a small Erté print on the wall to the right. Pale gray. *Rain.* Stylized raindrops paralleling tears on an Erté face. Simple. Appropriate. Anita probably passed, without seeing it, a dozen times a week. Tonight it held her. When she turned, her tears mimicked the Erté's. She grabbed him and clung as a child would. She was so small, her head barely reached his sternum. His arms closed around her reflexively.

"Oh God, Jack!"

She smelled faintly of Bain de Soleil. The scent brought to mind another beautiful Margolis, on a sun-washed beach, years earlier. Caleb felt the dismaying sense of loss before he could suppress the memory. Suppress, not repress. Put away for a more appropriate time.

He held her for a long moment, then said, "Let's talk about it."

She didn't let go as they entered the living room, pausing to turn up the lights. The room was an art gallery—vast stretches of white walls, each with original art displayed and lit to advantage, ceilings broken by skylights above luxuriant ficus and dieffenbachia. The furniture was modern and comfortable, selected to complement the art, not to be noticed for itself. The materials were for the most part natural—wood, glass, stone, wool, and leather. Anita's taste was exquisite if eclectic. Another Erté, *The French Rooster,* held the place of honor over the marble fireplace, in which a fire was laid between wrought iron firedogs of Celtic design. A Celtic bronze mug on the hearth held long-necked matches, and a *Phalaenopsis* lifted a spray of moth white blossoms over the mantle. Picasso, Miró, de Chirico, and a variation of Dali's *Persistence of Time* adorned other walls. A Harati warmed the polished oak floor. Everything was genuine.

Anita ignored the famous names as she led him toward the couch in front of the fireplace. Her eyes swept past the Erté to the five-by-five canvas between the fireplace and the outside wall with its spectacular view of the harbor.

The painting was of a sudden violent storm over the New Mexican desert. The artist seemed not so much to have fixed the light in time as to have captured live current within the four edges of the frame, where it resonated between sky and earth, and carried the eye with it to every loving detail. A trick. An illusion that made the scene flicker in memory like the afterimage of lightning on the retina. The strong black signature in the lower right-hand corner was David Bisti's.

"He had as fine a grasp of light as anyone. Ever!" Anita shuddered. "I may have to put it away for a while." She went back to the light panel and made the painting disappear in shadow.

Caleb didn't answer, but she wasn't offended by his silence. After a pause, she said, "Why would anyone . . .?"

"We like to delude ourselves that we're not like other beasts, that we're immune to the pull of the moon and the ancient stirrings of the blood. But it takes very little to make us revert. Less for those who are unprepared."

". . . 'Still we're bound by ancient chains. Sea water tides, still, in our veins . . .' "

He smiled wryly.

"You stand there like Gibraltar," she added. "How do you do it?"

He didn't need to ask what. "I've seen violent death before."

"In the war. I'd forgotten." She hugged herself and shivered. The room wasn't cold. "How do the police stand it?"

"They've grown calluses on their souls. And they didn't know the victim."

With another shiver, she went to the bar. "Drink?"

"Hmm."

She didn't have to ask what he wanted. Their tastes were remarkably similar. He sat down and studied the Erté, and in a little while, she handed him a brandy.

He switched his attention to her. She could have been the artist's model. Overwrought and disheveled, she was still exquisite. The few times in his life that he'd regretted being as he was were times spent with her.

The attention made her self-conscious, and she looked herself over as women do, spotting something on her dress.

"What's this?"

As he leaned closer for a look, the smell told him. "Blood, I'm afraid."

"Oh, God! I'll have to change."

"Hmm."

"You won't go?"

He shook his head. "Take your time."

She bent over to cradle his face in her hands and brushed his forehead with her lips. "I love you."

Ordinarily he would have made some flippant remark, but not tonight.

She backed away. "Make yourself at home."

"How 'bout some Mozart?"

"Not *Don Giovanni* . . ." she said, as she closed the bedroom door behind her.

He raised his voice a little so she could hear him through the door. "God, no! But the *Requiem* might be apropos."

She didn't answer, so he opened the cabinet housing the CD player and sorted through her Mozart. He located the *Requiem*. First that, then something lighter. The machine could take up to ten disks; he selected half a dozen.

To change your mood, you started with music that fit what you were feeling and gradually adjusted the music to fit what you wanted to feel. He wanted to feel well. And whole. He went to the fireplace and opened the flue, then lit the kindling. Then he got his drink and watched the amber liquid swirl and climb the glass in the firelight. And he let Mozart inundate his mind.

Anita didn't reappear until Mozart took a turn for the lighter. She was wrapped, chin to ankles, in a fluffy white robe, soft as cat fur. She'd showered, and her hair was still damp as she settled onto the couch, into the curve of his shoulder. The scent of Bain de Soleil was even stronger.

Déjà vu.

They'd been lying on the beach on the Côte d'Azur, she and

Christopher and he, celebrating Chris's birthday, grilling themselves under the Mediterranean sun. They'd taken turns slathering on Anita's suntan cream and laughing at how sweet it made them smell. Caleb sighed.

Anita said, "A penny for your thoughts."

"Those whom the gods love die young."

"You were thinking of Chris, too."

"Déjà vu."

It was too much. Anita pressed her face against his shirt and sobbed and screamed and squeezed the cloth of his sleeve and lapel until she'd pressed creases into it. Caleb took her on his lap and held her like a child.

Eventually, exhaustion stilled her sobs and her breath came in great shuddering gulps. Her breathing slowed. Her grip on his jacket slackened.

Caleb shifted his hold. He eased himself off the couch, lifting her slowly enough to not wake her, and carried her to her room.

Beneath another Erté, the bed had been turned down. Caleb settled her onto iris-patterned sheets and gently removed her robe. She was wearing little less than she had on that Mediterranean beach—that is, nothing at all. The Saint-Tropez tan had faded to her natural ivory skin tone, but she was as lovely as ever—small, perfect breasts and hips that were unmistakably female, but not overwhelmingly so. He bent and kissed her bare shoulder, murmuring, *"Bonne nuit, ma belle,"* then pulled the covers over her.

He set the security alarm before he let himself out.

It was dawn when he finally turned the key in his own lock. Sigmund Freud, Caleb's black cat, greeted him with his usual reserve, and Caleb bent to stroke him. He reset the security system and walked into the living room, where he looked long at the painting he lived with but seldom noticed anymore. Christopher's self-portrait.

Christopher Margolis, who had died more than five years

earlier, gazed at him from the wall with amusement and affection. Caleb felt a brief aftershock from the cataclysm that had shattered his life—Christopher's death.

Déjà déjà vu.

Those whom the gods love die young. Did that apply to David Bisti?

Caleb sat on the couch and put his hands to his face and wept bitterly. It was a strange reversal of roles for a therapist. But therapeutic.

TWELVE

When Thinnes ducked under the yellow POLICE LINE tape stretched across the elevator doorway, Bisti's body had been removed. The place it had been on the gray rug was outlined with masking tape and accented with dark-red blood stains. The crime lab had removed the remaining pieces of the exhibit that the murder weapon had come from.

Bendix held up the plastic bag holding the knife. "Finger-prints."

"The wife's," Thinnes said.

"There you go."

"Witness saw her pull it out. Nobody saw it go in."

"They see anyone else around?"

"No."

"There you have it."

"Just do your thing and leave the detecting to us."

Under orders from Andrews, the receptionist had checked off the names of invitees who'd actually attended. Lucky for the police. She'd also double-checked those who left, up until the hullaba-loo began. At that point, she'd forgotten all about such trivial pursuits. More luck. Dr. C. was a police consultant, familiar enough with police procedure to have asked someone to keep track of who was leaving. Once in a while you caught a break.

Thinnes didn't have to tell anyone not to talk to the press. The regular museum staff had standing orders to be discreet, and he heard their supervisor remind them that direct or anonymous quotes to the media would not be appreciated. The catering staff got a similar warning—their employer could be sued for breach of contract if they blabbed, which presumably would have a negative effect on their future job prospects. The guests only had to be offered an escort through the gauntlet of media reps outside. Most of them accepted.

After they'd gotten rid of everyone else, Thinnes and Oster went over the security arrangements and the night's events with the security staff. Several of them had been circulating in evening clothes, their radios discreetly concealed. They'd observed nothing after they threw out the crasher. No one bothered to notice which way she went when they dropped her on the sidewalk out front. Thinnes made a mental note to ask the reporters if they'd talked with anyone fitting her description. A long shot. If she *had* done Bisti, she'd be goofy to hang around. But then a lot of killers were goofy.

It was easier to run the security videos right at the museum than to go to the trouble of setting things up to see them at Area Three. Later he'd do that, if he needed to see them again, but he took notes as he watched, so he'd remember most of the details.

The security camera showed Todd Kent deep in conversation with a huge man—male Cauc, six two, probably 240 pounds, white hair and blue eyes, and a cynical, slightly amused expression. From his years of observing men with clout, Thinnes knew he was somebody powerful. Both men seemed to be enjoying some sort of joke.

The radio reporter was still out in front. Thinnes finally remembered his name—Rod Manly, a reporter for WMAQ. He'd been joined by his radio competition and Minicam crews from all the TV stations. Thinnes asked them if anyone had seen a woman fitting the description of the mysterious Irene. No one had. And Manly assured him he would have remembered.

THIRTEEN

Northwestern Memorial Hospital is the nearest trauma center to the Chicago Loop, but Lauren Bisti would've probably been taken there anyway. Gold Coast residents were presumed to have enough money to buy the best medical care available, and Northwestern was at or near the top of the list.

The woman at the reception desk told them that the resident who'd treated Mrs. Bisti was in the OR. They'd have to wait to see him. Mrs. Bisti was upstairs. They could see her now, although what good that would do was a matter they'd have to take up with the doctor. They elected to wait, and Thinnes went to get four coffees. He gave one each to Oster and the receptionist, and one to the doctor when he finally came out of the operating room.

They talked to the doctor in the hallway; the exam rooms were all full. They held the wall up while he sat on a gurney, back against the wall, swinging his feet as he sipped his coffee. "You can try her tomorrow morning," he said. "The paramedics treated her for the physical shock and we treated her for the psychological variety. With a sedative."

"She have any injuries, Doctor?" Thinnes asked.

"No physical injuries. Just shock. Your detective—Ryan, isn't it?—said she saw her husband murdered. That'll do it."

"She may have seen him killed, may have just found him afterward. We weren't able to get anything out of her."

"Any chance she was faking it?" Oster asked.

"You mean making her own pulse thready, skin clammy,

44

blood pressure drop?" He shook his head. "I wouldn't say it was theoretically impossible, but I can't imagine a Gold Coast resident pulling it off."

"Anybody tried to get in to see her?"

"You'd have to ask the nurses."

Thinnes asked him a couple of how're-you-doing? questions, and he filled them in on things going on in the Emergency department. "By the way," he said. "Detective Ryan insisted we hang that bloody dress up on a hanger to dry. Claims it's evidence. Maybe, when you leave, you could take it off our hands?"

FOURTEEN

The sign under the Western Avenue overpass still said:

POLICE DEPARTMENT
6TH AREA
HEADQUARTERS
19TH DISTRICT
HEADQUARTERS

nearly a year after Area Six had been renamed Area Three. Probably appropriate. People still thought of it as Area Six, still answered the phone "Area Six Detectives" when they were tired or distracted.

It was nearly light when Thinnes pulled the plainclothes Caprice along the curb east of the dark brick headquarters building, but the overhead sodium lights still gave an orange cast to the drive and sidewalk. Bare trees and litter and the November chill added to the feeling of depression Thinnes was working on. He shut off the engine. Neither he nor Oster spoke as they got out of the car. They entered by the north doors—the only ones open before six A.M.

A tired-looking woman was talking to the uniforms working in the square ring of the District Nineteen desk, and a tac officer in soft clothes leaned on the polished stone counter, listening to the beef. He gave the two detectives an index finger salute as they headed for the stairs, and both Thinnes and Oster nodded an

46

acknowledgment. The sergeant on duty held a note out for Thinnes but kept his eyes on the woman. Thinnes took it without breaking stride or interrupting her.

Upstairs, he and Oster hung their coats on the pegs along the wall inside the squad room entrance. Before Thinnes could even put his paperwork down, he was set upon by Rossi.

"Thinnes, that lush you sent in sobered up and is yelling for his lawyer."

"Okay."

". . . And Patrol wants the uniforms you've got baby-sitting him back on the street. *Now.*"

"My career's in the toilet!" The speaker, Lewis Andrews, was white, five eight, maybe 170 pounds, medium build, hazel eyes, and mousy brown hair. His tuxedo was rumpled and stained, and he smelled like he'd barfed on himself.

"Why is that, Mr. Andrews?" Thinnes asked softly.

Andrews looked as if he thought Thinnes was nuts. When Thinnes didn't say anything more, Andrews looked at Oster, who was no more helpful, then around the stark, white interview room. Finally, he stared at the two-way mirror behind Thinnes. He seemed to find his image disturbing, because he dropped his eyes to his hands, folded on his lap, and added, "The entire idea for the blessed show was a disaster."

"Could you be more specific?"

"My God! You saw that stuff. And then the son of a bitch gets himself murdered. Right in the museum! I'll never work again!"

"Just how did Mr. Bisti manage to convince you to let him have a show there without showing you the stuff he was going to exhibit first?"

"He showed me the brochure Anita Margolis made up for his exhibition at her gallery. He led me to believe he'd be displaying the same sort of things. God! And he showed me one work in progress—*Triptych*—that wasn't too offensive."

Thinnes glanced at Oster, who was taking notes, then nodded for Andrews to go on.

"We were getting pressured by some militant Native American group to show Native American art. I thought what they had in mind was that stuff you see in airports out west—that certainly would have been preferable to the—"

He didn't seem able to find an adequate put-down for Bisti's work. Thinnes raised his eyebrows.

Andrews continued. "One of the board members proposed that we try to appease the Indians by inviting one of their number to have a showing. And Bisti was recommended by someone."

"Who?"

Andrews raised his hands as if to make a who-knows? gesture, then seemed to forget what he was doing with them. "I don't remember. I don't recall if anyone even told me who it was."

"The same person suggested an Indian and recommended Bisti?"

"I can't remember."

"Can't or won't?"

For a second, Andrews looked startled or scared, then angry. *"I don't remember."*

"This is a murder investigation, Mr. Andrews."

"I am only too aware of that. Believe me, though I'd have liked to have killed him myself, I didn't. I don't know who did. I assure you, if I did know, I would tell you. I would do anything in my power to end this nightmare as quickly as possible."

Thinnes pulled the price list Caleb had given him from his pocket and pushed it across the table. "What can you tell us about this?"

"Oh Lord! It gets worse and worse."

Thinnes waited.

"You don't see something like that at the Art Institute, by God!"

Oster finally put his two cents in. "You don't see murder at the Art Institute either."

When Thinnes and Oster returned to the squad room, Ferris and Swann were sitting around, schmoozing. Both of them were assigned to second watch but because they worked for Lieutenant Evanger, they weren't slaves to the clock. Thinnes had worked Evanger's watch until he was shot. Coming back from sick leave, he'd been assigned to first watch because Rossi was shorthanded. Oster had drawn Rossi's watch because he lacked the seniority to opt out.

"How'd it go?" Swann asked. He was a middle-aged black man with an easygoing disposition and an uncanny resemblance to the late, beloved mayor.

Ferris, who was white, cynical, and also middle-aged, jumped in before Thinnes or Oster could speak. "I heard it was a real clusterfuck."

He was gloating, Thinnes decided, subtly rubbing it in that he'd escaped the draft. It was the sort of case he'd only work willingly as a principal, and then only if the killer was obvious.

"You doing anything right now, Ferris?" he asked.

"Why? You want me to take over for you?"

"No, I thought maybe we could send you out for doughnuts."

"She-it," Ferris said. He hurried away before Thinnes could say he wasn't kidding.

"I'll go," Swann offered.

Oster hooked a thumb in Ferris's direction. "You ever realize how much work that chump gets out of, just by being an asshole?"

"Management's worry," Thinnes said. "Not my job description."

FIFTEEN

Caleb was awakened by four small, cold feet kneading his side beneath the covers as Sigmund Freud began to purr. In the summer the cat slept on top of the duvet or, if it was really hot, on the parquet floor. But in the cold months, he burrowed beneath the sheets and slept curled against Caleb's hip or thigh, or in the curve behind his knees.

Caleb was simultaneously grateful for the small warm body—another living thing in an inanimate universe—and aware of the fragility of the cat's existence. His presence was at once comforting and frustrating, the latter because of his alien nature. Caleb could never embrace or relate to him as he would have to another human. They could communicate in a limited fashion, but they were symbionts, not soul mates. The cat could think, obviously, but not in human terms. Nor was Caleb deluded into imagining that a deeper commune was either possible or anything but a projection on his part. Though comforting, Freud's presence didn't assuage his loneliness or fill his need for human contact.

As Caleb stretched, Freud rolled on his back between the flannel sheets, the way a horse rolls in the dust. Then he wriggled over to the bed's edge and let gravity pull him from under the covers and down to the floor in a half somersault. He landed with a thud on all four feet.

Caleb rolled on his stomach to watch the cat wash himself and smiled. But, then, a profound feeling of self-loathing swallowed his pleasure. He felt ugly and unnecessary. He recognized depression coiled around his psyche like a constrictor around a small mammal, waiting to tighten its hold with every breath he took. He understood perfectly that David Bisti's death had brought back feelings from other untimely deaths—friends lost to AIDS and Accident and War, and another young man murdered. But recognition didn't vanquish the enemy; insight has its limitations.

He hadn't told the police, not even John Thinnes—though he considered Thinnes his friend—that David had been a client. Even mentioning the fact would have been a breach of confidentiality while David lived. And dead— Caleb wanted to review his file before mentioning it. Then if there was nothing that would compromise David's family, he would talk to Thinnes.

He dropped to the floor and did fifty push-ups on the moss-soft Harati, then rolled over and sat up fifty times. Freud followed him into the bathroom and watched with fascination as he urinated, showered, and shaved. Freud had been watching Caleb perform these tasks for six years, but his fascination seemed undiminished by repetition. The cat supervised as Caleb turned his attention to selecting the appropriate combination of shirt, suit, and tie from his extensive wardrobe.

By the time he was ready to leave for work, Caleb felt better.

When he got to his office on North Michigan, Muzak was leaking into the hall. The sound disappeared as he opened the door and Mrs. Sleighton spotted him. She always turned the radio down when Caleb or his partner was around, though they'd never asked her to. Years earlier she'd heard them agree that Muzak was the audio equivalent of nondairy creamer. Since then, she'd kept Half & Half in the refrigerator and kept the Muzak to herself. She was slim and gray haired, though still in her forties. And she was always ladylike, though she'd once come to Dr. Fenwick's aid with a broom when he was attacked by a distraught client.

The office was designed to be soothing, with subdued colors

and comfortable furniture. And the aroma of freshly brewed coffee added to the ambiance of solace. The Boston fern that usually hung above the fish tank near the windows overlooking Grant Park was missing. He didn't comment on its absence—two days a week Mrs. Sleighton took it down the hall to the janitor's closet for a shower and left it to drip-dry before replacing it. Caleb hadn't let Mrs. Sleighton decorate for the holidays yet—not until after Thanksgiving—but the man from the aquarium store was cleaning the fish tank in preparation for the season.

Mrs. Sleighton said, "Good morning, Doctor."

"Good morning, Mrs. Sleighton."

"Would you like coffee?"

"I would, thank you."

She poured it into the Laurel Burch cat mug, Caleb's favorite, and handed it to him along with three telephone-message slips. "You've had some phone calls already."

"Thank you."

"And Mrs. Willis cancelled."

Caleb didn't have to think about that. "Bill her."

Mrs. Sleighton pressed her mouth into a severe line and for a fraction of a second, something close to anger flashed across her face. She didn't approve of billing for missed appointments. But then, she didn't understand, either, how patients manipulated their therapists into assuming the role of parent, "giving" their time away. Caleb wasn't going to play. If Mrs. Willis wouldn't make the commitment therapy required, she would at least compensate Caleb for his time.

"Your eleven o'clock called to ask for an earlier appointment. I took the liberty of giving him Mrs. Willis's."

"Very good. Thank you, Mrs. Sleighton."

He took his coffee into his office and closed the door.

The office had been designed for his patients' comfort as much as for utility. His desk stood opposite the door, with comfortable chairs on either side. To the right, facing the desk, a conversation area—couch and armchairs, coffee table with ashtrays and designer Kleenex box—was arranged next to windows overlooking Grant Park. A cat lithograph by Jason Rogue graced the wall opposite the window wall, and below the lithograph stood a new PC.

He had an hour before his first client was due, so he started his morning game of phone tag with the callers.

He ushered his last patient of the day out at 11:04 and asked Mrs. Sleighton to intercept his calls for the next hour.

Back in his office, he swallowed the cold remains of his second cup of coffee before crossing to the impressive wall of bookshelves behind his desk. With pressure applied to the proper spot, the center third of the shelf swung out from the wall, like the door it was, to reveal a walk-in safe behind it. Caleb applied the combination to the dial on the safe door, and it opened noiselessly. The space inside was six feet wide and as long as the office. It was filled with metal shelves like those found in libraries. When Caleb and his partner bought the practice, the safe room had been overflowing with old records, all consigned now to computer disks occupying a single carton. The associates' current files took up even less space, residing—for the most part—on the hard disks of the partners' PCs. Backup copies of the files lived in the safe room with the few videotapes Caleb and Fenwick had acquired or made.

They hadn't let the liberated space go to waste. Caleb's art collection—carefully wrapped paintings and collages—was stacked between the shelves at one end of the room. The shelves were filled with other things that wouldn't fit comfortably in his apartment or safely in his storage locker. The shelves in Fenwick's half of the room were covered with books, all first editions.

Caleb found the six-year-old videotape he was looking for and took it back out to his office, where he opened the cabinet containing the VCR and television. He turned on the system and popped the tape in.

David Bisti came back to life on-screen. He was younger on

the tape but only slightly less confident. From off camera, Caleb heard his own voice ask, "Do you mind if we tape this interview?" Through the whole tape, he remained a disembodied voice.

"Why?" David said.

"It saves me having to take notes and insures I don't miss anything."

"Who else is gonna . . . ?"

"Under appropriate circumstances, I might share it with a colleague—only one whose confidentiality I trust. I'll stop the tape if you start to feel uncomfortable."

David shrugged. "Why not?"

Caleb had adjusted the volume and focus from controls in a desk drawer. "Tell me what brought you here?"

David seemed to be ordering his thoughts or—more likely—marshaling his courage. Caleb didn't rush him. Finally he said, "I can't work. I force myself to do my job, but it takes all my energy and I hate it. I don't have anything left for my *real* work."

"Which is?"

"I'm an artist. And I'm *good*. But lately, my ideas have been drying up. When I stand in front of a bare canvas, I panic."

"Tell me more about your work."

"Job or art?"

"Both."

The next twenty minutes of the tape chronicled David's tribulations with his job, at an advertising agency where he felt his talent was unappreciated and his time wasted on boring scut work.

When Caleb had had enough, he'd said, "Tell me about your family and educational background."

"How's that going to help?"

"I don't know yet. That's what we're trying to determine."

David gave another resigned shrug and said, "I'm twenty-three years old. I have a BFA from DePaul. I'm from a small family—just my mom and me."

Caleb waited for him to elaborate, and when he didn't, asked, "What about your father?"

"He died." Caleb let the silence go on. Eventually, David felt compelled to add, "When I was thirteen."

A significant age, Caleb thought but didn't speak it.

"They were divorced when I was ten. It was better after they split." He seemed to be trying to convince himself as much as Caleb, who didn't express the skepticism he felt. David continued. "They fought all the time—always about his drinking. He blamed it on her, because she wouldn't move to the Navajo reservation. She used to tell him, 'Listen, if you wanted to live on the reservation, you should have married some girl from there who never heard of indoor plumbing and higher education.' She'd be a real shrew sometimes."

"How did your father react?"

"He'd just say, 'Bitch,' and have another drink."

"How do you feel about your Navajo heritage?"

"I don't know. I've been doing a lot of reading on the subject."

"What, for instance?"

On the video screen, David grinned as his enthusiasm for the subject overcame the facade of cool he'd habitually maintained. "Oh, the usual—Campbell and Zolbrod. And everything Hillerman ever wrote."

Caleb had known who Campbell and Hillerman were, of course. He'd subsequently made a point to look up Zolbrod, author of *Diné Bahané,* the definitive English translation of the Navajo creation myth. He'd understood David's wanting to reclaim his father's heritage, but David had encountered major obstacles.

The first was his parents.

Like Jews, who are born to Jewish mothers, Navajo children are born into their mother's clan. As a non-Navajo, David's mother had none. And when Harlan Bisti followed his people's tradition and moved to the territory of his wife's family, he'd severed his connection to the *Diné* and to the land that gave his existence meaning. He'd lost his soul. Drinking himself to death, years later, had been a formality.

David's other and greatest problem had been himself. The rage that he'd repressed as a child, and his shame and contempt for a drunk father, were rekindled by a newborn interest in what that father lost. His anger explained the viciousness of his satire, but he hadn't been able to acknowledge rage. Like all bereaved, who sublimate their anger in their grief, he'd projected his rage outward.

"We can go into this further next week," Caleb's voice said, finally. "In the meantime, I'd like you to think about what's changed in your life since your creativity began to suffer. We'll start with that next time."

"That's it? You're not going to tell me why I can't work when I *do* get the time?"

"How long has this problem been occurring?"

"A couple months."

"Then why do you assume it can be fixed in fifty minutes?"

He hadn't had an answer. Caleb stopped the tape.

David came to therapy because he was blocked as an artist. It had been a simple matter to help remove the block, but that's as far as he would go. Perhaps, like Virginia Woolf, he'd feared losing his gift if he rid himself of his neuroses. More likely, as was true with most personality disorders, he'd seen no reason to change himself.

His death was as melodramatic as he'd tried to make his life appear and, in retrospect, there was a certain inevitability to the tragedy. But it was a Greek play rewritten for TV.

Caleb rewound the tape and put it in a desk drawer. He turned off the equipment, relocked the safe, and took his empty coffee mug out into the reception room. Before he crossed to the washroom to rinse the mug, he told Mrs. Sleighton, "That was excellent coffee."

SIXTEEN

David Bisti's mother lived on the eighth floor of one of the huge, impersonal, upper-middle-class buildings on Sheridan Road, east of Uptown. Thinnes and Oster got the super to let them in. After questioning him about the woman and her friends and visitors, they had him go up with them to her apartment. He knocked on the door and stood in front of the peephole until the door opened. He said, "Miz Bisti, these detectives have to talk to you," then he left.

Anne Bisti was Caucasian, about five eight, 140 pounds, blond haired and gray eyed. She said, "Something happened to David! I've worked ERs. I know cops on the mission when I see them. How serious is it?"

"I'm sorry," Thinnes said. "He's dead."

He watched carefully as he waited for her to respond. She was completely still for the moment it took the information to sink in, then she paled as what might have been a shiver passed through her and she very carefully took hold of the doorjamb.

"How?"

"He was stabbed to death."

He wasn't sure if she heard. She was completely still. Finally, she said, "By whom?"

"We don't know yet. We'd like to—"

"I don't know who'd kill him. Please come back tomorrow."

"We need—"

"I can't give you any help right now. Tomorrow." She backed into the room and closed the door as if they were already gone.

Oster said, "What the hell?"

Thinnes had seen it before. "Don't judge her feelings by that," he said. He turned away from the door. "We'd better ask one of her friends to keep an eye on her."

"You're gonna let her get away with this? This is homicide, for Chrissake."

"Her *son* died," Thinnes said quietly. "We'll come back."

SEVENTEEN

Thinnes turned in his preliminary reports and had just poured his fourth cup of coffee—since midnight—when Ferris hailed him.

"Hey, Thinnes, you lucked out. Custer's rematch didn't make the morning papers."

Thinnes walked over to look at the *Sun-Times* Ferris had spread out on the table. He flipped it closed and pointed to the headline: CARDINAL CHARGED WITH SEX ABUSE. "He seems to have saved our asses. God bless him."

Oster, seated at the other end of the table, demanded, "Ferris, what the hell are you doing here at this hour?"

Thinnes was surprised. Oster usually ignored Ferris's bullshit.

"OT," Ferris said.

"Like hell. You switched shifts with someone. Evanger finally ask you to do some work?"

"Take it easy, Carl," Thinnes said. He gave Ferris a look, then asked Oster, "So who killed Bisti?"

"The wife," Oster said. "It's always the wife. Or husband, or boyfriend. Nine times outta ten." He gave Thinnes a "you know that" look.

"Yeah, well. I'd like something more than statistics to take to the state's attorney."

"You got her, literally, red-handed. What more do you want?"

"A motive would be nice. You know. He was screwing

59

around. Or *she* was screwing around. Or she just took out a policy that'd pay off the national debt."

"Five'll get you ten, she's got him insured up the gazunk."

Thinnes's beeper started to vibrate. He shut it off and glanced at the number before he said, "You can check it out, along with their credit and whatever." It was Evanger's home number. He wondered what Evanger wanted. "And start looking for that Indian woman," he told Oster. "Irene. Check the American Indian Center, on Wilson. Maybe they got some kind of registry. She's probably Navajo."

"What're you gonna be doin'?"

Oster wasn't arguing, Thinnes knew. He'd made it plain he'd sooner let Thinnes divide up the work.

"Thought I'd drop in on the autopsy. You're welcome to come."

"No thanks. Seen one, you seen enough. I seen enough."

Thinnes had seen enough, too, but he didn't say so.

EIGHTEEN

Evanger was waiting in the upper level of the McDonald's at Dearborn and Randolph, at a table by the window. Thinnes was too tired to eat by the time he got there. He bought a large coffee—his fifth of the day—and joined Evanger. The window overlooked the State Street ice rink, which wasn't open yet. No ice.

Thinnes sat across from the lieutenant. If there'd been anyone to notice, they'd have made an odd couple—a lanky, laidback, rumpled white man, and the sharp, straight up, wideawake black. An odd salt-and-pepper team. But there was no one to notice. Two teenaged Hispanic males—employees—leaned on the tray-return/trash cabinet, shooting the breeze. A business type studied his *Wall Street Journal* while he slurped his coffee. A young black couple was all over each other in a back corner, staring into each other's eyes, doing who knows what under their coats.

"They stuck me on a jury!" Evanger said, with the same surprise in his voice Mob chiefs have been heard to show announcing that they've been indicted. "And this thing could last for weeks."

Nothing so far Evanger couldn't have told him over the phone. Thinnes looked at his watch.

Evanger took the hint and got to the point. "I need a favor." His face gave nothing away as his eyes made an inventory of the room.

Thinnes followed suit. No additions to the roster. No bad

guys. No other cops. He stared at Evanger. The lieutenant had always had a reputation for being clean—as clean as a man could be in a place as political as Chicago—but he'd never asked Thinnes for a favor before. A favor he couldn't ask over the phone had to be something against the law or against regulations. Thinnes didn't want to hear it. He felt like he had when he'd heard the news about Magic Johnson—like he'd been sucker punched. It seemed as soon as you found someone you could look up to, you found out something about him you didn't want to know. He wondered if Evanger, too, had AIDS.

On the sidewalk below them, pedestrians crowded and bumped one another. Traffic stopped for the red on Dearborn. A Streets & San truck parked illegally on the south side of Randolph, behind Thinnes's illegally parked Caprice. The truck driver took out a paper and made himself comfortable while his buddy dodged traffic, crossing to McDonald's.

Evanger removed a pile of file folders from his briefcase and put them on the table. He tapped the pile. "Old cases. I signed off on them but I didn't have time to read them. Now with this trial . . ."

Thinnes felt, suddenly, weak with relief.

". . . Would you read them over? See if there's anything we missed?"

The chief insisted on detective supervisors reading over all the open homicide cases every six months. Evanger wasn't supposed to delegate it. Especially not to one of the dicks.

Thinnes said, "Sure. Why not?"

"Then take them back to Records?"

Thinnes nodded.

"Thanks," Evanger said. "I owe you."

NINETEEN

The Robert J. Stein Institute of Forensic Medicine. Office of the Medical Examiner. Better known as the morgue. Thinnes parked behind the modern white stone structure and entered by the door near the loading dock. The guy on intake duty greeted him with, "Yo, Custer. Yo' redskin's already been scalped."

He was right. The autopsy was already underway by the time Thinnes entered the room. He wondered if someone with clout had called to expedite the process or if it was just a slow day. Dr. Cutler, the pathologist, was a light-skinned black man with a neat Afro, who reminded Thinnes of Greg Gumbel without the attitude. He said, "Detective," when Thinnes came in. "Your victim was killed by a single stab wound to the chest. Hit the heart. He bled to death."

"Tell me something I *don't* know, Doc."

"Off the record, your cutter is probably a woman or someone who's never been in a fight."

"Okay, Carnac. Tell me the question."

"How do I know?"

Thinnes waited.

"The angle of the wound suggests that, if the victim was standing—and I understand from your officer there weren't any chairs in the room—he was stabbed overhand. Like Jessica Walter did it in *Play Misty for Me*."

"Just one blow?"

"I thought I said that."

"You said he was killed by a single wound to the heart. You didn't say if there was any other damage."

"Picky. Picky. Picky. You want to get technical, I can give it to you in medicalese."

"I'm just trying to establish whether he saw it coming."

"I'd say no. No defense wounds. Beyond the fatal wound, not a scratch on him. He did have a hickey."

"I haven't heard of anyone dying of those lately."

Cutler laughed. "You *could* think of it as a hesitation mark for suicide by AIDS."

"*You're* an optimist."

"Comes with the territory." He pointed with his scalpel. "Look at the bruising around the wound. The knife went in far enough and hard enough to do that. I'd say it was someone really strong or really angry."

"Too bad you can't say which."

"Whichever suspect is one or the other. That's probably your doer."

Thinnes shook his head. "I've got one that's strong and at least a half-dozen that were pissed. Any chance he could have gotten out the name of who did him?"

"Nah. Well. Anything's possible, but probably not. But I understand you have witnesses. Why not ask them?"

"I will. But I always like corroboration."

TWENTY

Thinnes!" Rossi growled. "The museum just called. They want to know why we haven't released the crime scene. They'd like to open up sometime soon. I'd like to know, too."

"I wanted to get another look at it—maybe go over it with someone who knows something about art."

"Well, make it fast. It's bad enough we haven't got the perp. No use stepping on well-connected toes, too."

"Yeah," Thinnes said. "You never know if they're connected to an ass you might have to kiss." He was pretty sure Rossi couldn't tell if he was being sarcastic. Good. He picked up the phone.

"Who're you calling?"

"An art expert," Thinnes said, mildly. He held the phone in the air and looked expectantly at Rossi.

Rossi snorted and walked away.

Thinnes cradled the phone between his ear and shoulder while he punched in Jack Caleb's number. It was probably stretching things to call Caleb an art expert, but he knew a hell of a lot more about it than Thinnes.

At the next table Swann, who'd been listening, said, "You be dissin' the lieu?"

"You know what *loo* means in England, Swann?"

Swann showed all his teeth as he grinned. "No, but I'll bet it's fulla shit, too."

When Thinnes pulled over to the curb on Michigan, Caleb was waiting with two large Starbuck's cups. He got into the Caprice and handed one to Thinnes, who signaled a right and headed west. They were south of the museum, but it was easier to go around the block and make a left back onto northbound Michigan at a light than to try a U-turn in Loop traffic. Thinnes took a sip of the coffee, then wedged the cup on the dash. Caleb had noticed or guessed how Thinnes liked his coffee—two sugars, no cream. Little things like that made the doctor more likable but scary. It quickly developed, though, that the coffee was a kind of bribe.

"There's something I didn't tell you last night," Caleb said. Thinnes looked at him sideways. If he was nervous or repentant, it didn't show.

"Yeah?"

"David Bisti was a patient of mine—Briefly—Years ago."

Thinnes was suddenly furious, but he hid it. Caleb wouldn't reveal privileged information even to help the police. They'd had the argument before and had agreed to disagree, but he couldn't resist asking, "Whose side did you say you were on?"

Caleb refused to be needled. He handed Thinnes a videotape Thinnes hadn't noticed he was carrying and said, "For your eyes only."

"What's this?"

"The tape of a therapy session I had with him. At the time David asked for help, my partner and I were experimenting with videotape as a means of picking up on more of the nonverbal content of therapy sessions. I got David's permission to tape our conversation. I think he may have thought I meant on audiotape, though—our video camera is hidden. You never met David. The tape might give you some idea of what he was like."

"Why the sudden ethical reversal?"

"In a perfect world, we could choose between wrong and right. But in our imperfect world, we're stuck with choosing between more wrong and less wrong. And it's not as if you'll sell tickets."

Thinnes nodded. "Thanks." He slid the tape under the files

lying on the seat between Caleb and himself, where it wouldn't be seen by anyone looking in the windows. "What was your impression of him?"

"He was very talented, but narcissistic and manipulative. A passive-aggressive personality."

Passive-aggressive. That explained the nothing-happened-and-besides-I-don't-want-to-talk-about-him reaction they'd gotten out of so many who'd known the man.

"And there was something else." Thinnes waited. "I've heard writers say that what sets them apart from nonwriters is a sense of isolation, and a feeling of being different from others, of always standing apart, observing."

"So?"

"It's also true of fine artists. David was a *fine* artist. And he felt alienated. But I think he gave up therapy, in the end, because he couldn't bare his soul—not just to a white man, as he claimed—but to anyone. It was more an individual thing than racial. He never asked me for a referral to a Native American therapist. At our last session, he told me he'd joined a commune, and what its members had in common was that they were all artists who had enough Indian blood to make them outsiders to the mainstream culture."

The security guard who let them in told them the two men in blue overalls, sitting on carpet rolls in the lobby, were waiting on Thinnes's okay to replace the ruined carpet in the upper gallery.

Thinnes told the guard they'd be as quick as they could, then led the way up to the lower north gallery. He waited without showing impatience while Caleb looked around, and let him set the pace into the next gallery, the one below the mezzanine. Earlier, he'd gone over the room himself. Now, while he waited for Caleb's verdict, he studied one of the pieces.

Thinnes didn't get it. The price list Caleb had given him said, "Bids start at $15,000." Thinnes wouldn't have given two bucks for the thing—it looked like something some kid made before he was old enough to draw. The title was *Man Dying*. Thinnes would have liked to replace it with blowups of Bisti with the hole in his chest and his blood leaking out. *That* was a man dying.

Caleb came up behind him, and Thinnes said, "Fifteen grand, huhn?" He turned to see the doctor smile.

"Probably not a bad investment."

"You're serious!"

Caleb shrugged. "Scarcity usually drives up the price."

"That means someone'll pay fifteen grand for this piece of shit so he can sell it to an even bigger asshole for twenty. What if he can't find a sucker? He'll write it off?"

"That depends on what kind of collector buys it," Caleb said. "If he's just trying to make a profit and guesses wrong about it, he'll write it off. If he buys it because he likes it, and if he's lucky or has very good taste, he'll do well. But even if he's unlucky or has eccentric tastes, he won't lose anything."

"So, would you buy any of these?"

"I bought one."

Thinnes walked over to read the title of a landscape he'd noticed, earlier, the only thing in the place he'd have given houseroom. He ran down the price list until he found the description: New Mexico #27, oil on canvas. Courtesy of Dr. James Caleb. NFS.

"The rest of this stuff . . ." He waved to indicate everything and asked, "People like it?"

Caleb frowned as he thought about it, so his nod seemed contradictory. "People who understand it do. For the most part."

As they climbed the steps to the mezzanine, Thinnes said, "I guess I belong to the Lyndon Johnson school of art appreciation. I know what I like, and this ain't it. You might as well go down to Cabrini-Green and hang a frame around the shit they write on the walls, or shovel some of the crap from any vacant lot in the city into a box and call that art. What's the point?" Thinnes pointed to a Navajo sand painting advertising beer. "Besides taking someone for a bundle?"

"An artist usually tries to make the viewer experience something."

He sounded like one of those teachers who desperately wants his students to get it, and Thinnes was just half listening as he looked for anything he might've missed earlier. His only real interest in Bisti's stuff was whether any of it might have made somebody mad enough at Bisti to kill him. He shook his head and pointed at an abstract "installation" that gave him the creeps. "You couldn't give this stuff away at a Starving Artists' Sale."

"David's work may not be beautiful, but it seems to have achieved the ultimate in artistic expression."

"What's that?"

"Aroused one of his viewers to the most extreme of emotions. No artist can be more successful than that."

"What *is* art?" As soon as he asked he was sorry. The conversation was degenerating into an art lecture.

"A formal definition?"

Thinnes shrugged.

"The embodiment of form in a medium."

It was the sort of thing you got when you looked up something in the dictionary and got half a dozen other words that referred you back to the first word. It was like wrestling fog; he felt his eyes glazing over. "What's form? What's a medium?"

"Form is a sort of container for the idea behind the work."

"Like paint?"

"Not exactly. Paint would be the medium. What the artist does with it is form. David's use of paint, his form, is quite different from Picasso's."

They walked up the ramp to the exhibit's final gallery, the one where Bisti died. Thinnes stopped and faced Caleb.

"So if I got it right, an artwork is like the cylinder in an engine, and the idea behind it's the gas mix. If the design's good, and the compression and timing are right, the artist can get a lot of mileage out of a work."

"Exactly!"

"Some of the museum regulars were pretty worked up about this stuff." He pointed at the three-part painting titled *Triptych*. "Is it any good?"

The panel on the left was a still life, subtitled "City Indians," a vase of wilting flowers whose heads were whitewashed Indian faces. The right-hand panel, "Reservation Indians," was a parched, weed-choked landscape with trash and abandoned vehicles, sagging wire fences, and dilapidated buildings. The scraggly flowers in the foreground had white faces with a wash of Indian red. The large, central panel showed a panoramic view of forested mountains, streams teeming with fish, plains with deer and buffalo, and an overarching rainbow. The dark faces of the "Natural Indians" were sunny, smiling flowers in the foreground.

"It's not his best work," Caleb said. "It's too obvious and commercial. Great art works on deeper levels. Frequently, long after you thought you've gotten the idea of a masterwork, something will bring it to mind, and you'll have an experience of 'Aha! *That's* what that was *really* about!'"

TWENTY-ONE

What did you get out of the wife, Thinnes?"

The squad room was nearly empty—just Thinnes, Oster, and two Property Crimes dicks. And, now, Rossi. He was supposed to be working nights. In spite of the museum's involvement, the Bisti case wasn't sensational enough to keep supervisory personnel on OT. Rossi shouldn't have been in for hours. Thinnes wondered why he was still around, but he didn't wonder enough to ask. He said, "I haven't talked to her yet."

Rossi's jaw started to drop, then he snapped his mouth shut. "Then what the hell are you doing here?" Failing to talk to the next of kin was a major deviation from SOP.

"Wife's in the hospital, under sedation."

"So why aren't you over there waiting for her to come out of it?"

"Because I got better things to do." Thinnes didn't bother to say that detective Ryan was baby-sitting the wife and would take a statement if she made one. If Rossi was on duty, he should know it.

"Better than following procedure?" Rossi demanded.

"You want to take me off the case? Fine with me."

"That'd let *you* off the hook. Forget it. I want this shit cleared up today!" He turned abruptly and stalked out.

"What's eatin' him?" Oster said, mildly.

"Politics. Murder on the Magnificent Mile gets everyone stirred up."

"Shit!"

"Rolls downhill," Thinnes agreed.

About an hour later, Oster said, "Well, Thinnes, looks like you're two for two on this one." He put a sheaf of papers on the table, next to the file Thinnes was working out of, and headed for the coffeemaker.

When he returned and was sitting down, Thinnes asked, "How's that?"

"Looks like it might not have been the wife after all." Thinnes waited; Oster continued. "She's the one that had all the money. Nobody said Bisti married her for it, but a couple people said it didn't hurt him any. Everybody I talked to said they were devoted. She had a hundred grand life insurance on him, but that's chump change for someone in her bracket—from what I gather.

"If he was screwin' around, he was pretty damned discreet. Ditto for her. Neither of 'em's a drinker. I got a call in to Vice on whether he was a high roller."

Thinnes nodded. "What about their personal finances?"

"Separate checking accounts; healthy balances. Every credit card known to man—some rarely used—all current. They own the condo they live in—" Oster shrugged. *"Lived* in—and Bisti's studio loft on Wells. Joint."

"Let's go back and see the widow."

Ryan was sitting in the hall outside Lauren Bisti's room at Northwestern Memorial Hospital. She was reading, but she wasn't so deep into her book that she didn't see them coming. She looked tired and relieved to see them.

"You look like you been run hard and put away wet," Oster told her.

She pushed her red-blond hair back from her face. "I do you guys a favor and you insult me. Thanks, Carl."

"You are the most beautiful detective at Area Three," Thinnes said. She grinned. "What've you got for us?"

She hooked her thumb toward Lauren Bisti's door. "She's

still sleeping off whatever they gave her last night. And I've turned away two reporters—one posing as a doctor—and three people claiming to be relatives. Two of 'em named Kent."

"They come together?" Thinnes asked.

"Nope."

"Either of them mention the other being here?"

"Hun-uh. Todd Kent made some kind of noise about being a lawyer and said, 'We'll see about that,' when I told him he couldn't go in. But he hasn't come back."

"Who was the other relative?"

"Anne Bisti."

"Small world," Oster said.

"One more thing, Ryan," Thinnes said. "She remember what happened?" Ryan shrugged. "Thanks, Ryan. You can take off."

Oster took Ryan's chair. Thinnes went to find the resident they'd spoken with the night before or—failing that—to find someone who could be on hand in case what they asked Mrs. Bisti put her back into shock.

She was technically awake when they went in with the resident, but wouldn't have passed a sobriety test. She looked like the faded copy of a beautiful woman. Thinnes and Oster waited while the doctor took her pulse and explained that her visitors were police officers who'd come to ask her questions. They asked him to wait out in the hall or somewhere near by, and he said he'd be at the nurses' station.

The room brought last summer back to Thinnes. He'd spent it in the hospital. This hospital. He didn't remember the ER. He'd been in shock by the time Caleb—unwilling to wait four to sixteen minutes for a fire-department ambulance—had driven him to the emergency entrance. But he remembered the rooms well enough.

He pushed the memory away with a shudder and said, "Mrs. Bisti, could you tell us what happened?"

After a long pause, during which she seemed to be trying very hard, she said, "I can't remember."

He gave her more time. When she finally shook her head, he said, "What *do* you remember?"

"Going to look for David." She was sure about that. Then her face registered confusion again. "I don't remember finding . . . Something happened to him! What?"

"Why do you say that?" Thinnes said, trying not to sound like a cynic questioning a suspect.

"David's not here," she said. She sounded like a young child reasoning something out. "And you're policemen."

"Where's David?" Her voice rose on "David"; she sounded panicky. She grabbed for the call button and pushed it before they could stop her.

Oster said, "Mrs. Bisti—"

She ignored him. When the doctor came rushing in, she demanded, "Where's my husband?"

In the end, the doctor told her. He looked furious as he glanced from Oster to Thinnes and back—probably thought they should break the news. Then he took her hand in both of his and said, "Your husband's dead, Mrs. Bisti." He kept hold of her hand.

She didn't seem to hear, at first. Then—as suddenly and completely as ice in a microwave turns to water—her expression changed from fear to misery, and she started to whimper. Thinnes had heard the sound many times during his recovery— the sound of someone in great pain, too heavily drugged to be aware of it.

She pulled her hand away from the doctor and put it, put both her hands over her face. The whimper became a wail, then a scream, then a serious crying jag during which she curled into the fetal position.

An Academy Award performance, Thinnes decided. *Or* maybe *real pain.* It sometimes got to him that he automatically thought the worst. Occupational hazard. She hadn't been acting last night, when she went into shock.

After what seemed like a long time, the doctor said, "I'm going to order her another sedative."

Lauren Bisti uncovered her face and said, "No! It won't bring David back." She gave a few more involuntary sobs and sat up, pulling the covers up under her chin and shivering, underneath them, as if she were freezing.

Thinnes stepped closer to the bed and handed her a tissue from a box on the bed stand. She reached a hand out and took it, blew her nose, and wadded the tissue up in her hand. She looked at Thinnes when she asked, "What happened to him?"

"He was murdered."

She put her hand over the lower part of her face and sniffled, then took the hand away and said, "By whom?"

"We were hoping you could tell us?"

She shook her head. "What else can I tell you? That would help you find . . .?"

He had her go over the two days before the killing. It took a long time. She had to stop, often, to get her crying under control, and she seemed to drift off somewhere from time to time. Nothing she recalled seemed unusual. David hadn't seemed upset or preoccupied and hadn't had any threatening calls or visitors.

Thinnes finally gave her his card and asked her to contact him if she remembered anything else, no matter how trivial. "And we'd like to take a look at your condo and your husband's studio, if you don't mind, Mrs. Bisti, to see if we can find any clues as to who might've wanted him dead."

She seemed to bring her attention back from far away. "What? I'm sorry. Of course. Get me my purse, and I'll give you the keys."

TWENTY-TWO

Only the turquoise triangle with its tawny cougar curled inside advertised David Bisti's studio. The door it was mounted on looked like an artist's door. Made of polished hardwood planks—long sections of trees, seven feet in length and irregular widths—fitted together like puzzle pieces. No handle, bell, or knocker. It took Thinnes some time to locate the keyhole in a seam between the boards.

"Cute," Oster said.

Thinnes thought it was pretty ingenious. When he turned the key, the door swung open noiselessly and with the oiled precision of a safe.

What they found inside made him stop and wonder.

The entry hall had a standard, eight-foot ceiling, sandstone walls, and a blue slate floor. The sunset landscape on the wall facing the door was realistic enough to seem like a window into Arizona. Thinnes stared at it a full three seconds before he realized there was a couch below it and other furniture in the room. The painting had Bisti's signature in the lower right-hand corner. Thinnes wondered why it hadn't been in the show.

There were doors to the right of the entry that opened on an office and a john. A door to the right of the painting opened into the studio itself. Oster led the way.

The room was the size of a basketball court, with a sixteen-foot ceiling interrupted by skylights alternating with can lights for night work. The walls were brick with ten-foot windows facing pricey views of the near North Side, the river, and the Loop.

The floor was blue slate. And tree-filled planters divided the space into a work area—with painting and welding supplies, and works in progress; and a conversation area—with expensive-looking furniture, well-stocked refrigerator and bar, and a pond swimming with tiny silver fish. Oster walked around the entire place without saying a word, just shaking his head. Thinnes followed, taking enough notes so he could describe the place in detail in case he ever had to testify about it in court.

Oster climbed a circular staircase in the southeast corner to a small loft built over the entrance hall.

"Thinnes, check this out."

A king-size water bed was the central feature of the loft. Unmade. Satin sheets. The ceiling above it was a giant mirror. The north side of the loft overlooked the studio through a wrought-iron safety rail made of figures resembling those in Bisti's sand paintings. Full-length mirrors—including one hiding a closet door—hung on the other walls. Oster headed over to look at an easel facing into a corner while Thinnes crossed to check out the adjoining bath.

It was as upscale as the rest of the place—whirlpool tub, custom vanity, and fancy toilet. The towels on the bars were clean but not neat—used once or twice. Most of the things in the linen and medicine cabinets were brands you had to go to Fields or Neiman's for—except the aspirin, razor blades, and toothpaste, and the box of condoms. Large box. Half-gone. The wastebasket was empty.

Thinnes went back into the bedroom.

There was nothing of interest in the dresser, closet, or nightstand, not even dust under the bed. There was a wrapper and a used condom in the wastebasket. Thinnes put on one of the latex gloves he habitually carried these days and transferred the wrapper to a plastic evidence bag. He put the condom in a paper envelope and creased its sides so it would stay open for ventilation. He put both containers on the floor near the stair, where he wouldn't forget them, against the wall so they wouldn't be stepped on. He made a mental note to have someone check the room for prints before they took the key back.

"What's wrong with this picture, Thinnes?" Oster said. He was sitting on the corner of the bed frame, still breathing hard from the exertion of climbing the stair. He'd turned the easel around and was studying the nude portrait-in-progress resting on it.

Female Cauc. Young. Slim. Brunette. Knock-'em-dead gorgeous. She was lying on a couch in a pose he'd seen in an art book somewhere—a Spanish artist. This picture was as real as a photo. And unsigned. Mrs. Kent.

"It's not Bisti's missus," Thinnes said.

Oster said, "Yeah, and modeling isn't what she told us she does for a living. Maybe we oughtta go ask her about it."

"Maybe we should."

TWENTY-THREE

They located Amanda Kent at Water Tower Place, where she managed a boutique owned by Lauren Bisti.

"You haven't caught the son of a bitch yet, have you?" she demanded, when Thinnes handed her his card. She was a tall brunette with a model's figure and a Cover Girl face that would've been beautiful if her pissed-off mood hadn't been showing.

If something seems too good to be true . . . Wasn't it Caleb's impression of her that surface was all there was?

Thinnes said, "We'd like you to come in with us and make a formal statement."

They usually didn't bother with statements from nonwitnesses—and by all accounts, Amanda Kent was that. But the painting in Bisti's studio changed things. It suggested some beautiful motives. If she'd pose nude for the artist, what else would she do for him? How would the wife react? And the mysterious Irene? Thinnes had seen murder done for lesser reasons.

Amanda Kent said, "Oh, brother! David's killed, Lauren has a breakdown, and you want me to drop everything to help you do *your* job. Why should I?"

Bitch!

"You do want to catch Mr. Bisti's killer?"

She got her coat—a full-length mink—from the back and told her sales girl she'd be gone an hour.

They didn't talk to her on the way to headquarters. She sat in the back seat, clutching her purse on her mink-covered lap, and looked out at the Drive, then at Belmont. When they got to Western and Belmont, Thinnes pulled up by the north door, and Oster got out to open her door for her. She took his courtesy completely for granted, without acknowledging it. She looked bored as she stopped in front of the building door and waited for Oster to catch up and open it, too. Thinnes parked the car.

Oster had her in an interview room, upstairs, by the time Thinnes rejoined them. Impatience was beginning to replace her boredom—she fidgeted, took a cigarette out of her purse, and tapped it on the package. She let her irritation show when they said she couldn't smoke in the building. Oster excused himself and went out to take his notes on the other side of the two-way mirror.

In the interrogation room, Amanda Kent gave Thinnes one-syllable answers to his questions about David Bisti, and told him, "None of your damn business," when he asked how she got on with Kent. Lauren Bisti, she said, was her best friend as well as her employer.

To get a sense of her honesty, he asked her a number of questions for which he already knew the answers. Who? What? When? Where? Why? How long did you know Mr. Bisti? Where did you meet him? What time did you get to the museum?

Then he said, "Would you say Mr. Bisti was attractive to women?"

"Yeah, sure."

"And were women attractive to him?"

She smirked. "You know how men are." When he didn't answer, she added, "I heard painting wasn't his only talent."

"He fooled around?"

"*I* didn't say it."

"Did you ever sleep with him?"

"That's a hell of a question! No!" Her eyes tracked sideways, and Thinnes knew she was lying. And that she could tell he knew. She added, "I swear!"

He wanted to laugh. "You have any idea who might've killed Mr. Bisti?"

"Don't you think I would've told you?"

"That's not a yes or no."

"No!" This time, she didn't swear and she was much more convincing.

"Did Mrs. Bisti know you posed in the nude for her husband?"

That got her. "Who told you that?"

"I saw the painting."

"I never did," she said. Thinnes couldn't tell if she was lying. "David's little joke. He painted that same picture—the same pose anyway—half a dozen times. I don't know if anyone actually modeled for him—maybe the woman he went with before Lauren. But I'll bet he did one of those *Naked Maja* rip-offs of every woman he tried to seduce. Some of them even fell for it. Lauren did."

"Are you saying he painted your head on someone else's body?" Thinnes demanded. It *was* hard to swallow.

"What I'm saying is, he had a great imagination. I think it's called artistic license." Her manner said, "Just try and prove I'm lying."

He had her write out the gist of her story. When she'd signed it, he added his John Hancock, then offered to have Oster take her home.

"I'll take a cab," she told him. "I wouldn't go with one of you guys to a bar fight."

TWENTY-FOUR

Thinnes lived in a two-story brick and frame house in Sauganash, near Northeastern Illinois University. North Side. When he got home, there was nobody there but the cat: male, domestic shorthair, twenty-four inches long, ten pounds, yellow eyes, orange striped hair. Thinnes draped his coat and jacket over the newel post at the foot of the stairs, inside the front door, and went into the family room, left.

There was a couch and a recliner arranged around the fireplace, a healthy ficus by the front window, a coffee table on an area rug in the center of the room, and Rhonda's office—desk, computer, bookshelf.

He realized he'd grown uncomfortable in the house since he and Rhonda bought it. Over the years, he'd gotten the feeling it was *her* house. She'd found it, while he worked overtime to pay for it. She'd decorated it. She did most of the work. He only cut the grass—until Rob was old enough to do it. He'd farmed out anything more complicated to off-duty firemen and the few cops who had another life. As he and Rhonda'd drifted apart, the house had come to seem more alien.

His enforced stay, recovering from the gunshot wound, had made him face that fact. And deal with it. Little jobs he'd found to do—recalking the tub enclosure, reputtying and painting the kitchen windows, tuck-pointing a few places where the brickwork needed it—had helped him pass the time and given him a feeling for the place he'd never had before. It had finally become home.

His stay in the hospital and his recovery had made him face mortality. He'd come around in intensive care with Rhonda—white-faced—holding his hand, and Rob pacing like a caged wolf, and he couldn't avoid thinking he could've died. Rehab was a bitch, too. He hadn't been as weak or felt as helpless since childhood.

The cops had come to show their solidarity when he was in the hospital, when he would have liked to just sleep until the pain went away. They came in twos and threes. Even after the doctor forbid visitors, they'd sneaked past the nurses' station, as if the rules didn't apply to cops.

Later, when he was home, there was no one. Oster had come once and, oddly, Jack Caleb—who was a shrink, but not Thinnes's shrink—had showed up a week later. He'd phoned first and cleared it with Rhonda, then arrived with the cat.

The cat helped. Skinner—Skinhead to Rob—had come equipped with a carrier, litter box, litter, food, and instructions in the form of a book on the care of cats and training of their owners. Also a book for Skinner: *French for Cats—All the French Your Cat Will Ever Need to Know*. Skinner didn't care for it, but Thinnes found it amusing and Rhonda loved it.

Skinner kept him from going nuts. He hated to admit he'd become attached to a stupid animal that barely tolerated being held and wouldn't even come when called, but he had. Skinner followed him from room to room and sat next to him on the couch when he watched TV. Which was better than watching alone. Thinnes was sure, though, that Skinner secretly rooted for the Pistons.

Since the shooting, he found himself hypersensitive to every twitch or ache. Before that he'd been depressed—though he hadn't thought of the constant, dragged-out feeling as depression. The hospital had given him counseling along with the Darvon, so he could recognize depression now and fight it. But it seemed that when it lifted, he was left with aches and pains and stiff joints that he had never noticed before. "Getting old," the doctors told him. "Normal for a man your age." He hadn't thought of himself as old, not even when Rob said things like: "Dad, when you were a kid—back in the Stone Age—did they have TV?"

He took naps now. Naps—even as short as twenty minutes—got him through the twenty-four-hour watches that resulted from the city's astronomical murder rate.

He put his pager in his shirt pocket, slipped off his shoes, and stretched out on the couch. The pager would wake him.

He came awake slowly, feeling sleepy and not rested. Skinner was parked by his feet, nearly folded in half in the effort of washing himself. He stopped suddenly and stared at the door. As Thinnes eased himself off the couch, Skinner pulled himself together and tucked his feet and tail beneath him. Like a cop stepping out of his house, he was instantly alert. They both listened as the mailman dropped mail in the box.

When Thinnes opened the door to get the mail, Skinner streaked through the doorway. Thinnes didn't bother to try stopping him. He'd come back when he was cold enough. Thinnes kicked the door shut. He looked through the mail as he carried it to the kitchen, then dropped it on the counter by the message pad.

The message pad reminded him of Rhonda, and he decided to leave her a note:

Ronnie, High-profile case—working OT. I'll call later.
Love, John

He hesitated before writing "love." Not that he didn't mean it. He adored Rhonda. And he'd never loved another woman. He was just uneasy committing it to paper. It was the commitment part. Years ago, writing her from 'Nam, it'd been easy enough. But it hadn't meant much then. Now there was so much—*bag-*

gage was the word he wanted—it was depressing. He left the note taped to the counter.

He still wasn't hungry, but he hadn't eaten since dinner the previous night. He found soup and orange juice in the fridge. While the soup heated, he filled a Big Gulp cup with ice and juice.

The soup got him through three of Evanger's old files. Two were familiar—he'd gone through them before—and probably never would be solved. The third was the execution-style killing of a John Doe—someone had penciled *John Buck* on the folder—found in an alley off Wilson. Single shot to the head from a .25-caliber weapon. American Indian, probable robbery victim. The autopsy report showed that he'd had enough alcohol in his system to be legally drunk. Thinnes could see why no one had given the case much time. Alcoholic Indians—along with alcoholics of other races—were as common in Uptown as rats.

Ferris had done the initial investigation—just enough work so he could file the case and get on to the next one. "Victim doesn't match anything from missing persons," Ferris had written. "Nobody in the neighborhood could ID the ME's photo. No prints on file." Thinnes wondered if that meant Ferris had only checked the department's AFIS or that he'd also contacted NCIC and the Feds. He'd been known to skip the last two on occasion. Thinnes read through the evidence list to see if shell casings had been found. None were listed. He made a note for himself to have a look at the actual evidence to see if Ferris had missed anything in his report.

Skinner was waiting on the doormat, holding something in his mouth, when Thinnes went to let him in. Thinnes only noticed the contraband as the cat streaked through the doorway. Thinnes followed him into the family room, where he dropped his trophy in the middle of the rug. He stood over it, watching it and watching Thinnes. The mouse was still alive, dazed, and its whole body swayed slightly with the effort to breathe.

Thinnes said, "Dammit, Skinner!"

Skinner gave him one of his "What-did-I-do?" looks.

The mouse took advantage of the distraction to run for cover, scooting under the recliner. Skinner was after it like a tac team after drug dealers.

Thinnes grabbed his Big Gulp cup and dumped the remaining contents on the roots of Rhonda's ficus tree. Blocking Skinner, he tipped the chair on its side and shoved it against the wall, making a corner between the wall and chair, simultaneously trapping the exposed mouse. As Skinner leapt onto the chair, Thinnes clapped the cup over the mouse. Gotcha!

He slid the cup across the floor—carefully, so he wouldn't crush the mouse's feet or tail under the edge—to the bookshelf where Rhonda kept her typing paper. There was a pressboard protector sheet in the top of the box, which he removed and slid under the cup.

"Just like 26th and Cal," he told Skinner as he carried the captive to the door. "You bring 'em in—" He blocked the frustrated cat while he opened the door and released the mouse outside. "The system cuts 'em loose."

TWENTY-FIVE

When Thinnes got back to Area Three, there was an envelope waiting for him—carefully typed sheets containing detailed descriptions of the cars parked around the museum just after Bisti's murder, including VIN and sticker numbers, DMV expiration dates, decals, bumper stickers, and body damage. Clipped to the sheets was the DMV printout for the license numbers. On this, two of the entries were circled, and Officer Curtis had noted that the vehicles were also listed on the daily hot sheet. Bisti's car was on the list, too. A white Lexus. Illinois plate: BLUMTCT. Curtis hadn't bothered to run the plates on the city vehicles he'd listed, but he'd described both marked and unmarked cars in detail, as well as the squad roll and the fire department ambulance. On the bottom of the printout, Curtis's partner, Reilly, had noted that Thinnes's Caprice was currently operating out of the twilight zone as it was still assigned to Area Six.

Not content with noting parked vehicles, Curtis had called the CTA for the route and unit numbers of buses running the Magnificent Mile in the hours before and after the murder, and had gotten the bus drivers' vitals. He'd also called cab and limo services for the names and/or addresses of fares going to and from the area at the time. Thinnes was impressed. Thanks— probably—to Reilly, Curtis had a great start on being a good cop.

When he showed the stuff to Oster, Oster said, "Jesus X. Christ! Son of a bitch is gonna put us outta work."

A few minutes later, he asked, "Whaddaya think of Harrison

Wingate for a suspect? Bisti seemed pretty determined to show him up. How 'bout that for a motive?"

"Great—for the movies." Thinnes shrugged. "But I'll bet if you check, you'll find he's got some of the city's biggest lawyers on his payroll. He threatened to sue him, not kill him."

"Satisfaction?"

"Ruining him'd probably give Wingate a lot more satisfaction—especially watching Bisti's face when the verdict came down. Apparently he left before the murder—at least no one mentioned seeing him around."

"I think we oughta go lean on him anyway. He hasn't complied with our request to come in and talk."

"Good point. What've we got on him?"

Oster flipped through the pile of notes he'd been making as he talked on the phone to various sources. "Harrison Wingate. Fifty-eight years old. Divorced—three times. Head of Wingate Construction. He's Irish, by the way. Born here. Mother's name was Hanrahan. Big spender. Likes to drink and gamble, but apparently can quit while he's ahead—he's got a clean record with the underground credit bureau. No name check on criminal history. No wants or warrants. Not enough unpaid parking tickets to get the boot. Name didn't ring any bells with the Crime Commission or the Feds. A real straight-up guy."

"Who's his chinaman?"

"Nobody said. But if he's in construction . . ."

Oster didn't have to finish. Being in construction in Chicago meant having political connections or adding a hefty percentage to your bid to cover payoffs for unions, inspectors, and the folks who issue permits. Thinnes knew something about that. His father had been in construction. He'd refused to take jobs in the city just because of the underground "fees."

Of course you didn't *have* to pay. You could spend weeks of your time traipsing from rude to indifferent clerk and standing in lines Downtown, getting wrapped up in more and more red tape until, by the time you were done, you felt like a fly at a spider's picnic. And that was just the beginning. The city has some of the toughest building codes in the country, maybe on the planet. Codes written to protect the public. Codes used as a license to steal. He didn't know the current rate, but you'd better budget for plenty, because there were lots of inspectors. And lots of inspections. And God help you if you didn't have reliable subs, because that meant dealing with slugs from the unions. It was amazing anything ever got built.

They tracked Wingate to a South Loop building site that brought Bisti's installation, *Progress,* to mind. Though surrounded by streets, skyscrapers, and the usual mural-covered fence, instead of desert, it was the same building, in almost the same stage of construction. Bisti must've painted it from life or a damned detailed photo. Except there was a forklift, a crane, and a Komatsu loader instead of a tractor. And there were no bones—Thinnes looked.

When they flashed their stars, the mug doing the half-assed job guarding the gate pointed them toward an old construction trailer with its well-worn sign over the door—OFFICE. The trailer seemed familiar—like the one Thinnes had practically lived in all the summers he was growing up. Inside, the only difference from the trailer of Thinnes's memory was the plastic-draped computer system. The rest was all familiar: gloves—the brown jersey disposables and leather—invoices, and odd tools and parts covered the metal desk; lengths of chain, a wall phone, a come-along, coils of rope, and industrial-strength electrical cable decorated the walls; cans marked GAS and DIESEL, picks and shovels, a welding rig with extra cylinders of oxygen and acetylene, and surveyor's equipment stood in the corners; and boxes and barrels of other supplies were stacked along the walls. Three old folding chairs occupied the muddy space around the coffeemaker, and there were half a dozen hard hats with the Wingate Construction logo stacked on the drafting table.

The office was occupied: male Cauc, sixty maybe, five ten,

170 pounds, near-white hair, and faded blue eyes in a face the color of an old catcher's mitt. He was wearing jeans, worn work boots, and waffle underwear under a plaid flannel shirt and filthy sheepskin vest. His scarred, grimy white hard hat had GIBBS stenciled on it.

Oster held up his star. "We're looking for Harrison Wingate."

As he studied the star, Gibbs took his pipe and tobacco pouch from a vest pocket. He pointed out a filthy window with the pipe stem, at the freight elevator ferrying supplies upward. "Thirty-sixth floor. Meetin' the architects." He started filling the pipe.

Thinnes said, "Thanks," and opened the trailer door. The roar of the loader rushed in.

"You fellows planning to go up there . . ." Gibbs raised his voice to make it heard over the machine. He pointed to the pile of hard hats. "Better get you some hats."

They took the freight elevator up. The thirty-sixth floor was nowhere near the top, but it was the highest floor that had windows yet—no small consideration in the Windy City in November.

Even with windows, it was cold. As his head came even with the deck, Thinnes could see three men. Two wore expensive coats and hard hats like those he and Oster had been issued. One was carrying a briefcase, the other a portable computer and a rolled blueprint. Architects. The third man was hatless but otherwise dressed like Gibbs. Thinnes recognized him immediately— Todd Kent had been yucking it up with him in front of the security camera just before Bisti got punctured. *He* had to be Harrison Wingate. The impression of power Thinnes had gotten from the security video was confirmed by the man himself. Wingate had clout.

He took the two detectives for salesmen at first—probably because of the hats. He waved at them before they even got off the elevator. "Not now. Give your cards to the foreman."

Thinnes opened the safety gate, stepped onto the deck, and flashed his star. "We did. We still need to talk to you."

Irritation showed briefly on Wingate's face. "Shoot." He had heavy jaws in a square face. His expression could have been a grin or a sneer, but laugh lines around his eyes made it seem like he was enjoying some private joke. Up close, he seemed even bigger than when he'd been towering over the architects.

"In private," Oster said.

Wingate shrugged and pointed toward the other side of the deck. "Come into my office."

He was referring to the only other part of the thirty-sixth floor that wasn't piled head high with construction supplies. It was obviously the "lunchroom," littered with trash from every fast-food place in the Loop. And Wingate hadn't been kidding about it being an office. Building plans were rolled out and weighted at the corners on a four-foot-high pile of four-by-twelve drywall sheets. Miscellaneous junk, like the stuff in the office below, lay around on the plans. Someone had taped Wingate's hard hat, stenciled with his name and the slogan ONE WAY MY WAY, to the makeshift table with duct tape and added a note: BREAK SEAL IN CASE OF OSHA ATTACK.

Wingate stopped in the center of the open space and turned to face them. "Time is money, gentlemen."

Oster said, "Tell us about David Bisti."

"He's a fucking pain in the ass." Wingate squinted and laughed like a man who wants you to know he appreciates a good joke but doesn't think *this* one is especially funny. He planted his rump on a low pile of empty wooden pallets and pointed to another pile. "Have a seat." He seemed amused, and something about him reminded Thinnes of a big cat. Alert. Waiting for something to show itself so he could pounce on it.

They waited.

Finally he said, "How 'bout you just get to the point."

Oster said, "Bisti's dead."

"No kidding!" Wingate seemed more amused than surprised. "Somebody kill him?"

"Why do you say that?"

"Would you be wasting your time or mine if he ran his car into a bus?"

"Where'd you go after you left the museum last night?"

"The Berghoff."

"With?"

"Prospective investors. Gibbs'll give you the names."

"How long were you there?"

"We closed the place." He studied their faces. "That cover it?"

"You know anybody who'd want to kill Bisti?"

"I didn't know him—never laid eyes on him before last night. So I'd have no idea who'd want to kill him—besides whites and Injuns. But let me take a guess. Developers? Booze distributors? And everybody I talked to at the museum was pretty steamed."

Wingate grinned, and Thinnes could tell he was enjoying himself. His charm made you not take his outrageous statements too seriously. He was probably a big success with women.

"Why?" Thinnes said.

"Huh! Haven't you seen that crap he called art? Just go over to the museum and take a good look. You got any imagination at all, you'll come up with a whole roster of suspects."

"What was the nature of the business you had with Todd Kent?"

"I don't know any Todd Kent."

"You were seen talking to him at Bisti's show."

"I talk to a lot of people. Doesn't mean I know all of 'em."

"You didn't know Bisti?"

"No. And that makes his character-assassination scheme all the more bizarre."

"Why did you go to the reception?"

"It was a setup. Somebody told me a guy I've been trying to interest in a project would be there. And—what the hell—I'd never seen any of Bisti's crap before, so when I got the invitation, I decided to go. Somebody figured to annoy me. Figured right."

They waited for him to say more. That was a big part of interviewing—waiting. The wind tore through the open levels above, whipping a plastic sheet into a frenzy.

"Funny," Wingate said, finally. "I didn't hear anything about it on the news. But then they were so busy telling us about some alleged sex abuse that might have happened twenty years ago, they probably didn't have time. How'd he get it? Somebody shoot him?"

It was in the papers, so Thinnes didn't see any harm in saying, "Somebody stabbed him."

Wingate grinned. "I would have beat him to death."

TWENTY-SIX

Caleb finished at the office early; it was still light. He got his car and headed to Uptown. Spaulding House on Wilson. As he pulled the Jaguar into the fenced rear yard, he noticed, for the first time in a long time, how depressing the building's dirty stone looked, how the wire-topped Cyclone fence surrounding its weed-filled yard gave the exterior a concentration-camp ambiance. He would have to have the building cleaned in the spring, and maybe tuck-pointed. And ask a tax accountant if he couldn't write off a wrought-iron fence. Spaulding House had had one, years ago, when it was a Roaring Twenties domicile for the very rich. Its present residents deserved no less despite their poverty. He'd have grass planted in the spring, too. And try to get the inmates to help him plant some trees. It would be an act of faith. And hope. Spaulding House was a hospice.

He put the gearshift in first, turned off the engine, and let out the clutch. Too cold to use the parking brake. He hadn't used it in cold weather since the time his brakes had frozen on. He locked the car, didn't bother to turn on the alarm, but he closed and locked the gate.

"Rafe's a fucking burnt marshmallow!" Brian was saying as Caleb walked in. In case anyone missed the reference, he added, "Black on the outside, soft and sweet on the inside." He spoiled the intended effect by looking around for the others' reactions.

Bill and Lenny and Paul hid their amusement with varying degrees of success.

Rafe laughed. "What'd a honky faggot like you know about sof'n sweet?" He nodded at Caleb and said, "Jack."

Wanting to head off further wrangling, Caleb said, "It's nice to see you still love each other."

Rafe laughed again. Brian said, "Shit," but the ploy worked. It actually wasn't far from the truth, although the two men could scarcely have been more dissimilar—Rafe was huge, healthy, black, straight, and HIV negative; Brian, emaciated, white, gay, and in the throes of AIDS.

"I'm going out," Rafe told Caleb. "You're on."

"What needs to be done?"

"The market called; van's down. They can't deliver nothin' till tomorrow. You might could pick somethin' up for the meantime."

"All right."

"I'll go if I can drive your car, Jack," Brian said.

"It has a manual transmission."

"So?"

"Do you know how to set a car alarm?"

"Is the Pope Catholic?"

Caleb threw him the keys.

Brian clenched his fists and shook them in a victory gesture. "Yes!"

After Brian was out the door, Bill said, "You never let me drive your car, Jack."

"Do you have a license?"

"No."

"Me neither, Jack," Rafe said.

"You never asked."

"Jack, kin I drive yo car?"

"Surely."

Rafe gave him a sly grin. "Jus axing. *That* car's mo' trouble'n it's worth." He lowered his voice so only Caleb could hear. "You'd best look in on Manny."

* * *

The walls in Manny's room were covered with graffiti—whatever came to the minds of his many visitors. Caleb had started it off one night, when Manny was talking about giving up, by scribbling Dylan Thomas's imperative just below the ceiling with a Magic Marker: "Rage, rage against the dying . . ."

Someone had added, "Get well soon so we can go to the beach."

Advertising slogans probably not meant as double entendres soon followed:

BE ALL THAT YOU CAN BE.
UNCLE SAM WANTS YOU—SO DO I.
THE MARINES ARE LOOKING FOR A FEW GOOD MEN—
ME TOO.
JUST DO IT.

To the cliché "God is dead—Nietzsche/Nietzsche is dead—God," someone added, "But Manny's still with us. Thank Whoever."

Even Rafe had put his two cents in: "Hang in there, Mann."

Manny took Caleb's large hand in his small ones, which were like gloved skeletons. "Jack, I put on a good front but most of the time I'm terrified."

"Most of us are, Manny, even those without AIDS."

"But why? It's not like I have a brilliant future."

Caleb had no answer. He shook his head.

"I used to be so lovely," Manny said wistfully.

"You still are inside. Inside, you're the most beautiful man I know."

"I've forgotten how it feels to make love, Jack. I've even forgotten how it feels to want it."

Caleb put his free hand over Manny's skeletal one. "You haven't forgotten how it feels to love? To be loved?"

Tears brimmed over in the smaller man's eyes. "Of course not."

Judging by his flourishing practice, Caleb thought, there were healthy legions who *had* forgotten, but Manny needed to figure that out for himself. He said, "Well?"

"Why am I still so afraid?"

"It keeps you fighting?"

"Yes."

"When you're ready to let go, you'll stop feeling fearful."

"What will I feel?"

Caleb thought about patients who'd been lucid at the end. "Peace. Acceptance."

Manny sighed. "We've had this conversation before. Why can't I remember?"

"Human nature. Sometimes when what we're approaching is particularly awful or awesome, we can't bring ourselves to go straight at it. So we spiral toward it."

"Like Skylab on a decaying orbit?"

"I was thinking more of Dante in his descent into the Inferno."

"I never read that." Manny let his tone speak for the hard fact neither could say—he never would. He was too weak to hold a book or concentrate on printed words.

"I have a copy I'll bring in and read for you if you like. Ciardi's translation."

"I'd like that."

Manny's eyes drifted shut and his grip on Caleb's hand loosened as his breathing slowed. When he was finally asleep, Caleb turned off the light and went away.

TWENTY-SEVEN

They needed a professional opinion, so Thinnes and Oster took Caleb along when they went back to reinterview the widow.

"I remember waking up here," she said. "That's all." She paused, as if checking the statement against her memory, then added, "And a woman with wild hair was asking me questions."

There was a long pause.

Words leaked into Thinnes's awareness from the BS of his life. The time Before the Shooting. The vacuum of space. Nature abhors a vacuum . . . Fools rush in . . .

With words.

Lauren Bisti's spilled into the quiet. "I was dreaming, I think."

The silence returned, not an absence of sound, but the white noise from the heating system and the mind-numbing drug of daytime TV.

Thinnes was about to interrupt it when Caleb said, "Tell us about the dream." His voice was soft and comforting as a cat's purr.

Oster opened his mouth to protest; Thinnes stopped him with a look. Lauren Bisti didn't seem to notice.

"I was in jail. The cell was crowded with people yelling and pushing. And there was a window—not to the outside—but into another room full of people. Then a woman came running up to the window. She was covered with blood and screaming. And all the others in the room were trying to quiet her."

Caleb said, "Go on."

"That's all I remember." She smiled wistfully. "The rest faded away." She looked at Caleb as if confirming that he understood. "When I was little, I used to see fairies out of the corner of my eyes. But when I tried to look at them directly, they disappeared."

Oster said, "Who killed your husband, Mrs. Bisti?"

Carl must be getting tired, Thinnes decided. He was usually more subtle.

"I can't tell you."

Caleb said, "Tell us about your husband."

She pressed her fingers over the lower part of her face while she thought about him, and her eyes widened as if she were smiling behind them. Then she clasped her hands below her breasts. "He was beautiful. Physically, I mean, as well as talented. And smart. And considerate. Loving." She paused. Her face seemed to crumple; she sobbed as she added, "He's gone."

They waited for her to get herself under control. Caleb handed her a tissue, and she blew her nose.

Oster said, "Did he have any enemies?"

"Besides his own people—on both sides?"

"Yeah."

"There were the developers his installations ridiculed. And black-market antiquities sellers, and the preservationists. And some of the Navajos may have thought his works mocked them."

"Didn't they?" Thinnes asked.

"They didn't think he knew what it meant to be a Navajo. He knew! When he was out there, he didn't try to pretend he was a native, but he felt their connection to the land. He studied the language. He learned about the culture. He felt he was an exile returned home for a visit."

"But he was never accepted as a Navajo," Caleb said quietly.

She shrugged. "He understood the Navajo mind—my word. *He* would have said the mind of the *Diné*. He knew how it felt to be a stranger to the mainstream culture."

"So why did he make fun of them with his work?" Thinnes asked.

"Because he couldn't stand to see the old ways forgotten or exploited. Is what he did any more irreverent than gluing sand-paintings to cardboard to sell to tourists?"

They had her go over the twenty-four hours preceding the murder. Nothing had happened. They pressed her on the subject of stolen artifacts.

"The 'artifacts' David used in his works weren't real," she said, "even if they did have certificates of authenticity. They were all carefully crafted fakes."

"Crafted by whom?" Caleb asked.

"I don't know. I suggest you ask the 'experts' who authenticated them or whoever allegedly dug them up."

"You saying the paperwork was forged?" Oster demanded.

"The documents are probably as authentic as any you'll find for artifacts in private hands." She sounded defiant. "Though that's not saying much."

"Think someone he sold one of these artificial antiques to went away mad?"

"No one knew about that—except whoever he was working with."

"Who?"

"I don't know. When I asked, he told me the less I knew the safer I'd be. I thought in case . . . I thought it was a tax thing or something." She sobbed, nearly choking. "Maybe Todd can tell you. He handled all David's business."

While they went over the story with her again, Caleb compared her to the assured individual he'd observed at the museum. He knew it was relatively easy for women to fake depression—they just had to leave off their makeup and let their hair go wild. But she hadn't faked the shock that night. And he didn't believe she was feigning now.

He thought about names. David meant beloved. And there were ancient peoples who believed that knowing someone's name gave you power over him. Even today, if you had a name, even an alias, you were a long way toward having the individual. Blue Mountain Cat. David had been catlike in some ways: Withdrawn, self-centered, and cruel, in an impersonal way.

"What was the significance of the name Blue Mountain Cat?" he asked her.

"I think Blue Mountain refers to Mount Taylor, one of the Navajos' four sacred mountains. David told me but I'm not sure— It wasn't important to me, so I didn't pay attention. I think blue—turquoise, actually—is the color of the south, one of the four sacred directions. And everything is either male or female. Turquoise is male. The cat part refers to a mountain lion— David liked to play with words that way. I have no idea why he chose a lion."

They didn't talk until they were in the car and Thinnes pulled it out in traffic.

"Well, Doc," Oster said. "What d'ya think?"

"It may be my Freudian training, but I find it curious that she never said she didn't *know* who killed her husband, just that she couldn't tell us."

"So, you think this grieving-widow act is phony?"

"No. And that makes it more curious. Her grief seems genuine." Caleb shook himself. "So I may be reading something into what's simply an awkward choice of words."

"Maybe," Thinnes said. "But cops tend to believe in Freudian slips, too."

TWENTY-EIGHT

As long as we've got you out of your office, Doctor," Thinnes said, "what say we make another stop? I'd like your opinion of the victim's mother." He glanced at Caleb in the rearview and couldn't tell from his face what Caleb thought about it.

"Fine, as long as we're back to my office by twelve-thirty. I have an appointment at one."

Oster said, "What do we know about her?"

"I talked to three of her coworkers," Thinnes said. "She's a critical-care nurse at Weiss. According to everyone I talked to, an excellent employee, reserved, efficient, competent, and intelligent. Never talks about her personal life, though she sometimes mentions her son, the successful artist. Doesn't talk about her ex, either. Doesn't gossip, though she seems up to speed on what's going on around the hospital. She's good in a crisis. And her credit's in good shape. I checked."

"You know anything about her, Doc?" Oster asked.

"David told me his mother is Anglo-Irish," Caleb said, "with a stronger sense of her family's history than most third-generation immigrants. She was an army nurse when she met David's father, Harlan Bisti. He was a full-blooded Navajo. David said she was smitten with Bisti senior, in part, because of his strong tribal affiliation. But since her people simply took their tribes with them when they emigrated, she never understood how her husband's identity was so tied to his people's real estate. She finally wrote him off as a drunk and divorced him."

"Did Bisti hold that against her?"

"Not that he'd admit."

Oster twisted around in his seat to look at Caleb as he asked, "So he got on well with his mother?"

"That's what he said."

"You believed him?"

"I didn't have any reason not to."

Anne Bisti had herself under control when she opened the door for them. She wasn't wearing makeup. She looked strung out. She looked her age. She stepped aside to let them into a pristine white apartment, with polished wood floors and few but expensive furnishings. One of David Bisti's naturalistic paintings—one Thinnes wouldn't have minded having in his own living room— hung over the couch that she invited them to sit on. Thinnes didn't correct her assumption that Caleb was also a cop.

"Tell us about Lauren," Thinnes said.

"They wouldn't let me see her. I heard on the news that she'd been hospitalized and— I'm her only family."

"How do you feel about your daughter-in-law?"

"She's a very sweet girl, very fond of David."

"They ever have any trouble?"

"Not that I know of. But let me be frank with you, Detective. My son wouldn't have told me, even if he was planning a divorce. He just wasn't the sort to discuss his personal life with anyone—not even his mother."

"What about his business affairs?"

"I was led to believe he was doing well. And, in any case, Lauren has enough money—" She swallowed hard—the first sign she'd showed of any emotion. "Had enough for both of them."

"Have you had any thoughts, since yesterday, about who might have wanted to kill your son?"

"No."

"Do you know a woman named Irene?" Oster asked.

"Irene what?"

"We were hoping you could tell us—an acquaintance of your son's."

"He was once involved with a Navajo girl by that name. Irene Yellow."

"Was? What happened?"

"He met Lauren."

"You know if Irene Yellow might be upset enough about that to harm your son?"

She thought about it, going inside her head to work it out. Finally she said, "She struck me as a realist. I imagine she'd have been furious at the time, but my impression was that she's some sort of neo-traditionalist. And the Navajos don't believe in killing. I think she'd have gotten over it by now."

TWENTY-NINE

After they dropped Caleb at his office, Oster and Thinnes stopped at McDonald's. Neither particularly liked eating there, so they brought their Big Macs back to the office. Thinnes signaled right for the Police Business Only parking lot east of headquarters for District Nineteen and Detective Area Three, which also housed the First Municipal District Circuit Court. As he slowed to make the turn, a black Infiniti zoomed past on the left and cut back right to beat the Caprice into the lot.

"God damn it!" Oster said.

Thinnes said, "Find out who that son of a bitch is. I'm giving him a ticket."

"Right," Oster said—it had been years since he'd written a citation—but he did reach for the radio.

The Infiniti pulled along the curb dividing the drive from the plaza fronting the building, stopping across from the ugliest abstract sculpture north of the Picasso.

"Cancel that," Thinnes said, as the driver got out and he recognized Todd Kent. "I'll just hit him up with murder one." He tapped the horn to get Kent's attention and held up a finger to indicate Kent should wait.

He did. While he waited, he lovingly inspected his car. When they got close enough for conversation, he asked, "Like it?"

Thinnes had long since noticed the high correlation between expensive cars and incompetent drivers. And, since the war on drugs had turned drug dealers from every walk of life into millionaires, pretentious displays of money didn't impress him. "Must be a bitch to park legally," he said.

Just for a second, Kent's face fell. Gotcha! Then he pasted his public-offering smile back in place.

Thinnes walked around the car, and Oster sidled up to the lawyer. "Don't mind my partner," he said, too fast and too loud. He lowered his voice to add, "He must'a got up on the wrong side of the wife this morning."

Thinnes wasn't supposed to have heard that.

"*I* think it's a beautiful car." Oster patted it with all the appreciation of a luxury-car salesman.

That was how it was done, how the game was played. Mutt and Jeff. Good cop, bad cop. Even big-shot lawyers who were expecting it didn't recognize all the variations.

Kent waited to get even until they were inside the building, crammed into one of District Nineteen's tiny interview rooms. When they'd taken off their coats, Thinnes studied the lawyer while Oster went to get coffee. Kent wore contacts. His coat, suit, and smile were as expensive as his car. And given his age and the absence of wrinkles, he must've had a face-lift. Thinnes wasn't impressed.

When Oster came back, Kent said, "I ought to file a complaint."

Oster made it a point to look hurt, though Thinnes figured he didn't have a clue, either, about what Kent was talking about. Thinnes crossed his hands over his chest, tucking his fingers into his armpits. He hitched one hip up on the edge of the table, so he was half sitting, half leaning over Kent. "Is that so? What for?"

"My wife told me you dragged her in here and interrogated her."

Yesterday. "And you rushed right over here to defend her honor." Before Kent could blow his stack over that crack, Thinnes went on. "No, Mr. Kent. We didn't interrogate your wife. We asked her to come here and answer some questions to help us find out who killed your partner. And we interviewed her. We only interrogate people we're reasonably sure did something wrong."

"She said you accused her of having an affair with David."

"I *asked* her if she'd had an affair." Close enough to what he'd actually asked.

"How dare you?"

"Come off it. You may not be the world's greatest mouthpiece, Counselor, but you know how the game's played."

"And *you* know I've got the connections to make your life miserable."

"Okay. Now that we've gotten the strutting and posing out of the way, let's get to the point."

"Which is?"

"You didn't share Bisti's feelings about Harrison Wingate, did you?"

Kent seemed surprised. "What are you trying to say?"

It *was* a bit sudden change of direction. "You were seen yucking it up with him at the museum that night. It doesn't quite jive with the little scene Wingate played with Bisti just before he died."

"Well, some of that was just hype. You know—David's shtick. It's every artist's fervent hope he'll be banned in Boston. Or denounced by anyone with a following, any place with an active media."

"You saying he staged the fight with Wingate?"

"No. Of course not. But I wouldn't have put it past him to have done the installation, then invited Wingate just for the free publicity Wingate's reaction would generate."

"You tell that to Wingate?"

"Why would I? He's old enough to look out for himself."

"So, what were you talking about?"

"I don't recall."

It was a challenge. Prove it. With Bisti dead and Wingate as uncooperative as Kent, there wasn't a thing Thinnes could do.

"I think I'd like to leave, now," Kent added. He turned to Oster. "Would you be good enough to fetch my coat?"

"Nothin' I'd like better," Oster said. He made it sound like someone had just offered to take out the garbage.

Kent turned back to Thinnes. "By the way, I did an inventory, yesterday, of the pieces we had at the museum. We're missing an Anasazi bowl. Black and white. Indian designs. Andrews said your people took it. It's worth a lot of money."

"How much?"

"I don't know, exactly. Probably something close to what a cop makes in a year."

THIRTY

Dr. Caleb," Mrs. Sleighton's voice said, over the intercom. "There's a man here to see you, a reporter."

"What time is my next appointment?"

"Two-thirty."

"Thank you. Send him in."

The reporter was more than six-feet tall and slender, black hair—over the collar but neatly trimmed, as were his beard and mustache—fine but masculine features. The faded irises of his eyes—the only color to him—were rimmed with slate blue. With his charcoal-gray suit and suede shoes, pearl-gray shirt, and gray paisley tie, he could have been a Dockers commercial for gray.

"I'm Rick Patrick," he said. "I'd like to do a feature on a hospice. I was told you're the man to talk to about Spalding House."

Caleb recognized the signs of subtle interest and guessed Rick found him attractive but had no idea that Caleb was gay. And he could tell Patrick wasn't the sort to risk a hostile encounter by propositioning a straight man.

It would be easy enough to give him a sign, something noncommittal, that only someone who was looking would notice. But something—inertia? cowardice? maybe pragmatism—held him back. "I'm flattered," he said, "but I'd prefer not to have the publicity. AIDS hospices are not popular with neighbors, and we'd rather not call attention—"

"Isn't that the sort of prejudice a favorable piece would fight?"

"Our aim is to fight AIDS, not take on prejudice. I'm sorry . . ."

Patrick handed him a business cared—also gray, with black lettering. Tasteful. "If you should change your mind, give me a call. Please."

Caleb nodded.

"Thank you for your time, Doctor." He didn't seem to be indulging in any of the sulkiness people often display when their plans are thwarted. "I can see myself out."

"I'm sorry, Mr. Patrick."

This time Patrick nodded, then he left.

Caleb used the intercom to ask Mrs. Sleighton to give him time to make a phone call before she sent in the next patient.

He called his attorney. "I wonder if you could do a confidential background check," he said, "on a freelance reporter who's been asking about Spaulding House? Nothing too intrusive. Just what you usually do on a prospective employee."

"What do you know, so far?"

"Just what he has on his business card." Caleb read off the information. "And he's young, he seems to have adequate manners, and excellent taste in clothes."

"I'll see what I can come up with," he said, and hung up.

Caleb thought about Rick Patrick. He was certainly beautiful. And if he was successful as a writer, probably intelligent. Caleb's problem was that he knew what he wanted in a relationship. He'd heard it summarized on one of those Channel-11-self-help-pledge-drive specials. Passion and Safety. He'd had it once—so long ago that the loss had almost stopped hurting—but he remembered. He knew where he wanted to be; he just didn't know how to get there. How to find *the one*. Or someone who could be the one. He didn't know how to make contact, to get past the awkwardness and misunderstanding that his training and intellect—not to mention experience—told him he would have to survive to end up where he needed to be. Most of the time it seemed one couldn't get there from here.

He got the results of the background check by 4:30—a message to call his attorney's office ASAP. When he called, the lawyer told him, "Patrick got his undergraduate degree in journalism from Roosevelt and a masters from the University of Missouri. He works freelance as a reporter and feature writer, income's probably a quarter of yours. I could get you the exact figure, if you like."

"Never mind. I just wanted to be sure that he *has* a salary and doesn't have an arrest record."

"Oh, yes. A salary, a reputation for being tough but fair, and an apartment in Hyde Park."

THIRTY-ONE

Native Artists was strategically located on Broadway, between the yuppie cash in Lincoln Park and the disposable income of New Town. Thinnes parked in the upstream end of a bus stop, put his OFFICIAL POLICE BUSINESS sign on the dash, and asked Oster, "What've we got on this woman?"

Oster checked his notes. "Irene Yellow. Age thirty-four. Single. Address in Lincoln Park. Works at a tony gift shop belonging to her old man, Noah Hopewell." He pointed at the store. "This one."

"Let's see, one arrest for assault during an AIM meeting that got out of hand. Guy I talked to said he thought being in jail overnight must've put the fear of God in her, 'cause the only assault she's done since then is of a verbal nature."

"Good. I didn't wear my vest today."

The stuff displayed in Native Artist's front window ranged from pictures that looked like refrigerator art to sophisticated jewelry. Inside, there was a man sitting on a folding chair behind one of the display counters. He was reading when Oster and Thinnes entered. He was in his sixties, white haired, thin and gnarled, with a face as lined as a map of canyon country. He put a marker in the book and stood up.

"May I help you?" He was wearing a flannel shirt, Levi's, and worn cowboy boots. His voice was very soft but it carried well enough. He gave the impression of having all day to help them.

"You are?"

"Noah Hopewell."

Irene Yellow's old man. He was Caucasian, which surprised Thinnes. He put the book on the counter and rested his hands on either side of it. They were spotted and veined and arthritic, and his fingers wouldn't lie flat. Thinnes said, "We're looking for Irene." He showed Hopewell his star. "She's your daughter?" Hopewell nodded. "You know where we can find her?"

"Not at present. What's she done?" His pale blue eyes fixed on something behind Thinnes, shifting toward Thinnes only briefly. In a younger man, this would have given the impression he was lying, but they hadn't asked him anything, yet, to lie about. Thinnes wondered if it was some kind of cultural thing.

"We'd just like to ask her some questions," Oster said.

Hopewell waited at least fifteen seconds before he said, "If I see her, I'll tell her." He didn't look directly at Oster either, but Thinnes didn't think he was lying.

Oster said, "You know a David Bisti?"

"I did."

Oster waited.

Hopewell didn't seem retarded, but his answers were forever coming. "He was a friend of Irene's, years ago. An artist."

"Was?"

"You're here because someone killed him."

"How do you know that?"

"Irene told me. And it was on the news."

Thinnes said, "What did Irene tell you about Bisti's death, Mr. Hopewell?"

"She told me he was a witch and that someone turned his evil around on him and killed him with it. I think she was being sarcastic, though." He blinked slowly.

"What does that mean, exactly? How was Bisti a witch?"

There was another long pause before Hopewell said, "The People do not speak of such things to whites."

"You mean the Navajos? You're not Navajo."

"My wife was one of the People. She's dead now."

113

Thinnes nodded, not offering sympathy he didn't feel.

Hopewell finally got back to the question. "Witches are those who deliberately choose to harm others."

Oster started to interrupt. Whatever was eating him, lately, was interfering with his work. Thinnes caught his eye and he stopped. Thinnes looked back at Hopewell.

He was saying, "When someone has been injured by a witch, he commissions a ceremony to reverse the evil and restore the universe to harmony."

Thinnes waited until he was sure Hopewell was through, then said, "Tell us about your daughter, Mr. Hopewell." He thought the old man looked sad. "She claims to be a Navajo."

"She has that right. She was born to Two Gray Hills."

"Could you explain that?"

Hopewell said, "Her mother's family is called Two Gray Hills. When Navajos marry, they affiliate themselves with the wife's clan and the children are born into that clan. And they're born *for* their father's clan."

He didn't seem to be going to elaborate, so Thinnes said, "How long have you lived here, sir?"

"Since my wife died, three years ago."

"You daughter lives with you?"

He turned his head slowly from side to side. "She has her own apartment."

"Did you see her the night Bisti died?"

"No."

"Did she tell you about what happened at the museum?"

"My daughter has her own life. She doesn't account for her time to me."

"You haven't answered my question."

"No."

It was obvious Hopewell had said all he was going to. Thinnes handed him his card. "When you see your daughter, please ask her to call."

The old man took the card without looking at it and nodded.

THIRTY-TWO

Thinnes and Oster had court at 26th and Cal the next morning, after which they stopped by at Western and Belmont to answer a page. There was a woman sitting in the Community Relations office with her coat and hat on her lap. She stood up when the officer on duty pointed them out to her and said, "I'm Irene Yellow. I understand I'm wanted for questioning."

She was tall for a woman, maybe five ten, with hair and eyes as black as print powder, and high cheekbones in an oval face. She was wearing a red dress of some soft flannelly material that hugged her well-developed curves and came down over her boot tops.

"We appreciate you coming in to talk to us," Thinnes told her.

She gave him a smile that said, plainly, that her cooperation wasn't entirely voluntary.

Thinnes said, "Let's go someplace more quiet."

They took her into one of the District Nineteen interview rooms. Thinnes asked her to sit down at the small table that nearly filled the room, and she threw her things across the chair next to hers. He took the seat across from her. Oster sat on the same side as Thinnes, at the far end, and took out his notebook and pen. He waited, holding the book in a way that prevented her seeing what he wrote. Irene Yellow glanced around and relaxed enough to let her disdain show, then looked back at Thinnes, apparently not impressed by him, either.

"You're Ms. Irene Yellow?" Thinnes asked.

"I'm Two Gray Hills."

Out of the corner of his eye, Thinnes could see Oster blink, but he took down what she said. Thinnes repeated, "Your name is Irene Yellow?"

"That's my *belagana* name."

Belagana must mean something like "white man," Thinnes decided. He said, "You're Navajo."

"I sure am."

Thinnes waited the way old man Hopewell had waited. Irene must have been more white than she admitted because the silence had the same effect on her as on most of the people Thinnes interviewed. Eventually, she said, "What now?"

"Now you tell us what you can about David Bisti."

"It's considered a major faux pas to mention the name of the dead to one of my people." Her tone was neutral, and she hid whatever she was feeling behind a pleasant poker face. She had dangly silver earrings, a necklace of silver, and rings on every finger and both thumbs. She twisted one of the thumb rings around without seeming to notice it.

Thinnes wondered if she was serious or just stalling. He said, "So how do you refer to someone who's died?"

"We *refer* to him. We don't call evil on ourselves by naming him."

Thinnes nodded. "What happened Thursday night?"

"I saw the notice in the paper—for the show—and I was a little miffed that I hadn't been invited. I decided to drop in anyway."

Her smile was definitely sarcastic. "I waited till the receptionist was busy—there's always some nouveau—riche idiot who has to bully the help. I pretended I was waiting to meet someone until she was occupied with one of those and I convinced security that I was the sister of the guest of honor. Maybe the guy forgot to mention it to you. He was very young and had a gap between his front teeth. Ask him."

Thinnes remembered him. He hadn't mentioned any sister. "I will."

"Of course," she added, "he was so busy studying my cleavage, he never asked my name."

Thinnes heard a strangling sound to his right and looked to see Oster choking on that. Personally, he didn't blame the guard. "Then what happened?"

"I went through the museum, looking for the one who died, getting more angry by the minute—or, I should say, by the atrocity. When I found him— I don't remember my exact words but I believe I was less than tactful."

Thinnes waited. She didn't say more. "How did he respond?"

"He laughed. He always knew which button to push to get me going."

"You and this artist didn't get along."

"That implies . . ."

"Well?"

"He was a phony. I hate phonies—but not enough to kill one."

Thinnes waited.

"He was from here. He was *never* one of us. You can't be one of the *Diné*—what you call Navajo—and not be from the *Dinéhta.*" She looked from Thinnes to Oster. "Oh, he lived there for a while—rented a house, went to a few sings to soak up the local color, but he was always an outsider. His mother was white; he couldn't even name his father's clan.

"And?"

"He was an exploiter. Do you think anyone would have bought that junk he made if he hadn't claimed to be an Indian?"

"Why'd he do it?"

"I don't know. Well . . . Most of my people grow up being ashamed of being Native American. But how can anyone grow up *white* in this country and not be ashamed, sickened . . ."

The question seemed rhetorical, so Thinnes let it pass.

"Why did you go to the reception?"

"To see him. He'd been avoiding me—we used to be lovers, before he met that *belagana* bitch."

Thinnes waited.

"I just wanted to see him—you know?" When he didn't answer, she shrugged. "I wanted to see what he was doing artistically. I was out of town when he had his last show. He used to do tourist stuff when we were together—*Arizona Highways* landscapes, stereotyped Indian portraits, that kind of crap. I wanted to see how he could get rich and famous doing that."

"Did you?"

"Sure! He sold shit to suckers."

"You know who killed him?"

"No."

"Who might have wanted to?"

"Anyone who knew him well." Thinnes waited. "He had this way of making everything *your* fault. Nothing was ever his fault. He'd drive you to the edge of distraction, then ask you why you were upset."

"Specifically, who might have wanted him dead?"

"How about that developer he made fun of?"

"Wingate?"

"Yes. The publicity he was getting can't have been helping his business."

"Anyone else?"

"It's the custom of my people, when someone is being—like he who was killed—to avoid him. Whoever did it wasn't one of us."

"How long ago were you and he an item?"

"Five years ago. For a summer. Then *she* got her hooks into him and it was good night, Irene. To give her credit, though, I think she loved him. I think she'd have killed for him. And she could do more for him than I could have." There was a grudging tone to the last sentence that made what she said sound true.

"When was the last time you talked to him—prior to Thursday night?"

"When he told me he was dumping me for that *belagana*."

Thinnes remembered what Caleb had asked Bisti's mother. "What was the significance of Blue Mountain Cat? Why a cat?"

"I don't know."

"Is there such a thing as a blue mountain cat?"

"It would have to be a cougar. Blue Mountain is Tsodzil, in New Mexico. I have no idea what significance it had for him."

"Why a mountain lion?"

She shrugged. "I would have thought he'd have chosen a coyote."

After she'd left Thinnes said, "So if you can't be Navajo unless you live in Navajo land, what's Irene Yellow doing in Chicago?"

"The pot calling the kettle black," Oster said. "Why don't we get her back and ask her?"

"Next time. We haven't dealt with this Ivan character yet. Let's get that over with."

"You want me to go pick him up?"

"Sure."

According to the receptionist, Jack Caleb was with a patient when Thinnes called, but he rang back within fifteen minutes. When they'd gotten past the hellos, Thinnes asked, "What more can you tell me about this Ivan?"

"I don't know him very well. He writes reviews for several art magazines that I know of, and serves on the boards of a number of nonprofit corporations. He manages to get in the society pages."

"What kind of reviews does he write?"

"Witty but brutal."

"Bisti, too?"

"I don't recall. But I don't remember ever reading a positive review. In his own way, he's as much of a satirist as David was, and as skilled at manipulating perception."

"Where can I get one of his reviews?"

"I subscribe to a research service that's pretty efficient. I could have them fax you something."

Thinnes said, "Thanks," and gave him the fax number. "Yellow made the argument that no one would've bought Bisti's stuff if he hadn't claimed to be an Indian. What about that?"

" 'The lady doth protest too much, me thinks.' And I don't buy that 'he wasn't born here' argument. Joseph Conrad—one of the greatest writers of English prose—was born in Poland." There was a short pause, then Caleb added, "No. David's work is brilliant satire, and the fact that it infuriates both Navajos and whites indicates he had a foot securely on each continent."

THIRTY-THREE

Barbaric waste of talent," Ivan said when he'd accepted a cup of coffee and was seated in an interview room. Ivan the Terrible. Male Cauc, five seven, maybe 180 pounds. He had blue eyes and thinning brown hair—with blond highlights, Thinnes noted sourly. His three-piece suit was flamboyant but expensive. His shirt was silk. His tie, hand painted with flowers. He'd thrown his raccoon coat over one of the chairs.

Thinnes had trouble thinking of him as a man, though there was certainly nothing feminine about him. He seemed to use the stereotypical limp wrist as a weapon—an offensive one. Likewise the coy tilting of his head and his mincing walk.

His reviews had arrived twenty minutes before the man himself, so Thinnes had had time to skim them before Oster brought him in. Caleb hadn't exaggerated his negativity. Even a recommendation—like the one he'd given Bisti's work—came out as a put-down. It was even more obnoxious than the way he flaunted being gay.

Oster had elected to watch the interview from a distance—behind the two-way mirror, so Thinnes was on his own. He took a seat facing the reviewer and said, "I read your piece on David Bisti." The coffee must've been to give Ivan something to do with his hands; he wasn't drinking it. "I didn't think you liked his stuff."

Ivan pretended surprise, exaggerated it. "My dear, you didn't think I was referring to his artistic abilities!"

He was doing it to make Thinnes uncomfortable, and he decided to call him on it. "What abilities were you referring to?"

"You wouldn't understand." The flippancy masked enormous tension.

"Try me." When he didn't, Thinnes said, "Tell me about your relationship with David Bisti."

"Purely professional, alas. He created things; I reviewed them."

"You ever proposition him?"

"I?"

Thinnes looked around the room as if to see who else Ivan might have thought he meant.

Ivan said, "Of course not." A lie. He wasn't good at it.

"What happened when you propositioned him?"

"I didn't—"

"Did he laugh at you?"

"How dare you?" Thinnes raised his eyebrows. "I came in here to offer my help and you insult me!"

Thinnes stifled the urge to laugh. "Cut the crap. You came in here because Detective Oster brought you in. Save your—" He stopped himself before he said "fucking faggot routine." Not politically correct. And in a city with as many gay registered voters as Chicago has, career suicide. "Save your injured-innocence act for your fans. We both know you propositioned Bisti."

"What do you want from me?"

"I want to know what you can tell me about David Bisti?"

"He was a minor talent who could have made it. If he hadn't gotten himself murdered, he might have lived long enough to develop a following and create a body of work that'd outlast him."

The statement, or maybe the way he said it, gave Thinnes a reason for Ivan's vicious "reviews." Envy. Envy for artistic talent. Maybe even envy for straight men. The insight didn't make Thinnes dislike Ivan any less, but it made playing head games with him seem as mean-spirited as poking at a snapping turtle with a stick.

Thinnes said, "That's more like it."

And while envy is an occasional motive for murder, he thought, *there's no evidence it was the motive in this case.*

As if reading his mind, Ivan said, "Were you seriously think-ing *I* might have killed David?" When Thinnes didn't answer, he slapped the air in Thinnes's direction with a limp-wristed hand and said, *"Please.* If I *were* going to kill someone, I'd use gas or poison—something less messy."

THIRTY-FOUR

When Caleb entered his condo, there was a yellow Post-it note stuck to the wall near the door, above the alarm panel.

> Dear Dr. C. Einstein attacked my ankles today. I think
> he's bored. You should consider getting him a friend. L

"L" was Lucile, Caleb's housekeeper. She could never remember Freud's name and called him Einstein because Caleb had once told her *the* Freud was a genius. Caleb's Freud didn't seem to mind.

Caleb waved the note at the cat, who was perched on the chair back nearest the door. "What about this?"

Freud batted at the paper, tentatively at first, with one front paw, then ferociously, sitting up on his hind legs to grab it with both. He seized it with his teeth and bounced to the floor with it, mauling it, and rolling on the floor to disembowel it with all four feet. Then he streaked behind the chair and pounced, from the other side, on the unsuspecting paper, savaging it again.

"Freud," Caleb said, "I think Lucile's diagnosis is correct."

The fact of his sexuality wasn't constantly uppermost in Caleb's mind, nor did it color many of his casual relationships. He met men he found attractive whom he simply recognized as off-limits because they were straight or committed. And there were many he discounted because they were seriously flawed—something he was perhaps quicker to notice because of his profession. He recognized that he hadn't found an intimate because he wasn't looking, hadn't even been haunting places where he might be seen. He didn't frequent bars, in fact, hadn't been in one since before Christopher died. He was becoming like one of his female patients, who read romances and dreamed of tall, dark strangers appearing—like the answer to prayer—to solve her problems and give her drab life meaning. Magical thinking. He would never meet anyone by hiding out in his comfortable routine. And if he wanted to alleviate his awful loneliness, he would have to meet someone.

Not that his social life was lacking. He was often invited out. Couples asked him when they had an extra lady guest, male colleagues frequently asked him to squire their wives, happy he wouldn't seduce them. And he liked women, eighty-year-old grandmothers no less than teenaged ingenues. He enjoyed escorting most of them. But they didn't fill his needs.

Saturday, he forced himself to go out despite his misgivings. It took him all afternoon to get up the nerve.

The bar was on Clark, the northeast corner of an X-shaped intersection. He'd been there before, but not for years. Even as he was walking in, he felt great resistance. But what could happen? Some guy might make a pass? Wasn't that what he was hoping for? Some regular patron might challenge his right to enter? He could deal with confrontation. And the bar was a public accommodation. They'd serve even the most obnoxious homophobe if he didn't start a fight.

He stopped inside the door to analyze his reluctance. He recognized the illogic of his situation. He'd traveled some distance and set aside an afternoon to meet people, but couldn't cross the room to make the final connection. He hadn't thought of himself as shy since the service. After 'Nam, he'd thought he could face anything. But if merely talking to someone was so difficult, getting to the point—to intimacy—seemed a light-year distant.

Two men were playing darts. The bar was moderately full. Its patrons were integrated, assorted, mostly male, mostly in their twenties or early thirties. A few glanced at him, most didn't notice his arrival.

The decor was Southwestern—cowboy boots and cow skulls, Indian artifacts and old photographs. The music was contemporary and not unbearably loud, the ventilation good—air decent despite a number of smokers. Caleb made his way around the zigzag-shaped bar and took a stool between a papier-mâché totem pole and a woman wearing a man's shirt and suit jacket over Levi's. As he took Caleb's order, the bartender—cheerful, middle-aged but well kept—seemed almost too eager to please.

While he waited for his beer, Caleb studied the patrons. A dozen men flanked the north side of the bar in groups of two and three. A young black man in a dashiki leaned on the video game by the men's room, talking to an older black man wearing a Bulls jacket. Two women were playing pool in the back of the room, while waitresses hustled back and forth between the bar and the adjoining restaurant. A man with dark-framed glasses sat by the south window, watching passersby out on the street. And an urban cowboy sat at the bar with his back to the window and his arms around his lover.

The couple made him think of Christopher.

He was still discovering what he'd lost when he'd lost Chris. Before that, he'd been able to walk into a strange place and, without hesitation, initiate conversations with strangers. Losing Christopher, he'd lost the feeling that he was unique, that he was loved and treasured by one special person. He was liked well enough, now, by those who knew him, but he was indispensable to no one.

The bartender put a beer and a smile in front of Caleb, then began simultaneously mixing two tall, exotic drinks. The woman sitting next to Caleb watched with the avidity of Freud stalking birds. She had short, dark hair, thick glasses, and cat earrings by Laurel Burch. Caleb watched her twist her Sharps around in her hands as she visually fondled everyone and everything in the bar. She emptied the bottle and left a dollar for the bartender as she departed.

Before the door closed on her, a familiar figure swung it wide and entered like Melodrama, wearing a full-length raccoon coat. Ivan.

He minced his way across the room and took the seat the woman had vacated, gesturing to the bartender before giving Caleb a supercilious inspection. "So-ooo I was right about you. The great Dr. C is one of us after all."

"Just a bit of the continent."

Ivan slipped out of the coat and let it fall back over the bar stool. "Oh, don't go literary on me."

"Well, then drop the flaming-faggot routine and let me buy you a drink."

"I never pass up a freebie."

"It's not free." Caleb leaned into the angle between Ivan and the bar. "I want something."

"Me, I hope." He gave the bartender his order and turned back to give Caleb a simpering smile.

Caleb ignored it. "I want to know how David Bisti got a showing at the museum."

"Oh, that."

They both watched the bartender mix Ivan's drink—an electric-blue concoction—and set it in front of him. Caleb pushed a ten-dollar bill toward the barman, who smiled and nodded and deducted the price.

When he'd moved away, Ivan told Caleb, "A brilliant bit of misdirection, my dear."

Caleb waited.

"I showed Andrews the brochure Anita made up for the show at her gallery and let him believe that Blue Mountain Cat was still in his *Arizona Highways* period."

"Why go out of your way to promote David?"

"Cultivating my investment. I *do* own more of his work than anyone, including the widow."

It made sense. Gushing on paper about an artist in whose works he'd invested would destroy his carefully crafted reputation for impartial, critical savagery. Instead, he'd guaranteed priceless free publicity by setting up a situation that was bound to cause controversy. A brilliant strategy.

"Naturally, if you quote me, I'll deny it."

"Naturally." Caleb sat back and sipped his beer, then said, "I wouldn't think this was your sort of venue."

Ivan smiled, then leaned around him to speak to a waitress handing in drink orders on the other side of the totem pole. He pointed to a sign by the restaurant door—PLEASE WAIT TO BE SEATED—and told her, "My dear, I'm waiting."

She was a petite, conventionally attractive brunette. As she raised an eyebrow at Ivan, she seemed to be trying not to laugh. "Sure thing, hon." She took her drinks from the bartender and went back in the restaurant.

Ivan continued talking to Caleb as if without interruption. "It most definitely is not my kind of place. But the sweet young thing I'm dining with won't go near *my* watering hole."

"What would that be?"

"My dear, if you have to ask, you're too young . . ." He took a sip of his drink, managing to put the maximum of sexual innuendo into the gesture. Then, leaving the nearly full glass on the bar, he picked up his fur, said, "Ciao," and minced out. When Caleb turned back around, there was a new occupant on the next stool. Another acquaintance. Rick Patrick.

Nodding in the direction Ivan had taken, Rick said, "A perfect example of 'What's the use?' " He was wearing a turtleneck and slacks instead of a dress shirt and tie. He looked even more like a model for Dockers. Stunning. Too good to be true. Caleb felt a sensation akin to decelerating sharply in an elevator. His mind fogged and he could almost see the nervous vibes he was emitting. He took a deep breath.

Rick was saying, "Do you come here often?"

Caleb shook his head then forced himself to say, "No. First time in a long time."

"Serendipity, then," Rick said.

To Caleb's amazement, he seemed content to be making small talk. And he was attending closely to the conversation and to Caleb, not cruising the bar visually, not—apparently—marking time until someone more appealing wandered in. Caleb was almost flattered. But Rick had made it clear at their first meeting that he had an agenda, so Caleb withheld judgment and observed his own discomfort—the dissonance between what he wanted and what he believed possible—with proper scientific detachment.

"I haven't been here in years," Rick continued.

"What's special about today?"

"Luck?" He smiled, and Caleb imagined his own blood pressure rising. "I had an interview not far from here, and nothing special to do tonight. So I thought, what the hell . . ."

"And you spotted me and thought you might still get an interview?" Caleb observed his own alarm at the prospect and could see that Rick noticed it, too.

"Are all shrinks so paranoid?" He smiled.

"Why do you ask?" Caleb rolled his eyes from side to side as if looking for enemies.

Rick laughed. Other drinkers looked—stared actually. Caleb didn't blame them. He felt as if he'd won the office football pool. Rick was easily the most beautiful man in the bar.

"Off-the-record," Rick said. He pulled a little tape recorder out of an inside pocket and offered it to Caleb.

Caleb transferred it to his own and, parodying paranoia, said, "Where's your backup?"

"In the car. This whole evening is off the record."

They sat companionably until Caleb's beer was nearly gone. As the bartender approached, Rick said, "You hungry?"

"Not enough to go in there . . ." Caleb gestured toward the restaurant door. ". . . before Ivan leaves."

"I hear you. We could go somewhere else . . ."

Caleb had come on the bus, though he didn't mention that to Rick. They took Rick's car, an aging Chevy Blazer, back Downtown. Caleb suggested the restaurant, which was moderately expensive, so he also offered to pay. It was a test of sorts, the kind of place with real flowers and crystal and linen, and silverware in layers. The waiter presented them with a semi-interesting wine list; Caleb waited for Rick to make a selection.

After a few minutes's study, he put it down on the table. "I daresay I could tell cabernet from Chianti but, to be truthful, I've never had the money to develop a taste for the good stuff. I'd just as soon have a beer."

Caleb appreciated his candor.

Midway through dessert, Rick said, "I didn't see you at the march this spring." Washington, D.C. The gay-rights march. They'd progressed to the point in their relationship where he didn't have to explain which march.

Caleb laughed. "I was there." He thought about it for a moment. "Sort of."

Rick waited for him to elaborate.

"I went by myself, just for the day. It was a strange experience. I felt very alienated. Everyone else seemed to be *with* someone—friends or family, or loved ones. Or with an organization. I didn't feel as if I fit any of the categories. I didn't have a lover or a group, or any agenda beyond civil rights." He shrugged. "I promised myself I would join something when I got back, but I'm not much of a joiner . . ."

"Join me."

They headed back to Newton—Boystown, Rick called it—and barhopped until they found a place with live musicians and slow dancing. Between dances, they talked. It was nearly three when

Rick stopped the Blazer in front of Caleb's building. Caleb felt, simultaneously, relief and sadness, reticence and lust.

Rick said, "Aren't you going to ask me up for a drink?"

"You might get the idea that's not all it was for."

Rick leaned over and kissed him. "You had a good time tonight?"

"Yes."

Rick slipped his hands under Caleb's jacket to brush his fingertips up and down his sides. It was the first time they'd touched since they left the dance floor. Rick knew what he was doing—like the light man at *The Phantom,* orchestrating the magic. "You know I'm safe. You had me investigated."

Caleb blushed. "That was something else."

"So you know I won't mug you or steal the silver." He nudged Caleb's lapel aside and gently bit him on the *pectoralis.*

Caleb gasped.

"I have to admit," Rick went on. "I approve. You can't be too careful these days." He gently pushed Caleb away, then straightened his tie and smoothed his lapels. "We wouldn't want to scandalize your neighbors . . ."

Rick was suitably impressed with the condo. Caleb put jazz on the stereo and made them both drinks, then watched him explore the living room like a cat in a new territory. He pronounced his verdict as he settled onto the couch, intimately close. "Very nice." He made it seem to include his host as well as the surroundings.

Caleb was suddenly—and ironically—aware that he felt trapped.

"What's wrong?" Rick asked.

"I'm not prepared for this."

Rick seemed to relax. "Not to worry." He slipped his hand into his pocket and withdrew a small, flat, square, foil-wrapped packet for Caleb's inspection. "I am."

Caleb felt the hot wave of a blush color his face. "That's not exactly what I meant." With part of his mind, he could trace his own discomfort; part of it was numb with panic; and part of it noted—quite dispassionately—that Rick was enjoying himself. Caleb didn't hold that against him. Viewed objectively, the situation was absurdly amusing.

"You don't know the first fucking thing about safe sex, do you?" Rick asked.

"Theoretically, I'm a genius. But my last relationship was monogamous. And before that, it wasn't an issue."

"How antediluvian. Well, we're not all into rimming and fisting. By the time I was old enough to join the gay community, safe sex was 'in.' Most of my first lovers had lost someone to AIDS."

Caleb couldn't think of anything to say to that.

"You have a lover you didn't tell me about who's going to barge in on us?"

"No." He couldn't stop himself from glancing at Chris's portrait.

Rick caught the gesture. "You want to tell me about him?"

"Christopher," Caleb said, looking at the portrait, "died. I guess I haven't gotten over him."

"Ah," Rick said. "How long ago?" He studied the picture.

"More than five years."

"And how long since you made love with someone?"

"So long ago I've forgotten how."

Rick stepped closer and slipped his hands beneath Caleb's jacket. "Let me refresh your memory," he said, pulling Caleb closer. He glanced at Chris's portrait again. "Let's go somewhere more private."

A few moments later, in Caleb's bedroom, Rick put his hand on Caleb's shoulder. "You have to relax and relinquish control, even though I know what control freaks you shrinks are . . ."

"Tell me about your first time," Rick said. "Was it as awful as mine?"

They were stretched companionably on Caleb's bed, enjoying the aftershocks. Caleb rolled on his back and thought.

"We were in Saigon for R and R. I went with a number of my buddies to a bar. The idea was to pick up some B-girls and get laid. I was self-medicating for performance anxiety—with straight rotgut, the house brand. The problem was that, at nineteen, I was still a virgin. I wasn't sure I could get it up. I didn't know what to do. And without the usual urges, I couldn't just let the woman do her thing and trust nature to take its course.

Rick grinned—obviously savoring Caleb's retrospective discomfort. He balled the pillow up and propped his head on it.

Caleb didn't hold it against him—conflict is the essence of story. He continued. "Eventually, I devised a strategy. There was a singer there, a beautiful young woman—not a prostitute—who didn't fraternize. In fact, she had an escort watching her all the time. I think she might have been French or half French, and her escort wouldn't even let the patrons talk to her. I figured if I seemed drunk enough and got stubborn and refused to have anyone but the singer, my buddies would give up on me and go off without me. Then I could slink back to the barracks and sack out.

"My sergeant, a tough black man from Alabama, was watching the whole show and, a few drinks later, he peeled me off the bar stool and took me out of there. We walked until I was sober, then went to a hotel. He was gentle and considerate and he practiced what he'd been teaching us about safe sex."

"Got you off to a good start, I'd say."

Caleb was nearly asleep when he felt the familiar shaking that told him Freud had jumped up on the bed.

As the small, warm body curled itself against his thigh, a voice at his ear demanded, "What the hell's that?"

It took him a full three seconds to remember that he wasn't alone. Rick! "My cat," he said. "He makes himself scarce when I have company. I guess he's decided you're okay."

"Doesn't it give you the creeps to have it appear like that, without warning?"

"When you have a cat in the house, you're protected from all the strange, empty-house noises that would otherwise drive you mad. Whenever you hear something odd, you can tell yourself, it's only the cat."

THIRTY-FIVE

Matthew Dennison, PhD, ignored the detectives' invitation to come to Area Three headquarters and talk about David Bisti's death. So Thinnes and Oster invited themselves to the University of Chicago, to visit him. Having to go all the way to the South Side put Oster in a foul mood; the search for Frederick Haskell Hall, once they got there, did the same for Thinnes.

"He even gonna be here?" Oster demanded as Thinnes parked in a FACULTY ONLY space and threw their OFFICIAL PO-LICE BUSINESS sign on the dash.

"The woman I talked to said he has office hours from one to two and hadn't told her he wouldn't be in. If he's not here, we'll just use the time to see what we can find out about him."

Inside, they did an end run around the department secretary. Thinnes flashed his star at the student waiting in the chair next to Dennison's door. "We need to consult the professor about a technical matter. Maybe you could come back in half an hour."

The kid's eyes widened, and Thinnes could see Dennison's stock go up with him. "Ah . . . Sure." He took his book bag from the floor under his seat and left, looking back at them several times as he lumbered off down the hall.

Thinnes leaned against the wall, next to the door, to wait; Oster took the vacated chair. About ten minutes later, the door opened. Thinnes moved away from the wall. Oster stood up as Dennison escorted another student out.

Oster said, "Professor Dennison?"

Dennison looked from Oster to Thinnes and back, and said, "Yes," cautiously.

Oster held up his star and said, "We need a word with you."

"I don't think so." He backed into the room and tried to close the door.

Oster took hold of the door and stopped him closing it.

"You can't come in here," Dennison said, but he backed up as Oster stepped close to him. Oster followed him into the room and made a point of looking at his watch. "Office hours one to two. I got 1:38."

Trailing them in, Thinnes said, "We can go anywhere we need to in a homicide investigation, Professor." He closed the door behind them.

"I spoke with my attorney. I don't have to talk to you."

"That's true," Thinnes said. He thought, *It's funny how people use the word 'attorney' when they're trying to impress someone.* "But if you don't answer our questions, we'll have to ask your colleagues and students. And we won't be telling them that we're here to get your professional opinion."

"Is that what you told Fred?"

"That's right."

Dennison thought about that for a minute, then said, "What do you want to know?" He looked more like Thinnes's idea of a gym teacher than a college professor, but his office looked exactly like the kind of place an anthropology type would hang out, down to the skulls on top of the bookcase.

"Tell us about the night David Bisti was murdered."

He didn't have anything to add to what he'd told Viernes that night. He hadn't seen or heard anything, and he'd been put out that they made him wait several hours to tell them so.

"Murder's inconvenient for everyone, Mr. Dennison," Oster said.

"Doctor Dennison."

"Yes, of course. We're reinterviewing everyone who was there that night in hopes someone might have remembered something more."

"Not me."

"What brought you to David Bisti's show, Doctor?" Thinnes asked.

"I heard he was using genuine Indian artifacts in some of his pieces, possibly illegally obtained artifacts. I wanted to see for myself."

"Was he?"

"They certainly looked it."

"So why didn't you go to the authorities?"

"After his death, the question seemed moot."

"Had you met Mr. Bisti before?"

"He brought me a piece—a very fine Anasazi pot—to get my opinion before he bought it."

Oster said, "Black-market stuff?"

"He said it was from private property."

Thinnes asked, "The real thing?"

"I thought so."

"You don't still?"

"I mean, at the time, I told him I thought it was authentic. I haven't had any reason to change my mind."

"Okay," Oster said, "so how much was it worth?"

"I have no idea."

"C'mon. You buy these things for museums."

"No. I don't. I . . . We don't buy things like that any more—it encourages the vandals to destroy sites to get more. And once they're removed from their original site, the pieces have no archeological significance."

"There wouldn't be a black market for the stuff if it didn't have any value, Doctor," Thinnes said.

"I didn't say they didn't have value, Detective. Of course most of them have intrinsic aesthetic worth. And even the poorest examples of Anasazi work will bring something from collectors."

"Somebody mentioned a group of preservationists," Thinnes said. "You know anything about them?"

"I'm not sure what you mean by preservationists, but anyone of good conscience would try to put a stop to the black-market antiquities trade."

"What can you tell us about that?"

"Just that it's responsible for the destruction of hundreds of archeological sites every year."

Oster asked, "What makes the pot of someone who's been dead a long time so much more valuable than the pot of a living artist?"

"Scarcity, perhaps. There won't be any more Anasazi pots. Or it may be like the difference between the man who wins the lottery and the one who's left with a handful of losing tickets—just luck. Maybe today's potter's work will be worth $25,000 after he's dead, too—if it lasts long enough."

"The stuff just had the luck or whatever to last?"

"Or someone saved it. Or it lasted because it was better." Dennison smiled. "The indigenous peoples of the Southwest were consummate potters, although they never developed the potter's wheel. The people who made the bowl Bisti asked me to look at used the coil-and-scrape method. They built up the sides of the piece with successive coils of clay, then worked the coils together with a scraper—probably a shard from a broken pot—to make the finished sides smooth and thinner than the original coils. The designs were made of clay slip of a contrasting color, or with various indigenous mineral and plant materials."

"There's no test—for radioactivity or anything—to tell how old something is?"

"Only if it was once living—wood or bone. Then you can radiocarbon-date it. Ceramics and stone artifacts are usually dated by association. They're assumed to be the same age as the datable objects they're found with."

"Could they be faked?" Thinnes asked.

"I suppose it could be done. But why bother?"

"People go to a lot of bother for money."

"The people with the knowledge of the old techniques

wouldn't do it. And contemporary artists—with the potter's skills—wouldn't have the knowledge."

"So these things *can* be counterfeited?" Oster asked.

"No." Dennison seemed startled. "Well— I guess. If they were successful, who'd know?"

THIRTY-SIX

Sometimes what you fear is what you most desire," their therapist had told them. "If you're angry enough with a loved one, you might develop an obsessive fear of his being killed because to wish he'd die is unacceptable." She'd smiled. "It gets confusing because sometimes your fear for the safety of a loved one is normal and justified."

Rhonda had taken the biblical command to forsake all others to heart. In therapy she'd finally admitted her rage at Thinnes—she'd sided with him against her family only to have him abandon her, emotionally, for the department. In the hospital, after he was shot, she'd told him, "I've been waiting for this since you joined the force. I guess now we can get on with our lives."

Now she was still a little distant, a bit distrustful, still afraid, he guessed, that things would go back to the way they were. She was like a cop who's been lied to too often. He thanked God—figuratively. He didn't actually believe God bothers much with those who don't help themselves—that he'd woken up in time.

So he was keeping his hands where she could see them—so to speak. He was on parole and he wanted to go straight.

When he woke up Thanksgiving morning, he felt panic as he realized Rhonda's place in the bed was empty. He located her across the room. She'd started to dress—gotten as far as taking off her nightgown—and was standing, looking out the window through a narrow gap in the drapes, holding the bra she planned to wear.

The sudden want he felt was painful. He crossed the room slowly, not startling her. She had one hand on the window sash. She didn't turn. He put his arms around to cup her breasts in his hands. His own nipples brushed her back as he rested his cheek against her ear, then kissed the smooth curve between her neck and shoulder.

She leaned back against him.

Amazing! A year ago— Hell, six months ago she would have squirmed away or stood like a department-store dummy. Now, she rubbed her ass against him and tried to catch his cock between her thighs.

"Say it," she demanded.

He knew what. He kissed her neck again and let his tongue trace a path up to her earlobe. Why was it difficult? It seemed like a weakness, like admitting you were an addict—I'm John; I'm a Rhonda-holic.

"I need to hear it." She turned to face him as she said it. As she turned, he let his hands ride over her skin—still silky after all the years. She pressed against him. "I need to hear it."

When it was put like that, he couldn't help himself. He said it.

"I love you."

Thinnes parked his Chevy beneath the naked elm and maple trees overarching Forest Avenue. Wilmette. Snow dusted piles of leaves raked onto the street—between the parked cars—for pickup by the village crews. It caught in the cracks between the street bricks and the sidewalk squares. The winter-yellow lawn had an undercoat of snow.

Next to him, sprawled on the seat, Rob stretched and yawned and said, "Do we hafta go in?" Into the three-story gray stucco, with its imposing porch and tall windows. It was a rhetorical question.

"Look at it like this," Thinnes said. "You get through today, and you won't have to come back until Easter."

141

"Promise?" He had Rhonda's coloring and Thinnes's build, but his large hands and feet suggested that he'd be taller than both of them.

"Unless you want to fly down to Florida with them, over Christmas break."

Rob didn't bother to answer. He did laugh, and they both stared out the front window, not hurrying to get out of the car.

Thinnes had once heard Rhonda describe her parents' house as late nouveau riche. He didn't think it was that bad. They'd had the good sense to buy well-made furniture and had kept the brass and glass and the gaudy prints in trendy colors to a minimum. The overall effect was "We have money." The Coateses themselves were sort of like their house: basically decent, a tad too eager to impress. Bill got on well enough with Thinnes when they were alone together, but when Louise was around, he acted embarrassed that he was enjoying Thinnes's company. Louise didn't approve of Rhonda's choice of husbands. Her own was the ultimate yes-man, though he usually said yes in a way that made whatever he was agreeing to seem like his own idea.

The brass knocker on the Coateses' front door was hidden under a bunch of Indian corn, and a fat gray squirrel with a blond tail was clinging to the ears, munching the kernels. When Rob and Thinnes got near the door, it took off, flicking its tail.

"Look, Dad, a rat with a tailcoat." Under one arm, Rob was carrying a case of Miller Genuine Draft for Thinnes. Rhonda had brought the food earlier.

Thinnes laughed. "You want to start trouble, just tell your grandmother that." He reached behind the corn bouquet to rap on the door with the knocker.

"I got a better one than that for Grandma."

"What's that?"

The door opened as Rob said, "At the first Thanksgiving, they probably served squirrels."

Bill Coates—six one, two hundred pounds, blue eyed, and

gray haired—filled the doorway. He was wearing a red-plaid flannel shirt—L.L. Bean—and pressed designer blue jeans. He said, "Don't tell your grandmother that! Hello, son." He meant Rob. He'd never called Thinnes "son."

Rob shifted the beer to his other arm, and Coates shook his freed hand energetically, then hugged him. He said, "Hello, John," and offered Thinnes his hand.

Shaking it, Thinnes said, "Bill."

"Well, come in." Coates backed away from the door. "You're just in time. The game's starting."

Thinnes took the beer from Rob and said, "I'll just put this in the kitchen and say hello."

He followed the wonderful aromas to the kitchen, where Rhonda and Louise were elbow deep in potato peels. Louise's favorite thing to make for dinner was usually reservations, but on Thanksgiving, she made everything from scratch. She also made a production of serving it—candles and table linens and flowers, three kinds of forks at each place and two different glasses. Between setting up and cleaning up, it was a whole day's work for twenty minutes of eating.

"You've gotten much too thin, John," Louise said, after she said hello. She was five five, ash-blond, and gray eyed. And her statement was unintentionally ironic—she was thin as an anorexic.

Thinnes didn't bother to remind her he'd been sick. A bullet in the gut wasn't a reducing method he'd recommend, but he could testify to its effectiveness. He took a beer out of the case he'd brought and squeezed the rest into the refrigerator and the cooler near the door. He extracted a Coke from the cooler for Rob.

Louise wasn't finished. "Rhonda, you really should make him eat more."

"Mother, he's been feeding himself since he was six months old."

*　*　*

The rest of the Coates clan was gathered around the forty-six-inch TV, watching the Bears maul the Lions. Thinnes said hello to everyone, handed the Coke to Rob—sitting on the floor near his grandfather—and squeezed between Coates and his youngest daughter on the couch.

After a few minutes of the game, he found his attention wandering. Compared to the life-and-death problems he worked on daily, grown men fighting over a pigskin ball seemed silly. And adults getting worked up watching them seemed absolutely nuts.

Judith Coates Ashley, Rhonda's younger sister, was a rabid Bears fan and a bitch. Even Rhonda said so. She was carrying on about the game like a Pop Warner football mom. Her husband, Charles—only slightly less enthusiastic—was stretched out in Coates's recliner. Chuck—as everyone called him when they wanted to annoy him—was an attorney who'd always seemed to Thinnes like a pale imitation of Coates. He'd lost interest in Thinnes when he realized he wasn't going to give away any juicy details about open cases. Chuck and Judy's two spoiled brats were squabbling over a pocket video game close enough to the television to periodically interrupt the action with their own skirmishes. Thinnes figured it was going to be a long afternoon.

When Rob and most of the Coates clan headed outside, midafternoon, for a little touch football, Thinnes and Rhonda stayed in the TV room. They left the television on out of habit, but Thinnes couldn't have said who was playing. He sat in the recliner next to the couch and watched her. One of the teams called time-out, and she looked around. She seemed startled to find him watching, but—he could see her thinking about it—she didn't seem displeased. She gave him a little smile. "Penny for your thoughts."

The desire and love he suddenly felt made him feel as if his chest would explode from the internal pressure. He grabbed the chair arm. If he were to hold her—as every cell in his body cried out to do—he would surely crush her. He said, "Censored."

144

She smiled. "Let's throw a party. Just invite people we like." She looked around and lowered her voice. "No one here—your father. And my boss—people we'd like to get to know better."

"No cops."

"What about Carl?"

"Okay. Maybe him."

"Think about who else you'd like ask." She went back to watching the game.

Thinnes did think about it. Apart from Rhonda and his dad, he didn't have any close friends. Frank Flynn had been one. Frank had bought a .38 slug and six feet of Rosehill. Oster was the closest he could come, at work, to naming someone who'd miss him if he fell off the planet. And Jack Caleb.

But he's a faggot. And guys who make friends with faggots are faggots.

As quickly as he had the thought, he had another. It was queer—he immediately appreciated the irony of the term—how you could overlook someone's being gay if he was a relative, or if he'd saved your life. Maybe that was why the bashers were so busy—keep 'em away, keep 'em hostile, keep 'em from getting close enough for you to see the scared face on the head you were about to split. If you admitted they were human—like you—you might have to wonder if you were like them in other ways. Something Jack had pointed out to him once. He'd been right. And there were worse people you could be like.

Thinnes moved to the couch and put an arm around Rhonda. "Yeah, let's have a party. And maybe I'll invite Jack."

After dinner, Chuck borrowed Coates's Cadillac to go rent a movie. When he came back, and Coates asked him for the keys, he got a funny look on his face. Thinnes watched him pat down his pockets, becoming mildly alarmed at not finding the keys there, then look around the room. "They've got to be here somewhere," he said. "I couldn't have gotten back without them."

"Did you leave them in the car?" his wife whined.

He gave her a withering look, but handed her the videocassette and went out to look. "They're locked in," he announced when he came back. "Let me have your spare set, Bill," he said to Coates.

Coates looked annoyed. "It's at my office." His office was in the Loop.

"Shit!" Chuck said.

Judy rolled her eyes and said, "Oh, God!" then went to join Rhonda and her mother in the kitchen. Thinnes put a hand over his mouth to keep from laughing.

"I'll call the cops," Coates said. "Have 'em send someone over to get it open."

"They'll do that?"

"That's what I pay taxes for."

Cops breaking into cars. To order! Thinnes had heard rumors it happened, but he'd never quite believed it. At least Coates used the nonemergency number to call.

He felt sorry for the officer they sent. He had the pressed and polished look of a new academy graduate. Thinnes guessed suburban cops never had it worn or beat out of them, because this guy was at least thirty. He got out of his polished, no-visible-damage squad with a slim jim and an air of confidence. When they pointed out the car, he went back to his squad and adjusted his spotlight to shine on the Caddy's driver's-side door. As he slid the slim jim between the window and its rubber seal, the cop's face and breath—condensing in the frigid air—were lit by the reflection off the pale gray car. Coates and Chuck stood over him, their breaths also steaming.

Watching from the comfort of the Coates's living room, Thinnes didn't see how the cop could succeed. He was aiming for the wrong spot. But he kept trying. He gave it fifteen minutes—fourteen more than Thinnes would've—before he shrugged and got in his car and drove away. Comforting, somehow, to know the cops were inept car thieves.

Coates came in tight-lipped and tersely told Chuck to "forget it." Chuck headed for the kitchen; Coates headed for the phone. Thinnes heard him pick it up, then watched him listen to the message from the other end of the line. Then he slammed the receiver down and stalked out yelling, "Louise, where's the phone book?"

Good luck, Thinnes thought, *getting a locksmith on Thanksgiving.*

He got his coat and went out to his car. Under the passenger's seat, tucked into the springs, he had a flat strip of aluminum that had come from someone's lawn furniture by way of an apprentice car thief he'd busted. The strip had been modified to perform as a slim jim. It took forty-five seconds to get it out, slide it down next to the Cadillac's window, and unlock the door. Thinnes put the Cadillac's keys in his pocket and returned his slim jim to the Chevy. He brought the keys into the house and handed them to Rhonda as he kissed her good-bye. Before anyone could make an issue of it, or make the usual snide remark about him not having to work holidays if he had a respectable job, he got in the Chevy and left for work.

THIRTY-SEVEN

Friday. The day after Thanksgiving. The holiday had put together a lethal combination of booze and family members with long-standing grudges. Add a few knives and guns and baseball bats, and you had overtime for the police. All of the Violent Crimes detectives, except Ferris, were out when Thinnes got to the squad room. Even Property Crimes dicks had been pressed into service to catalog the mayhem. Thinnes was fifteen minutes early. He'd just gotten himself coffee when Rossi charged out of his office.

"Thinnes," he barked. "You're doing Indians this month. Here's another one for you." He handed Thinnes a paper with an Uptown address.

"Piece of cake, Thinnes," Ferris volunteered. "Just look for a male Cauc with long blond hair and a Seventh Cavalry uniform."

Thinnes watched Oster out of one eye and kept the other on the traffic ahead.

"Something's bugging you, Carl. What is it?"

The older detective often made pointed remarks about politics or current events, but he never talked about his personal life. Thinnes knew he had a wife, and three kids he was putting through college, but he rarely talked about them. He never said anything bad. Thinnes respected that. Guys who bad-mouthed their own wives had no idea how stupid they made themselves out to be.

"Nothin'," Oster grunted.

Thinnes waited.

"Aw, what the hell. I found out yesterday my daughter's gettin' a divorce. Be final in three days. Guess the father's always the last to know."

Thinnes felt like saying, "Not always, sometimes it's the husband," but he didn't think that would go over well.

"That's not the worst," Oster continued. "She's pregnant!"

Thinnes vaguely remembered Oster mentioning—months ago—that he was going to be a grandfather. He'd been disappointed. Oster was a great believer in education and wanted his children to finish college before they complicated their lives with kids.

"I take out a second mortgage and work OT for a year so she can marry the bum in style, and it doesn't even last a year. Go figure."

Thinnes shook his head by way of answering. He signaled left and didn't answer until he'd made the turn. Two blocks up, he could see the flashing blue lights of the patrol car at the scene, but he kept to the speed limit. The Indian wasn't going anywhere, and the uniforms were on the clock. He stole a glance at Oster and said, "If the guy's such a bum, maybe she's better off raising her kid alone."

"Oh, she won't be raising him alone. She wants to move back in with Norma'n me. Just when we got the last one outta the house . . ."

"Just say no."

"Where else she gonna go? Cabrini?"

Moot question.

Thinnes pulled the car over to the curb behind the beat car. He put it in park and shut off the engine. "Keep telling yourself it could be worse, Carl." He pointed beyond the parkway, to the vacant lot surrounded by yellow POLICE LINE tape, lit by portable lights, and guarded by the uniforms. "It could be a lot worse."

* * *

The Indian was the American variety, male, five eight, Thinnes guessed, though it was hard to be sure given his position. He was dressed in the traditional city-Indian garb—Levi's, jeans jacket, and cowboy boots. No attempt had been made by his assailant to take the silver and turquoise-trimmed belt or watch. So, he'd had some money, but he didn't look like a drug user or seller.

It was a fresh kill. Steam rose from the blood trickling from a star-shaped entrance wound in the man's temple and from his groin region, where urine seeped onto the freezing ground. Among the deep shadows thrown by the portable lights, it seemed like a soul escaping from the body.

Thinnes took an extra glove from his pocket and pulled it on over the one he already had on his right hand. Poor SOB probably didn't have AIDS, but no sense taking any chances. He probed the center of the head wound with his little finger. Small-caliber weapon, probably a .22. Mob hit?

As he stepped back and pulled the outer glove off, inside out, Oster walked up.

"We got a witness says she saw your shooter." He pointed toward the shadows beyond the sidewalk, where one of the uniforms was talking to a bag woman. "Poke Salad Annie there says Elvis did it."

"Get her statement."

"I was just kidding. She's so high you could get tipsy breathing in the same room with her."

"Get her statement," Thinnes said.

While the technicians hustled around the crime scene, chased by their own long shadows, Thinnes stood outside the police-line tape and tried to reconstruct the murder in his head. The victim hadn't struggled. The expression on his face suggested surprise—though you couldn't count on that. He hadn't been a bum or wino—a blue-collar worker, by his clothes. The boots were new or—probably—his dress boots.

As soon as the photographer was finished, Bendix ambled over and began to go through the deceased's pockets. Thinnes and Oster ducked under the yellow tape and moved closer to watch. He removed a piece of paper and put it in a plastic bag, which he held up so Thinnes could read and copy what was written on it. A telephone number. Unfamiliar area code.

"No wallet," Bendix announced. "And no keys. But you may be in luck."

"How's that?" Thinnes asked.

Bendix held up a plastic evidence bag containing a .22-caliber shell casing. Then he pointed to a slight dip in the terrain that had collected residue from a snow shower earlier. "And someone left a footwear impression. What d'ya wanna bet it's the perp's?"

"No takers," Oster said.

Bendix's crew had finally finished casting the "footwear impressions" and were packing up when Thinnes yelled out, "Hey, Bendix, get the dog shit, too." He pointed the flashlight he'd borrowed at a pile of shit just inside the crime-scene perimeter.

Bendix hurried over and gawked. "What kind of crap is this? I'm filing a complaint."

"It's physical evidence, Bendix. Officer . . ." Thinnes checked his notebook for the patrol officer's name. "Officer Enright observed that pile of shit steaming when she arrived. Since it was only six minutes between the 911 call and Enright's arrival on the scene, we can assume that whatever dumped that pile was here during the killing or pretty soon after."

"What the hell d'you expect me to do with it?"

"What ever you do with any unstable evidence. I want to know whether it's from the two- or four-legged variety of dog." Thinnes turned to Oster. "Have everyone doing the canvassing ask who around here has a big dog. And maybe you could check with animal control and see if there've been any complaints."

While he was talking, they watched Bendix amble over to one of his junior partners.

"You really hope to learn anything with this dog shit?" Oster asked.

"At the very least, it'll piss Bendix off." Thinnes shrugged. "And who knows, maybe the dog's owner knows something."

"Maybe the dog is the two-legged variety and he *did* something."

THIRTY-EIGHT

Dr. Caleb," Mrs. Sleighton said, when Caleb came back from lunch, "a Mr. Wang called. He'd like you to get in touch with him as soon as possible."

Wang was the manager of Caleb's condo. He was efficient and discreet and would never contact Caleb at work for a trivial reason. Caleb's only client for the afternoon had canceled, so he decided to go see Wang. When he entered the lobby of his building, the doorman handed him a note from the building manager. "Please see me at your earliest convenience. Thomas Wang."

Wang was in his office, and he looked very relieved when he opened the door for him. "Doctor, so good of you to respond promptly. You received an . . . animal." With a sweep of his hand, he indicated a small, wire-and-plastic animal shipping crate in the center of his oriental carpet. Affixed to the outside of the carrier was an envelope. Caleb opened it and read:

> 29 November
>
> Dear Jack,
> Tampa is exquisite! Divine weather, beaches with sand
> white as granulated sugar and littered with bronze
> gods, water warm as blood, brilliant, saturated colors.
> The rocks could have been sculpted by Henry Moore.
> It'll take ten years to pay for all the film I've exposed.
> If I didn't have the show coming up, I'd never come
> back. You must come.
>   But you won't. So here's a little souvenir. I rescued

it from a pack of SAVAGE urchins. But then what? I know I can trust you to keep it safe or, at least, dispose of it in a P.C. manner. It's had all its shots—courtesy of a divine DVM I met on the beach. (I'm going to immortalize him—or at least parts of him.).

Anyway, I'll be here another week if you change your mind.

Ciao.

love,
Jeremy

Health and rabies-vaccination certificates accompanied the shipping manifest in another attached envelope.

The crate contained a tiny kitten, white underneath, with bright splotches of orange and black above. It had a white blaze on its face, yellow eyes, and long, graceful, white whiskers. Caleb picked it up—her, he noted—and put his hand under her. The kitten planted all four tiny feet on it and tucked her tail around them. Looking around, she took in the room as if Caleb's hand was her usual observation post and his assistance her right. He laughed. So perhaps, Freud had his friend.

He turned to Wang. "Would you mind putting the crate down by my storage space?"

"Of course not."

"Thank you."

The kitten was asleep by the time Caleb got upstairs with her. Inside, he put her on the floor by the door, and she stood at his feet, scanning the room with eyes and ears and nostrils.

Freud was not amused. He sauntered into the room like Abdul Aziz surveying his domain. He ignored Caleb, who'd had the nerve to arrive home at an odd time, and sat in the center of the Harati doing his Sultan of Turkey routine.

Then he spotted the kitten and switched, instantly, into

hunter/killer mode. His eyes widened as he crouched. His tail whipped from side to side. He froze.

The kitten, who'd been watching this performance with great interest, toddled forward.

Freud pounced but landed just short of the smaller cat. His hair stood up. His mouth opened in a snarl.

The kitten beat him to the attack. Simultaneously, she fluffed her hair out—doubling her apparent size—and hissed and struck Freud with her needle claws. Almost faster than Caleb could follow, her tiny paw batted the larger cat.

Freud retreated with a face-saving hiss.

Caleb laughed and picked the kitten up, all fears for her safety vanished. And as he stroked her to settle her ruffled temper, he told her, "I think we'll call you Psyche."

THIRTY-NINE

Eastbound on Belmont, waiting for the light to change, Thinnes noticed the bumper sticker on the rusty Econoline stopped in front of their unmarked car. I GOT A GUN FOR MY WIFE—BEST TRADE I EVER MADE. The van had Michigan plates.

He was about to point it out to Oster when his partner said, "That kid's up to something." He jerked his head in the direction of an Hispanic male, five three or four, about eleven years of age, loitering two storefronts east.

Truancy, if nothing else, Thinnes agreed. Two elderly women waiting at the bus stop seemed to be the objects of the kid's interest. One was built like a brick shit house, and a pro tackle would have hesitated to confront her. The other was a purse snatcher's dream, tiny and feeble. "See if there're any wants—" The rest of his sentence was cut off by the horn blaring from the car behind their own.

The light had changed. The line of traffic started up, and the Econoline took off. Thinnes glanced in his rearview and saw the guy in the car behind theirs giving him the finger with his right hand, leaning on the horn with his left. Thinnes glanced toward the kid they'd been watching and saw him disappear into an alley midblock. The jerk behind them kept honking.

"That does it!" Thinnes jammed the gearshift into park and opened his door. As he rolled out of his seat, the honking stopped. Stoplight-red Chevy Cavalier, he noted. Not new but clean, Illinois plate, current city sticker.

The offender rolled his window down as Thinnes approached his car and yelled, "Move it, asshole!" Westbound traffic slowed. Gawkers. Thinnes waved them on. He put his left hand on the roof of the car and leaned over the window. White male, midtwenties, medium build, probably medium height.

"Are you in need of assistance?" Thinnes asked.

"Move your fucking car, asshole."

Below-average intelligence, Thinnes added to his mental inventory. Even the street kid recognized the Caprice as an unmarked police car—half a block away. Thinnes flipped open the right side of his jacket so the offender could see the star fixed to his belt. He kept his voice even. "Detective Asshole, to you, pal."

The man paled. "I didn't realize . . ." He seemed more disturbed by the discovery than the situation warranted. "I'm sorry, Officer Aa— I was just in a hurry. I'm late. Sir."

And you're gonna be later, Thinnes thought. He said, "Step out of the car, please."

"I didn't do anything."

"Out of the car!" Thinnes kept his right hand above his belt—not too far from his piece—as he opened the car door with his left. He kept his eyes on the subject.

The man sat with his hands on the wheel, eyes straight ahead. No doubt weighing his options.

Thinnes put a hard edge in his voice. "Do it *now!*" As the subject started to comply, Thinnes said, more softly, "Keep your hands where I can see them." He backed up as the subject stood up. "Turn around. Lean forward and put your hands on the roof. Spread your feet." The man complied slowly. "You have any needles on you, or anything that might hurt me if I search you?"

"No."

"Okay. I'm going to do a quick check of your jacket, then we'll talk."

"Am I under arrest?"

"You're temporarily detained." As he spoke, Thinnes did a quick pat down. No weapons. "Okay, step around here." He pointed to the space between the Cavalier and the Caprice, which now had its portable blue Mars light flashing—Oster doing his part. With his peripheral vision, Thinnes could see him talking on the radio.

Motorists behind the Cavalier were backing up to go around them. No one else honked. "See your license?" Thinnes asked the offender.

The man took out his wallet and handed over his license. Thinnes watched him while pretending to study it. Mark Leon. Address on North Kenmore.

Oster got out of the squad and started back toward them.

"This your car?" Thinnes asked Leon.

Leon was watching Oster. "Ah, no. My girlfriend's."

"She have a name?"

Leon dragged his attention back to Thinnes. He was sweating although it was cold enough for his breath to form a cloud around his head. Thinnes wondered why.

"Listen, what'd I do?"

Oster said, "Car's registered to—"

Thinnes shook his head sharply, cutting Oster off, and said, "Well?" to Leon.

"You checked the registration. You know her name." He spoke to Oster, who didn't answer. Oster sidled along the passenger's side of the Cavalier peering in the windows. He spotted something and gave Thinnes a thumbs-up.

Thinnes said, "The question is, Mr. Leon, do *you* know her name?"

Leon's eyes darted from side to side. "What?"

Planning to make a break, Thinnes decided. "What's your girlfriend's name?" He kept talking, not letting Leon have time to think clearly, not letting him watch Oster open the car door and start his search. "You don't remember your girlfriend's name?"

Before Leon could answer, Oster said, "Look what I found."

He came toward them holding up a plastic bag of a dried plant material. "Bet this isn't catnip."

Suddenly Leon dived toward the space between Thinnes and the unmarked car. But Thinnes was ready. He grabbed Leon's left wrist with one hand and the shoulder of his jacket with the other, using the man's own momentum to swing him around and slam him onto the Cavalier's hood.

Oster stepped to Leon's other side, moving quickly for a man of his bulk, and pinioned the suspect's right hand behind his back.

"Nice try," Thinnes told the prisoner. "Close, but no cigar." He snapped the cuffs on him and frisked him more thoroughly while Oster called for backup.

"I haven't done anything!" Leon snarled, as Thinnes opened the back door of the Caprice for him.

Oster held up the plastic bag.

"That's my girlfriend's stuff."

"What's her name, Mr. Leon?" Thinnes asked.

"You had no probable cause to stop me!"

"What're you, a lawyer?" Oster demanded.

"I know my rights. You got no case."

"How about interfering with the police?"

"I want to talk to a lawyer."

Thinnes started to say, "Get in," when he was interrupted by a stream of profanity from the bus stop that would have done credit to a teamster. An old, rusty voice. The smaller of the two older women they'd seen earlier was swearing like a stevedore as she and her heftier companion struggled with the previously observed juvenile, trying to drag him toward Thinnes and Oster. "Police!" the larger woman yelled.

The kid kicked at his captor's ankle and jerked free when she flinched away. He took off.

Leon leaned forward from the waist and said, "Yeah!" Both

Thinnes and Oster grabbed him and hustled him onto the sidewalk closer to the action.

"Get him!" both women screamed at the detectives, pointing after the kid. When they didn't immediately take off running, the smaller woman screeched, "You worthless bastards! You're wasting time on speeders while God-fearing women are attacked under your noses."

"You tell 'em, Grammaw," Leon urged.

She charged closer and snarled at him. "You shut your yap."

"Just our luck," Oster told Thinnes.

Thinnes shrugged. "It corroborates the police investigation we were conducting."

"Thinnes," Oster said, "they warned me not to get involved with you." When Thinnes didn't answer, he sighed. "I'll call for backup." He climbed into the Caprice to use the radio, leaving the door open while he talked. By the time he'd finished transmitting, Thinnes had heard more than anyone would ever want to know about the purse snatching. There'd been smaller ruckuses raised over bank robberies. Thinnes was a captive audience, standing holding Leon's arm to prevent him from bolting.

Oster got out of the car rubbing his hands like a used-car salesman with a likely prospect. "Maybe you ladies would like to sit in the backseat of our car—to stay warm?"

They decided they would, and Oster closed them in with relief.

"What about me?" Leon demanded.

"You can sit in there with 'em if you like."

Patrol took forever to show up, but when they did, they had the purse snatcher in the back seat. They'd heard Oster's initial call, one of the officers explained, about wants on a juvenile suspect fitting the detainee's description. When they saw him come running out of the alley with a woman's purse, they'd picked him up. Then they'd heard Oster call in the crime.

"Nice work," Oster told them.

In the back of their car, the little woman—Thinnes was starting to think of her as a human mynah bird—started bouncing up and down, banging on the window and demanding to be let out, promising, "I'll kill him!"

"They're all yours," Thinnes told the beat coppers. "You got the perp, there are your victims."

"Jesus," one of them said.

"Your reward for fast, efficient service."

When they got back to Area Three, Thinnes and Oster split up. Oster went to get lunch. Thinnes left Leon to cool off in an interview room while he did his paperwork—case report, arrest report, and complaints. When he'd had them approved by the Watch Commander, he took Leon to the lock-up.

"Run his prints," Thinnes told the booking officer. "It'd be nice to get the paperwork done before this guy's back in circulation. And just *maybe* there's an outstanding warrant on him."

Before he went upstairs, he stopped at the District Nineteen desk and showed the sergeant the Cavalier's registration. "You got a car you can send over to look for this woman and ask if she loaned her car to anyone?"

Up in the squad room, he started on a warrant to search the Cavalier. Jolene Wilson, the "girlfriend" Leon hadn't been able to name, was the car's owner of record. Or maybe an unrecorded victim. Maybe the real owner of the dope. Thinnes didn't much care. He was more than sorry he'd ever gotten involved, but he had to follow through, if for no other reason than to prevent some shyster lawyer from suing for false arrest on Leon's behalf.

If he had time, Thinnes always wrote the text of his search warrants out on scrap paper so he wouldn't have to revise on the typewriter. It made them look more professional. He was halfway through transcribing the narrative when Oster came into the squad room with McDonald's for the two of them.

"What're you doing?"

"Search warrant for Jolene Wilson's car."

Oster dropped his bag on the table. "Are you crazy?"

Thinnes looked to be sure Oster was really listening. "Leon was too nervous for just a little grass. He's into something heavy. Trust me on this."

"I'm trying." Oster eyed the polystyrene cup next to the typewriter. "You want a refill?"

"Thanks. Hey, five bucks says Wilson never loaned her car out."

Oster shook his head. "No deal."

As Thinnes was reading over the finished draft of the search warrant, Rossi came in waving a sheet of paper. "What we got here is a bust for petty theft. Juvenile—he won't even do time. And possession of marijuana—probably a misdemeanor amount. For this you guys tied up two detectives and a beat car for half a day?"

"Two beat cars," Thinnes said mildly. "Can't transport victims and perps in the same car."

"And you still haven't figured out who killed the Indian. Either one," he added before anyone could ask which.

"That's about it."

"I'm having you transferred!"

"That a promise?"

"What's a promise is you better have Bisti's killer on the wall by the end of the week or I'm having you transferred—to crowd control at the Harold Washington Library. And I'm not authorizing any overtime—you don't need it if you got time for this bullshit!"

"Are you asking me to avoid doing my sworn duty to uphold *all* the laws just because I happen to be assigned to Violent Crimes?"

"You? Shit! Cut that asshole loose and get back to work."

"Maybe you'd better put that in writing."

"I put anything in writing, it'll be writing you up for insubordination."

Thinnes didn't say anything more, just looked at Rossi until he turned and walked out of the room. Then he went back to reading his search warrant.

The phone rang and, when Thinnes picked it up, the booking officer asked, "Detective, you want me to cut this guy loose?"

"Nope," Thinnes said. "We're going to throw the book at him."

The judge didn't consider Thinnes's hunches probable cause, but he liked to hear them anyway—so he said. He *was* swayed by the fact that Mark Leon had had a controlled substance in his possession and was unable to name the owner of the car he'd been driving.

Thinnes had put drugs and guns in the warrant as a matter of course.

"He really has no standing to challenge a search," the judge said, "but I can see where you might want your evidence admissible if Ms. Wilson turns out to be involved."

Thinnes nodded, and the judge signed the paper with a flourish.

"What'd ya bother with this for?" Sergeant Houlihan of the motor pool handed the warrant back to Thinnes. "You wanna see what's in a car, just ask. Nothing in here I can't open."

"The term 'inadmissible' mean anything to you?"

Houlihan raised his hands and waved them at Thinnes. "Waste of time—you look. You find something, *then* you get a warrant."

Thinnes didn't bother to argue. He followed Houlihan to where the red Cavalier was parked and held his hand out for the key. Oster, who seemed fed up enough to walk out, said nothing to anyone.

Thinnes inserted the key and popped the trunk. Before he could even look, Houlihan said, "Christ!"

"Shit!" Oster said.

Thinnes looked down at the human form wrapped in sheets of polyethylene, trussed with clothesline cord. "I believe we've located Jolene Wilson."

FORTY

Jolene Wilson's mother lived in an old, yellow brick building that was wrapped around a small dirt courtyard cut in half by a cracked cement walk. The Wilson apartment was in the rear with its front windows facing Belle Plaine over the court. The lobby was typical for the building's age—walls darkened by years of neglect, wainscoting by countless coats of old varnish. The space smelled of mildew. The white, octagonal ceramic floor tiles were stained and cracked. The lightbulb was dead in its high ceiling fixture overhead. One mailbox in the bank of six had been pried open. Few of the doorbells were intact; loose wires poked from the hole next to the Wilson name. 3B.

The glass panes in the security door were intact, but the lock was broken. Thinnes and Oster entered a pumpkin-orange stairwell grayed with grime. Each landing was lit by a sash window—two-and-a-half by five feet, with an old, ornate, cast-iron radiator below it. The wooden steps and door and window frames were blackened by the same accumulation of dirt and old varnish as the woodwork in the lobby. A gaudy, threadbare striped carpet clung to the steps.

Thinnes took them two at a time out of habit. He ended up waiting for Oster on the third-floor landing, noticing—really for the first time—how out of shape his partner was. When Oster finally got to the top, he had to lean over the landing rail, resting on his forearms and breathing hard for several minutes, before he was ready to face the mother. He wiped a glaze of sweat from his face and neck with a handkerchief.

Thinnes rapped on the door of 3B, and it opened a crack. He could see a chain and a pale blue eye. He held his star up.

A woman's voice said, "If it's about Rory, I ain't seen him since he went to jail." Her accent was vaguely Southern. One of the city's scores of Appalachian immigrants. A hillbilly.

"Could we come in, ma'am?"

The door closed, and he could hear her fumbling with the chain. She opened the door six, then eight inches but didn't move to let them in.

Caucasian. Five five. Rail thin. No makeup. Washed-out blond hair. It had been a while since she'd dyed it; the dark roots outlined a center part. Thinnes wondered why she'd chosen such a lackluster color. He guessed her age about forty-five, but an old forty-five. Marking time. Ground down by poverty or poor health or loss—he didn't want to know. She wore a faded flowered housedress and cheap slippers of a clashing pattern. She looked wary, fearful but resigned, as if she'd been expecting bad news all her life and was seldom disappointed. Thinnes had met her many times before. Victims' kin.

He didn't try to sympathize. Her kind was different. They may have been created equal, may even have been born equal, but a lifetime of living without hope had changed them into something else, something smaller and meaner than most people or than what they, themselves, might have been. Knowing that kept him from having delusions about making a difference. He was doing his job. Nothing more he *could* do.

He said, "Are you Mrs. Emmalynn Wilson?"

Her right hand gripped the doorjamb above her shoulder. It was rough skinned and heavy veined, with enlarged joints. "Somethin' happen to Len?"

"Not that I know of. Len your husband?"

She seemed to relax. She nodded.

"Are you the mother of a Jolene Wilson, North Leavitt?"

It seemed to take her a minute to understand the question, then her initial panic seemed to return in spades. "Oh, Lord! Not

Jolene!" She sagged away from the doorway, letting the door gape open.

Thinnes reached to touch, then take hold of her forearm. "Mrs. Wilson, maybe you'd better sit down."

She backed into the room, pulling her arm free with an absent sort of annoyance that didn't seem to apply specifically to Thinnes. He followed her—not too closely.

She couldn't seem to meet his eyes. "What happened to my baby?"

There was no way to break it gently—nothing soft about homicide. "I'm sorry, Mrs. Wilson. Jolene's been murdered."

He waited. The first stage of grief is disbelief—denial, the shrinks called it. Thinnes called it shock. Emmalynn Wilson looked like she'd been poleaxed. He looked around. The room was clean but bare, symptomatic of poverty of the spirit if not actual lack of money. There were no pictures, no family mementos. A reclining chair posted in front of a thirty-two-inch TV set told him plenty about the Wilsons.

Thinnes took Emmalynn's arm and steered her to the faded couch at right angles to the recliner's line of sight. She moved like an automaton. "Mrs. Wilson," he said, as he settled her on the couch, "is there someone I can call for you?"

Oster, who'd followed Thinnes in, crossed the room and disappeared through a doorway at the far side.

"Mrs. Wilson," Thinnes persisted, "would you like me to call your husband?"

She seemed to find the question puzzling. She shook her head. "Be soon enough when he gits here."

Why not? The girl had been dead two days already.

Oster reappeared with two glasses. One was three-quarters full of water, the other had what looked like a double shot of bourbon in the bottom. He offered her the latter glass.

The woman took it, sniffed it. Her expression told Thinnes Len was probably a drinker and that his wife didn't approve.

"Medicinal," Oster said.

Emmalynn shuddered but took it and swallowed the contents in a single swig. Oster took the glass and handed her the water.

"Mrs. Wilson," Thinnes repeated, "is there someone we can call for you?"

She had to think for a minute. "Marge. Downstairs."

Even before the double shot took effect, questioning her was like interrogating a drunk. Her answers came after pauses long enough to make him wonder if she'd heard him, and not all the answers made sense. Gradually, he ascertained that Jolene Wilson had been a medical transcriber, the first—and only—in her family to go to college. She'd been a good girl. "The best thing I ever done," to quote her mother. She'd had no close female friends her mother knew of. She'd dated several men from work—none extensively. Her mother couldn't even imagine anyone wanting to hurt her.

Thinnes finally sent Oster downstairs to find Marge, who turned out to be the building manager. Then the two of them escaped the apartment with relief.

"God!" Oster said, when the outer door had closed behind them. "I need a drink!"

For once Thinnes—who generally was scrupulous about not bending an elbow while on duty—had to agree.

FORTY-ONE

It wasn't as bad as a child's autopsy would've been, but Jolene Wilson's post mortem was getting to him. Usually Thinnes could ignore the smell of meat and bleach that permeated the back rooms. Not today. What did they say about it? *Not so bad if you don't think about it.* Impossible today. He was glad he hadn't eaten. Dr. Cutler was the same pathologist who'd autopsied David Bisti. Dead children bothered him, too. And this death— viciously intended—was getting to him. Thinnes could tell. There was none of the black humor that usually lightened the gravity of the situation. When his assistant started cracking jokes, Cutler silenced him with a dead stare.

Thinnes felt like a fighter too tired even to raise his gloves, and every insult to the body of the young woman laid out before him was another blow.

Jolene Wilson had been pretty, well developed, and well-groomed. Mostly, she'd been young. The autopsy assistant, in his blue gown, removed the black plastic sheet covering her and straightened her out on the stainless-steel tray that formed the top of the gurney. The photographer pulled his wheeled stepladder up and began documenting the injuries Jolene Wilson had suffered. Bruises and contusions. Massive blunt-force trauma. Bites, both on her breasts and thighs—these post mortem, according to Dr. Cutler. There was a small, round hole in her left temple, surrounded by gunshot residue. The bruises on her throat resembled those Thinnes had seen before—on other murder victims.

When everything was photographed and Cutler had described it in detail to his pocket tape recorder, the AME turned her over and the process was repeated. Then they turned her over again.

Thinnes handed Cutler the rape kit he'd brought, its labels already filled out with name and case number. He watched with feigned uninterest as the doctor swabbed the remains for semen and combed through its pubic hair for foreign fibers. Its. Not hers. Not ever again. Otherwise, Thinnes wouldn't be watching. But the dead suffer no embarrassment. Damn good thing. They have no privacy.

Then the AME took his scalpel to the back of the victim's head, cutting the scalp along the hairline. He flipped the whole scalp forward. Covering the face of the dead was an old tradition Thinnes thought of every time he saw it done. Ironically respectful. The sightless eyes wouldn't look on the next indignities.

Cutler muttered into his tape recorder as his assistant opened the body: cut through the skull and ribs with a little stainless saw that made a noise like a vacuum cleaner and created a small cloud of bone dust, and sliced the skin in an obscene Y, shoulders to sternum to pubic bone.

Thinnes took careful notes against the time he would be called to testify, forced to recall the details replaced by more recent images, details of autopsies yet to be performed on people not yet murdered. It was the only thing he could do for Jolene Wilson.

"Cause of death was manual strangulation," Cutler told Thinnes, finally. "The gunshot wound was overkill."

It wasn't an atypical death. A disorganized killer had found a moment of opportunity. The victim had been unlucky—wrong place, wrong time. She'd probably struggled, and he beat her, put his hands around her throat and squeezed until she stopped fighting. Then, unwilling to pass up a silent, passive victim, he'd raped her. Never mind she was a corpse by then. She was available and uncomplaining. Forever. The gunshot wound had probably been to hide the necrophilia. Trading up, some doctor once told him. Murder was more acceptable than the violation of a corpse.

FORTY-TWO

Thinnes, you be the bad guy and I'll be father confessor,"
Oster said. "Leon already hates your guts."

"Yeah," Thinnes said. "After what I've just seen, I promise
you, the feeling's mutual."

They were standing outside the interview room where
Thinnes had deposited Mark Leon. He was handcuffed to a giant
staple in the outer wall of the room—hanging on the wall, they
called it—opposite the see-through mirror, slouching on his
spine in an uncomfortable, plastic contour chair.

"I'm going to try a variation of one of the chief's old rou-
tines," Thinnes said. "Wait out here until he starts to look real
uncomfortable."

Various detectives in the squad room had been watching
Leon for two hours through the open door. The door was closed
now. Leon hadn't yet been informed of the charges against him
or advised of his rights. In fact, apart from periodically asking if
he needed to relieve himself, no one had spoken to him since
before Thinnes went to watch Jolene Wilson's autopsy. He
looked like he was sleeping—a dead giveaway he was guilty.

Thinnes went in and closed the door behind him and didn't
try to hide his dislike as he recited Miranda. "You understand
your rights as I've explained them to you?"

"Yeah."

Thinnes put one of the state's attorney's statement forms in
front of Leon and pointed to the part on the top that said he
understood his rights. There were spaces for a date and a signa-

ture. Thinnes pointed at the form. "Okay, then sign here." The form was Thinnes's only deviation from SOP. The department didn't have such forms because an unsigned form gave defense lawyers something to work with they wouldn't otherwise have had. Thinnes didn't really have any business asking Leon to sign a state's attorney's form, and he'd have had to stop everything until the ASA arrived if Leon got cooperative and decided to sign it. But Thinnes had a very strong hunch he wouldn't.

Leon didn't even look at the form. "I ain't signing nothing till I talk to a lawyer."

"Why'd you kill her?"

Leon shifted and squirmed on the hard plastic seat. "I didn't kill anybody."

"Jolene Wilson."

"I don't know any Jolene Wilson."

"Maybe you didn't know her, but you killed her."

"Bullshit!"

"How do you explain the fact that we found her in the trunk of the car you were driving?"

Leon was quiet for a minute, no doubt trying to come up with something plausible. Then he said, "I stole the car. I didn't know there was a body in the trunk."

Thinnes stood up and let some of his pent-up rage show for a minute. He pointed at Leon, suddenly, with his index finger, thrusting it forward with the weight of his whole arm behind it. "You're a fucking liar!" He pointed again. "And I don't want to talk to you anymore. I don't need your fucking statement to make a case. In fact, if you talk to me, you might give me some extenuating circumstances that would prevent me from hitting you up with murder one. So you just *shut up*."

He went out and got a small wheeled stand on which he put a typewriter, several blank departmental forms, and some blank sheets of paper. He wheeled the stand into the room, in front of a chair opposite Leon's. He sat down and put one of the forms in the typewriter and began to fill in the blanks. He used only two fingers, although he was an excellent typist. Two fingers take longer. It didn't make sense for Thinnes to be doing his paperwork in the interview room, but if Leon was smart enough to figure that out, he probably wouldn't have killed Jolene Wilson.

After about twenty minutes, Oster opened the door and stood in the doorway. "Phone for you, Thinnes."

Thinnes motioned him into the room. "Yeah, okay." He finished typing the line and pulled the sheet out of the typewriter. He picked up the SA's form and motioned Oster to a chair between the door and the two-way mirror. "Keep an eye on this bastard, will you? But don't talk to him. He hasn't consulted with his lawyer yet, and we don't want to violate the SOB's civil rights. The asshole won't even sign that we read him his rights."

Oster shook his head as if he thought that very sad.

Thinnes added, "Just as soon as I get done with this goddamn paperwork and decide how many counts I can hit him with, he can talk to all the fucking lawyers he likes."

"Okay." Oster said it as if he didn't want to set Thinnes off further. He sat on the chair.

Thinnes left the room, slamming the door. Outside, he stopped and crumpled the papers he was carrying and tossed them at a wastebasket. The balled paper teetered on the rim and tipped out onto the floor. Thinnes whirled and faced the see-through side of the two-way mirror through which Ferris, Swann, and Viernes were watching the drama in the interview room.

Oster was studying his hands, recleaning his immaculate fingernails.

Leon fidgeted, twisted around to look at the clock over his head and around again to stare speculatively at the mirror. "Now what?" he said, finally.

"Sorry," Oster told him. "I can't talk to you. Thinnes is the boss. And you refused to sign that we've given you your rights."

A long silence passed before Leon said, "Can I ask you a question?"

"You understand your rights?"

"Yeah."

Oster waited.

"Get the paper back in here," Leon said. "I'll sign it."

Oster shook his head. "I'd like to do that, but Thinnes is probably halfway Downtown with it by now." He shook his head again. "I'm not supposed to talk to you."

"I just want to ask you something."

"What might work," Oster said, as if he was working it out as he went along, though he wasn't, "is if you just wrote something out."

"Like what?"

"Just that you understand your rights and I'm not forcing you to say anything against your will."

Leon seemed to be thinking about it.

"Hey, kid," Oster added. "We'll get through this."

Leon licked his lips and nodded. "Okay."

Oster shuffled through the papers Thinnes had left on the typewriter stand, locating one that was blank. He handed it to Leon along with a pen. Leon held it up as if not sure what to do with it, and Oster quickly removed the extra papers and the typewriter from the stand, putting them on the floor near the wall. He pushed the stand over in front of Leon. "There you go, son."

Leon put the paper down and looked at it, then at Oster. "What do I say?"

"Well . . ." Oster fumbled in his pockets and "found" his Miranda card. "What if you just copy this? It about covers everything."

Leon took it. Read it. Shrugged.

On the other side of the view-through window, Ferris said, "He's not stupid enough . . ."

Thinnes and Viernes smiled.

Swann laughed. "You want to put five bucks on that, Ferris?"

Ferris looked in at Leon and said, "No."

Leon was copying the card. When he finished, he asked Oster, "I just sign it?"

Oster said, "Hold on a second." He crossed to the door and opened it, stuck his head out. He looked them all over quickly and said, "Viernes," motioning "come in" with a jerk of his head and backing into the room. Viernes followed him in and closed the door. Leon looked alarmed. Oster told him, "Go ahead, son."

Leon jerked a thumb at Viernes. "What's he doing here?"

"Just witnessing your signature."

Leon glared. The two detectives waited.

Out in the squad room, Swann ventured an opinion: "He's got too much invested to back out now."

Thinnes agreed. "If he signs, you go find the ASA. And tell him to bring his statement forms."

Inside the room, Leon was signing the paper. Oster nodded. Solemnly. Like a father approving a son's work. Then he took the pen from Leon and printed "witnessed" below Leon's signature. He wrote the date and signed his own name. Viernes took the pen and did the same.

"Now," Oster said to Leon, "what was it you wanted to ask me?"

Leon was still glaring at Viernes. "Does *he* have to be here?"

Oster shook his head. "Not if you don't want him here." To Viernes, he said, "Could you wait outside?"

"Sure."

Viernes closed the door quietly on the way out. As he resumed his place in the audience, Swann, who'd just left the squad room, reentered it with the ASA in tow.

The assistant state's attorney's name was Cipareli or Ciparini. Something Italian. Thinnes could never remember. Everyone called him Columbo because he wore a ratty-looking raincoat and was a lot smarter than he seemed.

Columbo said, "Detective Thinnes, are you looking for me?"

"We have a guy about to confess to murder," Thinnes said. "We'd like you to take his statement in a few minutes." He and Viernes moved aside to make room for Swann and Columbo in front of the viewing window.

"What's he said so far?" the ASA asked.

"Nothing, but he will."

"Watch and learn," Ferris told him.

Thinnes tried to catch Ferris's eye, to let him know he should shut up, but Ferris was too busy trying to impress Columbo with his wit to notice.

"Like the chief always says," he gushed, "these guys ain't rocket scientists."

The usually easygoing Swann said, "Lucky for you, Ferris." Ferris was even getting to him.

Inside the little room, Leon said, "What's gonna happen to me?"

On the other side of the glass, Thinnes said, "That depends on you, you son of a bitch!"

Inside the interview room, Oster said, "That depends on you, son." He might have been a priest counseling a penitent. "You left enough evidence around so we got you dead to rights. With this new DNA test, there's no way you're gonna get out of it, and Thinnes is probably getting a court order right now for a sample of your blood. The only way he wouldn't go for murder one is if there was extenuating circumstances. But nobody knows the circumstances but you. And you're not talking."

"What's extenuating circumstances?"

"It's like an excuse—you know, a reason. Like it was an accident or something."

"Like she laughed at me an' I got mad and went nuts?"

"Like that. Is that what happened?" Oster seemed completely sympathetic. Only the sweat pouring off him gave any hint he wasn't totally sincere. He wiped his face and neck with his handkerchief as he waited for Leon to answer.

"I can talk to a lawyer when I want?"

"Anytime you like. But you want to tell me about this. I can feel it. And I've heard that talking about these things can be a great release."

On the other side of the window, Thinnes said, "Good thing he didn't say for who."

Inside the room, Oster told Leon, ". . . good for the soul, even."

Thinnes said, "What if you haven't got a soul?"

"Shut up, Thinnes," Viernes said suddenly. "This is *good.*"

"Better than a soap," Columbo agreed.

"Shut up, you guys!" This from Swann. "He's giving it up."

Oster glanced at the mirror, telling Thinnes to pay attention on the other side. Thinnes got his notebook and pen. And took notes while Leon talked.

"What's going on here?" Rossi's face was redder than usual. Embarrassed to be out of it in front of so many of his dicks, Thinnes thought. He let someone else answer.

"Oster just got a murder suspect to give it up," Swann volunteered.

"Nice work. Which case?"

"The Jolene Wilson murder," Thinnes said.

Rossi nearly did a double take, then said, "Why wasn't I kept up to speed on this?"

"The paperwork's on your desk," Thinnes told him. "If you'll excuse us, we'd like to get this guy's statement before he has a chance to think about what he just told Oster." Thinnes handed Columbo a page from his notebook.

"What's this?" the ASA asked.

"Questions Oster needs to ask this guy while you're getting his statement."

"Aren't you coming in?"

"And louse up a perfectly good confession? Oster's doing fine. If I go in there, Leon's gonna get belligerent and clam up. Trust me."

Columbo shrugged. "I'd have thought you'd want to be in on the kill."

Thinnes looked sideways at Rossi and said, "I set it up. That's enough for me. Just make sure you don't blow it."

Three hours later, they had the whole story on paper and Mr. Mark Leon was on his way to 26th and Cal. Columbo came into the squad room, looking like a man who's won the lottery, and headed for the coffeemaker.

Two minutes later, Oster followed along, dragging his ass. He put his paperwork on a table and sat next to it, resting his head on his hand. Columbo brought his coffee over, and Oster asked, "Are we done?"

Columbo tapped the papers. "This is pretty good." He turned to Thinnes and said, "But he didn't name the guy he got the gun from."

"We'll wait till ballistics gets finished with it," Thinnes told him. "See if it was used in any other felonies. If it was, we'll have a little more leverage."

"This guy's no rocket scientist," Oster added. "He's got no priors, so chances are this is his first real fuckup. Probably got the gun from a friend or bought it from a neighborhood gang-banger."

"And we don't want to deprive you of the opportunity to get in on this fish hunt," Thinnes told Columbo.

"Fish hunt?"

"Shooting 'em in a barrel," Oster said. "After you've laid out just what the consequences are of all Mr. Leon's told us, I'm sure he'll be happy to give us his friendly local gun dealer. Also his neighborhood pushers and his grandmother if she cheats at bingo."

179

FORTY-THREE

Rossi had taken to calling the victims of Thinnes's two unsolved homicides the Downtown Indian and the Uptown Indian, as if they were some kind of joke. But even *he* couldn't fault the investigation of either murder. Convincing evidence just wasn't available. Thinnes was prepared to wait for it—no statute of limitations.

In addition to the Wilson case, Thinnes and Oster did clear three other homicides during the weeks following Thanksgiving. Two were routine cases where the shooter was known and clearing them was a matter of canvassing the neighborhood, taking witnesses's statements, and writing up reports. The multiple perps in one of the shootings gave such wildly conflicting stories that interrogating them was a piece of cake. Getting confessions was easy. There were no witnesses to the third killing, and the suspect wouldn't talk at all. But there was plenty of incriminating physical evidence—semen, saliva, fingerprints, bite marks. And the victim's blood was all over the perp's shoes. The only hard thing about it was the reams of paper the detectives had to fill out—days' worth. Few of the sob-sister reports about the national murder epidemic ever mentioned how expensive it was in terms of police overtime.

On Friday, Thinnes came in during the day to tie up some of the loose ends on the Wilson murder. Ferris was the only Violent Crimes detective in the squad room. "Hey, Thinnes," he said, "we got the tox report back on your John Doe—or maybe I should say John Buck."

That brought to mind something that had been niggling at the back of Thinnes's mind ever since he first spotted the unidentified corpse. John Buck. Evanger's unsolved case. Same MO.

"Thanks, Ferris." He walked away, leaving the other detective to wonder about his lack of response to the slur. He took the tox report to a table with a phone and put in a call to records, looking the report over while he waited for someone to answer.

No trace of drugs or alcohol in the victim's system.

When a voice from the phone said, "Records," Thinnes said, "Thinnes, Area Three. I need a case report on a John Doe homicide." He paged through his notebook for the RD number, gave it to the clerk, and waited while he went to find the report.

When the clerk came back on the line, he said, "Sorry, not here."

"Who's got it?"

"Search me. Not here. Not signed out."

"Well, look around. I dropped it off three weeks ago."

"Why didn't you say so?" He went away again, then came back on the line. "Bingo."

"Hold on to it," Thinnes told him. "Someone'll be by later to pick it up."

His next call was to Ballistics. As soon as he said, "Thinnes, Area Three," the tech told him, "We're working on it, Detective. Check back this afternoon."

"You're not working on anything of mine," Thinnes said. He'd gotten the ballistics report for the Wilson case the day after the autopsy. "I wanted to ask you to check an old open case as soon as you get time."

"What?" He sounded tired.

Thinnes gave him the number of Ferris's John Buck case and said, "The MO matches that John Doe we had recently. Maybe you could compare the slugs and see if we've got the same shooter." He gave him the John Doe case number.

The tech sighed. "Yeah. Okay. We'll get on it."

"Thanks." Thinnes put the tox report into the Uptown Indian's case folder and went out to talk to the state's attorney.

Ferris was gone by the time Oster showed up. "What're we doin' today?" he asked. Neither of them commented on the fact that they weren't scheduled to be in for hours and, consequently, weren't on the payroll.

"I was about to bring the commander up to speed on the Wilson and Bisti cases." He meant the commander of Area Three detectives.

"You want me to come?"

"Not unless you want to."

"Not particularly. You got something else for me to do?"

"Feel like going Downtown?"

Oster shrugged.

"I need an old case file from Records." He gave Oster the case number.

"Yeah, okay. I'll do that. You want I should ask about the tox report on Wilson?"

"They'll fax it to us when it's ready. It isn't as if we don't have enough to hold him on without it."

"Then why am I going all the way Downtown for one lousy, *old* case report?"

"I'd like you to personally take it up to Fingerprints and have them run the victim through NCIC."

"Why?" He meant, Why, when that's been done already, or should have been?

"It was Ferris's case."

"Say no more."

"Same MO as our Uptown Indian."

Thinnes spent exactly twenty minutes with the CO, then had the next two hours free. He and Swann went to lunch at a sit-down restaurant where they could get a steak sandwich and a beer. They were in good spirits when they got back. Oster, on the other hand, came back from 11th and State looking so dragged out that Thinnes was sorry he'd sent him. He had a McDonald's bag with him that he put on a table and tore open. He got himself coffee before he started in on his Big Mac.

Swann hung up the phone and finished jotting something on a piece of paper. "Hey, you guys know there was such a thing as a Navajo Tribal Police?"

Thinnes was getting coffee. "No," he said, "but it makes sense." He brought his cup over to where Swann was sitting.

"He sounded like he knew what he was doing. Use-ly, when you're dealin' with some *po*dunk sheriff's department, you got a better chance of gettin' somethin' from Deputy Dawg than from Deputy Redneck."

"An Indian tribal police force probably doesn't have any rednecks."

"That'd explain it."

"How 'bout you guys just cut the crap," Oster said. He glared at Swann. "Just tell us what you found out."

Swann gave him a what's-with-you look, which he ignored, then shrugged. "The shipping company you asked them to check out—near Farmington—from the phone number you found on your victim, the Uptown Indian? Officer Tso told me, as far as he's been able to find out, it's legit. According to the owner, they haven't shipped anything to Chicago in the last two months. They do send art supplies to Wisconsin. Regularly."

"What kind of art supplies?" Thinnes asked.

"According to the shipping manifests, clay, clay slip, glazes, and botanical dyes. That kind of stuff."

"He give you the address?"

"Yeah." Swann handed Thinnes the paper.

"I don't suppose they're missing any citizens?"

Swann shook his head. "None matching your Uptown Injun."

FORTY-FOUR

Saturday morning Rhonda had to work, so Thinnes's hopes of a day alone with her were dashed. He followed her around the house until she was ready to leave, then asked Rob if he'd like to go to Wisconsin. Rob wasn't interested; Thinnes left alone.

Before hitting the highway, he stopped in at headquarters and went over the Uptown Indian file. In case he'd missed anything. And out of habit.

When he went back out to start his Chevy, it gave a discouraging groan, followed by the stomach-churning click of a dead battery. Damn! He spent the better part of an hour trying to get the car started, borrowing jumper cables and bumming jumps. It was freezing; the car kept dying. Finally, he gave up and went inside.

"What d'ya 'spect?" Mike asked, when Thinnes called. "Gotta get serviced now 'n' then."

Thinnes arranged to have the car towed to Mike's shop, on Fullerton, and left the key at the District Nineteen desk. He'd just walked back into the detectives' squad room when the sergeant said, "Phone for you, Thinnes."

He picked it up and said, "Area Three detectives. Thinnes."

"John," a familiar voice said.

Thinnes racked his brain for a name to put with the voice. Jack Caleb!

"Rob told me you'd gone to Wisconsin for the day. I was going to leave a message."

"My car broke down," Thinnes told him. "Looks like I'll

have to go another time. What can I do for you?"

"Would you like me to drive you?"

Thinnes said, "Why?" without thinking. "That's not why you called. You don't even know where I'm going."

"Sun Prairie. Rob told me."

"Why? And why'd you call?"

"Why not?"

Refusing to be sucked into the I-asked-you-first trap, Thinnes waited.

Finally Caleb added, "My car could stand the break from city driving, and I haven't anything better to do this afternoon."

Thinnes suddenly felt very strange. He hadn't really worked out how he felt about the idea of being alone with Caleb for any length of time. Intellectually, he was aware that he and the doctor weren't so different, but his gut feeling was—

He still wasn't sure *what* he felt about him.

Caleb had brought the cat to the house and stopped by several times to see how it was doing, but most of their conversations were strictly business, especially now that the doctor was a department consultant.

"Why did you call?" Thinnes repeated.

"I was wondering what progress you'd made on David Bisti's murder."

"I wish I could say we were getting close, but we've run out of leads."

"I'm sorry to hear that. I'm serious about the lift. And I'd be happy to let you drive."

Caleb drove a Jaguar. XJS 4.0 liter coupe. Silver-blue. This year's model. Thinnes usually had contempt for yuppie cars and their drivers, but he knew Caleb was very good. He was relieved, though, when the doctor got out of the car and walked around to get in on the passenger's side.

The car had a manual transmission. As a kid, working for his dad, Thinnes had driven a pickup truck—and damn near every other vehicle used in construction—so the Jaguar's gearshift didn't throw him. But it still took a few blocks to get used to it.

The doctor leaned back in the corner between the door and the seat and watched him without commenting, even when Thinnes ground the gears going into third. By the time they hit the Kennedy, Thinnes was shifting up and down automatically and could concentrate on traffic. The car was a pleasure to drive, responsive and comfortable. He could see why someone with the cash would own one. He had to fight himself to keep from doing Daytona as they spun north off the Kennedy, onto the Edens.

Traffic increased and Thinnes was forced to slow down. As they passed the Touhy exit, he pointed to the CD player. "You got any disks for that?"

"Yes," Caleb said. "But how do you feel about opera?"

"Forget it."

"What have you found out, so far, about David's killer?"

There wasn't much to tell—nothing new. Beyond saying that the lead they were following wasn't part of it, Thinnes didn't go into detail about his reason for going to Wisconsin. He did confirm that his supervisor had refused to authorize the use of a department car for the trip. Caleb was as good a listener as any of the best dicks Thinnes knew. They quickly exhausted weather—standard for the Midwest; sports—they were in agreement about the Bulls, the Bears, and the Cubs, and neither gave a damn about hockey; and current events—the Cardinal *didn't* do it, but the Rock Star probably did.

For a while, after that, they rode in silence—Caleb staring out at the winter-yellow scenery; Thinnes appreciating the merits of the Jaguar as he maneuvered it around lesser vehicles. He could easily see the horsepower going to his head, like a drug. He backed off the accelerator and said, "Have you always had money?"

"I suppose by most people's standards. Yes. My father's a surgeon. And, as a workaholic . . ." He paused, then laughed.

"The first accident I ever had, I wrapped his Cadillac around a tree."

"My old man drives a '75 Ford F150. Changes the oil every two thousand miles. He's had bodywork done on it—twice—but he won't even consider getting a new one."

North of Waukegan the land flanking the highway began to look and smell more like farm country—miles of yellow grass; paler, stubble-striped cornfields; and hedgerows of naked trees poking through threadbare snowdrifts. "What made you decide to become a shrink?" Thinnes asked.

" 'Nam."

"How's that?"

"My father always wanted me to be a surgeon. We didn't get along, so, naturally, I planned to do anything else."

Caleb paused. Thinnes let the silence be.

"I was majoring in history when I was drafted, registered as a CO. One of the geniuses who assigns PhDs to the motor pool must've found out my father was a doctor and decided that would make me a natural medic. It made sense, in a Catch-22 sort of way. I forced myself to learn to do it well, and I kept my sanity by studying my buddies' descents into madness.

"After the war, rebelling against my father seemed trivial, and I had to find something useful to do with my life. Since they wouldn't let me practice psychiatry without a medical license, I put aside the oedipal thing and applied to med school."

Thinnes had known plenty of guys who'd had their lives changed, their middle-class values challenged, by the war. Some had been sobered and tempered by it, others broken.

"I was drifting through classes at Oakton Community College," he said, "trying to decide on a major that would fit with my half-assed plan to go to work for my dad when I finished. I never gave police work a thought until I was drafted. I spent my year in 'Nam in Saigon, as an MP."

North of the state line, traffic thinned, and the green highway signs announced places like Sturtevant and Franksville. Signs on the right-of-way said, WISCONSIN ARRESTS DRUNK DRIVERS, FIREWORKS, and $500 FINE FOR THROWING LITTER OR TRASH ON HIGHWAY—KEEP WISCONSIN CLEAN. They took the 894 bypass, around Milwaukee, and continued toward Madison on I94, passing exits for exotic places like Heartland, Wales, and Oconomowoc. Snow covered the fields and rights-of-way, but the road was clear and in good shape. Just past the Lake Mills, Waterloo, Aztalan State Park exit, they were doing close to eighty when Caleb said, "John, I think we're being followed."

Thinnes glanced in the rearview and felt the twinge of panic motorists always get when they spot the flashing lights. Police. Wisconsin state troopers. Men rumored to give each other tickets.

He signaled and pulled over. The trooper sat in his car for a while—no doubt checking the registration—before he got out. Caleb was decent enough to not comment.

Thinnes rolled down the window and passed his driver's license through. He stared at the highway while the trooper studied the license, his breath condensing in the frozen air.

Finally he said, "What brings you fellas up our way?"

"We're on a little hunting expedition," Thinnes said.

"You have a hunting license?" He didn't point out that it wasn't hunting season.

Thinnes showed him his star.

The trooper raised an eyebrow. He took a step back and looked pointedly at the Jaguar. "Guess you must be bagging some pretty large game in Chicago."

Thinnes shook his head. "No. Jack offered to let me try her out and I couldn't resist opening her up a little. Guess I got carried away."

"Yeah," the trooper said. "Well, sorry, Detective, but your hunting license isn't good this side of the state line."

"I was going to stop in at headquarters and take out a local permit."

"Did you talk to anyone from here?"

"Sergeant Blackburn."

"Let me give him a call. See if he can meet you somewhere."

They waited in silence while the trooper radioed from his car. Five minutes later, he leaned over the Jaguar to give them detailed directions on where to go to meet Blackburn. Then he handed Thinnes his license and a sheet of paper.

"What's this?"

"A warning citation, Detective. Wisconsin tickets speeders. Drive safely."

Sergeant Blackburn had done his homework, but he didn't have time to go with them to the address the NTP had provided. County Road N pushed north through open farmland, past flat hills, cornfields, and barns with silos. Their destination was a place called The Pottery Factory, located just east of Sun Prairie. It looked more like a retail greenhouse than a ceramics outlet. The long, single-story building looked warm. Its entire south wall—the gable end—was windows filled with green plants, some as tall as the cathedral ceiling of the showroom. The northern two-thirds of the structure was hidden behind a forest of overage Christmas trees.

"What they call a cash crop in Wisconsin," Thinnes said, pointing.

An OPEN sign showed in the front window. Inside, no one was in sight, but overgrown houseplants leaned over the doorway and encroached on the walkways between display counters. The sign next to the cash register advised: RING BELL FOR SERVICE. An old church bell with a hemp pull rope hung from the ceiling, amid pots of ivy and philodendron suspended from the rafters. Thinnes pulled; the bell sounded.

They looked around as they waited. East and west walls of the store were filled with shelves of ceramic gimmicks varying in quality from dime-store cheap to really pricey art objects. Caleb inspected everything, even the cheap junk, by hand. Thinnes kept his hands in his pockets. He glanced over the merchandise, then studied the security arrangements, wondering why they needed motion detectors *and* a security camera *and* the infrared interrupter beam across the doorway. Hefty security for a few knickknacks and pots.

Caleb had dragged an Egyptian cat statue and a reproduction Anasazi bowl to the cash register by the time a saleswoman showed. Female Cauc—or light-skinned Indian, he couldn't tell for sure; five four; 110 pounds, maybe; early twenties. She was dressed in a bulky sweater, jeans, and men's work boots. Betty, according to the tag on her sweater. She asked, "May I help you?"

Thinnes took the Polaroid of the Uptown Indian out of his pocket. "Do you recognize this man?"

She looked suspiciously at Thinnes but took the picture and glanced at it. "Looks a little like Tom Redbird. Only this guy looks dead." When neither Thinnes nor Caleb said anything, she said, "That's him, isn't it?"

"We were hoping someone could tell us," Thinnes said. "He was shot to death in Chicago. He'd been robbed. There was no identification on him."

"You're cops." They didn't contradict her. She looked at the picture more carefully. "I think it's him."

"Who was he?"

"A truck driver. I don't—didn't know him well. He delivered supplies and sometimes took a shipment of our stuff places. I didn't know him very well—just to talk to when he came in." She paused and sighed. "He seemed nice. Not like some of the jerks who drive trucks."

While Betty rang up Caleb's purchases, she told them Redbird was an independent owner/operator who had relatives somewhere nearby but lived in Chicago. "He had a big Kenworth he was really proud of, kept it really clean."

She gave them Redbird's business card. Chicago PO box and phone. The zip code was for Uptown.

Thinnes was ready to leave it at that, but Caleb started asking questions about The Pottery Factory. Who were the artists who contributed? How did they come to set up shop here in Wisconsin? Did they have a catalog? Et cetera. Betty didn't seem to find this sudden interest odd, but to Thinnes, it was peculiar. He could hardly wait to get away so he could ask.

But back in the car, it was Caleb who got the first question in: "What now?"

"What's with the sudden interest in pottery?"

"The cat's a Christmas gift. And I needed the bowl as a sample for a comparison before I said anything about a theory I've formulated. It looks like one I saw in a catalog from a store called Native Artists."

"That's interesting."

"What are we going to do next?"

"I think we'll try to locate Redbird's family while we're here—maybe save someone a trip back later."

FORTY-FIVE

None of the Redbirds listed in the local directory, or the Madison or Milwaukee directories, were unaccounted for or missing any relatives that they'd admit to. The DMV *was* able to confirm a Chicago resident named Thomas Redbird as the holder of an Illinois Class A commercial driver's license. The address was in Uptown, which jibed with the phone exchange and zip code on Redbird's business card. Thinnes didn't get an answer when he dialed the number.

"What now?" Caleb asked, as they walked out of the state police station in Madison. Salt, scattered across the sidewalk, crunched underfoot. His breath condensed around his head. The air smelled like snow.

Thinnes sighed, creating his own cloud. "I guess we call it a day."

"Let's eat first."

It was nearly dark by the time they got to the Edgewater Hotel, on Wisconsin Avenue. Caleb's suggestion. The restaurant was pricey—not the sort Thinnes would normally frequent—but the food was very good. Rhonda would have liked it. They sat in the dining room, watching the lights of ice fishermen replace the fading daylight across the frozen surface of Lake Mendota. Caleb drew Redbird's story out of Thinnes with his seductive listening.

"It may have just been random," Thinnes concluded. "But I have a hunch Redbird knew his killer. He couldn't have been naive enough to let a stranger get that close without some . . ."

What? Protest? Disturbance? Struggle? He shrugged, not sure what he meant. "And it's incredible that there should be two unrelated murders with the same MO in the same area."

"There *is* a school of philosophy that holds that there aren't any coincidences. Did the victims know each other?"

"We don't know. We don't know who the first victim was, just that he was Indian."

"And they're not uncommon in Uptown."

"For that matter, dead Indians aren't uncommon in Uptown."

As Thinnes pulled the Jaguar into the lot at Western and Belmont, he noticed his Chevy was where he'd left it. Damn! Mike hadn't gotten to it. Oh well. He probably wouldn't get home tonight anyway. He curbed the car, put it in neutral, and set the parking brake. He and Caleb got out together, and Caleb walked around to the driver's side.

Thinnes said, "Thanks, Doc," as they shook hands. "Jack," he added, remembering Caleb hated *Doc*.

"Keep me posted."

"Will do."

Inside the Nineteen lobby, Thinnes was hailed by the desk sergeant, who tossed him his car keys. "Detective, the little shit that brought back your car made a federal case when he couldn't put it back where he got it. Wouldn't leave till we moved two squads for him."

"Thanks," Thinnes said. "I'll talk to him."

Thomas Redbird's apartment—according to the address on his CDL—reminded Thinnes of the old "Ajax was here" commercials. It stood out, the only spotless building in a row of dingy, dilapidated structures. In front, the parkway was free of trash and dog shit. The walk, clear of broken glass and even old chewing gum, sparkled with a glitter of salt. Dark evergreen bushes, inside the perimeter of the sidewalk, were squared off and clear of dead wood, the winter-yellow grass sheared and raked. And the building itself had recently been sandblasted and tuck-pointed—no graffiti. Thinnes was able to observe all of this because, when he got inside the hedge, motion sensors activated wire-caged security lights that flooded the building's courtyard.

A clean, well-lit place, he thought, when he entered the pristine vestibule. Who said that? The security door had a frosted glass panel in its upper half and a security peephole. The mailboxes were polished brass, as was the doorbell panel. He pushed the button next to the sign that said: MANAGER—SENSKI.

A fuzzy, heavily accented voice came over the security speaker. "Come back later." Eastern European accent. Polish, probably.

Thinnes pushed the button again. "Police."

There was a long silence, then, "I coming."

Thinnes held his star up in front of the peephole. He heard shuffling footsteps, then a woman, five four and solid—maybe 150 pounds—opened the door. She had curly blond hair—not her natural color—blue eyes, and was somewhere between forty-five and sixty. She had on a pink apron over her flowered, below-the-knee dress, and a cardigan over the apron. And thin white socks folded over ugly tie shoes. She said, "I no want trouble."

"No trouble," he said. He spoke slowly and clearly, careful to keep from raising his voice. "I need help." She waited with a fearful expression. Thinnes held up the autopsy photo. "Do you know this man?"

He could see she did, even before she said, "Two B. No trouble," she repeated, plaintively. "Please no trouble." She worked on the hem of her apron, pressing creases in it with her work-rough hands.

"Can you let me into 2B?"

The request frightened her, but she nodded. "I clean him. Nice man. No trouble."

She opened Redbird's door for Thinnes and stepped away

from it. He reached in and flipped the light switch, then entered, signaling for her to follow.

She stopped just inside and waved a hand at the room. "I clean."

He nodded to acknowledge that. "Stay here."

Eager to avoid trouble, she nodded and said, "Yes, Meester."

A message from his childhood flashed through Thinnes's mind: *Blessed are the meek, for they shall inherit . . .*

He did a quick look around—the apartment was even cleaner than the hall and stairs. Bad luck for the cops. Not much chance that Evidence would find anything, but . . .

The woman was standing where he'd left her by the door.

"You speak Polish?" he asked.

"Polish, yes. I Polish."

He put on gloves before using Redbird's phone to call in. "I'm gonna need Evidence," he told the watch commander. "And a Polish translator. And send me somebody to help do a canvass."

Redbird's living room was sparsely furnished—a couch, a comfy-looking armchair in front of a TV wired for cable, Indian rugs on the floor and couch, and coffee and end tables that didn't match. The coffee table had scratches on it about where you'd put your feet if you sat in the chair to watch TV. Everything was polished and dust free. The only interesting thing in the room was a neat pile of unopened mail, including two packages, on one of the end tables. Thinnes resisted the urge to touch it before Evidence got a shot at it.

A muffled sob brought his attention back to Mrs. Senski, who was fighting tears and looked ready to pass out. He pointed to the couch. "Maybe you'd better sit down."

She did. He went in the kitchen to get her a glass of water, finding what you'd expect to find in a kitchen. Nothing new or expensive. Everything spotless, down to the clean liner in the garbage can. He filled a glass with water and returned to the living room. Mrs. Senski hadn't moved. She was shaking and crying silently, breathing with little hiccups. She took the water gratefully and sucked half of it down.

Evidence arrived a few minutes later. Thinnes buzzed them in from the panel next to Redbird's door. When they got up to the apartment, he said, "Fast work."

"Slow night."

He had them process the mail first, so he could look through it. Most of it was junk, but there was a Kodak mailer—processed film—and a padded envelope with no return address.

The package contained Redbird's wallet. His license, credit cards, pictures, and insurance cards were all there. There was no cash. The anonymous "Samaritan" who'd dropped it in the mail said, in a note he'd attached with a rubber band, that it was found in the garbage, where—presumably—it had been tossed by a thief. Thinnes handed everything to one of the techs. "You want to dust for prints and log this in as evidence?"

"You think the killer was stupid enough to leave prints?"

"There's always the chance our Good Samaritan is the killer, and sending us this is his way of laughing at us."

"Cy-ni-cal."

"Occupational hazard."

While the technician brushed his black powder all over the note, the wallet, and its contents, Thinnes opened the Kodak mailer. It contained photos from a family gathering, taken in September—he guessed, from trees just starting to turn in some of the backgrounds. Lots of shots of a young Indian woman and a boy. And one of Redbird, sunlit and smiling, with his shirt open and a Coke can in hand. Carefree. Happy. Alive. Thinnes handed the mailer and all but two of the photos to the tech. "May as well keep these with the rest of his stuff." He held up the shot of Redbird by himself, and one of him with his arms around the boy and woman. "I'm holding on to these for now." The tech nodded.

Thinnes looked at the picture of Redbird. "I'm gonna get the son of a bitch who shot you," he told him, as if the man's spirit was trapped in the emulsion and could hear.

Mrs. Senski, who'd been watching Thinnes, pressed her hands over the lower half of her face and sobbed.

Thinnes walked over to the phone, dialed the dispatcher, and identified himself. "Where's the interpreter?"

"Tied up. Interviewing a rape victim."

"Great. Don't you have any beat guys that speak Polish?"

"How would *I* know?"

"Ask!" He hung up the phone and went to see how the Evidence team was doing.

The cop who spoke Polish was a young black man who looked like a college student and talked without a trace of any accent—a Midwesterner. When he noticed that Mrs. Senski was afraid of him, he put the coffee table between them, squatted down—like he would to talk to a kid—and kept his voice very soft. She had to listen carefully to hear him. The strategy worked. Gradually her sniffling subsided and she began to give them the story.

Redbird had lived there two years, during which time he'd been a model tenant. He didn't drink or bring home loose women. He drove a truck and was away for weeks at a time, so he'd paid Mrs. Senski to do his cleaning and bring up his mail. She hadn't seen him since Thanksgiving, when he left to spend the day with family in Wisconsin. He had a sister and nephew that she knew of—she didn't have their name, but the rental office would. It was Mrs. Senski who'd left the Kodak mailer and the package on the table, with the rest of the mail, per her agreement with Redbird. She couldn't imagine who'd want to kill him. She couldn't even imagine him dead.

Thinnes did the paperwork before he went home. He spread out his forms and the notes he'd made on a table in the squad room and went to get coffee. Someone had slapped a BIOHAZARD

WASTE decal on the pot. The coffee tasted like it, but it had enough caffeine in it to do the job.

Two hours later, he handed his report and Redbird's photo over the desk. "We got a name and better picture of our Uptown Indian," he told the sergeant. "One that doesn't make him look dead. He was Thomas Redbird."

The sergeant nodded. "We'll put together a photo lineup and trot it around."

Thinnes handed him another sheet. "Here's the list of neighbors I talked to. Get whoever's doing the canvass to cover between Redbird's place and where he was found."

"Yeah."

"And you think you could check for this missing truck being sold lately?" He meant, could someone else do it, before he came back on duty.

The sergeant shrugged. "If our perp was snatching kids instead of bumping off Indians it wouldn't be a problem. I can see if it's been impounded."

"Thanks. Monday, I'll pick up where you leave off. I'm not coming in tomorrow. I haven't seen my wife in a week."

He left the search-warrant request for the PO box with the sergeant, to give to the first ASA who showed up. Normally, he'd have called the state's attorney, but he needed sleep, and neither the post office nor the rental office would be open until Monday. One more day wouldn't matter. Redbird wouldn't get any deader in the meantime.

By the time he got home, Rhonda was long since asleep. But she came awake as he kissed her good night. . . .

FORTY-SIX

Caleb got the phone on the second ring and sighed inwardly when he recognized the caller.

"How was your day?" Rick asked.

The question had an intimacy Caleb found himself resenting vaguely. It was the sort of question he and Chris had asked each other at day's end. He tried to analyze his reaction, tried to remember at what stage of their relationship he and Chris had started calling each other "dear" and caring deeply, had started asking "How was your day?" and really giving a damn.

"What're you doing tonight?" Rick asked.

He'd planned to catch up on all the things he hadn't done yesterday because he was with Thinnes. He hadn't told Rick about Wisconsin. "I really hadn't any firm plans."

"Come to the game."

"I can't," Caleb said, trying to remember if the baseball play-offs were finally over and which of the three winter teams he'd heard mentioned on the news earlier.

"You just said you don't have any plans."

"Who's playing?"

"That's a good one, Doc," Rick said.

"Jack," Caleb reminded him. He hated *Doc*.

"I got two tickets for the best seats in the house—center ice, front row, first balcony."

The Blackhawks.

When Caleb didn't respond enthusiastically, Rick reminded him, "This is the last season in the old stadium."

Caleb had never been to see the Hawks at the stadium. In fact, he couldn't recall having attended a live hockey game since high school. And he was too tired to think of a plausible excuse not to go. So he didn't argue when Rick told him, "I'll pick you up. No use two of us driving. And no sense taking a chance with that car of yours. See you tonight."

Hawks versus Sharks. Bread and circuses or, in this case, beer and circuses—there were at least twice as many beer vendors as at a Bulls game. The crowd was mostly male and almost universally white, as well as merciless, vociferous, and vulgar. Regulation jackets, hats, and other Hawks paraphernalia—with the high cost of tickets, and more than forty home games—marked many of the fans as truly dedicated. Rick was one of them.

Below Rick and Caleb, on the main floor, the fans seemed more civilized and better dressed. Above, in the second balcony, the crowd was rowdier and more inebriated. Above and below, people were plugged into personal radios—addicted to the constant prattle of other people's voices or, perhaps, unable to interpret things for themselves.

The huge neon Indian glowed on the scoreboard above the ice, and colorful ads glowed from the boards around it. The teams came out at opposite ends of the arena and circled like the predators they were named for. Warming up. Unashamed to be labeled patriotic, the fans stood for the National Anthem, clapping and whistling, increasingly louder, until the roar was like the shock wave of an explosion in slo-mo. Caleb recognized that the appeal was as old as time, though he felt personally alienated from the spectacle. His perceptions began to blur from the sensory overload.

The game was very fast and not too subtle. It resonated in the cerebellum, the old brain, and the collective unconscious. The players were ritual killing machines, their fans drawn like predators to blood. Caleb didn't grapple strenuously with the rules.

Base chords from the stadium's organ vibrated below the human noises. The pressure of the sound wave swelled Caleb from within like the first waves of a building orgasm. Ecstasy.

Eight minutes into it, a Shark shot the puck past the Hawk goalie, scoring. A fight broke out. Joyful mayhem compared to the carefully choreographed battles of professional wrestlers, but catering to the same needs. High on the most ancient drug, the crowd tongued its cheerful blood lust. Then there was outrage from the crowd as the announcer reported Cam Russell being ejected.

Moments later, the Hawks evened the score, and Rick jumped to his feet screaming, "Yes! Kimble!" When Poulin scored as well, two minutes later, the whole audience rose to its feet to recite his name.

As Caleb watched Rick pound the air in a Dionysian frenzy and give high fives to the equally insane fans around him, he thought the younger man's face, in the reflected light from the arena, seemed as beautiful as the god's.

And then, the first period was over.

Smoking was prohibited in the stands, but a hazy miasma floated above the lines waiting, between periods, for beer. As they stood meekly in the queue, Caleb felt withdrawal setting in—the wolves were turning back to cattle.

Second period, there was a lot of activity but no action. Caleb found himself devoting as much attention to the fights in the stands as to the activity on the ice. The man to Caleb's left became progressively drunker. He put each new beer inside the previously emptied cup, and by the end of the second intermission, he'd collected nine of them.

"The *off*ense really sucks tonight," Rick told Caleb, shortly after the third period began.

A fan behind them reiterated: "Yeah, fuckin' pacifists!"

"They seem tired," Caleb said.

"Yeah. Well, they did play yesterday," Rick admitted.

"Who?"

Rick looked at him as if he were suddenly psychotic, and the fan behind him demanded, "What planet are *you* from?"

Rick leaned over to shout, "Boston!" in Caleb's ear.

"But they won?" Caleb persisted. He found himself comparing Rick to Thinnes. Unfavorably. The two men were as unlike as dog and cat, and that—he realized with an unpleasant shock—was what bothered him about Rick, what made him unsuitable as a companion. Rick was one of those who needed constant reassurance; Caleb knew his charming narcissism would lose its appeal. Like Freud, he failed to fill Caleb's deepest longings, but unlike the cat, he made demands the doctor found annoying.

A few minutes further into the period, Caleb began to feel that the stadium was warmer. The crowd seemed closer and louder. A free-for-all erupted in the upper levels, and security guards in yellow jackets pushed their way among the boisterous to eject the instigators. Rick leaned over and said, into Caleb's ear, "This isn't going anywhere. What say we blow this pop stand?"

Caleb agreed.

As they climbed into Rick's Blazer, he consoled himself with the thought that it could have been worse. It could have been next Sunday and he'd be missing *Trovatore*.

The worst of it was that any of the guys at Spaulding House would have killed for his ticket.

FORTY-SEVEN

The blinking readout on Caleb's answering machine was announcing five messages when he got home. He would have ignored it—in an emergency, he'd have been paged—but Rick's eager, "Aren't you going to check your messages?" seemed like the perfect excuse to call off the rest of the evening.

The first message was: "Yo, Jack. Need to check the Mann." Rafe.

The next was a hang-up; it was followed by calls—each sounding more concerned—from Brian, Lenny, and Paul asking Caleb to get in touch. Manny was obviously having some sort of crisis.

Caleb picked up the phone and hit the auto-dial button for Spaulding House.

Brian answered. "Jack! Thank God!" Caleb waited. "Manny's IV came out, and we can't find a vein we can get a needle into."

"Why didn't you take him to the hospital?"

"He won't go. He's afraid they'll keep him."

It was a realistic possibility.

"I'll be right there." Caleb put the phone down and turned. "I heard," Rick said. "A suicidal client?"

"A friend with AIDS."

"At Spaulding House?"

Caleb nodded. He went to the closet and got his medical bag. "There's probably no point in your waiting. I could be half the night."

"Let me go with you."

Caleb felt a stab of disappointment. Was that what Rick had been angling for all along—a chance to get in at Spalding House? He shrugged mentally. If he was that determined, he'd get in somehow, sooner or later. And it might be a good test of character—to see how he'd react. "Only if you promise you'll respect our right to privacy."

Rick's gray eyes widened, a model of injured innocence. "Of course."

Brian, the cynic—who, under normal circumstances, would have slit his wrists before he'd show concern for anyone—was waiting by the yard gate. Hands in pockets—he never wore gloves—he shivered in his too-large coat. His hair looked black in the orange glow of the alley light. His eyes were dark holes in a skeletal face. When they got close enough, Caleb could see tears glistening on his cheeks. And his breath rose like a ragged prayer.

Rick had driven west down the alley. So Brian could see Caleb through the window of the Blazer as it approached. He opened the gate for them and closed it when they'd passed. Caleb scarcely waited for the car to stop before he was out, running to the house.

He took the stairs two at a time, with Rafe on his heels. The others followed, Rick bringing up the rear. They filed into Manny's room and surrounded the bed like a pack of interns on rounds. Worry made them forget their usual manners and crowd in where they usually gave visitors time and space to get used to them. Objectively, they resembled escapees from a horror film. Paul, the most attractive, could have been a possessed Holocaust survivor, his movements manic, his eyes glittering with fever. Bill's face was pocked with herpes sores, Brian's blotched by Kaposi's lesions. Lenny displayed a textbook case of thrush run amok. Rafe, who wasn't afflicted with HIV, was scowling with worry and looked like the heavy from a violent action film.

Caleb felt, rather than saw, Rick shrink back from them. What-ever he'd expected from Spaulding House, this—apparently—wasn't it. With a single glance at him, Caleb took in all the signs of stress, then put Rick out of mind. He wasn't the patient.

The hospital bed, the medical supplies on the bureau, and the IV stand with its pendant envelope of fluid, furthered the hospital atmosphere. On the center of the bed, Manny looked like an Egyptian mummy—sans wrappings—desiccated and faded to a jaundiced yellow. He seemed to have shrunk to child size and looked dead. The noise of their arrival reanimated him. He smiled at Caleb. "Hi, Jack."

Caleb put on the surgical gloves Rafe handed him and sat down on the edge of the bed. "Making trouble again?"

"Right up to the end. Job security for you."

Distracted, Caleb nodded and pushed first one, then the other of Manny's oversize sleeves up his arms in search of veins. He decided the left arm showed the most promise and looked at Rafe, who handed him the black rubber tourniquet. There was complete quiet, and everyone seemed to hold his breath as Caleb put it on Manny's arm and swabbed the arm with cotton soaked in alcohol. Then he squeezed Manny's hand and rubbed the fore-arm to raise a vein. Rafe handed him a syringe with its needle bared. Caleb carefully threaded it into the vein, and dark blood began to seep into the syringe. A collective sigh broke the silence.

"With a little practice, you could get quite good at this, Jack," Manny said, as Caleb carefully traded an IV line for the syringe.

"Not something I want to have to practice, Mann."

"Just until January," Manny said. "Don't want to fuck up Christmas with a funeral."

Caleb nodded, feeling his eyes liquefy. He took a deep breath to distract himself—Manny didn't need tears.

"Holding out for Martin Luther King Day," Manny went on. "It's already pretty lugubrious. That the right word, Jack? Lugubrious?"

"It is."

Rafe ended the awkward moment by turning to the spectators, growling, "Don't you chumps have sumpthin to do?" He swept the used syringe and cotton into a plastic box labeled BIOHAZARD WASTE and threw his gloves in the wastebasket. Then he pushed between Bill and Lenny, who were blocking the doorway, and vanished.

Rick had watched Caleb work on Manny with the fascination of a spectator at an accident site. Now his attention wandered, as if Manny's symptoms were too terrible to consider. He stared at the wall covered with graffiti.

Manny smiled. He noticed Rick and said, "You'll have to excuse Rafe. He went to the Mr. T school of etiquette. But he's a sweetheart."

Rick nodded dumbly, looking shocked.

"He's beautiful, Jack," Manny continued. "I'm happy for you. I was afraid you were gonna die an old maid."

Rick blushed.

Paul, Bill, and Lenny used the pause that followed to come up and put their hands on Manny under the guise of hitting him on the chin and shoulder. Brian edged his way around the bed and sat on it, back against the headboard, and took Manny's right hand in both of his, resting them on his lap. "What's he do?" he asked Caleb.

"Rick's a writer."

"You going to immortalize us?" Brian asked, his sarcasm restored by Manny's improved prognosis.

"If you'll let me." Beyond that he seemed at a loss for words. So much for his determination to write about a hospice.

Manny's eyes were creeping shut. He opened them wide and looked at Rick, yawning. "Maybe tomorrow."

"I'll hold you to it." Rick still seemed uncomfortable.

Manny yawned again and turned his head to look directly at Caleb. "Bring him back tomorrow. When you come to read . . ."

Caleb glanced at the copy of *Inferno* on the bedside table. The bookmark had advanced noticeably. They were all worried Manny wouldn't live to hear the denouement and were hurrying things along by reading it to him whenever he was lucid. Rafe had told him it was replacing the soaps, for some of them, as a filler of time. Caleb bent and kissed Manny on the forehead. When he stepped away from the bed, Manny opened his eyes again and turned his head toward Rick. "Nice meeting you." His hand quivered.

Caleb watched a sardonic smile form on Brian's face as he recognized Manny's effort to offer Rick his hand. He stared at Rick and lifted Manny's hand up. It was a test. It was like the climax moment in a TV disease-of-the-week movie, where the protagonist must confront his fear of AIDS by embracing a disease-ravaged victim.

Rick held Brian's gaze long enough to make it clear he understood what was going on. He stepped over to the bed and gently closed his hand around Manny's and raised and lowered it. "The pleasure's mine." He let the hand down gently on the bedcover and backed away.

Rick stopped the Blazer in front of Caleb's building and put it in park but didn't turn it off.

"Aren't you coming up?" Caleb asked.

"It's late. And I have to be up early."

Relieved, Caleb nodded.

"Were they all friends before they came to Spaulding House?" Rick asked.

"None of them had ever met, to my knowledge."

"They seem so close."

"Is this off-the-record?"

"Nothing you tell a writer is ever off-the-record. Everything he sees, or hears, or feels goes down on paper." He smiled. "But I've been known to change names to protect the guilty."

"I have a theory about attachment."

"Which is?"

"Humans can't remain neutral about anything they give their time or labor to. Whatever we take care of, we either come to love or hate."

"Will Manny make it?"

"Past Christmas?"

Rick nodded.

"I doubt it. But then, I wouldn't have bet he'd last as long as this."

FORTY-EIGHT

At the morgue, there was a different kind of show-up—only one subject, one who wouldn't turn to offer his profile for identification. And a fearful witness—fearful for what she'd see, not for who would see her. Thinnes had been in the room a hundred times, and it was still unnerving.

He'd called Wisconsin and asked them to break the news to Redbird's sister and make arrangements for her to come to Chicago to ID the body officially. He'd picked her up at O'Hare. Now, in Room 131, he stood with her in front of the window into the cooler, the cold room where the dead awaited their ultimate disposition. The assistant medical examiner pulled the curtain, and they could see the gurney through the viewing window, with its shrouded burden.

She was dry-eyed, a lifetime older than the young woman in the photos. As she stood at the window, without fidgeting, and waited for the man on the other side of the glass to pull back the cover and make her brother's death real, Thinnes could sympathize with her lack of hurry.

Then the man lifted the cover, and Thomas Redbird's sister nodded and turned away. "That's him."

Thinnes signaled, and the AME re-covered the body and pulled the curtain closed. Thinnes opened the door into the next room and waved her in. Room 133. Gray-and-black furniture, built to withstand the onslaught of distraught humans; reddish carpet and orange door; tan walls and ivory curtains; and, near the ceiling, the preferred medium for introducing people to the hard facts—closed-circuit TV.

At his request, she sat on the sofa. He thought she fit the stereotype—the stoic red man. Or, in this case, woman. "Do you have a place to stay?" he asked.

"Yes."

"I'm sorry to have to ask you questions at a time like this, but I need help finding those responsible." She nodded. "When was the last time you saw him alive?"

"The morning after Thanksgiving. He came for dinner and left after breakfast the next morning."

"Did he have any enemies?"

"No."

"Anyone hate him enough to kill him?"

"No."

"Can you think of anything that would help me?"

"I know why he was killed." He waited. "He knew who killed the artist. Bisti."

"Who?"

"He wouldn't tell me. He knew, though."

"Did he know Bisti?"

"He knew *Mrs.* Bisti. He loved her. He wanted to marry her—before she met Bisti. But she didn't love him. So she married Bisti. I told him, go to the police."

"Was he afraid?"

"My brother was never afraid. But he should have gone to the police."

FORTY-NINE

Hey, Thinnes. Looks like we got a line on your dog." Viernes slapped a note sheet down on the table in front of Thinnes. "Beat copper—Noir—ran him down for you."

"Dog?"

"Yeah, you know. The one that took a dump on your crime scene."

"Oh." Thinnes picked up the paper and read a name, Abner West. Address in Uptown. The address was familiar: an SRO—single room occupancy—hotel, an odd one in that its former suites had been converted to one-bedroom apartments. "Noir still on duty?"

"Should be."

"Do me a favor?" Thinnes waved the paper. "Call over to Twenty and ask them to have him meet me."

Gray and dismal even in summer, Uptown was hell in December. Thinnes parked; before he and Oster could get out of the car, Officer Noir and his partner pulled up with their Mars lights flashing.

Thinnes got out and walked over to the patrol car. "Noir?"

"Yup."

"Kill the lights, would you please?

"Sure."

"You guys with us?" Oster asked.

Noir gave them a thumbs-up and got out of the car, closely followed by his partner. Young and blond and fit, Noir could have been a poster boy for the Hitler Youth. He was pressed and polished, clean-cut and clean shaven. And macho. His partner was dark, taller, heavier, and laid-back enough to seem half-asleep by comparison. He wasn't. He gave Thinnes a succinct account of their discovery of the dog's owner—from memory. Thinnes was impressed. An "attaboy" was in order, he decided, maybe a good word to the team's supervisor.

The man who opened the office door looked like a Hell's Angel, from long, greasy hair tied back with a bandanna to chain-clad motorcycle boots. Dirty sleeves from his thermal undershirt showed below the rolled sleeves of a plaid work shirt, and his jeans were held by both suspenders and a belt with a Harley Davidson buckle.

"We're looking for an Abner West," Oster told him.

"Yeah. Well, like I told the beat cop earlier . . ." He focused on something behind Oster—spotted Noir, guessed. He seemed to calculate briefly whether Noir would consider it an insult to be called "cop" by a civilian. Thinnes could almost see the wheels turning and the internal shrug as the man decided he didn't care. He brought his full attention back to Oster. "I ain't seen him in a couple days."

"That unusual?"

"Well . . . He's a boozer. You know how they are some-times."

"Tell us about him," Thinnes said.

"Not much to tell. Lives alone—no family he's ever men-tioned 'cept a nephew that's a bum. Served in Korea. Pays his rent pretty regular."

"What does he do for a living?"

"Ya got me. Some kinda pension, maybe?"

Oster said, "What's the nephew's name?"

"Elvis Hale."

"What kind of bum is he?"

"The kind that's got a prison record."

"Know where we can find him?"

The manager shook his head.

"Tell us about West's dog. What kind is it?"

"Damned if I know. Yellow."

"Big?"

"It will be when it gets done growing."

"How long has he had it?"

" 'Bout two months. Not sure. It's quiet. No tellin' how long he had it 'fore I found out."

"Why'd you let him keep it?"

"Like I said, it's quiet. And he cleans up after it."

They waited. Nothing he'd said so far explained why a land-lord would let a tenant keep a dog.

Finally he said, "Well. He gave me two months rent up front for security."

They kept waiting.

"To be honest, I figured if he had some company, he wouldn't be pestering me all the time. He gets lonely and gets tanked up, then he comes down here wantin' to talk—a real pain in the ass."

There was no answer when they knocked on West's door, and the woman in the next apartment was worried. She hadn't seen him in two days, though he usually came and went walking the dog.

It was obvious, as soon as Thinnes opened the door, that their concern was justified. Blood was everywhere. Dark, clotted blood. Half-dried. Still smelling like death. The dirty, scarred linoleum was splattered with it as if someone had taken a bucket and splashed it from the center of the room to the doorway on the far side. And then padded through it barefoot. And slipped on one of the splotches and gone down on hands and knees, squeegeeing the blood aside, leaving scrabbled handprints on the filthy floor.

Right behind Thinnes, Noir said, "Christ!"

Thinnes said, "Stay here."

Noir stopped in the doorway. Thinnes pulled latex gloves from a pocket and put them on before stepping carefully across the room. The overhead light reflected dully off the clots that hadn't dried. It was hard to find places, as he reached the far doorway, to put his feet without stepping in it. The short hallway beyond the doorway was dark, and Thinnes stopped before entering it. "Noir, throw me your flashlight."

Noir, who'd drawn his gun, complied.

Thinnes hugged the left side as he continued, holding the light well away from his body and trained on the bloody handprints along the right wall. He didn't really fear an attack. The blood was old, the killer likely gone. But Thinnes advanced cautiously.

The trail led to the end of the hall, a bedroom if the layout was the same as the neighbor's, back out into the hall, and through a doorway in the right wall of the hallway—what had to be the bathroom. The door was closed. Thinnes picked his way through the bloodstains, stepping carefully on dried patches where there wasn't enough blood-free space for his feet. The flashlight beam found dried blood on both jamb and doorknob. And bloody daubings along the door's edge. Thinnes turned the knob and pushed. There was momentary resistance. Then a grotesque, familiar smell. The smell of death—feces and a body left lying in the steam heat. How many days?

The resistance was from weight, not power—something heavy leaning on the door. Thinnes shoved the flashlight in his belt and leaned backward so he could look for an attacker through the crack between the jamb and the hinge side of the door. He saw only a dirty bathtub and an old steam radiator. He pushed the door open wider. The white tile floor of the room was dark with blood, blood following the grout lines, outlining the small hexagonal tiles. He peered cautiously around the door.

The room was about five by eight, with sink and toilet on the right, tub opposite the door, and radiator opposite the toilet. The body of a Caucasian male, mid-sixties, 250 pounds, lay on its left side, facing the toilet with its arms bracketing the space occupied by the fixture and its feet against the door. Worshipping the porcelain god even in death. The body was clad only in a sleeveless undershirt and boxer shorts.

Without entering the room, Thinnes looked closely at the remains. Abner West's face, hands and feet, forearms and knees were covered in dried blood. And blood matted his thinning white hair. His half-mast eyes were darkened by the dry air, as were his lips and the numerous small scrapes and scratches on his flabby legs and torso. His skin looked jaundiced under a fluorescent light yellowed by years of cigarette smoke. The purple blotches of *livor mortis* darkened the lowest-lying body parts, except on the feet, which had been moved when Thinnes shoved the door. West's flaccid limbs and the greenish tinge of his distended abdomen told Thinnes that rigor had come and gone and putrefaction was settling in.

There was a spent cigarette butt dissolving in the toilet—lid and seat were up—and black crud growing under the rim. Yellow drip stains decorated the outside of the bowl, trailing to a crust of filth around the base. Not a foot from Abner West's dead face. Apart from the blood, there was no sign of a struggle. Thinnes looked everything over twice to be sure. Then he backed out of the room and let the weight of West's feet against the door push it shut.

The room at the end of the hall was dark. Thinnes shone the flashlight around and was momentarily startled when a pair of red eyes flashed back at him. Then he remembered West had a dog. He found the light switch and flipped it. Light changed the red eyes dark brown and the darkness around the eyes to almost white. The dog looked like a Labrador retriever that had been bleached almost white. A red nylon collar around its neck and a red nylon leash tied to the leg of the bed kept it from crossing the room to greet Thinnes. There was a large damp spot on the faded rug at what looked like the maximum distance the dog could get from the bed. The dog wagged its tail, timidly at first, as if expecting to be punished, then more enthusiastically.

Thinnes looked around the room. At first glance, it appeared to have been tossed by the DEA—clothes and old newspapers and empty booze bottles were strewn everywhere. But the drawers were still in the dresser, and the closet door was shut. And nothing in the room was broken. Abner West had simply been a slob. The only neat thing in the room was the dog. And even the dog was splashed with the blood that trailed into the room and back out again.

Thinnes returned to the front room.

Oster was standing just inside the front door, looking around. "Not much of a housekeeper, is he?"

"Was," Thinnes said. "Looks like natural causes, but in case I'm wrong, let's get a mobil unit in here to take a few pictures. And call the ME—see if they want to send an investigator—the usual drill."

Thinnes spent the next twenty-five minutes talking to the neighbors up and down the hall, learning nothing helpful. When the district evidence guy showed up, Thinnes told him, "Victim's not in any hurry. Go take pictures of his dog, first, so we can get it out of here. End of the hall."

The photographer took pictures of the hall, itself, before he picked his way down it, through the blood. From just inside the bedroom door, he shot pictures of the floor and three walls, then crossed to the opposite side of the room to shoot the door wall. He took two close-ups of the bloody dog, one from each side. The dog sat quietly and wagged its tail.

"What've we got here, Detective?" the tech asked.

"In spite of the blood, I think we got natural causes," Thinnes said. "Guy was a boozer. Looks to me like it finally caught up with him."

The technician nodded. "Where is he?"

"In the bathroom. Let me get rid of this dog before you shoot in there."

Thinnes crossed to the bed and untied the dog, then carried it out of the apartment, trying to hold it away from his body to keep from getting blood or hair on his clothes. The animal was heavy—twenty-five or thirty pounds—and he was glad to set it down in the hall.

The two beat coppers, lounging against the wall opposite the door, came to attention when he appeared.

"Noir," Thinnes said, "see if the manager'll take this dog off our hands. If not, call Animal Control, then take it out for a walk before it has another accident."

Noir nodded, without enthusiasm, and took the leash. Thinnes went back in the apartment to watch the tech photograph Abner West.

FIFTY

What're you doing tomorrow night?" Rick's voice.

Caleb stood at the window of his office as he listened to the phone, watching the traffic crawl down Michigan Avenue. The Loop was aglitter with lights and feverish with the urgency of the season. Christmas shoppers. He tried to picture Rick in a Christmas context—shopping, stringing lights, or singing Christmas carols. What came to mind was a fantasy involving red ribbon and mistletoe. He blushed at the thought and said, "I have tickets for the opera."

"Tickets?"

"Wagner. *Die Walküre.*"

"You're going with someone."

Nothing like being subtle, Rick, he thought. "No . . ."

"Well?"

Caleb took a deep breath and wondered why he couldn't just say no. It was symptomatic that he felt he was being pressured into what he should have freely offered. And he resented it. *What am I doing, going with this man?*

"I've never been to an opera," Rick was saying.

"*Die Walküre* is not the one to start with."

"I'll be good."

"That's not what I meant."

"What's the drill?"

"Business attire—"

"No T-shirts?"

"The performance starts at six-thirty and runs nearly five

hours. Latecomers aren't seated until there's a break or an intermission. Clearing one's throat is frowned upon; talking is grounds for murder."

"Sounds pretty stuffy."

"You don't have to come."

"Where do I meet you?"

He took a cab. The usual hustle and rush of Loop traffic was intensified by the urgency of the season. Hanukkah. Headlights and brake lights flashed, and turn signals and Four-ways. There was the usual glitter and neon of the Loop, and all the Downtown trees were bejeweled with white Italian lights. For the first time in years, he felt the manic joy of the season. Ebenezer Caleb transformed by Christmas spirits. The words for the song, "You're Just in Love," mingled in his head with the carols and madrigals he'd heard recently on WFMT—*Wassail* and *Oh Come, Oh Come, Emmanuel*. Being in love—he recognized it as infatuation—was closely akin to insanity and probably biochemically congruent with the manic phase of bipolar affective disorder. He was—in strictly clinical terms—hyperrthymic. But as the "dis-ease" was strictly self-limiting, he decided to enjoy it.

As the cab let him out in front of the opera house, Caleb's excitement built like an electric charge in the dry, cold air. Rick was waiting.

He looked gorgeous in a dark-gray mohair coat, gray suit, and gray paisley tie with traces of red and the same slate blue as his eyes. His only concession to the season was a small cloisonné wreath of holly leaves with a tiny, red AIDS-awareness ribbon in place of a bow. His greeting was more effusive than Caleb felt comfortable with under the circumstances—an awkward hug.

For a brief moment, Caleb felt like an old cat in the company of a puppy. "Shall we go?" he said.

The art deco doors opened, creating a temporary vacuum, and a great whoosh of cold air propelled them inside.

"The Lyric is a world-class ensemble," Caleb said. "And the

Civic's one of the world's premier houses. It's acoustically perfect, and there aren't any bad seats."

They had drinks, then went to their seats. Caleb had a box, on the mezzanine, with a superb view of stage, orchestra, and audience. The spectacle was dazzling: bronze and marble, gold and glitter, and golden light.

He tried to see it as Rick must. There were upper-middle-class people, middle-aged and older couples, gays as well as straights.

"So what's the appeal?"

"Ritual, spectacle, and drama." Bread and circuses. Opera and hockey. Different metaphors for the same spiritual experience. In opera, the emphasis was on verbal assault. "It fills the same need as soap opera, professional wrestling, and Kabuki. Or Greek tragedy."

"Pretty heavy."

He was being polite. Ponderous was the word more often applied, particularly to Wagner.

"How did you get interested?"

"My mother was the quintessential opera buff."

As a child, Caleb had resisted his mother's efforts to interest him in opera. But, since his father always managed to have "emergency" surgery on opera nights, Caleb accompanied his mother to performances from the time he was seven. He'd never enjoyed it. The music wasn't bad, but as with Gregorian chant, he'd liked it better before he understood the words—which in translation frequently were insipid. And there'd seemed no point in ruining a perfectly good drama—or dressing up a silly one—with songs in foreign languages.

Then one day he'd heard Maria Callas on the radio. It had been an epiphany.

"So tell me about this show," Rick said.

"In Act One, Siegmund, the hero, arrives destitute and exhausted at Hunding's house, built around the trunk of an ash tree. Hunding's wife, Sieglinde, offers him sanctuary. When

220

Hunding arrives, he reiterates the offer of shelter—until he hears Siegmund's story and discovers Siegmund is his kinsmen's enemy, whom he's sworn to kill. He tells his guest that he can safely stay the night, but in the morning, he's a dead man. Hunding and Sieglinde go off to bed, but she drugs him and returns to Siegmund. She shows him a sword a mysterious stranger once drove into the trunk of the ash. Siegmund retrieves the sword. They talk and discover that they're siblings, separated long ago. They fall madly in love and elope—"

" 'Vice is nice, but incest is best,' eh? Who said that?"

"Oscar Wilde, I think."

"So, does this sordid little tale of disfunctional family living have a happy ending?"

"I'm afraid not."

Just before the lights went down, he spotted a profile that was infuriatingly familiar, but which he couldn't connect to a name. The man was tall and powerfully built, and considerably older than the blond beauty on his arm. She was patently bored by the conversation he was having with two men Caleb recognized as real-estate heavyweights.

Then the lights began to fade—he never failed to feel a surge of joy, of anticipation—and the magic drove all else from his notice.

He could tell, before the end of the overture, that Rick was going to hate it. At first, he divided his attention between Siegmund and Sieglinde and watched the surtitles translating for them. Then he began to study people in the audience. By the time Hunding arrived onstage, Rick was examining the architecture, and the pattern of the carpet. He shot his cuffs, adjusted his tie, and surreptitiously scraped imaginary dirt from under his fingernails. Then he shifted around in his seat to the sleep position adopted by bored students worldwide. Just as well, Caleb thought.

* * *

Caleb was no musician. Apart from long exposure and a general music-appreciation course in college, he'd had no formal musical training. Over the years he'd learned to listen and to understand beyond the literal translation of the story. Maybe it was only the morbid fascination engendered by all tragedy, from DUI accidents to *Hamlet*—he hadn't seen enough Wagner to have thought of analyzing it—but he found he was hanging on every word. Even if you hated Wagner, there was power in the words and in the story. It reminded him of old newsreel films of Hitler's speeches a German teacher had showed him, long ago, trying to fire his students with some passion for the language, some inkling of the power in the words.

And there were moments between the pomp and pomposity that overwhelmed his senses, moments that sent him home sated, moments when the glorious sound swelled him like an orgasm, threatening to burst his skin and explode his entire being like a star gone nova.

Maybe part of the anomie in the country was the absence of relevant epic and contemporary myth. There were occasional attempts—the hero's journey in *Star Wars,* the creative retelling of the Christian incarnation tale in *Starman* and *The Terminator*—but for the most part, modern mythologizers retold the old stories without understanding. *JFK* was not really *Macbeth, Apocalypse Now* missed the point made in *Heart of Darkness.* Caleb thought of David Bisti and the old chestnut "Those Whom the gods love die young." What he knew of the Navajo way of life—with its balance, and honesty and abhorrence of incest—was so opposite this story of incest, power struggle, and deception, that it must belong to a different species.

"Who's my rival?" Rick sat up and yawned as the lights went up.

"I beg your pardon?"

"The old gent with the expensive suit and the Barbie doll on his arm? You've been watching him all night."

It was the sort of exaggeration that was fueled by pique;

Caleb didn't consider jealousy a virtue. "His name is Harrison Wingate, and I've met him once."

"Well, he obviously made an impression that once."

"Your claws are showing." As soon as he said it, Caleb was sorry. Rick stiffened as if he'd been slapped. To make amends, Caleb said, "He was one of the attendees at a reception where the guest of honor was murdered."

"The Bisti case!"

"Yes."

"You were there! You've been holding out on me."

"It's a police matter—an open investigation. I was asked not to discuss it."

"I'll quote you as an anonymous source."

"I'm afraid it would be a conflict of interest."

"And *you'd* know."

"Maybe we should get a drink."

After intermission, as they were making their way back to their seats, Caleb noticed Wingate going the other way. He was obviously not a fan.

The "flight" of the Valkyries, in the third act, held Rick's attention. Young women—gymnasts—had been drafted for the parts and armed with "neon" weapons. They bounded across the stage, from one hidden trampoline to the next, giving the appearance of flight. It was a damned good show.

Then Rick began to cough softly, and he excused himself and went out. Caleb made up his mind that he wouldn't let it spoil his enjoyment of the rest of the performance. But just as quickly, he decided he would have to leave.

He spotted Rick outside the front doors, just lighting a cigarette. He seemed embarrassed to be caught, but nevertheless took a deep drag before saying, "Caught me."

"Hmmm."

"Listen, I didn't mean to spoil the show for you. I could meet you here afterward." Caleb shook his head. "Well . . . You've seen it before, right?"

"We can leave if you'd like."

"As a matter of fact, I'm starved." Caleb nodded. "Do you think you could get us into Planet Hollywood?"

FIFTY-ONE

Thinnes was in the front room, directing the photographer to shoot all the empties, when Oster came back from talking to the manager. Thinnes had sent him to get addresses for the next of kin. There were two burly uniforms trailing behind him, one carrying a stretcher, the other an empty body bag.

"The ME's going with your call on this one, Thinnes," Oster said, "but he wants a copy of your report ASAP. And he wants us to find out who West's doctor was." He added, unnecessarily, "Oh, and Bendix is here."

Bendix had come up quietly and was standing right behind him.

"I was in the neighborhood," Bendix said. "Thought I'd offer to help you guys out."

"There's nothing for you to do here," Thinnes said. "There's no crime, so there's no crime scene."

"Then why'd you call for evidence?"

"Documentation. Just a death investigation—natural causes. I thought those were beneath you."

"Long as I'm here, mind if I have a look?"

"Be my guest."

Bendix walked into the front room, followed by the uniforms. Oster pointed to the hall and led the coppers to the john.

Meanwhile, Officer Noir came back with the dog and stood in the hall outside, waiting for further orders. The dog sat, quiet and alert, at his side. Its huge feet and off-white coat were black, in spots, with West's dried blood.

"Landlord said he won't take it," Noir told Thinnes. "And Animal Control can't get here for at least an hour."

Situation normal, Thinnes thought, *all fucked up.*

"Well," he told Noir, "tell the landlord, if he wants us to take it away, he's gonna have to let us hose the blood off somewhere."

"Us?"

"Please."

"This isn't in my job description."

"Sure it is. We *serve* and protect."

Noir looked ready to do murder himself.

"Hold on a minute," Thinnes told him. He went back into West's bedroom, to the closet where he'd seen what looked like clean laundry. There were towels folded beneath the other stuff. He pulled out three and brought them back to Noir. "I'll owe you one."

Noir swallowed whatever he was going to say and took the towels. He stalked off, with the dog trailing.

Bendix had finished with the scene and hauled his box of tricks away, and the coppers had packed West up and shipped him by the time Noir returned with the dog. He waited with it in the hall. The animal was wet but clean. Noir had changed his leather duty gloves for latex. His uniform was damp and splattered with what Thinnes hoped was just mud.

"I used up all my disinfectant," Noir told him. "And they're going to be able to skate down the alley. Oh, and I tossed the towels."

"Thanks, Noir." Thinnes pulled out his wallet and extracted a ten. "This cover cleaning your uniform?"

Noir looked surprised, then as if he wanted to say something. He *did* say, "Yeah, thanks," as he took the bill.

Thinnes handed him a twenty. "You and Azul have one on me when you get off."

"Thanks," he said again. This time he sounded like he meant

it. He pocketed the money. "What do you want me to do with the dog?"

It was still sitting where Noir had parked it when they'd come back from its bath.

Thinnes got out his keys. "Put him in the back of my car. And start it up so he doesn't freeze. We'll be down in a minute. Oh, and give Animal Control another call. Tell 'em to pick him up at Area Three."

Before Noir could comply, Bendix came back into the hall. "Thinnes, you—" He broke off when he spotted the dog, then grinned slyly. "That a witness?"

"What do you want, Bendix?"

Bendix never passed up a chance to get his licks in. "It's your perp in the Uptown case, isn't it? Great detective work, Thinnes. You got him cold—for littering, anyway. And if you play your cards right, maybe even conspiracy to commit loitering."

Noir folded his arms across his chest and covered his mouth with one hand, but he still couldn't stop his shoulders shaking as he laughed. Thinnes glared at him, and he turned quickly toward the door Bendix had entered by. The dog was up and after him like an obedience-trial champ.

Thinnes turned on Bendix. "What?"

Bendix checked the hall, then said, "I been thinking. Even though this looks like a busted pipe, I'll bet it was murder."

Oster came out of the apartment to stand in the doorway. Folding his arms, he leaned against the jamb. His presence seemed to make Bendix more belligerent.

"Twenty bucks!" Bendix said. He pulled out his wallet, removed a twenty, and waved it in front of Thinnes.

Thinnes said, "You're on!"

Bendix handed the bill to Oster. "You can hold it."

Oster took the money and shrugged. Thinnes got out his wallet. He had a twenty and a five left; he gave Oster the twenty. Bendix turned and walked away.

* * *

Noir and Azul were sitting in their squad, making sure the Caprice was safe from car thieves and dognappers. Oster and Thinnes got in it, and Thinnes waved to them. They turned on their lights and took off.

Inside, the Caprice was warm as Florida in August, but the car smelled like the wet dog shivering on the backseat. It figured. Thinnes turned off the heat and cracked the window before he pulled away from the curb.

When they'd gone about eight blocks, Oster put his hands over his face and said, "Christ! Six more hours."

Until quitting time.

"You could call in sick, Carl."

Oster thought it over. "Nah. I'll be okay soon as I get some coffee in me."

The long silence, as they drove, was interrupted when the dog thumped its tail against the backseat. Oster twisted around to look at it. "Poor bastard probably hasn't eaten in days. Maybe we oughta swing by McDonald's and get him something."

Thinnes had been trying to figure out why Bendix would make a sucker bet, when West obviously died of natural causes. He dragged his attention back to the car. "Huhn?" *McDonald's.* "McDonald's?"

Oster gave him a hurt, you-weren't-paying-attention-again look.

"Why don't you just take the damn thing home with you, Carl?" They came even with Addison, and Thinnes turned west. Toward McDonald's.

"Can't. My daughter's allergic."

"How's that working out?" He stopped for the light at Western.

"So far, so good." Oster looked out the window as he answered. Even at 10:30 PM there were plenty of people out and about, and a fair amount of traffic on both Addison and Western. "She seems to have ditched her attitude with the bum." The light changed, and the car started forward. "It's like having my little girl back."

Neither of them said anything more until Thinnes stopped to give their order at McDonald's drive-up. He looked back at the dog and said, "What do you want?"

The dog wagged its tail.

Oster started to take out his wallet, but Thinnes beat him to it. "Just coffee, or d'you want something else?"

Oster sagged back in his seat. "Coffee'll do it."

"A large coffee and a Quarter Pounder," Thinnes said into the speaker. When he pulled up to the pay window, he gave the girl his last five dollars. He stuffed the change she gave him into his pocket without counting it. The girl at the next window asked, "Cream or sugar?"

"Yeah."

She dropped a handful of paper sugar packets and three plastic cream containers in a cardboard tray that already held a large polystyrene cup and a paper bag decorated for Christmas with the golden arches. When she handed the tray to Thinnes, he passed it to Oster and drove on.

The dog was sitting up on the backseat, watching hopefully, brushing the car door with his tail. Oster balanced the tray on the seat while he unwrapped the Quarter Pounder, broke it in quarters, and offered one to the dog. The animal took it delicately, then swallowed it in one gulp. By the time a break in traffic gave Thinnes the chance to pull onto Addison, the Quarter Pounder was history.

When they got to headquarters, the dog created only slightly less of a stir than a lost toddler. Western and Belmont was, after all, the station where they cordoned off a scene with police-line tape so Maggie the duck, a not-so-wild mallard, could incubate her eggs undisturbed in a planter near the door. And the same hardened cops had given the duck and her family a police escort to the river when the hatchlings were ready for their first swim.

Thinnes walked the dog on the little fringe of grass east of the parking lot before he brought it inside, and before he got it upstairs, four people offered to walk it and three others offered it food. Nobody wanted to take it home. One of the Property Crimes dicks raided Lost and Found for an old coat, so it wouldn't have to lie on the bare squad room floor.

Upstairs, Thinnes put his papers on the table and threw the borrowed coat under it. He tied the dog to a table leg and ordered him to sit on the coat and go to sleep. It did.

"Rossi!" Oster whispered fiercely. He grabbed his McDonald's cup and rushed to the coffee machine, near Rossi's office door.

Both of the Property Crimes dicks sitting across the room got up and came over to stand in front of Thinnes. One spread his *Tribune* out on the table and leaned over it as if fascinated by the story.

"What the hell . . . ?" Thinnes said.

"You want to have to explain your friend to the boss?"

As Rossi neared the table, he was distracted by the sound of a large cup of coffee hitting the floor near his office, followed by Oster's resounding, "Goddamn it!"

The ploy worked. Rossi rushed past the table to survey the damage, and the Property Crimes detectives hurried after him, positioning themselves between him and the sleeping dog.

Rossi muttered a curse and shook his head. "Clean it up," he said, and hurried into his office. Oster went to get some paper towels.

There was something familiar about the name of Abner West's nephew, more than just because he was named after a sainted celebrity. Thinnes got the files out for his three unsolved cases—the dead-Indian cases—and began to page through them. He found what he was looking for in the Uptown Indian file—recently rechristened for Thomas Redbird. "Poke Salad Annie."

The drunken bag lady who'd insisted, "Elvis done it," when the beat cop questioned her.

"Carl," Thinnes said, "what do you think would make a long-winded old boozer like West keep his mouth shut about a shooting he witnessed?"

"Fear," Oster said.

"Maybe. But it looks like he was close enough so the shooter must have seen him. What do you think would keep a stone-cold killer, like the one who did Redbird, from killing a long-winded old boozer like West? Just for insurance?"

"They were friends, maybe?"

"According to his neighbors, West didn't have any friends but his dog."

"Kin!" Oster said. "Relatives. 'The kind of bum that's got a prison record.' What was the nephew's name?"

"Elvis Hale."

"Then we got a witness. Poke Salad Annie *said* Elvis did it."

"I wouldn't want to try to convict anyone on her say-so, but it's a start."

Oster stood up. "I think I'll just go put a wanted-for-questioning out on Elvis, and we'll see what he has to say for himself."

"And get me a copy of his arrest record, will you?"

First watch had begun by the time Thinnes was done working on the preliminary for Abner West's death investigation. He couldn't finish the report until he got the ME's report or the autopsy report—if they decided to do an autopsy. West had been old and sick and under a doctor's care, and there'd been no suspicious circumstances. Thinnes outlined the case for the watch commander—Rossi'd left by then—and put away his open case files. He had his coat on and was on his way down the stairs when the sergeant called him back.

"Thinnes, you forget something?" He pointed to the table

Thinnes had been sitting at to do his paperwork.

Thinnes looked. Under the table, the dog was curled up like a sled dog.

"Animal Control was supposed to come for him," he told the sergeant.

"Well, they didn't. So it's all yours."

"I don't need a dog."

The sergeant shrugged, shook his head, and held his arms away from his sides in an it's-out-of-my-hands gesture. "Well, then *you* take it to the pound. You're not leavin' it here."

Damn!

Thinnes went to a phone and called Animal Control.

"Whadda ya mean, when're we gonna show? We sent a truck out for that dog an hour after you called. They said they never heard of any dog."

"Who did you talk to?"

"I don't know. Whoever was on the desk."

Thinnes called down to the District Nineteen desk, even though whoever was on duty when Animal Control allegedly showed would've gone off by now.

When the desk sergeant came on the line, he chuckled. "They probably went to South Cal."

Damn!

It happened all the time. You told anyone who'd been around a while to go to Area Three, and they went to 3900 South California, which had been Area Three headquarters until January.

Thinnes said, "Thanks," and hung up. He went over to the dog and untied it from the table. "Come on, dog. Animal Control will have to pick you up at my house."

He got home at 9:00 AM. He stopped by the door to hang his jacket on the newel post, at the foot of the stairs, and put his .38 on the top shelf of the closet. The dog, meanwhile, sat where he told it to, even when Skinner came bounding down the steps, stopped with his fur all fuzzed out, and hissed. He didn't even move when Skinner flew back up faster than he'd come down.

Surprised, Thinnes said, "Good dog." He judged the animal to be just past half-grown; he hadn't seen as much self-control in middle-aged police dogs. When he started toward the kitchen without it, the dog stood and wagged its tail, but stayed put. "Oh, all right. Come on," he told it. The dog was instantly at his heels.

The kitchen was light and cheerful, thanks to Rhonda's flair for decorating and the weeks of OT Thinnes had put in to pay for it. Rob was sitting at the table, breakfast laid out in front of him—milk and cornflakes. There was a banana peel next to his bowl, on one side, and the *Sun-Times,* open to the funnies, on the other.

"Hi, Dad," he said. "Whose dog?"

"No one's." Thinnes pointed at the dog and it sat. "Animal Control was suppose to pick it up but they never showed. Aren't you late for school?"

"You must be getting old. Don't you remember about Christmas vacation, or didn't they have it in the Stone Age, when you were a kid?"

"No. And I had to walk five miles to school in the snow."

Rob laughed. "Yeah. I'll bet you've got this great bridge you'd like to sell me."

"Actually, it's lakefront property just east of Monroe Harbor. You gonna be here a while?"

"Till ten, anyway."

Thinnes nodded. He got a glass from the cupboard and filled it from the gallon on the table in front of his son. He drank half of it before going to the phone. When Animal Control answered, he said, "Thinnes. Area Three Detectives. I need a dog picked up." He gave them the address. "Someone'll be here until ten." He hung up. "I'm beat," he told Rob. "Give the dog to Animal Control when they get here, will you?"

"Sure." Rob looked at the dog, who was wagging its tail

tentatively. "Can I give him something to eat?"

Thinnes shrugged. "If you walk him afterward."

"What do dogs eat? Can I give him some of Skinhead's food?"

There was something about cat food that was bad for dogs. . . . "It'll give him the runs." Funny the trivia you picked up investigating homicides. "See if there's any meat loaf left. But don't tell your mother what you did with it."

As he left the kitchen, Thinnes looked back to see the dog watching intently while Rob rummaged through the fridge.

Skinner was sitting on the corner of the bed, looking like he owned the place when Thinnes woke up. He came awake enough to think about it and decided Animal Control must have finally picked up the dog. Downstairs, he found a note stuck to the refrigerator:

Dad, Gone to Greg's. Back ? Love, Rob.

FIFTY-TWO

Oster was already in the squad room when Thinnes got back to work. He didn't look well—he was gray and sweaty, though he insisted he just needed coffee. "Don't be stupid, Carl," Thinnes told him. "Go home and get some rest. Call in sick."

"It's just indigestion. Nothin' a little Maalox won't take care of."

Oster had been trying to get into Violent Crimes since he made detective, back when there was a separate homicide division. After Thinnes's last partner, Crowne, was murdered, Oster'd put in a transfer from Property Crimes. The help he'd given Thinnes nailing Crowne's killer put him in well enough at Area Three to insure his request for a transfer was granted. He went at homicide detecting all out, like a starry-eyed rookie instead of the overweight fifty-year-old he was.

"You're not gonna miss anything," Thinnes told him. "After I interview Poke Salad Annie, I'll probably spend the rest of the day on the phone. If anything goes down, I'll call you."

Thinnes had asked the District Nineteen, Twenty and Twenty-three offices to keep an eye out for the bag lady. Patrol found her sitting on the steps of a doorway to the apartment over a store on Argyle. She had all her earthly belongings in a wheeled wire shopping basket, and she knew her rights well enough to insist the officers bring her stuff along to the station. They brought her to the District Nineteen desk and waited with her until Thinnes came down to take custody.

He hadn't spoken to her at the scene of Thomas Redbird's murder, but he recognized her—a small, skinny black woman, much older, according to her record, than she appeared. Her teeth were too perfect to be original equipment, and her hair, too black. The wig was so excessive it reminded him of Dolly Parton's. She was sitting on the bench next to the Community Relations office. He watched her for a few minutes before going over to introduce himself. Poke Salad Annie, a.k.a. Layde Bird Johnson, a.k.a. Melanie Moonshine, a.k.a. Alice Mayhem. She must have had enough gray matter, once, to have a sense of humor. Now, she seemed kind of vacant.

She also had an extensive arrest record: possession, prostitution, assault, and aggravated battery. Her most recent arrests, though, were bullshit: trespassing, disorderly conduct, and petty theft.

He didn't even consider dragging her upstairs with her stuff. He sat her down at a table in one of the district interview rooms. It was small and close, and breathing the same air with her was almost enough to make you high. She must have had a BAC two or three times the legal limit. She took off her coat—a ratty fur—and carefully laid it on the far end of the table. She seemed to be wearing a whole jewelry box–full of costume jewelry, and three or four outfits, one on top of another. It reminded Thinnes of a little girl playing dress up. He didn't comment as she fished a pint of cheap whiskey out of a pocket, opened it, and took a swig. Her trinkets jangled as she threw her head back and slugged it down. "You know why they call me Poke Salad Annie?"

Thinnes grinned. "You were busted for marijuana possession and told the arresting officer it was poke salad greens."

She gave a whiskey-voiced laugh and nodded. "I was beautiful once. Men wanted me." She leaned back and squinted at him. "Bet you find that hard to believe."

"No. You've got a sense of humor. That's more important than looks."

She pointed at him with an index finger bent by arthritis.

"You all right. I s'pose you want I tell you 'bout the man was killed." He nodded. "Elvis done it."

"*The* Elvis?"

"Hunh! I ain't that drunk. I *never* been that drunk."

"You know Elvis's last name?"

"Naw. Jus' Uptown Elvis."

"Did you see him shoot the man?"

"I seen 'em together. Then I heard a shot. Then Elvis was gone, and the other man was daid. What'd *you* figure happen?"

"You think you could identify Elvis?"

"Sure."

Thinnes handed her a pack of pictures, a dozen in all. The sixth in the pile was the smiling, sunlit picture of Thomas Redbird; the tenth, Elvis Hale's "graduation" picture, taken when he was last released from jail. The rest were pictures of men whose descriptions matched Elvis's, including one of the *real* Elvis, and one of an Elvis impersonator arrested last year for flashing.

Annie began to lay the cards out on the table in a pattern, the way a gypsy lays out fortune-telling cards. When she got to Elvis Presley's picture, she said, "Humph." She put Redbird's picture directly in front of her, against the table edge, and Hale's next to it. When she'd laid out the rest of the cards, she tapped Elvis Hale's photo with the fingers of her right hand and said, "Uptown Elvis." Then she did the same for the picture of Redbird. "This the man he killed."

It was only 1:30 PM when he parked on Larrabee, in front of Terry's Red Hots, and flipped his OFFICIAL POLICE BUSINESS sign onto the dash. The parole office across the street looked as depressing as everything else in the immediate neighborhood except the hot-dog stand. Number 1543–47 was a three story, gray-tan brick building sandwiched between a weed-filled vacant lot and the El tracks, suspended between the poverty of Cabrini-Green and the money of Old Town. He locked the car before he crossed the street.

A substantial desk stood between Elvis Hale's parole officer and his visitors. It looked secondhand, like everything else in the room, and the man behind it looked more like an accountant than a "corrections parole agent." Thinnes knew better than to judge him on appearances. After all, his own partner looked like a used-car salesman. He accepted coffee and a seat, and decided the agent was probably a lot sharper than he looked.

"What can you tell me about Elvis Hale?" Thinnes asked.

"He really looks like Elvis. I'm not sure that's good, because it's gotten him off the hook often enough he thinks the rules don't apply to him. And he can be quite charming when he wants to.

"His father was a Native American—denomination unknown. Abusive. Drank himself to death when Elvis was young. His mother was a hooker and heroin addict. Died about five years ago. He does have a maternal uncle for whom he's expressed mild affection."

"Did have."

"He didn't . . ."

Thinnes shook his head. "Natural causes."

"The Department of Corrections has become his family, over the years, and county jail, his home away from home. He hasn't done any hard time. Yet. But his future's not what I'd call promising. You've seen his rap sheet."

"Yeah."

"Has Mr. Hale done something of which I should be apprised?"

"Too early to say yet. Anything else?"

"He was assessed as having antisocial personality disorder. Are you familiar with that term?"

"What they used to call a sociopath?" The agent nodded. "What—exactly—does that mean in Hale's case?"

"That he came off the assembly line without a conscience and with an appalling inability to learn from his mistakes."

"You got a current address?"

The parole officer nodded and pushed a paper across the desk. "I thought you'd want it. An old girlfriend. He claimed she was going to put him up."

"Claimed?"

"He's about a week overdue reporting in."

"You didn't report him."

"His last offense was criminal damage to property—not people. Since the jail doesn't have enough room for killers and rapists, I tend to cut nonviolent offenders a little slack. How long ago was this last alleged—"

"More than a week."

Elvis Hale's parole officer seemed relieved. "Parole officers are like teachers. We burn out after a while and, in the meantime, we concentrate our efforts on those of our charges who seem to give a damn. Mr. Hale isn't one."

When Thinnes got back to Western and Belmont, there was a message to call the crime lab. Mabley answered.

"This is Thinnes. Got a message to call ASAP."

"Did you get the report on the Jolene Wilson shooting yet?"

"Yeah." The report matched the bullet that had killed Jolene Wilson to a gun found in Mark Leon's possession—no surprises there.

"Well, there's another on its way over, but you might want me to fax you a copy in the meantime."

"Why?"

"You'll see."

Thinnes was waiting by the fax machine when the report came out. As soon as he read it, he called Mabley back. "Nice work!"

The reason Mabley'd called was that the same gun that killed Jolene Wilson had fired a bullet into the brain of the John Doe found dead in a vacant lot in Uptown nearly a year earlier. The case christened "John Buck." Thinnes felt a strong sense of déjà vu. Small world. And there was a connection to the Redbird case—different guns but same MO. It'd be nice—but too much to expect—if Leon turned out to be the perp in those cases, too. Thinnes didn't get excited. He remembered an old *Hawaii Five-O* episode about a murderous handgun that passed from shooter to shooter, leaving a trail of shattered lives. But maybe the asshole who shot John Buck sold the gun to Leon. And maybe Leon could be persuaded to give his name to the cops.

FIFTY-THREE

When he got back from inspecting the plumbing, Thinnes dumped his stuff on a table and went to get coffee. Back at the table, he hadn't even started to spread out his paperwork when his pager went off. The number showing was suburban. Seven-o-eight area code. He rang it.

"Highland Park Police. Bell."

"Thinnes. You paged me?"

"Mr. Thinnes, you need to talk to Officer Reyes. Please hold."

After a few minutes a female voice said, "Reyes."

"This is Thinnes. What can I do for you?"

"We're holding your son, Mr. Thinnes."

Rob arrested! Other guys' kids got arrested. Other *cops'* kids! Not Rob. Thinnes felt like he'd been sucker punched. "What'd he do?"

"He and a buddy brought a dog into Kmart."

"And?"

"And what?"

"What'd he do to get arrested?"

"They brought a *dog* into Kmart and they refused to leave." Thinnes waited for the punch line; finally Reyes said, "That's against the law."

"You got nothing better to do than bust—"

"Mr. Thinnes, if you come right now and pick him up, we'll let him off with a warning and release him into your custody."

"I can't come right now. I'm working." He didn't add that

he was working on something more serious than disorderly conduct.

"You'll have to leave work, sir. It's the law. He's a minor and you're—"

"I know." No sense arguing. And he wasn't anxious to tell Reyes he was a cop. "Give me the address." He remembered it as he scribbled the number down: 1677 Old Deerfield Road. The Northern Illinois Police Crime Lab was housed in the same building. "I'll be there as soon as I can."

After he'd hung up, he looked for Oster, then remembered he'd sent him home. Ryan was in the squad room, however. "I got to take care of something," he told her. "I don't know how long I'll be. Cover for me, will you?"

"Yeah, sure. But what do I tell Rossi if he asks?"

"Tell him I went to see someone about a juvenile offender."

The Highland Park Police station, actually the Public Safety Center, was just west of Route 41. It was a flat-roofed, brown brick structure, with a two-story central core flanked by single-story wings. In addition to the crime lab, the cop shop shared quarters with one of the city's fire stations. Thinnes had been there before.

He parked in front of the building. In a grudging concession to the season, someone had stuck huge snowflakes to the glass walls of the upper-level offices. Below them, Thinnes went through two sets of glass doors into a small lobby. The dispatch area, on the left, was separated from a hall leading to RECORDS by a wood-paneled, glass-topped wall, and from the public by a security window that looked like it belonged in a currency exchange. A door to the right of the window led to the back rooms of the cop shop. To the right of that, a small reception area boasted a bulletin board, several chairs, and a small table, stairs going up and down, and a door leading to the FIRE DEPT.

Thinnes went to the security window, feeling as if he should produce a check or a filled-out form.

The dispatcher asked if she could help him.

"John Thinnes," he said. "You're holding my son."

She said, "Yes," then talked into the radio, then listened. "Officer Reyes will be with you in a minute," she told Thinnes. She didn't bother to ask him to have a seat.

No one came or went. A public-service message on the bulletin board—A FEW DRINKS COULD GET YOU A FREE RIDE— seemed to summarize Highland Park's biggest crime problem. The paranoid security arrangements were ironic for a city with fewer murders in a decade than District Nineteen had in a week.

After what seemed like fifteen minutes but was probably four or five, an officer—female Hispanic, under five feet, and 110 pounds—came out of the back with Rob.

"Mr. Thinnes?"

Thinnes nodded. Rob kept his hands in his pockets and his eyes on the floor.

"May I see some ID?"

Thinnes reached for his wallet and suddenly the officer was pulling her gun. "Put your hands over your head! NOW!"

Rob's mouth flew open. Shock twisted his face.

As the woman's gun sights found him, Thinnes felt the familiar flush of adrenaline that insanity or sudden danger causes. It was only slightly lessened as he realized Reyes must've spotted his gun, and it took all the self-control he had to put his hands out. "I'm a cop! Hold it!" He noticed Rob had turned white.

He raised his arms as ordered. Body bladed, she held her gun in both hands. A Glock. Perfect form.

"Assume the position!"

Thinnes put his hand on the public-service message and leaned forward, spreading his feet.

"ID!" Reyes barked.

"On my belt, left side."

She stepped closer and lift his coat hem, then let the coat go and plucked the star from his belt, stepping backward in an extension of the same motion. There was a long silence—ten seconds, going on forty-five minutes—while she studied it. Finally, she said, "Relax." She holstered her gun and handed back his star. "Why didn't you identify yourself as a police officer?"

"I wasn't on police business."

Neither Reyes nor he could think of anything to say, and there was a long, uncomfortable silence. Anticlimax.

The moment ended when a white-shirted cop charged out of the back. A sergeant. "What's going on?" he asked Reyes.

"Just a little misunderstanding."

"What was that about a gun?"

"Detective Thinnes is armed."

The sergeant looked from Reyes to Thinnes to Rob, then shrugged and went back where'd he come from.

Reyes let her breath out with exaggerated care. "I guess I can save the sermon."

Thinnes glanced at Rob, who looked like the survivor of some major disaster. Served him right. "Yeah," he told Reyes. "Sorry."

She must've have given Rob the word before Thinnes got there, because she nodded and said, " 'Bye, Rob."

Rob's good-bye sounded like a small, scared child's.

The only time he'd ever hit the kid was accidentally, while trying to teach him how to defend himself against bullies. Thinnes had been hit as a kid and raised to believe hitting was a parent's right. But when Rob was small, he'd been afraid to hit him, afraid he'd hurt him. And Rhonda'd been opposed. As the boy grew older, Thinnes discovered he didn't need to hit him for discipline. Rob had him on such a pedestal that a simple "No!" would almost send him into a depression.

And seeing the horrifying results, in his job, of parental discipline gone haywire made Thinnes come to accept the idea that parents shouldn't hit their kids. Ever.

But there were times you'd like to. Like now.

As they walked out of the Safety Center, Rob said, "I'm sorry!"

"Hmpf."

"Aren't you going to say anything?"

Thinnes stopped. "What's to say? You know better than this."

"She could've shot you!"

"She didn't. Don't worry about it. And don't say anything about it to anybody."

"Don't you even want to know why?"

"Why?"

"Forget it."

Thinnes didn't push. Sooner or later, Rob would tell him. "Why didn't you call your mother?"

"I did. They said she was gone to a meeting and wouldn't be back for the rest of the day." He started walking again, stopping when he got to the car. He looked in. "Where's Toby?"

"Who's Toby?"

"Our dog."

"We don't . . . You mean the one I brought home yesterday? The one Animal Control was supposed to pick up today?"

"Yes." Rob seemed almost afraid to say it.

"Maybe you'd better start talking."

"I heard you call them. And after you went up to bed, I called them back and said they didn't need to come after all. I used redial."

"I see. How long did you think it would be before I found out?"

Rob looked at him out of the corner of his eye; Thinnes could see the wheels turning.

"Not long. Just until you asked me what I want for Christmas."

"What do you want for Christmas?"

"Toby."

"What about your mother?"

"She's cool." Thinnes waited. "She said, 'Ask your dad.' "

Thinnes sighed. "I can't promise anything. Technically, he belongs to West's nephew, but I'll see what I can do. Go wait in the car."

Thinnes walked back into the Safety Center, up to the window. "What's the procedure for bonding out a dog?"

FIFTY-FOUR

Ordinarily, Animal Control would take the dog to the pound, where it would be adopted or gassed. Then it wouldn't be a problem for the police. But Thinnes wanted the dog—God knew Rob asked him for little enough. And he wanted it without compromising any case he'd make in the future against Elvis Hale. If Evanger had been around, Thinnes would have asked him what to do about the situation. He'd have been helpful. Rossi wouldn't be. So Thinnes asked the ASA who was hanging around the felony review office.

He was a new guy. "Jesus," he said, "That's property law—not my bailiwick. You're Thinnes, aren't you? They warned me about you."

Thinnes was beginning to wonder who "they" were.

When Abner West's building super didn't return three calls, Thinnes decided he'd have to resolve things face-to-face.

"Have you been able to contact West's nephew?" he asked the super when the man opened the door. He could see him thinking about how to answer and added, "Just tell me the truth," before he could think of a plausible lie.

"Yeah, well. He was here. He didn't seem too surprised that the old fart croaked." Thinnes waited. "I axed him what he was gonna do with the old man's stuff. He said I could have it all."

"You happen to get that in writing?"

"Yeah, as a matter of fact."

"Mind if I see it?"

The super shrugged and went over to a table, against the

wall, that was piled high with papers and obviously served as a desk. He found the one Thinnes wanted and brought it to him.

Thinnes looked it over before saying, "I'd like to borrow this so I can make a copy."

"Sure. If you gimme a receipt."

Thinnes nodded. "What're you planning to do with the stuff?"

"I got this nigger'll take everything I can't use for what he can get for it."

"You mind if I look it over one more time?"

The super shrugged and walked back to rummage through the stuff on the desk. He came up with a key, which he tossed to Thinnes.

"What about the dog?" Thinnes asked.

"What . . .? Hell, I thought you guys were gonna take care of that."

"Well, I guess technically it's yours."

"Technically, I don't want nothin' to do with it."

"You mind putting that in writing—in case there's any question later about why we took it?"

"Yeah, okay." He got another piece of paper from his desk and scribbled, "I don't want West's dog. I gave it to the cops." He held it up for Thinnes to read. "That okay?"

Thinnes looked at it and shrugged. "I guess so. Sign it."

The super scribbled his signature across the bottom of the paper and handed it to Thinnes. "If I ain't here when you're done, shove the key under my door. And if you take anything, I want a receipt."

The apartment had been searched. It hadn't been tossed, but whoever'd gone over the place had been thorough and hadn't tried to hide what he'd been doing. Thinnes didn't find anything new. Until he was leaving.

In a corner of the filthy living room, where it would have landed if someone missed the wastebasket with it, he found a small, balled-up paper. Instinct—or good habits—made him put on gloves before he picked it up. It turned out to be a liquor-store receipt—dated the day the ME figured West'd croaked—for the cheap wine he'd half finished before he died. Thinnes put it in an evidence bag and wrote the super a receipt.

When he got back to Western and Belmont, Oster was in the squad room. He had the Redbird file spread out on a table and was playing Thomas Redbird's answering-machine tape on a little portable tape recorder. He looked marginally better.

"You just can't stay away from this place, can you Carl?" Thinnes asked him.

"Huh. You know how many talk shows they got on TV now?"

"Who said you gotta watch TV when you're home sick?"

"My wife's addicted. What're we doin' today?"

"Why don't you keep doing what you're doing? I've got a few loose ends to tie up on the West case."

"I thought that was cut-and-dried. According to the autopsy report, you were right about his drinking finally catching up with him."

"I'm beginning to wonder about that."

Thinnes got out the Abner West file and shuffled through the photographs of the scene. Even at eight by ten, the shot he wanted wasn't big enough for the detail he needed, but when he studied it under a magnifying glass, he was able to find the balled-up receipt next to the wastebasket. Bingo! He took the receipt downstairs, to one of the District Nineteen evidence technicians, who dusted it for prints. The black print powder raised what looked like a clear thumb print from the paper's surface, so Thinnes asked the tech to run the print through AFIS. When he got back up stairs, Oster hailed him.

"Hey, Thinnes, listen to this."

He turned on the tape recorder and Thinnes heard: "Redbird, if you don't get this damn truck out of my yard, I'm gonna sell it for scrap!"

"Be nice if we knew who's talking," Thinnes said.

"Some guy named Dietz. He left another message earlier. I thought I'd start with the yellow pages—see what I can do. If that doesn't work, I may just take a little spin around Redbird's neighborhood. It makes sense he wouldn't park it too far from where he lived. Damn, I wish we'd found his address book!"

"Probably left it in his truck."

While Oster started trying to locate Dietz by phone, Thinnes got to work on another open case. Other detectives came into the squad room and went out. The coffeepot ran dry and there was a discussion between Swann and Ryan about whose turn it was to refill it. Thinnes got tired of the wrangling and set up a fresh pot himself. At some point, Oster took off. He was gone two hours. When he came back, he was excited. "I found the truck," he announced. "Three blocks from his apartment."

"Nice work," Thinnes said.

"You were right about the address book—in the truck. I've got it right here." He held up a plastic evidence bag containing a brown leather book smudged with fingerprint powder.

"They get anything off that?"

"No, but they did get a few prints off the truck. Let's see what we got here." He took the book out of the bag and began to page through it.

Thinnes got out of his chair to read over his shoulder. Most of the entries seemed to be companies Redbird had done business with. Oster pointed out a few names—people who'd left messages on the answering machine. When he got to the Bs, he pointed to a familiar entry: BISTI.

"Bingo! You believe in coincidence, Thinnes?"

"Sure. And Santa Clause and the Tooth Fairy. Keep going. Let's see who else we recognize."

They recognized two other names, Kent and Wingate. Both had phone numbers but no address.

Oster asked, "Which Kent do you s'pose this is?"

Remembering the painting in Bisti's studio, Thinnes

laughed. He paged back to the H section and pointed to a number penciled in without a name. "Let's see if we can find out who this belongs to."

"I'll do it." Oster reached for the phone.

Thinnes flipped to the back of the book and pointed to another number, in the W section, without a name attached. "This one, too."

The phone rang. Once. Swann called out, "For you Thinnes."

Thinnes picked up the nearest phone and hit the lighted button on the console. "Thinnes."

"Thinnes," a familiar voice said. "Got a match for you on the prints on that liquor-store receipt. One Elvis Hale. An individual well known to the *po*lice."

"Thanks, Mabley." Thinnes hung up the phone and turned to Oster. "It looks like it was Elvis who bought West his last drink."

There were four other Violent Crimes detectives in the room, a few minutes later, when Rossi stopped in front of Thinnes on his way to the coffeemaker.

"Have you had that Indian's wife in here for questioning yet?" Rossi demanded. He obviously meant Lauren Bisti. Redbird hadn't had a wife.

"No," Thinnes said.

"Why the hell not? Any rookie knows—"

"According to two different shrinks, she's suffering from trauma-induced amnesia," Thinnes said. "She doesn't remember a thing about it, and any further upset could make her break down completely."

"That's bullshit! She's got the money to buy a hundred doctors."

"One of the shrinks is our own department consultant."

"You get her in here. That's an order!"

A wave of anger surged through Thinnes, making him feel almost light-headed. He took a deep breath and let it out slowly. When he was a rookie, that sort of officious stupidity would

251

have sent him through the roof. Now he tried hard to not sweat it, not to let Rossi see his rage. "No," he said. "You want her pushed over the edge, you do it. And *you* can explain it to the brass when Royko or Bob Greene gets hold of the story." Thinnes shook his head. "I've done all the usual things and followed up on all the leads. And I'm watching the mouse holes to see what ventures out. I can wait—there's no statute of limitations on murder."

"Yeah, well, there's a statute of limitations on my patience and you just exceeded it."

"Oh yeah? What are you gonna do about it, banish me to working days?"

"You could get time off for insubordination."

"Oh, Christ! Please no! Not that!"

Rossi pointed to the door of the squad room. "Get out! Right now, get out!"

Thinnes had pushed enough suspects to the point where Rossi was to know that the man was very near his breaking point. He didn't like Rossi, even a little, but he didn't want to be the one who pushed him over. He got up and walked out. He was barely through the doorway when he heard Rossi demand, "Where the hell are *you* going?"

Swann's muffled voice replied, "Goin' out for some air."

Fifteen seconds later, Oster walked out of the room, followed by Swann, Ryan, and Viernes—all the Violent Crimes detectives who'd been in the squad room. Oster stopped as he came even with Thinnes, the others nodded or shrugged but kept moving, heading for the locker room or the stairs.

Oster said, "Effing desk jockey!"

"Peter Principle," Thinnes said. "Don't give him another thought."

"How'm I s'posed to do that?"

"If he yells at you for anything, just tell him it was my idea."

FIFTY-FIVE

The unidentified phone number in the H section of Thomas Redbird's phone book turned out to be that of a Teresa Moreno, address on Western. Ms. Moreno didn't answer her phone and didn't have an answering machine. Assured of anonymity, and under the vague threat of being hauled down to Western and Belmont for questioning, several of her neighbors confided that she'd gone to stay with unidentified relatives—maybe in Pilsen, maybe Mexico—until her abusive boyfriend forgot about her. The boyfriend's name? Elvis.

Thinnes left his card with a request for Ms. Moreno to get in touch. "Maybe we can help her with her problem."

The second odd number in Redbird's book was issued to Blank Storage on the near North Side. Located in a changing area, it was an old factory built when everything in the city was made of brick. It had been divided into a dozen small, self-contained warehouses, each with its own loading dock. The windows were protected by decades of grime and by chain-link grilles. The whole building and its parking lot were surrounded by a healthy chain-link fence topped with razor wire. A small sign near the gate stated: BLANK STORAGE M–F 8–5, S 8–12, CLOSED SUN.

The owner-manager was Blank. Male Cauc, two-hundred-plus pounds, brown eyes, thinning brown hair, missing right index finger. He recognized Thomas Redbird's picture immediately and also IDed Oster's Polaroid of the truck.

"Who does he work for?" Oster asked.

"No one. He's independent."

"Who does he deliver to?"

"No one. He's got a key."

"I meant, what company?"

"Mount Taylor Distributors."

"Where have we heard that name recently?" Thinnes asked Oster.

"Somebody we interviewed in the Bisti case. I can't remember who, but I can sure look it up when we get back." Thinnes nodded. "What does he deliver?" Oster asked Blank.

"Damned if *I* know." They waited to see if he'd elaborate. "Contract says they can't store any flammables, incendiaries, or explosives, or caustics, acids, radioactives, or controlled substances. Also stolen property or foodstuff unless it's in ratproof containers. That pretty much eliminates foodstuff."

"That's pretty comprehensive," Oster said. "What's it leave?"

"Search me. But I haven't had a vacancy in years."

"You ever do any inspections?"

"Nah. Unless I notice something suspicious—like a funny smell."

"I notice you got hours posted. What happens if someone's got a delivery after hours?"

Blank shrugged. "They can make arrangements with me ahead of time, or I got a security company that has the key. They'll open up, hang around, and close up for fifty bucks an hour. Most of the tenants just keep business hours."

"When was the last time you saw Redbird?" Thinnes asked.

Blank thought about it. "Day before Thanksgiving. He dropped off a load."

"Where's the office of this Mount Taylor outfit?" Oster asked.

Blank shrugged again. "Some P.O. box. I got it in the office along with the lease."

"Mind if we see?"

Blank hesitated.

"We can do this two ways," Thinnes told him. "You can help us out here—save everyone a hassle. Or we can get a subpoena."

"If we have to do that," Oster said, "you're gonna have fun trying to convince us you're not part if it."

"What did Redbird do?"

"Got himself killed."

"Oh, shit! C'mon. Let me show you what I got."

Back at Area Three, it took Oster all afternoon on the phone to track down Mount Taylor Distributors. When he finally put the receiver down, he turned to Thinnes. "Bingo!" Ferris and Viernes, who were sitting nearby, looked interested.

"Bisti was one of the owners," Thinnes said.

"Bisti was *the* owner."

"Okay. Who do we talk to about getting permission for a look-see?"

"Kent's the executor."

"Well, then. Let's call his bluff on his 'anything I can do to help' offer." He picked up the phone and dialed the lawyer's number.

When he finally got past Kent's secretary, Kent didn't sound convincing. "What warehouse?"

Thinnes wished he could see Kent's face as he gave him a carefully edited version of the Redbird case and its apparent connection to Bisti's death. "Bisti's name is on the lease, and the warehouse manager said his lawyer handled the paperwork."

"That must have been before my time."

"We'd like your permission to go in and look around."

"Certainly—anything that will help you catch David's killer. Obviously, I can't give you a key."

"We'll get a locksmith."

"Let me know what you find?"

"Sure thing." Thinnes hung up.

Oster said, "Let's get something to eat before we do anything else. I'm so hungry, I could eat *escargot.*"

Ferris said, "What's a escargot?"

"That's a big, expensive name for snails, Ferris," Oster said.

"Snails! Christ!"

Viernes grinned. "What do they taste like?"

"Who the hell would eat one?" Ferris said. "I'd rather eat roadkill."

"What does roadkill taste like, Ferris?" Oster didn't keep the dislike out of his voice.

Thinnes answered for him. "Chrome."

The warehouse turned out to be empty. There wasn't even a cardboard box or a gum wrapper. "Think it'd be worth having Forensics go over it for prints?" Oster asked.

Thinnes shrugged. "They didn't leave anything else."

His pager went off before Evidence got there, and he answered it from Blank's office. Viernes.

"Woman named Moreno wants you to call her, Thinnes. She wouldn't leave a message."

Teresa Moreno was five three and maybe weighed a hundred pounds. When Thinnes interviewed her in her aunt's living room, she sat on the couch, beneath a picture of the Virgin of Guadalupe, with her feet tucked up underneath her. She was very young and very pretty, in a revealing blouse and tight Levi's. The yellowing bruise on her left cheek corroborated her claim that she'd been beaten.

As she recited the details of her sordid relationship with Hale, Thinnes listened for something he hadn't heard before. Hale had been charming and attentive at first. And he really did look like Elvis. When he got out of jail and needed a place to stay, he'd talked her into putting him up. When he first moved in, he looked for a job—or pretended to. But pretty soon he was spending his days sitting around, watching TV and drinking. He'd first slapped her when she asked how his job hunt was going. He'd begun to suspect her of seeing other men. Finally, he'd asked for money and beat her when she told him to get a job and earn his own. That had been the end. He might have killed her if the neighbors hadn't pounded on the door in response to her screams. That was novel—someone getting involved. Moreno had taken advantage of the interruption to climb out a window and take off down the fire escape. She hadn't gone back. Not only did Hale outweigh her by seventy or eighty pounds, he also had a gun.

"What kind of gun?"

"A little gun." Teresa Moreno wasn't fooled by the size. It was just such a little gun that killed her *primo,* Emiliano.

Thinnes made her wait in the hall while he pulled his gun and checked to be sure the one-bedroom apartment was empty. It had been searched—thoroughly but not maliciously. Nothing was cut open or dumped out. He guessed Hale had been looking for Moreno's valuables.

Beyond the evidence of the search, the place had the look of a bachelor pad—sink, sideboard, and table piled high with dirty dishes, garbage overflowing, cockroaches. There was a box of .22 shells on the table.

When he gave her the all clear, Moreno stopped just inside the front door. *"Dios mio!"* She crossed herself then stood swearing softly in Spanish and quietly crying.

Thinnes pulled on gloves and held up the box of shells. "These yours?"

"No!"

He picked up the phone. "I'm going to get us some help. We'll need to know if anything's missing. And I'll give you a ride back to your aunt's. Best you stay with her till we get this guy."

She nodded and pointed to a large open carton on the coffee table. *"Esa no es mía.* Er . . . That's not mine."

The carton contained half a dozen ceramic bowls, seemingly identical to the Anasazi artifact in the evidence lockup.

FIFTY-SIX

Dr. Caleb, Mr. Patrick is here."

A little shock of pleasure caused Caleb to shiver. He hadn't seen Rick since Tuesday night, after he'd tried to compensate Caleb for the missed opera, an effort that had left Caleb literally as well as figuratively breathless. "Send him in."

The door opened and all the clichés used to describe the feeling he felt rushed to mind. He inhaled sharply and mentally sighed—ahhh!

Rick was beautiful, hatless, in a black leather jacket and boots, charcoal-gray slacks and scarf, and a pale gray, hand-knitted sweater. His eyes were the color of the lake reflecting winter skies. As he crossed the room, Caleb told himself that part of Rick's attraction was his fierce beauty, and the indefinable something that reminded Caleb of Christopher.

"I'll be out of town for a few days," Rick said, after kissing Caleb. "Think you can live without me?"

Caleb sighed. Whenever he'd almost convinced himself they could work things out, Rick said something like that. It, too, reminded him of Christopher, but Chris's intimacy had been the genuine thing—born of long association and mutual . . . What? Respect? Sensibility? Christopher had been an artist. Rick referred to himself jokingly as a hack and didn't seem to take his gift for words seriously or see his work as art. It was a form of insecurity Caleb found off-putting. He said, dryly, "I'll try."

It didn't take a genius, much less a psychiatrist, to recognize that part of Rick's attractiveness was Caleb's own loneliness, but the metaphors of psychology's great pioneer seemed especially apt. To use Freud's terms, he was exhausted by the war between his id and ego—the conflict between his human need for warmth and touch, to be cared for by one special other, and his intellectual misgivings about his lack of *fit* with Rick. Rick was certainly capable, intellectually, of learning to appreciate opera. And perhaps in time, Caleb would come to see the finer points of hockey. In time. That was the problem. Rick was twenty-seven, Caleb forty-two. He didn't have the time.

"I checked on something for you," Rick said. "The name Wingate struck a chord, so I called a friend in Albuquerque and asked him to refresh my memory."

"And?"

"The name was familiar because when I was there last, it was in the news and on signs at construction sites everywhere. Wingate is very big down there. They really didn't have much bad to say about him. He employs a lot of people."

"But?"

"Among other things, there's a rumor that he's a thief of time. And he was arrested, once, for DUI, but there's no longer any record of it. He obviously paid someone off to have it expunged—of course you didn't hear any of this from me."

After Rick left, Caleb made a few calls—people he knew in development and zoning. What they had to say about Harrison Wingate confirmed what Rick had said.

A crated painting had been delivered for Caleb when he got home that afternoon. Mr. Wang flagged him down as he waited for the elevator and offered to bring it up. "I'll get it," Caleb said.

Wang seemed surprised, as he had the first time Caleb refused help with a menial task. Caleb easily carried the crate upstairs. It was five by five by one foot—awkward but not heavy—and decorated with a huge red bow and the caricature of a gift tag with Caleb's name on it. Margolis Gallery was scribbled in the upper left-hand corner. There was no note or packing slip.

The crate contained David Bisti's painting of a storm over the desert that Caleb had last seen at Anita's. He felt enormous pleasure. He unpacked it in the living room and wondered where to put it. The obvious place—over his mantle—was occupied by Christopher's self-portrait. He leaned the landscape against the fireplace and sat on the couch to consider the problem.

A soft thud—the sound of a small body hitting upholstery—interrupted his rumination, and was followed by a larger thud. Then a tiny, silky head—orange and white and black—rubbed against his hand. Psyche. Freud was right behind her. He crowded in and began to wash the kitten's head and ears vigorously.

Suddenly they were wrestling—feinting and boxing, claws withdrawn—and pretending to bite. Freud grabbed the kitten by the throat, and she stretched out along the edge of the couch, then rolled off. He let go. She took off as if demons were chasing her, and he sat and began to wash himself with exaggerated dignity—like an elder statesman settling his suit coat.

Caleb picked up the phone and dialed Anita. When he'd thanked her for the painting, she said, "You remember the woman at the museum who called David a wolf-man?" It was a rhetorical question; she didn't wait for an answer. "Ivan may have a picture of her."

"Who is she?"

"I don't know, but I came across an old list of David's paintings, and one was titled *A Portrait of Irene*. I called around and found out Ivan bought it."

"So he may know the story behind her fight with David?"

"Yes. I'd ask him but . . ."

Caleb laughed. "I'll ask him."

"And you'll tell the police?"

"Surely."

People on the museum board, mutual acquaintances, told him Ivan had bragged of owning paintings of several of David's mistresses. Caleb stopped at the critic's condo/office and bullied his way in.

"What do you want?" Ivan said. His body language belied his curt tone.

"I want to see your etchings."

FIFTY-SEVEN

Thinnes laid everything he had on the Bisti murder out on one of the squad room tables. It made an impressive collection. There had to be *something* he'd missed. Bisti was killed in a small space, containing a limited number of people. And of those, there were few who had the motive or the stomach to stick a sharp object in Bisti's chest.

He picked up the guest list and read it over. Nothing. Then he started in on the list the secretary had made of people leaving early and a name jumped out at him. Thomas Redbird! He would have been willing to bet Redbird's sister was right on. He had known who killed David Bisti. And the knowledge had gotten him killed.

Ferris, Ryan, Swann, Oster, and Thinnes were sitting around the squad room when Caleb came in.

"Well, if it isn't our new pet shrink," Ferris said. "How's business, Doc?"

"Business is always good in this city, Detective Ferris."

"You making house calls now, Doc?" Ferris looked pointedly at Thinnes.

"No, but I'm having a special this month on neuroses, phobias, and personality disorders. Half-off. You ought to come in and take advantage."

Thinnes, who was sipping his coffee, couldn't help laughing, making the coffee go down wrong. He coughed, suddenly, spraying it all over the table in front of him and over Ferris.

Ferris didn't laugh. "She-it!" he screeched, before snarling at Caleb, "Tell Thinnes." Then he headed for the door.

"There's a first, Thinnes," Swann said. "No one in recent memory," he explained to Caleb, "has gotten Ferris's goat like that."

"What can we do for you, Doctor?" Thinnes asked.

"I made a few inquiries. It may be irrelevant to David's death, but rumor circulating in Albuquerque has it that Harrison Wingate's projects are never held up by the discovery of archeological artifacts because anything found on his sites disappears on the black market."

"Told you, Thinnes," Oster said. "Son of a bitch . . ."

Caleb continued, "There's been speculation that he helped finance more than one development by selling artifacts to Japanese collectors."

"They have the money," Oster said. "But why the Japs?"

"Wingate has several Japanese investors. And you said it—they have money."

"And why should we expect Japanese collectors to be any more virtuous than the American kind?" Thinnes asked.

"I think David knew about it, but couldn't prove anything. Hence the installation. He may have hoped he'd call enough attention to Wingate to stop him or to interest the authorities."

"It sure gives Wingate a motive," Oster said.

"Among others," Thinnes said. "We heard Bisti was using black-market stuff in his work," he told Caleb, "though his wife swears they were fakes."

"What do you s'pose the connection is between those two items?" Oster asked. "And not to change the subject—what's your professional take on this Ivan character, Doc? Without all that psychobabble, what makes *him* tick?"

"He hates himself. And because he can't love himself, he can't believe anyone else can love him. In order to avoid the pain of being rejected—as he's sure he will be by anyone who knows him intimately—he keeps everyone away with his hurtful remarks. Essentially, he rejects everyone else before they can reject him."

"So how do you like him for our murderer?"

Caleb shook his head. "If he ever let anyone get close enough to become intimate, and that individual betrayed him, he might be sufficiently enraged to commit violence. But otherwise, I doubt it."

"Maybe he and Bisti were an item."

"I rather doubt that. David wasn't gay. And Ivan wasn't enamored of his talent—although he owns quite a few of David's pieces. Including compromising portraits of Lauren Bisti and Irene, the woman David quarreled with the night he died."

Thinnes finally jumped in. "What's the story on those?"

"Ivan told me David painted the women he slept with. When he broke up with them he sold their portraits."

"Jesus!" Oster said. "He sold his wife's picture and started painting Kent's wife." He looked at Thinnes. "I told you the wife did it. What about that, Doc?"

"It's a possibility, but . . ." Caleb took the Polaroid snapshot of an unfinished nude portrait out of his pocket and handed it to Thinnes. "Ivan gave me this."

Thinnes recognized the unfinished painting they'd seen in Bisti's studio.

"Ivan swears David gave him an option on that painting."

"He say who it's of?"

"Amanda Kent."

"So our killer could just as well be Mrs. Kent," Thinnes said. "Or Kent. We'll have to go back and talk to them all again."

"Maybe Ivan killed Bisti to drive the prices up," Oster said.

Caleb smiled. "Not for another ten years. In ten years, David might have been a name."

It took Thinnes a while, long distance, to locate Officer Tso, the Navajo Tribal Policeman Swann had talked to. He figured it was worth the wait when Tso told him it was rumored Wingate's projects never got held up by strikes or requests for zoning variances, and confirmed what Caleb had said about archeological remains. "And it's common knowledge that mysterious, nameless investors are lined up waiting to help him with funding."

"Money laundering?" Thinnes asked.

"Search me," the cop said. "But you'd think the IRS would be on to him if that were the case."

For kicks, Thinnes asked him to look up David Bisti.

"Arrested for criminal trespass to property. *Hel*-lo. Harrison Wingate's property."

"See if you can find out how it turned out."

"I can tell you that already. Probation."

After he finished other business in the building, Caleb stopped back in the squad room. Ferris was back. "Doc," he asked, "how many psychiatrists does it take to change a lightbulb?"

"Just one, but he has to be really motivated to change."

"How many *lawyers* does it take to screw in a lightbulb?"

Coming back from the coffee machine, Swann joined the game. "Just one—he stands still while the whole world revolves around . . ."

"Naw," Ferris said, "you're thinking of attorneys. Lawyers don't screw lightbulbs, just people. How many ex-wives does it take to screw in a lightbulb?"

Swann shook his head. "I don't know about lightbulbs. . . . And let's not talk about ex-wives screwing."

Oster glared at the two of them. "Lady present!"

"That's no lady, that's just Ryan."

"Thanks, Ferris."

"What do you think, Ryan? How many *cops* does it take to screw in a lightbulb?"

"What time warp have you been in, Ferris? Lightbulb jokes came and went decades ago."

"Some guys are slow studies, Ryan," Thinnes said.

"You just don't know the answer, Thinnes," Ferris insisted.

"How 'bout it? How many cops does it take?"

"Cops don't do lightbulbs—against union rules."

"Yeah," Oster added, glaring at Ferris. "We're all sick of lightbulb jokes, and lawyer jokes, and Rock Star jokes. And *I* don't want to hear one more damn word about priests."

Ferris had gotten what he wanted. He laughed and said, "I'll see if I can't come up with something about old dicks who can't get it up anymore."

Oster turned to Caleb. "You'll have to excuse Ferris, Doc. The department's toughened up its standards on who it hires, but some of the old assholes are grandfathered."

FIFTY-EIGHT

When Thinnes and Oster walked into the squad room after lunch, Viernes hailed Oster. "Carl, some perp you busted is screaming for you down at County. Name of Leon. Mark Leon."

"Now there's a coincidence," Oster said. "Just so happens, *we* want to talk to Mr. Leon."

"Let's see if Columbo would like to get in on this," Thinnes said. "Maybe he can meet us down there."

An hour later, they brought him into the conference room at 26th and Cal, and Leon went ballistic. He took one look at Thinnes and did an about-face. When the guard wouldn't let him out, he aimed an impressive stream of profanity at them, finishing with a demand for his lawyer.

"Learns fast, doesn't he?" Thinnes asked.

"Take him back," Columbo told the sheriff's deputy.

"Wait!" Leon said.

Thinnes could see the conflicting desires at work. "Are you waiving your right to have your lawyer present?"

Leon thought about it for a minute. "No! I wanna talk to my lawyer first."

It was another hour before they could locate the public defender who'd been assigned to represent him. A woman. Just under five feet and a hundred pounds—fully clothed and soaking wet. She was in uniform—power suit, female version; expensive, unrevealing blouse; and three-inch heels, matching briefcase. She'd been angry when she'd found out how Leon had been duped into talking to Oster in the first place, now she was furious. "Where do you get off—"

Columbo interrupted. "There're two more murders, Counselor, in which your client's implicated."

That rattled her cage. But she said, "You're bluffing!"

Columbo shook his head. Thinnes said, "So far, it's purely circumstantial, Counselor, but the ballistics test done on the gun we found in Leon's possession shows it was used in a killing last year. And the MO of *that* killing matches one we had a few weeks before Leon killed Jolene Wilson. If he doesn't have an alibi for the times those shootings occurred, we could probably clear up both of them by making him the perp."

"What's stopping you?"

"Just the fact that he talked to Carl about Wilson," Thinnes said.

Her mouth actually dropped open. "Did I miss a step?"

Columbo was staring, too.

"He cooperated," Oster said. "We'd like to cut him some slack."

Both attorneys looked skeptical.

"We'd like to get the real killer in those cases, but we don't know that wasn't Leon unless he helps us."

"What're you offering?" the PD asked.

"He cooperates," Columbo said, "and we'll let him plead to murder two."

"Manslaughter!"

Columbo shook his head. "C'mon, Counselor. He was driving around with her in the trunk."

"You didn't know that when you stopped him." She turned to Thinnes. "How many traffic citations have you handed out in the last year, Detective?"

Thinnes managed to avoid smiling. Gotcha! "I didn't write the citations, but I made three stops. And all of them were cited."

That got her.

"We'll put in a good word at the sentencing hearing,"

Columbo said, "if he'll plead second and cooperate on these other homicides. That's the best we can do."

The PD shrugged and sighed. "I'll talk to him."

Leon looked faded and scared as he sat across from Oster in the conference room, and he started his statement with, "He said he'd kill me if I ever narked."

"We just need his name and address," Oster told him. "We'll get a search warrant and if we find any guns, we'll nail him for that."

"You're lying! He'll know as soon as you ask about the gun."

"You can't be the only one he's sold a gun to," Oster said.

"If you won't give us a name," Thinnes said, "we'll have to assume it's because there isn't anyone else, and you did the two killings yourself."

"No!" Leon buried his face in his hands and sobbed, mumbling, "Just the girl. That was a accident."

Oster stood up and leaned over the table to put a fatherly hand on his shoulder. "You'll feel better after you've told us everything. And you'll clear yourself on these . . ." He tapped the Indian case files on the table between Thinnes and himself. ". . . other two shootings."

Leon wiped his face on his sleeve and snuffled. "Little kid— said his name was Chico—sold it to me."

"How little?"

Leon shrugged. "What do I know about kids?" He held his hand up, palm down, about midchest level. "This tall, maybe. Little spic kid. Oh, and he had a scar under his . . ." Leon had to move his own hands to figure out right and left and translate to where'd they'd be facing him.

The guy was dumber than a box of hammers.

"Left eye," Leon finally said. "I gave him fifty bucks and he went away and came back with the gun."

* * *

270

The tactical officer folded a copy of the *Daily Bulletin* into an airplane and sailed it into the wastebasket between Thinnes and Oster. Then he took his feet off his desk and said, "The kid's Chico Galardo. Ten years old going on fifty. He's a gofer for Xaviar Ocampo, a.k.a. Hielo, the neighborhood gang chief."

"Ocampo," Oster said. "Must be Irish."

"Yeah. Just like the IRA."

"It would be nice," Thinnes said, "if we didn't have to name our source. Maybe we could set up a buy and use that for probable."

"We got a little problem there—finding someone they won't spot in a Chicago second."

"A fresh face?" Thinnes said.

"Yeah."

Oster looked at Thinnes. "What about Azul?"

"Who?" the tac cop asked.

"He's a beat copper," Oster said. "Very sharp and he'll fit the profile."

The tactical cop looked skeptical but said, "We'll check him out and let you know."

FIFTY-NINE

There was a brown van parked in front of the apartment building they were watching, with the C removed from the name CHEVY on the front—a HEVY van. A sign on the dash, propped against the windshield with an oversize ghetto blaster, said: THE DRIVER OF THIS VEHICLE IS ENGAGED IN THE DISTRIBUTION OF TELEPHONE DIRECTORIES.

Across the street, inside the surveillance vehicle, Oster said, "S'pose it's bogus? That'd be great cover for somebody up to no good. Anybody spotting it wouldn't give it a second look."

The tactical officer sitting next to him said, "Maybe it was stolen, but it's real. If you were gonna make up a sign, you'd just say something like, 'Driver delivering phone books.' Anybody would. Only a utility company would come up with bullshit like 'engaged in the distribution of telephone directories.' "

"Well," Thinnes said, "when he comes out, let's ask him."

The phone-book delivery man was able to draw them a pretty good diagram of the building. The gang had let him in because Chicago directories are useful but heavy, and none of the gang-bangers wanted to carry them up to the second and third floors. He hadn't seen anyone who looked like the picture they showed him of Ocampo, but one of the kids who lived on the second floor had asked, "You gonna go up where Ice live?"

Just in case he might be tempted to drop a dime to "Ice," they sent the phone-book guy Downtown to look at mug shots while they did a background check.

They wore their vests. And jackets with POLICE stenciled on the backs. Thinnes led, followed by Oster, two tactical officers, and two hefty uniform cops. Inside, on the third-floor landing, they waited while Oster caught his breath and the tac cops coordinated, via radio, with the troops covering the rear, the roof, and the back alley. Then, guns drawn, Thinnes and Oster flanked the door. Thinnes pounded on it with his free hand. "POLICE. OPEN UP!"

He counted five before the cops attacked the door with their battering ram. On the first hit, the jamb splintered, and the door flew open. Four Maglite beams played around the interior as Thinnes led through the door, with Oster covering.

Thinnes got an impression of clutter and chaos. Guns. Smoke. Hostiles. Two people across the room; one close.

Thinnes focused on him—male Hispanic, stretched out on the couch, reaching for a nine millimeter on the end table near his head.

"Don't try it! FREEZE!"

Behind him he heard one of the tac cops yell, *"No se mueva!"*

The man froze, pinned to the couch by fear and flashlight beams.

As the tac cops swarmed across the room, Thinnes pointed his .38 at the man's head. He shoved his flashlight in his belt and grabbed the nine millimeter. He noticed a man and a woman across the room, naked, on a mattress on the floor, caught by the lights and confusion, and shocked into consciousness. He held the captured gun out behind him and said, "Take him, Carl."

Oster said, "Yeah," as he moved to cover the goof.

Thinnes took the flashlight from his belt and rushed the bedroom, glancing into the can as he passed it. The tac cop who'd been third into the apartment covered him while he kicked open the bedroom door. It slammed against the wall inside the room and rebounded. Thinnes pushed it wider as he dived through the doorway. In the bed to his left, a woman screamed. Hispanic. The color of half-milk coffee. Alone.

Holding the light away from his body, Thinnes ran to the far side of the room. No one. A shotgun under the bed. The woman sat against the headboard, with the covers pulled up around her neck, and kept screaming.

"Shut up!" he told her. *"¡Cállase!"* He knew that much Spanish. *"¡Silencio!"*

She covered her mouth with a hand and whimpered.

The tac cop switched on the room lights. Thinnes put his flashlight away. He and the tac man converged on the closet. "COME OUT, OCAMPO!"

Nothing happened. They stood to either side of the door, guns pointed. Thinnes cautiously turned the knob, then yanked the door open.

The closet was full of guns—rifles and shotguns, boxes of ammunition, and an Uzi. And booze—cases of it. There wasn't room to hide a cat.

Thinnes turned back to the woman and jerked the covers off her. She was naked and pregnant, and only about fifteen. A child. She stifled a scream. Thinnes's disgust for Ocampo made him feel like puking. He pointed to the foot of the bed and the girl scrambled on all fours to curl up there in the fetal position. He threw the covers over her, and she clutched them around her, leaving only her face exposed. He flipped over the pillow she'd been sitting on, revealing a .357. Nickel plated. Cocked.

The tactical officer said, "Christ!"

Thinnes decocked the gun and put it in his pocket. "Where's Xaviar?" he asked the girl. Her eyes widened. *"¿HIELO?"*

"No sé," she said, but her eyes tracked toward the window.

Thinnes pulled out his radio and said, "Ocampo's escaped. He may have gone out a window." He put away the radio and went over to look. The room was hot, so the quarter-inch gap between the sash and sill seemed innocent. He carefully moved the curtains aside. Light from the room showed a brick wall two and a half feet beyond the glass. Thinnes cautiously pushed up the sash. No shots. He heard the tac cop call the roof squad to ask what they could see.

"Nothing up here" came back over the air. Ferris's voice.

Thinnes stuck his head out and looked. Above him, the roof team probed nearby rooftops with their lights. Below, the searchlight from a marked squad played over garbage and litter in the gangway. Something moved. A human form materialized from the trash and slunk, like a giant rat, away from the lights, toward the alley behind the building. "OCAMPO, FREEZE!" Thinnes shouted. The figure kept running. Thinnes backed into the room and grabbed his radio. As he keyed it, the tac man climbed out on the window ledge and leaned back until his shoulders hit the wall of the adjacent building. He wedged himself between the two walls and started downward like a mountain climber in a rock chimney.

"Don't shoot!" Thinnes said into the radio. "Spiderman's a cop! The suspect just ran in the alley!"

He looked around. The girl was still curled up on the bed. Out in the hall, Ryan was holding another girl, of about five, wrapped in a towel. Two older boys were holding onto Ryan, and a male uniform was carrying a toddler of indeterminate sex.

"Ryan," Thinnes said, "there's a female juvenile in here who needs to get dressed."

Ryan came into the room. The girl she was holding put her two middle fingers in her mouth and began to suck them.

Thinnes pulled the .357 far enough out of his pocket for Ryan to see. "Don't be fooled by her age and condition," he said. "She was sitting on this." He laughed when Ryan did a double take. He let the gun drop back in his pocket and went into the front room.

The lights had been turned on. There was a strong smell of cigarette smoke and pot. The man Thinnes had disarmed and the naked couple—now clothed—were cuffed and sitting on the couch. Oster was watching as narcotics and tactical officers systematically searched the room, piling contraband on a table for one of the tac cops to tally.

"Reinforcements are on the way," Oster said. He looked tired. "Rossi's coming."

"Good," Thinnes said. "He can talk to the press. Let's go. Ocampo's getting away."

The street was lit by the orange glow of the sodium-vapor lights and the blue-and-white strobes of police squads. Exhaust from the cars and the cops' breaths condensed in clouds in the frigid air.

"Any sign of our perp?" Thinnes asked a patrol officer leaning against his car. He was a rookie, Thinnes guessed, from his energy and fitness level.

The rookie's heavier, more jaded partner answered. "Naw, but we got cars covering the alley and street at both ends of the block. He's probably lying under a car or squatting in the bushes somewhere along here. We'll get him when it gets light. Or maybe we'll get a dog."

Spiderman wandered up, warming his hands in his armpits, and Ferris joined them. Then patrol announced over the radio that they'd flushed Ocampo. "We're heading him back your way."

They tracked the chase by the transmissions. The first team was joined by other cars. When they'd herded Ocampo into the alley behind his own building, just west of the detectives' location, Ferris, Spiderman, and the rookie joined Thinnes trying to head him off. They tore down the gangway between the buildings, their flashlight beams raising weird shapes from the trash. Suddenly, the rookie tripped and slid—swearing—into the shadowy debris. Following too close, Spiderman went down on top of him. Thinnes had to jump over both to avoid joining the pileup, and the cramping in his gut reminded him he wasn't yet fit enough for such maneuvers.

When he got to the end of the gangway, he stopped. He saw

Ferris skid to a halt, midalley, and crouch in a fighting stance. Thinnes took out his .38 and aimed as Ocampo charged up just ahead of a blue-and-white with its lights blazing. Ocampo feinted toward Ferris's left, then charged right and bowled him over, high stepping to avoid tripping on him. He was so busy, he didn't see Ryan fly down the apartment steps. She caught him off balance and shouldered him into the overhead door of a garage facing the alley.

Ocampo bounced off the door and swung at her. She deflected the punch, then landed a solid kick to the side of his thigh. Thinnes could see his jaw drop. Ryan spun Ocampo around and slammed him back against the door.

"GRAB THE WALL," she shouted. "SPREAD YOUR FEET."

Spiderman and the rookie cop swarmed up, guns drawn, and took positions to either side of her. Thinnes put his own weapon away.

Ocampo screamed, "FUCK!"

"For Unlawful Carnal Knowledge," Ryan said. "Are you confessing? ASSUME THE POSITION!" When he tried to turn, she shouted, "DON'T LOOK AT ME!" She lunged forward and slammed him against the door again. "HANDS ON THE DOOR! SPREAD YOUR FEET! SPREAD 'EM OR I'LL SPREAD 'EM FOR YOU!" She swung her left foot against the inside of his right, nearly causing him to do the split. She got her cuffs out and snapped one on his right wrist, then let go of the cuff and grabbed his fingers.

"FUCK YOU!" he screamed.

"That your alma mater? Or the last institution you attended?" She swung his right arm in a big circle that ended with the arm behind his back. She kept hold of his fingers, bending them back just enough to hurt if he struggled.

He offered only token resistance. "BITCH!"

"Best In Throwing, Catching, and Hitting," she agreed. She patted his lower back. "Bring your other hand around here."

When he'd complied, she grabbed his fingers and pulled the wrist straight, then snapped the second cuff on.

"Fuckin' pig," he said.

Ryan patted down his jacket and pockets. "Pride, Integrity, and Guts. You got that right. You also got a name?"

"CUNT!"

"That's a funny name. *I'd* change it." Ignoring the guffaws of the men enjoying the show with Thinnes, she told Ocampo, "You have the right to remain silent, and I strongly suggest you exercise that right. If you give up the right to remain silent . . ."

When she'd finished reciting Miranda, she looked around at the others and said, "One of *you* gentlemen can search him."

SIXTY

Rick said he had to make an early night of it, so they met for dinner at Orly's, on South Hyde Park Boulevard, near the U of C campus and Rick's apartment. The restaurant was a small, comforting place with dark, wood-paneled walls and furniture, hanging plants, and a red, patterned carpet. The evening's specials were listed on a chalkboard near the entry.

When they were seated, and the waitress had vanished with their drink orders, Rick said, "How's Manny?"

"The same."

Rick nodded and looked around the room as if he'd exhausted his line of small talk. He was working up to something. Out of habit, Caleb let the silence be, let it draw out what was on Rick's mind.

"You going to your family's for Christmas?" he said, finally. His body language confirmed Caleb's suspicion that he really didn't care.

"I have a standing invitation from friends." Caleb looked around the room. In the darkest corner, a man and woman were locked in an ardent embrace. At another table, a dark woman in a sari conversed with a man resembling Rasputin. And further down the room, two young men and a woman hung on the every word of an older man, U of C students and their professor, Caleb surmised. At the table nearest Rick and Caleb's, two men underdressed for the venue sat with their backs to the wall and watched the door, the waitress, and the other patrons. Caleb recognized the breed: policemen—tactical officers or undercover cops. They chatted amiably with the waitress but kept their eyes moving. Caleb looked back at Rick, who was also studying the room. His drink was half-gone. A snatch of an old '60s song ran through Caleb's head—"The Dangling Conversation," by Simon and Garfunkel.

The waitress came by, and Rick said, "Why don't you give us five minutes and another round?" She gave him a nice smile.

Rick said, "I'd like you to look at something."

"Surely."

Rick took a sheaf of paper rolled into a cylinder from inside his jacket pocket and handed it to Caleb. "I'm not Bob Greene but . . ." He shrugged. "I'd like your opinion."

Caleb unrolled the paper, titled, "A Ribbon for Your Easter Bonnet." He read:

> This started out to be a ho-hum human-interest piece—the obligatory heart tugger about an AIDS hospice—but in the course of researching the story, I met someone who taught me that a hospice is just a place without human interest. What makes human-interest stories is human beings. People, individuals like Manny . . .

The waitress reappeared with their drinks. Rick asked Caleb, "Are you still hungry?"

"No."

"Just a check," Rick told the woman.

Caleb kept reading.

> I reject the idea that there has to be suffering involved for something to be pure or true or noble. Bullshit! If someone's suffering, it means there's been a fuckup. The continued rapid spread of AIDS is the ultimate fuckup . . .

Caleb was nearly through when Rick interrupted. "It's good enough so it won't embarrass me—my editor's accepted it—but I'll never stick my neck out like this again."

Caleb understood. The article notwithstanding, Rick couldn't or wouldn't talk about deeper issues. He was intelligent and sensitive—or sharply perceptive—in his writing, but it was obvious he wasn't comfortable with emotion or introspection.

. . . As we come together to celebrate the resurrection, maybe we could resurrect some hope . . .

When Caleb finished reading, he studied Rick's face. They thought in different metaphors—as irreconcilable as opera and hockey. Caleb was like a cat, emotionally cautious and reserved; the writer was a dog man, superficially uncomplicated and instantly affectionate.

"Well?" Rick said, figuratively holding his breath.

He *wasn't* Bob Greene, but the article was— "Very effective."

Rick relaxed. "Thanks."

"May I keep it? For Manny."

"Sure. I was going to send him a copy."

There was silence while they sipped their drinks. Caleb felt a twinge of guilt for being snobbish, but he was becoming tired of Rick's preoccupation with the trivial, his effusiveness, and his instant assumption of familiarity. And he taxed Caleb's tolerance for talk of sports and weather.

"We're not working out, are we?" Rick asked. A mind reader.

"To be honest, no."

"Well, as long as we're being honest, I hate opera. And I think all cats should be declawed behind the neck." He said it with a smile.

"What is it you want in a relationship?" Caleb asked.

Rick smiled. "Oh, I don't know." He was being evasive. "But I bet *you* do."

"Passion and security."

"Would you settle for one out of two?"

"No."

"I'm not ready for commitment."

"I know."

"I guess you've got me analyzed."

"What makes you say that?"

"Don't do that shrink thing on me."

"What is it you're feeling guilty about?"

"I'm not feeling guilty!"

Caleb raised his eyebrows and smiled knowingly.

Rick reddened. "All right. We don't have anything in common but good sex." Caleb waited. Rick blushed again.

"You want out and don't know how to say so," Caleb finished for him.

He looked relieved, then looked away. "I feel as if I've been taking advantage of you."

Caleb felt an almost overwhelming sense of relief. He laughed. "I'm over twenty-one. And I've been capable of saying no since I was two years old."

"That's it, then." Rick sighed. "The trouble with being sensitive is you get hurt a lot."

"Your capacity for joy is only as great as your capacity for sorrow."

"Well, you can go for the joy. I'll settle for good sex once in a while." He put his hand out. Caleb gripped it. "No hard feelings?" Rick said.

Just shaking hands felt awkward after everything, but Caleb said, "No." He reached for the check, but Rick beat him to it.

"I got it. If you're ever just horny . . ." He grinned, then emptied his glass in a single long swallow and put it down. "Take your time; finish your drink."

Caleb sat back and nodded and watched him put on his

jacket. He felt simultaneous relief and sadness, but not grief. He had found Rick. He would meet others. *You have to kiss a lot of frogs* ... And somewhere, in a city the size of Chicago, there had to be someone for him. Someone who loved cats and enjoyed opera.

As he followed Rick's departure with his eyes, he noticed that the amorous couple in the corner had come up for air. He realized he'd seen the woman recently—naked, in Ivan's collection. It was Irene Yellow. The man she was with was Professor Matthew Dennison. Caleb got up and went to look for a phone.

Instead of calling a cab, he dialed Area Three.

SIXTY-ONE

Thinnes was waiting when Caleb came out of Orly's. "Where's your car?" he asked.

"I took a cab. I didn't want to worry about parking in unfamiliar territory."

They sat in the Caprice and waited. Even with the windows cracked, their breath condensed on the glass, shutting them off from the surrounding neighborhood. Shutting them in together. Thinnes felt less uncomfortable than he had on the Wisconsin trip. As they discussed the Bisti case, Caleb seemed like a new partner he was finally getting used to.

"We still haven't figured out why," he said, "but we're pretty sure we know who killed Redbird. And Redbird may not have been his first victim." Caleb waited attentively, so Thinnes told him about the circumstantial case against Elvis, including everything about the dog. He noticed, by the time he finished, that the heat had leaked from the car. He restarted the engine. "His parole officer told me Hale hates Indians even though his father probably was one. Is there such a thing as a Custer complex?"

"Sounds more like an Oedipus complex to me. Or a child's quite logical hatred for an absent or abusive parent."

They followed Irene and Dennison to an apartment building—not the address either had given the police—and sat in the car, watching through the windows of the landings as the pair made their way to the third floor, pecking and pawing each other like actors in a steamy movie. When they paused for a long clinch in front of one of the apartment doors, Thinnes sneaked a sideways look at Caleb. What was he thinking? Was watching a straight couple any kind of a turn on for him? Caleb's face gave away nothing.

After a bit, Caleb said, "Professor Dennison told me he was at the reception to investigate a rumor that David was using genuine Anasazi artifacts in his pieces. The implication was they were illegally obtained. Can we put any credence in that?"

"People lie to the cops. That's the First Law of Detecting. And the Second Law is: People lie to the cops."

"People lie to psychiatrists, too."

"What do you do about it?"

"Same thing you do. Have them go over the story so many times they confuse the details. Then confront them with the discrepancies."

"Let's do it, then."

They gave the subjects a chance to get comfortable, then they followed a tenant into the building lobby. Thinnes flashed his star before the security door closed, and the man dropped any objection he might have had to their following him in. Upstairs, Dennison opened the door.

His face showed disbelief and shock. Irene came to the door behind him, and her expression mimicked his. Thinnes said, "Can we come in?"

Dennison shrugged and stepped back, bumping into her. He had just a towel wrapped around him, and he tucked the edges in at his waist as he led the way to the living room. Irene was wearing a man's shirt as a robe, with the sleeves rolled. It looked like she had nothing on under it.

Thinnes and Caleb hung their coats on a coatrack by the door and followed the pair into the living room. They sat on the couch. Irene and Dennison sat on the love seat, opposite. He crossed one leg over the other, not caring whether the other men could see up his "skirt." Thinnes laughed to himself. The professor would probably be a little more modest if he knew Caleb was gay.

With a little prodding, the couple told their story: Both, it turned out, were on friendly terms with Bisti, who'd headed up a group of artists, Indians, and archeologists bent on putting black-market antiquities dealers out of business—both by dropping a dime to the fuzz whenever they came in possession of incriminating evidence, and by flooding the market with brilliant fakes implied to be the real thing.

"That's fraud," Thinnes said.

"Fraud?" We never represented them as anything other than what they were—pots made by Indian artists."

"You didn't say they were Anasazi?"

"No. We circulated pictures without saying anything except that they were for sale. And they got a chance to look at what they were getting before they put their money down. If they jumped to the wrong conclusions . . ." He shrugged. "Caveat emptor."

"What about your spat with David the night he died?" Caleb asked Irene. "You were very convincing. Was it staged?"

She blushed. "Thanks. Yes. We thought a fuss would get free publicity for David's show and call attention to our "Anasazi" artifacts. There wouldn't have been any point if it wasn't convincing. We even had a reporter on the guest list. The plan would have worked if someone hadn't murdered David."

"A reporter?" Thinnes said.

"She must've caved in to pressure from someone to hush the whole thing up, because there wasn't a word about it on the society pages, and the only thing in the rest of the paper about David made his death seem like just another semianonymous urban tragedy." Irene looked at Thinnes. "After David died, Kent pretended not to know about our plan or what happened to all the fake Anasazi pots David had squirreled away."

"We think he might be selling off the inventory," Dennison

said. "But we have no way of knowing. Each part of the operation was separate. David would bring things to me for my opinion, or have people call me, for advice on how something should be, without giving me their names. David was the linchpin. He had all the names in his head. When he died, they were lost."

"Who got the money?"

"We all got a little. Various foundations got anonymous gifts. How he did it sometimes was, he'd show a piece to some rich collector and tell him it would be delivered when his check to AIM, or the Smithsonian, or the Heard Museum cleared."

Irene added, "We weren't ever in it for the money, so we decided to keep quiet, especially since Kent threatened to tell Matt's wife about us if we didn't just go away. Whatever Kent has in mind undoubtedly involves him getting rich, and probably involves fraud—which we've carefully avoided. But since it'll have the same effect on black-market profits as the original plan, we decided to just bow out."

Thinnes said, "Tell us about Thomas Redbird."

"I know him slightly," Irene said. "He does deliveries and odd jobs for David. . . . Did."

"Did?"

"Now that David's gone, I don't imagine there'll be much work for him."

Thinnes turned to Dennison. "Doctor?"

"I don't believe I've met him."

Thinnes pulled out Redbird's photo. "Look familiar?"

Dennison shook his head.

"What did he do?" Irene asked.

"Got himself killed."

Irene's shock seemed genuine. Dennison was indifferent. Why not? If you didn't know him personally, he was just another Chicago statistic.

They said that all they knew about Harrison Wingate was what David told them; he was a land-raper who never let archeological remains get in the way of a project. They agreed David

287

couldn't have proved that or he would have turned his evidence over to the police, and were pretty sure that was why he was killed.

"What did you mean when you told your father Bisti was a witch and someone turned his evil around on him?" Thinnes asked Irene.

She made a disgusted face. "I was angry. I was just mouthing off. I didn't mean it. Ah— David could be a real jerk, sometimes."

Remembering the question Caleb had asked Lauren Bisti, he said, "What's the significance of the cougar in Navajo mythology?"

Dennison answered. "In the Bead Chant, members of the cat family give medicinal plants to the People. In other connotations they're snitches or messengers."

"Like the Greek god Mercury," Irene said. "David loved that."

"Though in Navajo tradition," Dennison added, "Coyote also performs some of Mercury's functions. Like Mercury, Coyote's a thief, and he's responsible for mischief and chaos."

"David *had* to have intended for people to make the connection," Irene said, "between cougar as a messenger, and artist as messenger."

"So who killed the messenger?"

When they were back in the car, heading north on the Drive, Thinnes said, "What can you tell me about Navajo witches?"

"Most of what I know, I got from reading Hillerman's novels," Caleb said. "I gather you have to understand Navajo philosophy to comprehend witchcraft."

"Can you put it in a nutshell?"

"They don't have an organized religion with formal doctrine. It's more a way of life—in harmony with others and with Nature—like the Tao."

Thinnes decided not to ask what *that* was. And he stifled the urge to ask Caleb to get to the point.

"If I understand it correctly, it's something like the Force in *Star Wars*. When you follow the Navajo way, the Force is with you. If you embrace the Dark Side, you're a witch or skinwalker or Navajo wolf—all metaphors for an evil person."

SIXTY-TWO

The interview room was lit by overhead fluorescents. Three of its walls were painted cinder block, with hard, molded plastic seats attached to the walls by brackets; the fourth held the door and a one-way mirror window. Xaviar Ocampo was "hanging on the wall"—handcuffed to a giant staple between two of the seats. Outside the room, Thinnes stood with Oster, Viernes, and Rossi, and watched him.

"What page are we on here?" Rossi demanded.

"He's facing a number of state and federal gun charges at this point," Thinnes answered. "We think he'll finger John Buck's killer to avoid adding murder one."

Rossi made a face. "When're you gonna come up with a perp in the Downtown Indian case? *That's* the one generating all the heat. I'm still getting a call a week on that one. Who cares who killed some drunk breed?"

Thinnes turned to Oster, as if Rossi hadn't spoken, and said, "Let me work on this guy." Oster nodded. "Viernes, would you get hold of Columbo?"

"Sure." Viernes turned away without a word to Rossi.

Oster pulled his notebook out of his pocket.

As Thinnes sauntered toward the interview room, he watched out of the corner of his eye as Rossi stood flat-footed while the others walked away, then hurried off.

Thinnes entered the interview room. "Mr. Ocampo, I'm Detective Thinnes." Even though he'd heard Ryan run through the drill, he asked, "You've been read your rights?" He'd come to the force after Mapp, Miranda, and Escobedo, so he'd never found the landmark decisions to be a particular hindrance. He had heard veteran cops—good men—swear that the controversial decisions actually made for better policing. Not that they'd say so at a gathering of cops.

Losing a beef over Miranda meant either that you'd gotten sloppy and hadn't done your homework, or that the fix was in. He was always careful to avoid being sloppy. And if the case was fixed, there was nothing you could do. So either way, he did his job and didn't worry about it.

"No hablo Inglés," Ocampo said.

Thinnes shrugged, concealing his annoyance. He went back to the door and called to Oster loudly enough for Ocampo to hear clearly. "Carl, go get Viernes, would you? Mr. Ocampo seems to have forgotten how to speak English."

He backed into the room and sat opposite Ocampo, staring without fidgeting or blinking until the dealer looked away. It was going to be easier than he'd thought.

Viernes came in. "What's with *this* dipstick?"

"Mr. Ocampo's feeling so pressured, he can't remember his English."

Viernes nodded. "So you need a translator. Shoot."

"Maybe you'd better start by reading him his rights."

"Sure." Viernes took out his Spanish version of the Miranda card and read it. He could have recited it from memory, but some prosecutors liked to have it read so smart-ass defense attorneys couldn't question the officer's interpretation. When he finished, he asked, *"¿Lo entiendes?"* Do you understand?

Ocampo nodded.

"¡Dime, sí o no!" Viernes demanded.

"Sí."

"Mejor." Viernes looked at Thinnes. "He says he understands."

"Tell him who I am and what I do," Thinnes said. "Tell him I'm investigating a murder." He listened while Viernes translated and Ocampo responded. Thinnes had studied Spanish in high school, but all he remembered was a few commonly used phrases—*¿que pasa?* or *gracias*—and the profanity he'd learned on his dad's construction sites. Viernes was using some of that. He was also using the familiar form of his verbs—treating Ocampo like a child or a dog. It was part of the old good-guy, bad-guy routine, although Thinnes was usually the bad guy when questioning Hispanics. Viernes started shouting. Thinnes recognized *¡Pobre putito!*

"Viernes, ask him where he was November sixth last year."

Viernes translated.

"Con amigos," Ocampo said.

"They have names?" Thinnes spoke directly to Ocampo.

"No recuerdo."

"Your bad luck. Tell him we're talking murder one, here." Thinnes held the .25 they'd taken from Mark Leon in front of Ocampo's face. The heavily engraved, nickel-plated, .25 caliber Browning, a Baby Browning, was not a gun he'd be likely to forget. The semiautomatic held one in the chamber and five in the clip. It had only taken one to kill John Buck. "This look familiar?"

Ocampo wiped his face with his sleeve. "No."

Viernes laughed. "The iceman's melting."

"This is a collector's item," Thinnes told Viernes. "They stopped making these. I'm surprised you'd part with it," he said to Ocampo. He handed the gun to Viernes. "It was used for a hit. Someone put it to the head of a poor, drunk son of a bitch and blew him away." He looked pointedly at Ocampo.

Ocampo said, "So?"

"The guy we got this from said you sold it to him."

"Huh!"

"He's got an alibi for last November sixth. Have you?"

"I want to talk to a lawyer."

* * *

"Here's the deal," Columbo told them. "Ocampo gives us a name and testifies if we need him. We let him plead to a single weapons count, simple battery, and contributing to the delinquency of a minor."

"Cops, one; bad guys, two," Oster said sourly.

"He wasn't caught on the premises," Columbo said. "His name's not on the lease. And his girlfriend isn't going to testify against him."

"So what's the name?" Thinnes said.

"Elvis Hale."

SIXTY-THREE

District Three, on the South Side, had a lot in common with District Nineteen on the North. Both contained extremes of wealth and poverty. Headquarters was located at 71st and Cottage Grove, an aging white fortress of a building with its few street-facing windows set high up in the walls. Thinnes pulled through the lot north of the POLICE ONLY entrance and parked among the employees' cars, west of the building. A bumper sticker on one of the cars jumped out at them: WE COME FROM DIFFERENT WORLDS—MINE HAS SOAP AND TOOTHPASTE. Oster shook his head and said, "Yeah." They went in through the police entrance, and Thinnes led the way down a hall that ended in the front lobby at a square counter.

The district commander was educated and had an excellent rep for handling personnel. It showed. However wild the neighborhood, the interior of the building was clean and calm, with freshly painted walls and polished floors—no fingerprints or gum wrappers anywhere. The officers on duty were fresh and polished too.

"Detective Thinnes?" the sergeant asked as Thinnes approached the desk. Thinnes couldn't remember having met him before.

Oster started to ask, "How . . .?" but looked around and trailed off. Theirs were the only white faces in the room.

"Yes," Thinnes told the sergeant. He had a sudden flash of understanding of how Swann must feel sometimes, walking in the door at Nineteen. He didn't think he was racist, but he was suddenly acutely aware that his and Oster's were the only white faces in sight. It was something he never thought about at Western and Belmont, where the personnel roster was also integrated but was more noticeably white, and where the human division was into cops or not-cops.

The sergeant smiled. "Officer Madison's waiting for you in the tac office." He pointed back the way they'd come. "Down the hall, on the right."

The door of the tactical office was open, and Madison was sitting inside the room on one of the desks, sipping coffee from a Dunkin Donuts cup. Black, five eleven, 190 pounds, with a medium complexion and a neat afro. He was wearing old Levi's, new Nikes, and a Bulls jacket. He had his ID on a chain around his neck, in compliance with the posted regulation: IDS WILL BE DISPLAYED BY ALL PERSONNEL WEARING STREET CLOTHES WHILE IN THE BUILDING.

Madison said, "You're Thinnes."

Thinnes nodded.

Madison finished his coffee, crumpled the cup, and lobbed it into the wastebasket beneath a neatly printed sign: THERE'S NO REASON FOR IT. IT'S JUST POLICE POLICY. "Let's go get your boy."

They followed him into another office that had its own interview room and a holding tank with a small window in the door. A second tac officer—black, male, five eight, 160 pounds—was sitting behind the desk with his legs stretched out beneath it and his fingers laced together behind his head. He was dressed as a laborer and had his ID stuck to his shirt pocket with an alligator clip.

"My partner, Harold Leroi," Madison said.

Oster peered through the window in the holding cell door, looked back at Thinnes, then pointed into the cell. "Hey, see that? The *Enquirer*'s right. Elvis isn't dead."

"Not yet, anyway," Leroi said.

"So, what's the story on this guy?"

"We respond to a complaint of a male Cauc hanging around the U of C campus, acting suspicious," Madison said. "And we spot him just over the line, here in Three."

"Naturally," Leroi added, "we ask ourselves, 'What's wrong with this picture?' "

"So we stop him and do a Terry, and we find a gun."

"And we turn out his pockets and find the keys to a *big* truck. This guy doesn't look like he can afford the beater he's driving."

"So we search his car and find some very interesting dinnerware in the trunk." Madison lifted a cardboard box from the floor onto the desk and flipped open the top. Inside was a pottery bowl almost exactly like the ones Thinnes found in Teresa Moreno's apartment, like the Anasazi bowl Bisti used in his fatal installation. "Mr. Hale claims he bought this down on Maxwell Street," Madison continued. "And he was going to try'n sell it to some professor over at the U. He conveniently forgot the guy's name."

"Probably Matthew Dennison," Thinnes said.

"This some kind of black-market thing?" Leroi asked.

Oster said, "We're still working on that. We've gotten several different versions, so far."

Leroi nodded. "Well, he told us his name was Oliver North, but then we ran his prints . . ."

"We'd like to arraign him first thing in the AM," Madison said. "Of course murder one beats unlawful use any day. . . ."

They didn't try the Mutt-and-Jeff routine on Hale. It would have been a waste of a performance. He'd seen it before. And they didn't want a hassle over whether they'd read him his Miranda rights.

Thinnes was pretty sure they had a good circumstantial case, even without Poke Salad Annie's ID. It would be up to the state's attorney to sober her up and make her appear credible on the witness stand.

"We don't give a shit why he did it," Thinnes told Oster before they joined Hale in the interview room. "So long as he's willing to admit he did it."

In the room, Oster said, "Why'd you do it, Elvis? We know you did it. We got a witness."

A witness that will never stand up in court, Thinnes thought, *but we're not telling you that.*

"Don't try that witness shit on me. The old asshole's dead. Who's your witness, his dog?"

"Don't you wish. No, we got a human witness."

"Who'd the *old asshole* be?" Thinnes said.

"I ain't saying anything more."

"You just said enough to hang yourself, Mr. Hale. Your best bet is to come clean and try to cut yourself a deal."

"Someone named your name," Oster added. "How else would we connect you up?"

"Prove it!"

"We will. In court." He let Hale think about that for a minute.

"I want a lawyer."

"Fine," Oster said.

"Elvis's lawyer just showed up," Oster told Thinnes, later. "They're conferring."

Oster and Thinnes, Swann, Viernes, Ryan, and Ferris had just polished off a pizza and were washing it down with coffee. Just then, Columbo walked in.

"What's five hundred lawyers in the bottom of the lake?" Ferris asked, loudly enough for the assistant state's attorney to hear.

"Jesus!" Viernes said. He pronounced it *HAY*-SOOZ. "What'd a lawyer ever do to you?"

"I'll tell you some day when we got more time."

"Sorry, Columbo," Swann said.

"Oh, Columbo's not insulted," Ferris said. "He'd be the first to admit state's attorneys are all wannabe cops or apprentice politicians."

"I have a theory about lawyer bashing," Columbo told them.

"Jealousy?" Thinnes asked.

"Yup. Those who can, do; those who can't, criticize."

"Yeah, Ferris is a great critic."

"You know, Ferris," Viernes said, "when you retire—assuming you're not shot first—they're gonna throw a party and everyone's gonna come."

"To make sure he's really leaving," Thinnes told Columbo.

"Yeah," Viernes added. "And if he dies with his boots on, even Thinnes won't be able to solve it—"

Ryan finished for him. "Too many people with a motive and a weapon."

SIXTY-FOUR

Lauren Bisti was depressed. Thinnes recognized the symptoms. He could even still remember—barely—what they felt like. "How're you feeling?" he asked.

"Depressed. My doctor wants me to take Prozac, but it's normal to feel bad when you've lost someone." She smiled; it didn't reach her eyes. "I'm sorry, but I don't remember."

"Thinnes, I got six calls this week from people in high places," Rossi said, "wanting to know when we're gonna solve this Downtown Indian murder."

Only six? Thinnes thought.

"The commander wants to know. The *chief* wants to know, and so do I."

"You read my reports. What more do you want me to do?"

"Find the fuckin' killer!"

Half an hour later, the sergeant handed Thinnes a handful of telephone-message slips. "Thinnes," he said, "I got good news for you and some bad news."

Thinnes glanced toward Rossi's office. "I could use some good news."

"The good news is, they matched the shell casing found at your Uptown Indian scene with the gun District Three took off Elvis Hale."

"That's nice. What's the bad news?"

"Hale's escaped."

Thinnes shook his head. "How'd that happen?"

"He took some other prisoner's court call and got let out on an I-bond. Just walked away."

"Why doesn't that surprise me?"

Thinnes hung up the phone and sighed and told Oster, "Wingate's secretary says her boss is out of town—indefinitely. And Kent's lawyer—I'm sorry, *attorney*—is gonna sue me for everything I've got if I don't stop harassing his clients."

Oster laughed and hitched a thumb toward an interview room. "Maybe we should start calling 'em harassment rooms."

"Kent and Wingate are in cahoots, but good luck proving it."

"Kent and Wingate," Oster repeated thoughtfully. "There's a match made in heaven."

"Where?"

"You know what I mean—Kent's got the product. Wingate the buyers."

"The sixty-four-thousand-dollar question is, does Wingate know what they're really peddling?"

SIXTY-FIVE

Caleb stopped at the Margolis Gallery to give Anita the cymbidium he'd gotten her for Christmas. It wasn't as unique or expensive as Bisti's painting, but he knew it would please her. "Carlos said you could bring it back and exchange it for something else when it stops blooming," he told her.

"I'll let him board it for me until it blooms again, but I won't give it up. It's lovely."

"What are you doing Christmas Eve?"

"I was hoping you'd ask me out."

"Would you join me for dinner?"

"I'd be delighted. By the way, I came across the name of someone else who sells dubious artifacts, if you're still interested. . . ."

"I want something for Christmas," Caleb told the man. "Maybe something Anasazi. I'm willing to pay a premium."

"I haven't got anything right now."

"I'd be willing to pay a broker's fee if you could give me a name."

"All I have is an address."

"That's a start."

The address was a Gold Coast high-rise. It was late in the evening by the time Caleb got there. The doorman was just turning a shabbily dressed man away from the door. He greeted Caleb quite differently.

Since he didn't know who he was looking for, Caleb tried the absentminded-professor routine. "A friend of a friend's," he said vaguely. "I'm so stupid. I left home without the name. And there's no one home I can call to ask." He waved his hands as if to conjure up the name. "Native American art, pots and—"

"You must mean Mr. Wingate."

"That's him. Is he home, by any chance?"

"No. Sorry. Maybe you ought to phone first next time."

Caleb nodded as if he found the advice profound. "I'll do that, of course. Thank you."

When he got into his car, he phoned Thinnes's pager.

The vagrant Caleb had noticed when he arrived was still loitering near the entrance to the building's parking garage, where the doorman couldn't see him. There was enough light for Caleb to notice something familiar about him, so he looked more closely as he got in the Jaguar. The man looked just like Elvis Presley!

Caleb realized he had to be the Elvis Thinnes was looking for—Elvis Hale—and Hale apparently realized, simultaneously, that he'd been noticed.

He stepped closer until he stood just forward of Caleb's door and said, "What the fuck are *you* looking at?" Then he reached under his coat and drew out a gun. It was a loaded revolver. He pointed the weapon at Caleb's head. "Park it."

Caleb put the gearshift in neutral and set the parking brake.

"Open the door!"

He did.

"Now get out—"

Again, Caleb complied. Hale kept him covered as he stepped closer to the car. He glanced at the interior before getting in. "What the hell—?" He pointed to the gearshift lever with the gun. "That a manual?"

"Yes."

"I'll be damned."

Very likely.

"You're gonna be my chauffeur," Hale continued. "I never drove one of these. Get in and unlock the other door." He kept the gun on Caleb while he walked around and got in the passenger's seat.

Caleb sat very still. If Thinnes was right, Hale was already a killer. Caleb was struck by how much the young man resembled the late singer at the rock star's zenith. What a total waste.

Hale kept the gun pointed at him, but below the level of the windows. Caleb could only hope they'd pass an observant truck driver, who'd notice and call the police. At Hale's urging, he started the engine. Then the phone rang.

Hale jumped. "What the hell's that?"

"My phone."

"Don't answer it."

After several more rings it occurred to Caleb to say, "That's probably a friend I'm supposed to meet for dinner. If I don't answer and don't show up, he'll call the police."

"They won't find you, will they?"

"They might. I have one of those homing devices in the car— to locate it if it's stolen."

"Where?"

"How would I know?" When Hale looked as if he were getting angry, Caleb added, "Do I look like someone who works on his own car?"

Moot question. The ringing stopped. Hale stared at the phone thoughtfully. When it rang again he said, "Answer it."

Caleb picked it up and said, "Hello."

"What's up?" Thinnes's voice.

"I can't make dinner tonight, after all. Something's come up."

"That so?" Thinnes said. There was caution in his voice as he played along. "Why's that?"

"An old friend just showed up. Remember the guy who gave Rob the dog?"

"You're kinda breaking up. You using a speakerphone?"

"No."

"Elvis Hale?"

"That's correct."

"You got one of those antitheft locators in the car?"

"Yes."

"That's enough," Hale said. "Hang up."

Thinnes must have heard. "Say ciao when I get to the brand." He rattled off the major car-security suppliers. When he got to the right one, Caleb said, "Ciao."

"Okay," Hale said, "Let's get outta here."

"Where?"

"Just . . . head for the Drive."

It took some calling around to find someone who knew the unpublished number, but eventually Caleb got through to Wingate. Hale took the phone and told him, "We need to talk."

Wingate's anger must have caused him to elevate his voice; Caleb could hear him say, "What do *you* want?"

"Money. I need to get outta town. It'll cost me plenty to start someplace else."

Wingate lowered his voice, and Caleb could only hear Hale's side of the conversation. "How 'bout your job site? Call your watchdog and tell him to get lost. Bring lots. And don't call the cops, cause I'll cut a deal with 'em, if I have to. I'm lookin' at murder one here."

Wingate got there ahead of them. The gate was open and a car was there, though Wingate wasn't in sight. Caleb drove in. The site was lit only by the glow of the city's lights reflected from a sullen sky, the head- and taillights of the Jaguar, and the glow from a window of the construction trailer barely visible in the gloom. Other large, dark shapes were indistinguishable. In the rearview reflection, Caleb could just see the gate swing shut and make out a dark-clad form fiddling with the lock. The figure moved along the passenger side of the car and leaned over against the roof.

Hale jumped.

Harrison Wingate opened Hale's door and said, "Let's go inside where it's warmer." He indicated the trailer.

Hale pointed at Caleb with the gun. "What about him?"

"Bring your friend, by all means." Wingate seemed arrogant or amused, even bored, but not the least worried.

"Shut off the motor," Hale told Caleb, then, "Gimme the keys." He took them and said, "If you try anything funny, I'll kill you. What's one more?"

Caleb felt light-headed from a rush of adrenaline. Then he realized Hale was speaking to Wingate, who didn't seem to take the threat seriously.

"Who's your accomplice?" Wingate asked.

Hale laughed. "A dead man."

Wingate didn't respond. Caleb wondered if he were inured to murder, or if this was a demented game they played. And where were the police?

Hale told Wingate and Caleb to precede him into trailer, then closed the door behind them. He looked around. Caleb looked, too. It was a former house trailer, perhaps eight by thirty feet, with a desk and metal folding chairs, tools of various sorts, hard hats, boots and gloves, gas cans, rope and chains, and numerous things he didn't recognize. There were papers, building plans, a computer, and assorted office supplies on the desk. The floor was gritty with tracked-in dirt.

Hale lifted a coil of rope from its hook on a wall and tossed it to Wingate. He pointed the gun at the developer, then jerked his head toward Caleb. "Tie him up. Tie his hands behind his back."

Wingate caught the rope. He didn't seem any more frightened, but he looked apologetically at Caleb as Hale asked him, "You got any Indian blood in you, Mr. Rich Bastard?"

"Not to my knowledge."

" 'Not to my knowledge.' What're you, a politician?"

"A doctor."

"You look familiar," Wingate told Caleb. He stepped around behind him and began to tie his hands together "Where've we met?"

Caleb tried, unobtrusively, to tense all his muscles. Somewhere he'd read that was the way to escape from rope bonds. "At the museum—the reception for David Bisti." It occurred to him, that as unreal as the situation seemed, it wasn't a movie. He was truly in danger. He began to sweat.

"Someone's been prying into my affairs," Wingate said, "beside the police. You." He pushed Caleb down into one of the folding chairs. "Why?"

"Fuck it, Wingate," Hale said. "He's not living long enough to tell anyone what he knows. Where's my money?"

Wingate turned on Hale and said, "He may already have told someone what he knows. And I won't be party to murder."

Hale laughed. "Quit stalling. The money."

"It's outside."

"Let's go." He made a circle with the gun barrel to take in both other men and signify movement outdoors.

Wingate hooked a thumb toward Caleb. "He doesn't need to come."

"Yeah. As soon as we're out the door, he's off and running."

Wingate grabbed another coil of rope and knelt to loop it around Caleb's feet and the base of the chair. When he looked up from the task, he winked at Caleb. Then he stood and preceded Hale out the door. It was a matter of seconds for Caleb to work the rope off his wrists. He waited a tense minute, to be sure they weren't coming back, and freed his feet. Then he slipped out of the trailer, closing the door behind him.

He hadn't time to adjust his eyes to the darkness before the action started. He heard what sounded like a fist striking flesh and an oath from Hale. Two human forms differentiated themselves from the dark background. A gun discharged. Something struck something else metal. Hale swore again. One of the figures broke and ran toward the incomplete building; the other appeared to be feeling around for something on the ground. Hale must have dropped the gun. There was a sound of machinery, and Caleb could see a human form silhouetted against one of the few, dim lights lit in the building. Wingate was in an open elevator, going up.

Then Hale must have recovered the gun, because he screamed, "WINGATE!" and fired at the moving platform, too late to do any damage. The elevator was high enough so that only its underside presented a target, and even that was just a dark form against even more obscure shapes. Hale fired nevertheless. Caleb decided to escape before the killer remembered him and came back to the trailer. He moved slowly toward the gate, keeping to the gravel walk and driveway so he wouldn't trip over equipment and supplies invisible in the dark. He tried to see something, as he went, that he could use for a tool to pry the gate open when he got to it. He passed Wingate's car and his own Jaguar.

Suddenly lights went on above the fence on two sides. Caleb was blinded by them, then confused by the plethora of elements thrust into his visual field. He picked out the locked gate, and human forms standing or hunching above it, and to either side. He looked back and got a glimpse of Hale staring around. The unfinished building looked like David's installation/painting come to life. A figure and a tiny point of blue flame appeared high up in the building's skeleton. A shout made him drop to the ground behind his car; the fear in the voice boosted his adrenaline to an unbearable level.

"JACK, DUCK! INCOMING!"

Thinnes had spent the intervening time well. He'd put out a city-wide flash on Elvis and the blue Jaguar—carjacking, possible hostage. He'd called the security company and waited impatiently as they triangulated the car's location. Then he'd alerted the pertinent individuals and divisions, and set a land-speed record getting to Wingate's building site. When he arrived, the site was locked, dark, and quiet, surrounded by marked and unmarked vehicles—all with lights off to avoid alerting Hale. Without any obvious signs of a crime in progress, or any unequivocal complaint of auto theft, there was nothing they could do but wait. Thinnes had someone back a squad roll up to the fence so he could climb on top and have a look. He gave orders, via radio, for someone to set up scene lights around the perimeter, so they could see what they were doing when the search warrant arrived. They were nearly ready when the shot was fired. The fact was reported over the radio. Someone was struggling in the darkness. Machinery started up in the building. Someone yelled, "WINGATE!" Someone fired again.

Then the lights went on.

Thinnes saw the gunman first. Elvis Hale. Then Caleb, staring, confused, at the suddenly lighted scene. Then someone high up in the unfinished building. Lighting an acetylene torch. It flashed orange as the spark caught, then turned blue and shrank as he added oxygen. Thinnes knew, suddenly, what he was planning. He made himself speak slowly into the radio. "Head for cover! He's gonna blow the place up!" He remembered Caleb and screamed, "JACK, DUCK! INCOMING!"

Trapped inside the fence by the closed gate, Caleb dived behind his Jaguar. Alerted by Thinnes's warning, Hale ran for the trailer.

Thinnes didn't take his own advice. He stood on top of the squad roll and watched the tiny, high-up figure push the acetylene rig off. Thinnes only dived for cover as the tandem tanks twisted down through the air, hoses and torch handle whipping behind like the tail of an angry cat.

The explosion shook the fence. Then there were giant thuds and metal screaming as—they reconstructed later—the oxygen tank, transformed to a rocket run amok, punched through the trailer. Fuel cans inside ruptured and ignited. The trailer walls blew outward around the openings. The ball of flame and burning gases raced the flying tank outward. The tank punched through the Jaguar. Tank and shock wave flattened fence against squad roll. And Thinnes had the wind knocked out of him as he was slammed beneath the flying gate. Then the oxygen rocket punched through the brick wall of the building across the street. As the shrapnel and dust settled to the ground an awed voice whispered over the radio, "Jesus X. Christ!"

At the sound of "incoming," Caleb hit the dirt. It was a reflex from the war. And he was instantly transported back by what followed: an explosion and a chaos of fire and shrapnel. A missile tore through his car, the fence, the wall of the next building.

Reflex made him check the aftermath, drove him from cover. Training as a medic got him up and running toward the flames, into the fiery debris of the trailer, at the human torch staggering away from it.

Elvis Hale's eyes held Thinnes's. "I'm not gonna make it, am I?"

Thinnes looked at the EMT, who shook his head. "No."

"I want to confess."

"Why?"

"I got nothin' to lose. Somma bitch's gonna get away with it."

Thinnes felt his heart rate rise, but he made himself take a deep breath. What were the rules for dying declarations? You had to *know*. Check. You had to say you knew. "Hale, you want to make a formal statement? A dying declaration?"

"Yeah. What've I got to lose? I can't feel anything . . ."

"Hale?"

"I'm here." He tried to turn his head to look at Thinnes but couldn't.

Thinnes moved so Elvis could see him. "You have to say that you know you're dying." He looked at Caleb and the EMT to see if they were paying attention. Both of them seemed to be holding their breaths.

"I'm dying," Elvis said. "I'm telling you I killed three people. Wingate ordered the hits." He had to stop to get his breath, and it came out in ragged, steamy clouds.

Thinnes held his. What to ask first, in case there wasn't time for second? "The hits—who were they?"

"Two red niggers. The trucker. And some lush named Albert something or Something Albert. I don't know . . ."

"Why?"

There was a long pause. Thinnes wasn't sure he was going to answer. Could answer. Finally he said, "Afraid they'd spill their guts."

"About what?" Thinnes forced himself to speak slowly and keep his voice level. "What did they know that would've hurt Wingate?"

"Selling stuff. Old Indian stuff . . ."

"Who was the third person you killed?"

Elvis seemed momentarily confused. "Third? . . . Uncle West." He seemed to be fading. His breathing seemed harder.

Thinnes remembered the liquor-store receipt. "Why?"

"Saw me shoot the trucker."

"How?"

" 'Wasn't s'posed to drink . . . Said his doc told him . . . It'd kill him . . . Bought a jug. Old fart never could hold his tongue or liquor."

"Detective," the paramedic said, "we've got to get going."

"One more question. Hale, did you stab David Bisti?"

There was another long pause as Elvis worked the question out. "Th'artist?"

"Yeah."

"No. I done . . . the others. Not him."

"Thanks, Hale."

"Get the SOB . . ."

SIXTY-SIX

Late the next afternoon, Thinnes saw Evanger in his office talking to the detective sergeant. Evanger spotted Thinnes and jerked his head in a come-here gesture. "Come in," he said, when Thinnes got to the door. The sergeant nodded and excused himself.

Thinnes left the door open and leaned against the jamb. "Nice to have you back."

"Thanks," Evanger said. "You're the only one who thinks so."

"Just the only one who'll admit it."

"Have you got the details worked out on the Hale case?"

"We're going on the theory that Hale became a liability the minute we connected him with Redbird. When he put the touch on Wingate, he signed his own death warrant. They were supposed to pour cement this morning. If Dr. Caleb hadn't been there, it's pretty sure Hale would've ended up as part of the foundation, but when he showed up with Caleb, Wingate had to change his disposal plan to include two bodies." Thinnes shrugged. "There wasn't any other reason to start up that torch, much less push it over the edge. Wingate wasn't in any danger at that point—Hale couldn't have gotten at him up there. All he'd have had to do was sit tight till the cops arrived."

"Anyway, nice work."

"Question is, can we make it stick?"

Evanger shrugged. "Time will tell. Wingate can buy the talent . . . Anyway, thanks for clearing that old John Doe shooting."

"He fits the description of a missing person on file with the Albuquerque PD. A Navajo Indian named Sam Albert that worked for Wingate. He had a drinking problem. I can't prove it—yet—but it looks like he was a loose cannon, and Wingate just told Hale to get rid of him."

"I owe you one."

"Then you can transfer me to days."

"Sure. Ryan's working solo."

"I've *got* a partner."

"Rossi's got to have some—"

"Let him have Ferris. They deserve each other." Thinnes started to leave, then had an idea. "I don't suppose you could get *Rossi* transferred?"

"Oh, no. We need Rossi. What else can we threaten you guys with?" Thinnes laughed. "Seriously," Evanger said. "The only fly in the ointment is, the museum case is still open. We're still catching flak for that."

"You know how it goes—the difficult we do immediately, the impossible . . ."

"Tell you what. If you and Oster close it before New Year's, you can write your own ticket."

"We'll see what we can do."

Thinnes didn't feel like moving. The ordinary business of the squad room went on around him while he sat and thought about relationships. In balance. Deadlocked. Sometimes when the cops started poking around, they threw things off-kilter, and things got fucked up. Or maybe it was Bisti's death that had set things in motion. Certainly if he hadn't died, Hale wouldn't have shot Redbird. And if the police hadn't been poking around in Hale's life, Wingate wouldn't have felt the need to get rid of Hale.

A phone rang, and the sergeant called from across the room, "Thinnes, where's your better half?"

"Who wants to know?"

"His missus."

"He left half an hour ago. Should be there any time."

"Thanks." The sergeant relayed the information and hung up. Then he walked over to stand near Thinnes. "You 'bout done with your paperwork on last night's activities?"

"About."

"Rossi wants you to wait for him, to brief him before you leave."

"In that case, I left with Carl." When the sergeant gave him a look, he added, "The boss said we could have off until Monday."

"Then what're you doing here?"

"Just knotting some loose ends."

The sergeant nodded and went back to what he'd been doing. Thinnes called home.

Rob answered his hello with, "Hi, Dad. You working late tonight?"

"Just a couple more hours. What're you up to?"

"Ma and I are going Christmas shopping. We're going to shop till the stores close."

"That'll be about ten o'clock Christmas Eve."

"Oh. Well, maybe we'll just shop till we drop. Want to come?"

"No thanks. I'm already ready to drop. Maybe you and I could go tomorrow. You could help me pick out something nice for your mother."

"Sure."

"Have fun."

He called Evidence next. He identified himself and said, "Bendix on today?"

"Yeah," the tech said. "Just got sent out to a scene on North Kenmore." He gave Thinnes an address south of Bryn Mawr.

Thinnes said, "Thanks," and hung up.

The sergeant called from across the room, "You still here, Thinnes?"

"Depends who's asking."

"Some doctor—Caleb."

"Which line?" When the sergeant told him, he punched the number and picked up the receiver. "How're doing, Doctor?"

"Fine, thank you. How's Mr. Hale?"

"He didn't make it."

"Ahhh. Have you been able to verify what he told us?"

"We're working on it. But if he was telling the truth, we're back to square one on Bisti's murder."

"Perhaps we could meet and go over the facts again together. There may be something we've overlooked."

"I have a couple of errands to run. How 'bout in an hour or so?"

"Could you meet me at Clark and Balmoral?"

"What's at Clark and Balmoral?"

"A nice little restaurant where we can break bread and try to narrow our suspect list."

Our suspect list. Funny, Thinnes thought, how they'd drifted into partnership.

Bendix was standing in the apartment doorway with his hands on his hips and the usual unlit cigar in his mouth. If Thinnes's arrival surprised him, he hid it. "You come to gloat?"

Thinnes shook his head. "Came to pay up." He took two twenties out of his wallet and handed them to Bendix.

The aging cynic scowled. "What the fuck is this?"

"West was murdered."

"The hell, you say. I saw the autopsy report—natural causes. Booze."

"I can't prove it, but his nephew gave it to him, just to kill him. It's moot now; the nephew's dead. But a bet's a bet, and you were right."

Bendix took the money, shaking his head. "You're some-thin' else, Thinnes. A real piece of work."

SIXTY-SEVEN

Noah Hopewell was waiting on customers when Thinnes entered Native Artists, so Thinnes had plenty of time to look around. The store was laid out like an old-time trading post without the food, and with a few guns mounted out of reach for show. Small valuable items were displayed like pawn in the glass display case that served as a counter. Everything else was stacked on shelves or tables, or hung from the walls or ceiling. Indian art. And stuff made in Taiwan to look like Indian art. Fabulous animals and plants painted in bright colors on brown bark panels—HECHO EN MEXICO. Wool blankets with Southwestern designs, and *ponchos*—or were they *serapes?* He didn't know. Leather shirts and leggings with fringe and beadwork, and beadwork belts, and belts with silver *conchas*. Silver jewelry. Jewelry made of coral, shell, and colored stones. Pottery. Kachina dolls. Feathers and feather headdresses. Drums and baskets. A small totem pole. Painted animal hides. Paintings of animals and Indians. Sandpaintings. What had Lauren Bisti said about those? "Is what he did any more irreverent than gluing sandpaintings to cardboard to sell to tourists?"

He remembered Rhonda telling him—in the once-upon-a-time when she was still a teacher and life was simpler—that children and primitive artists—or very sophisticated ones—represented things symbolically rather than realistically. Which is why children's drawings have such large heads and hands and small bodies. The figures in the sandpaintings seemed childlike, but were obviously abstractions. And in an abstraction, everything is removed that isn't absolutely necessary to identify the thing. It jibed with what Caleb had said about an artist's purpose—to manipulate perception. Thinnes tried to figure out the purpose of the sandpaintings but, beyond guessing they were symbolic, he was mystified.

When Hopewell finished with his customers, he came over to Thinnes. His knees must have been as arthritic as his hands; he moved very slowly. "May I be of assistance?"

Thinnes pointed to one of the sandpaintings and said, "What does it mean?" It showed four tall, thin cornstalks, with leaves and ears of corn, that had human hands, feet, and faces, and corn tassels for hair. Surrounding them on three sides was a thin rainbow, also with human features.

"I can only tell you what it is," Hopewell said. "Corn *yei*—spirits. To understand all the implications would require a lifetime of study."

"Somebody told me it was sacrilegious to glue sandpaintings down and sell them. That right?"

Hopewell sighed. "Yes and no." Thinnes waited. "If these were the actual dry paintings used in the healing ceremonies, it would be unthinkable—some would say—even to photograph them, because when they're correctly rendered, they have great power. But when they are not drawn correctly, or when details are omitted, they have no more power than any other work of art."

Thinnes waited to see if he had anything to add, then asked, "Which one of these is a cougar?"

Hopewell pointed to the sandpainting of an animal that looked like a straight-bodied lizard with a trapezoidal head and the same humanlike hands as the *yei*. "You've come to ask more about the artist who died," he said.

Thinnes nodded, resisting the urge to use Bisti's name. Irene Yellow had made a big deal about not speaking the name of the dead. And Hopewell hadn't mentioned his wife's name when they interviewed him before. "Where did you meet him?"

"I met him in New Mexico. When he came out there. That's when he met my daughter. He was a *belagana* but he wanted with all his heart to be one of the *Diné*."

"I thought his father was Navajo."

"Being one of the People is more than a matter of genetics." Hopewell paused for a long time. "My wife was a teacher. She used to read about all kinds of things and tell me—because I never had time to read, but I like to know things. . . . Funny. Since she died, I read all the time." He shrugged and there was a long pause. Thinnes began to think his train of thought had derailed. Finally, he said, "One of the things she told me is that people have to be taught a language when they are very young—before the age of two—or something happens to the language part of their brains and they lose the ability to learn, or they can never be *fluent*." He said the last word as if it were a foreign term and waited to see if Thinnes understood.

Thinnes had heard the theory. He nodded.

Hopewell continued. "I think that being of the *Diné* is like learning a language. It is very difficult to be fluent unless you were born to it. Not just the language, but everything. It's a way of life, a way of looking at everything, from solitude—which is highly prized—to revenge, which traditional Navajos think is insane. They probably wouldn't worry too much about catching a killer. They would say that anyone who'd do something so bad was sick—in need of healing, or a witch—someone to be avoided."

Two women came into the store. Caucasians with blue eyes and pale faces. One was wearing a fringed buckskin dress under a coat patterned like an Indian blanket. When Hopewell moved away to wait on them, Thinnes studied the sandpaintings. He lifted one down from the wall for a closer look—two characteristic Navajo figures, tall and thin with headdresses and weapons. Blue and black triangles, in the background, formed stylized mountains pointing toward each other from the top and bottom of the picture. A card stuck to the back said:

The Hero Twins, Monster Slayer and Born For Water.
Sons of Changing Woman. They slew all of the
Monsters but those helpful to the People—Hunger,
Old Age, Poverty, and Dirt.

The last time he'd talked to Hopewell, the old man told him
Navajo children were "born for" their father's clan. That made
Born For Water the son of water. He tried to remember where
he'd seen something like it before.

When the woman left, Hopewell came back. Thinnes
pointed to the Hero Twins and said, "What's the meaning of the
blue mountain?"

"It's one of the four sacred mountains that mark the bound-
aries of the *dinéhta*. It was made of sand and turquoise." He
nodded toward the painting. "Some versions of the story have it
that Born For Water didn't kill any of the Monsters, that he only
witnessed their extermination. According to Waters, he's a passive god, the child of the benign, blue south."

"How does that relate to— the artist who died?"

"He was a *belagana*," Hopewell said, "because he thought
in the language of the *belagana*. Like so many young people, he
was caught between two cultures with very different values. It is
hard to know how he would interpret anything."

"That a problem for your daughter, too?"

"What my daughter needs is to go back to the *dinéhta*, and
have a curing ceremony."

So Hopewell knows about Dennison, Thinnes thought.

"She will not be happy until she does that. But she's not ma-
ture enough to know yet."

Or maybe she'd forgotten the language, Thinnes thought. It
was a pretty good analogy. Maybe if she went back to New Mexico, it would come back to her.

"What brought you to Chicago, sir?"

"I grew up here. I thought it would be as good a place to go
as anywhere. And my daughter was in school here."

Thinnes waited. He hadn't said why he had to go.

"And to be truthful," Hopewell continued, "I was fleeing my wife's shade. The *Diné* fear ghosts—what they call *chindi,* which are residues of all of the evil in spirits of the dead. Only the very old—those who've earned a reputation for great wisdom and integrity—die without leaving such a residue. I'm sure my wife left no *chindi.* But I had to leave New Mexico when she died. Everything reminded me of her—every mesa, every cloud, every smiling woman was a reminder."

As he drove north on Clark, Thinnes told himself that Rhonda would like the corn *yeis,* even if it was the strangest thing he'd ever given her. He thought about what Hopewell had told him. It was comforting to know there were still people on the planet with their heads on straight—even if you had to go to the other side of Bumblefuck to find them.

The Dellwood Pickle was on Balmoral. The restaurant consisted of two small storefronts connected by a double-arched opening in their common wall. The arches and the chair rail around the room were decorated for the season with green garlands lit with white Italian lights. Red bows brightened the newel posts on railings around tables set in the storefront windows. There were fewer than a dozen tables in the place. The decor consisted of local artists's work and the do-it-yourself efforts of patrons, who were encouraged by small baskets of crayons nestled among the condiments on each table, and heavy white paper sheets over the cloths.

At Thinnes's request, the waiter seated them against the back wall, where he could keep an eye on the door. Lifelong habit. For a cop, a lifesaving habit.

"The restaurant doesn't serve alcohol," Caleb said, "but customers are free to bring their own, and the waiters will serve it. Would you like something?"

With his mind's eye, Thinnes could see a portable bar in the trunk of Caleb's rental car. It wouldn't have surprised him. "A beer?"

"Surely."

Caleb handed his keys to the waiter who eventually brought glasses and two chilled bottles of Dos Equis. He started to open one for Thinnes, but he waved him away. Caleb opened his own and decanted it. They looked at the menu while they finished the round, and the waiter brought another when he came back to take their orders.

Then they shifted their chairs so they were on the same side of the table, and Thinnes pushed everything off the middle. He drew a grid on the paper with a black crayon and wrote "Means," "Opportunity" and "Motive" down the left side. In the spaces across the top, he wrote in "Mrs. Bisti," "Kent," "Mrs. K," "Yellow," "Dennison," and "Wingate." "Anybody could've gotten hold of the murder weapon." He put an X in the "Means" box under all the names.

"And based on our interviews and my personal gut feeling that half of them are lying, this is what we know about who could have been alone with him at the right moment." He put an X under "Mrs. Bisti," in the "Opportunity" line, and a question mark under all the other names. "That leaves us with motive." Under "Mrs. Bisti," he put a question mark.

"If she knew about his infidelity," Caleb said, "she had a motive."

Thinnes put an X under "Kent," "Mrs. K," and "Wingate." "Bisti was fooling with Kent's wife, probably planning to dump her, and he was giving Wingate headaches. He put a question mark under "Yellow" and "Dennison." "These two, it hinges on whether we believe their story. Anything else?"

"That seems to summarize it."

"Speaking of motives, what keeps you at this, even risking your life? Bisti wasn't close or a client."

"I'm outraged by the waste of life and talent."

Someone had to be. Thinnes usually saved his anger for the most brutal cases—those involving torture or children. But even in the other cases, his rage went somewhere—if only into hunting down the killer.

As if mind reading, Caleb said, "This case is about rage or passion. Whose?"

Thinnes nodded. Lauren Bisti's anger could be said to have been turned inward—if you bought that particular school of thought. Todd Kent's anger seemed more for the inconvenience to himself. Wingate could be it. Or Irene Yellow. Money may have been involved, but it was a crime of passion—rage, jealousy, or greed. Thinnes nodded. The ME'd suggested someone strong or very angry. "Redbird's sister said *he* had a thing for Lauren Bisti. If she was a widow . . . Think he could have done it?"

"Was he angry?"

Thinnes thought about the smiling photo and shook his head. "Not as far as I know. Maybe I need to know more about Bisti."

"He was a paradox—essentially a white man who tried to be more Indian than an Indian, a narcissist who tried to shield his wife from knowledge of his affairs, a greedy individual who gave generously to certain causes."

Thinnes told him what Hopewell had told him about Navajos and art, about the Hero Twins and the Blue Mountain. "I remember where I saw them before" Thinnes said. "Bisti had something like the animal figures in his studio."

"The artist as a hunting animal," Caleb said thoughtfully. "Or as observer.

"Active and passive. Yin and yang. Animus and anima. Art always boils down—in the end—to the most elementary themes and passions. I believe David rewrote his life to fit some epic outline in his head. He once asked me, during a conversation about the autobiographical nature of art, 'Is it autobiography or artifice? People never know for sure unless you tell them. And I won't.' Life subservient to art is useful to an artist, not so helpful for a therapist."

"I hate to admit it," Thinnes said, "but the wife looks like our best bet." Tell me more about amnesia. Could she fake it?"

"Possibly, but from what I saw, I doubt it."

Thinnes thought about what the resident had told him—she hadn't faked being in shock. "If she's not faking it, what're the chances she'll remember?"

"Some amnesias are caused by brain injury—the memories are literally destroyed. Others occur when the brain fails to convert short-term memories to permanent ones. And in the occasional case, emotional trauma causes the mind to block shocking information, sometimes things as basic as the victim's own identity. This form can often be reversed by time and therapy. Without knowing more about Lauren Bisti, I wouldn't even guess at a prognosis. If she did kill David, she might have blanked it out. Or she may have just seen him killed by someone she can't accept as his killer."

"In which case, if she remembers, she's in deep shit."

"It's also possible she was just overcome by the shock of finding him dead."

"We may never know. When we questioned her the first time, she seemed pretty zonked. When we tried to question her again, her lawyer insisted on being there. He's threatening a harassment suit if we don't leave her alone till she gets her memory back." Thinnes shrugged. "People get away with murder all the time, and if she killed him, she just might, too. All she's got to do is just *not* remember. And if I was her lawyer, I'd tell her to just forget everything."

SIXTY-EIGHT

J ack!" Anita sounded worried. "Lauren Bisti was just here."

"And?"

"She left suddenly. She said she was Christmas shopping and she started browsing. The next thing I knew she was gone."

Caleb waited.

"She dropped her packages where she was standing and took off. Mark told me she sounded scared. She said, 'David,' and he thought she was crying as she ran out."

"Any chance he saw which way she went?"

"No, but she hailed a cab."

"Right out front?"

"Yes. And he got the number."

"Thanks." As he wrote the information down, he said, "I'll get on it immediately." He disconnected and rang up Area Three. "Detective Thinnes, please."

"Sorry, he's not here. Somethin' I can help with?"

"Please ask him to call Dr. Caleb. It's urgent."

"He got the number?"

Caleb gave it to him, in case he didn't, then disconnected and dialed Thinnes's pager. While he waited for Thinnes to return the call, he rescheduled his afternoon appointments.

"What's up, Doc?" Thinnes was feeling pretty good about things in general, but he had a lot of paperwork to do, and he would've preferred to talk to Caleb another time.

"Lauren Bisti may have just remembered. And if she did, she may be in danger."

"Where is she?"

"That's where I need your help. She took a cab. I might be able to talk them into telling me where, but not in time."

"Let me have the details. . . ."

Caleb got as far as Diversey before a radar cop pulled him over.

"Fifty in a thirty-five, sir. You got an excuse?"

Caleb explained the problem and stood impatiently next to the squad, with its blue lights blazing, while the officer checked his story via radio. He willed himself to be patient. When the patrolman finished his transmission, he handed Caleb's license back and said, "Follow me, Doctor."

Thinnes didn't have as far to drive. He got to the address ten minutes after the cab-company dispatcher gave it to him, twenty minutes after the cabby dropped her there. If Caleb was right, twenty minutes could be a lifetime. Thinnes floored it going through the gates, then realized he didn't know which way to go. The cemetery was a huge place. He wasted precious minutes stopping at the office to ask.

She was standing over David's grave, looking just as she did the first time he'd seen her. In shock once again. With blood on her hands. Only this time, she had the knife in them.

He wished he'd had more training for this kind of thing or that the doctor would hurry. He got out of the car slowly. He was about fifteen yards away before she noticed him.

She said, "Stop!"

He stopped. And kept his voice low. "Where'd you get the knife, Lauren?"

Her camel-hair coat was open. Her long hair hung loose, and there was a slackness to her face that made him think of a performance he'd seen in school of *Hamlet*. Ophelia. Only the lines were changed. Wasn't it something like 'Out, out, damned blood'?" He could smell the blood.

"Where did you get the knife, Lauren?"

It took her moments to remember, or maybe to come back from wherever her mind was. The vacancy faded momentarily. "Hammacher Schlemmer. The cab driver waited for me. I gave him a tip."

Did she ever! A hundred dollars. The driver'd remembered her instantly.

"Not a very good knife," she added, looking at her mutilated wrists. "Should have done the job by now. Not like David's knife."

Blood dripped from her wrists and soaked into the frozen dirt. Her eyes dropped to the grave. Beneath the Blue Mountain Cat logo on the headstone, the inscription read, DAVID BISTI 1964–1993 VITA BREVIS EST, ARS DURA. *Latin.* It seemed as inconsistent as the two cultures of Bisti's origin.

Lauren said, "David's dead."

"Yeah."

"I can't *live* without him." The knife moved toward her throat, paused. Her eyes started sweeping from side to side, as if to find something hiding in the field of her peripheral vision.

Thinnes said, *"Lauren."* He kept his eyes on her so that he wouldn't draw her attention, by a glance, to anyone who might be in a position to creep up on her. *Where the hell is Jack?* Or the cops? Or anyone?

"I have to be with him," Lauren said.

"You won't if you do that," he told her quietly. "They don't allow suicides in hallowed ground."

She thought about that. It took her a long time, maybe thirty seconds. Then she gave a little shrug that caused her to sway like a drunk. "That's that, then." The knife moved upward.

"Wait!" Thinnes said, softly. "Why?"

"Why? David's dead." The knifepoint touched her throat, teasing a bloody drop from its smooth whiteness.

"Lauren!"

"I killed him." A straight statement, without defiance or anger. And scariest of all, without apparent remorse.

It was all Thinnes could do to hide his surprise. "What for?"

The knife sagged as she thought about it. "He stopped loving me."

"Why kill yourself?"

"He stopped loving me." As if it were elementary. As if living without David's love made the thought of living unbearable.

The knife started back toward her throat. Christ! Where was the cavalry? Thinnes tried to judge how quickly he could cover the distance between them. Lauren said, "You can't stop me."

Then a huge hand closed over her knife hand, and a long arm circled her from behind.

"No, but *I* can," Caleb said, quietly.

She fought him, but he was a bear of a man and in good shape. Fighting him was like wrestling a tree. After a while, she stopped and went limp. The knife slipped from her hand and clattered onto the headstone.

For the first time in half a century, Thinnes took a breath.

SIXTY-NINE

Sunday morning, Thinnes tracked Caleb down at the Grace-land cemetery. Not the one where David Bisti was buried. He waited in his car, parked near Caleb's rental car, until the doctor turned away from the modest grave near Lorado Taft's great sculpture.

As Caleb neared the cars, Thinnes got out of his own and folded his arms on the roof, waiting to be noticed. Caleb seemed far away in his thoughts. Then he stiffened. Thinnes could see alarm cross his face momentarily.

"Sorry to intrude, Doctor," he said. "I remembered that you come here sometimes on Sundays."

"No intrusion. It's time I let Christopher go and get on with my life." He smiled wryly. "How may I help you?"

There were things in his work that Thinnes could do with phone calls—this wasn't one. He needed to see Caleb's face when he talked to him—to better judge the effect of his words and see if Caleb understood them—but he felt uncomfortable. "I wanted to thank you," he said. "For the other day with Lauren Bisti."

There was more. Caleb seemed to sense it and waited while Thinnes put it together. It seemed stupid to thank a man for doing the right thing, but damn few people were willing to do the right thing if it meant going to any trouble. And fewer still—usually only the cops, who were paid to—were willing to stick their necks out for strangers. But that was what was wrong with the world. And when you found someone who was willing to do what needed doing, you had to say something.

"Elvis Hale may have been an unmitigated bastard," Thinnes said, finally. "But he didn't kill Bisti. Thanks for helping me set the record straight."

Caleb nodded. "We all do what we can." He turned to face the same direction as Thinnes, toward the *Crusader* statue. Barring vandalism or act of God, it would still be guarding Victor Lawson's grave when all their bones had crumbled to dust. Artists seemed to leave their works everywhere.

"What will we leave behind?" Thinnes asked.

"In your work, you've probably influenced countless people for the better. And you've raised a decent son. Rob will pass your goodness on to his children, and they on to theirs—perhaps for as long as there's life on this planet."

The blatant compliment caused Thinnes instant embarrassment. But he thought about it. If he'd turned out well, it was because of his parents' skill as parents . . . Jesus! It could really get maudlin if you thought about it too much. Then again, Rob could be killed tomorrow—by accident or gang bullet.

But you didn't plan it that way. Chances were good that Caleb was right, about Rob and about descendants. "What about you?" he asked.

"I can only hope *my* art will help others express their talents."

"The words on Bisti's headstone. What do they say in English?"

Caleb seemed, suddenly, very sad. "I think it's a bastardization of a quote from Seneca.

" 'Life is short, only art endures.' "